THE
KINGDOM
BEYOND
THE
SUNSET

THE KINGDOM BEYOND THE SUNSET

A Grand Adventure

by

Diane H. Larson

First Edition

Printed in the United States of America

ISBN-10: 978-1477510889
ISBN-13: 1477510885

Library of Congress Catalog Card Number: 2012909619
CreateSpace. North Charleston, SC

Sunny Bay Press
P.O. Box 655
Fox Island, WA 98333-9998

www.thekingdombeyondthesunset.com
dianehlarson@gmail.com

A Word to Parents. Grandparents, and Other Adults From the Author

In our technology-obsessed, fast-paced, and all-too-violent world, young people have little time to celebrate their innocence, develop a connection with nature, and explore their imaginations.

Yet it is through the wonder and magic of our childhood innocence, a deep and enduring relationship with nature, and the experience of our inner lives that we learn to know and love our own hearts.

The Kingdom Beyond the Sunset is an adventure story for contemporary times that models this journey of self-discovery. It illustrates for young people how to develop a sense of their own value and power in the world without resorting to violence to themselves or to others.

This book is written for age eight and above, yet the story has multiple levels so that it can be enjoyed not only by young people but also by adults who like to read to children and by adults who simply enjoy reading ageless stories for themselves.

Since the story of *The Kingdom Beyond the Sunset* also appeals to children of an even younger age, a series of six illustrated books for this age group is in the planning stages.

Thank you for reading *The Kingdom Beyond the Sunset*. May it touch your heart and the hearts of your loved ones.

Dedicated to

my beloved grandchildren,

Jordan, Noah, Sam, and Mara Grace

and to

all the innocent children of the world

including

those adults who still remain children at heart

TABLE OF CONTENTS

Book Four—FACING THE DARKNESS

Book Five—FINDING THE WAY BACK

Book Six—FIGHTING FOR THE LIGHT

Epilogue

Acknowledgements

About the Author

Prologue
A Darkening World

The dark vessel maneuvers through the tumultuous seas as masterfully as Noah's ark prevailing over the rising waters. The Forces of Darkness are on the move again, and this time, nothing will get in their way.

Mother Nature protests with great vehemence; an epic storm rages around the intruder. Angry clouds tear across an inky-black sky. Fierce winds hurl seething waves against the enormous dark ship, all to no avail. The power of each mighty wave diminishes in an encounter with such an unyielding force.

For some peculiar reason, the ship is growing larger. It resembles a hungry sea monster gorging on an endless supply of fattening fodder, an image enhanced by eight arm-like attachments extending out from the hull. One of these slippery arms reaches far across the water as if in greedy readiness to grab whatever might be there for the taking.

Unknown to those on board, for whom such information might, or more likely, might not, be of concern, gooey black blood oozes out through a microscopic hole in the underside of this arm and dribbles down into the ocean. Defeated waves carry the slimy stuff away with them as they travel back toward the shore.

The heart of this sea monster throbs with activity. Hundreds of shadowy figures haul equipment across the heaving deck, stopping only to brawl with one another. From time to time, one of these figures breaks loose from the scuffling mob and plummets overboard, vanishing into the churning depths; the roar of the storm muffles any screams of anguish.

The bridge of the vessel, a round booth overlooking the deck, functions as the massive head, with lights gleaming into the darkness from behind shaded windows, its watchful glowering eyes.

From inside the bridge, a harsh voice bellows, "What's taking so long? Everything waits in readiness. We need to finish. Do what you have to do, but make him decide. Make it happen now, or suffer the consequences. Now get out of here!"

Something shatters against a wall, the noise reverberating across the deck. A heavy door slams shut. Boots clank on metal stairs. A few moments later, a boat engine starts up; the sound, loud at first, slowly fades away into the distance.

An eerie stillness descends on deck as the shadow figures stop moving and fighting. Their dark faces contorted with fear, they remain motionless, staring up at the windows of the bridge. What captures their attention is a bizarre frightful silhouette pacing back and forth with the ferocious energy of a caged beast.

If a plane or ship happens upon this isolated spot, not even a remote sensing system will detect any movement. All that might be visible, if one knows just where to look, would be a puzzling sort of shadow on the horizon.

Thus, the only possible witnesses to the ominous behavior of this phantom ship are the curious and vigilant creatures of the sky and of the deep.

Some of the weary waves find their way back to a point of land where the weather remains clear and the night calm. A golden moon and glittering stars light up the evening sky, illuminating the shore and prompting the darkness to heel.

Gliding across the crest of a tree-covered hill, the glow spreads over a large modern house built upon the bank nearest the shore. Creeping up to the top floor, it slips in through a skylight to shine down on the room below, arriving just in time to spotlight three mysterious night visitors in the midst of what appears to be an important discussion.

"Do you really think she is the one who can assist us?" the tallest figure of this strange trio asks in a slow meticulous voice. Except for the blue of his eyes and a sparkling jeweled crown on his head, he is white from head to foot. His maturity, noble bearing, and majestic clothing indicate that he is a person of great distinction.

"I am not absolutely positive, Your Highness, but yes, I think she may be the one," responds the dwarf-sized man standing next to him. Creased leathery skin, drooping ears, and a straggly white beard, almost as long as he is tall attest to his considerable age. Miniature wire spectacles balance precariously on the end of his thick, sagging nose. Even the high point of his wide-brimmed black hat slumps down in resignation over his right shoulder.

Perched on this shoulder is a tiny gray screech owl, its feathers sticking out in all directions. Blinking one hooded eye, it trills, "Hoot Mon!" Its other eye remains focused on a large black and brown striped tabby cat snoring softly at the foot of the bed next to them.

The *she* to whom they are referring is a little girl who lies fast asleep in the bed. Her long wavy red hair spills across the white pillow like blood upon snow. Brown freckles sprinkled on her cheeks emphasize the fairness of her skin. Shifting slightly in her sleep, she breathes out a gentle sigh, causing the cat to stir. The owl snaps its hooded eye open to scrutinize the cat with both eyes until it settles again.

The moonlight's expanding glow reveals a menagerie of stuffed animals surrounding the three observers. Amongst an assortment of fuzzy bears of differing sizes and colors sits a gray wolf with shining amber eyes. A pocket-sized scruffy owl, much like the miniature bird on the little man's shoulder, leans sideways against the wolf.

A grinning green frog in denim overalls, a multi-colored snake, and an otter clasping a small rubber ball, make up another unusual trio. An oversized white bison stands guard in a place of honor, with a woolen bighorn sheep and a glossy satin unicorn reclining beside it.

Rounding out the abundance of stuffed creatures are a couple of soft furry seals, a squashy black and white whale, and a comical fat-butted duck of many colors.

On a shelf above her bed, a ceramic seagull and an ebony raven watch over the girl. Rocks and seashells scattered around the birds add a touch of seashore to the room. Bronze eagle bookends prop up several musty dog-eared collections of fairy tales set next to a reading lamp on a bedside table.

An antique carousel horse, the rich red of its original color now mottled with age, maintains its proud prance in a nearby corner.

Her bedroom looks as neat as a pin with everything carefully coordinated except for the old handmade quilt on her bed, the collection of creatures, and perhaps more to the point, her three out-of-place visitors.

"What we require," continues the little man, "is someone young and innocent who holds much Light inside… someone who cares deeply about her world and has the courage to face the Darkness ahead. We have been watching her for some time. She has these characteristics. Her concern for her world is as great as is her love for all living things."

"Shall we put her to the test then to see if she will pass muster?" asks the king, for a king is who he is. Coming from someone else, this would be a question; from him, his words issue a command.

"Yes, indeed," agrees the little man, whose wisdom matches his age. Although he has already made up his own mind about the girl, he knows that the decision belongs to the king.

The owl opens both eyes just a slit to say in a broad Scottish brogue, "Hoot Mon, but she's a bonnie wee lassie. Ach aye, look at her rare red hair and those braw fernitickles! Do ye no ken she might be a wee bit small for such a big job? It's no an easy one! Hoot Mon!"

"We do not have a choice," declares His Highness. "Time is running out. We need assistance immediately. Our kingdom faces great danger, and her world is in desperate peril. Come let us go. The sunrise will soon be here. We must be gone before she awakens."

Whereupon, the white king, the old man, and the tiny owl disappear back to where they have come from… into the mind and heart of the child in the bed.

Absorbed in the enchantment of her dream world, the little red-haired girl is enjoying the time of her life. Barefoot in the lush green grasses of a wildflower-filled meadow, she twirls about with whimsical fairies and magical creatures of every color. All her favorite birds and animals have joined in the frolic.

Snow-capped purple mountains, an evergreen forest, a sparkling silver ocean, and a wall of glorious colors surround the meadow. Above, wisps of cotton candy clouds drift across a sapphire blue sky. A brilliant rainbow stretches over the meadow. The girl has never felt as content as she does in this peaceful place.

Without warning, numerous shadowy figures begin sneaking into the corners of her dream. At first, light gray and transparent, they grow darker as they creep in her direction. With the passage of time, countless numbers of these strange shadows invade her dream landscape.

Then something much more threatening comes into view. A dark shadowy ship looms on the horizon of her dream ocean. The ship appears to be increasing in size, causing the light around it to shrink in proportion.

While watching the shadow figures multiply and darken and the shadow ship expand, a horrible notion dawns on her. If this continues unabated, in no time at all, the light will extinguish and a Dreadful Darkness will fall upon her world. She quivers with foreboding,

BOOK ONE

ON THE SHORE

Chapter One
The Rainbow Ribbon

"Wake up, Sleepyhead. Wake up!" Priscilla tried to shoo Mathilda off the bed with little success. Her silly cat was such a night owl; this morning she was out like a light. The heavy tabby asleep on the quilt complicated the task of making the bed, but Priscilla tackled the challenge with her usual determination.

Once the bed met her exacting standards, she flopped down beside the snoozing cat and gently stroked its soft thick fur. The familiar warmth under her fingertips eased the shakes left over from her scary dream. Some of the creepy dark shadows had followed her back into the early morning light.

Remembering what day it was, her thoughts turned to Granny. Sitting up, she reached into the pocket of her overalls and pulled out her rainbow ribbon. The brilliant colors of the lustrous striped fabric chased away any sinister shadows still lingering in her bedroom.

The ribbon transported her back to her tenth birthday, one year ago to the day. The memory of the moment her beloved grandmother had given her this precious gift slipped along a well-worn pathway into her mind. Early that morning…

… just as she was waking up, she heard a light tap on her bedroom door. Calling out a sleepy, "Come in", she was relieved to see Granny enter her room and not Jessica or Jennifer wanting to borrow something as usual. The small box in Granny's hand reminded her of what day it was. She sat up with great excitement.

"Good morning and Happy Birthday, Sleepyhead!" Granny announced with a cheery smile, as she sat on the bed and handed Priscilla the box. "This is a special gift for you, my little granddaughter. I wanted to give it to you before you got too busy with your birthday activities."

Bursting with curiosity, Priscilla examined the old-fashioned wooden box. An upholstered inlay of rose-colored flowers and green vines decorated the attached lid. The pristine condition of the antiquated box suggested it held something long-treasured.

With trembling fingers, she lifted the lid and carefully peeled apart the layers of thin gold paper tucked inside. Nestled within the delicate paper was an old hair ribbon, striped in every color of the rainbow. The ribbon still shone with the vibrancy of a real rainbow.

Delighted at first, disappointment soon followed. Even if she wanted to wear a ribbon, which she definitely did not, the colors were so intense they would only call attention to the rare color of her hair, something she tried to avoid at all cost.

Granny's serene smile indicated her understanding. "This is a cherished ribbon, Priscilla. My grandmother gave it to me on my tenth birthday when my hair was exactly the same color as yours. I wore the rainbow ribbon for many years."

Priscilla stared at her grandmother in astonishment. Granny's hair was a deep chestnut color, not blood red like her own. She had never said one word about it being anything else.

Granny laughed at the expression on Priscilla's face. "Yes, dear, I know you're surprised. When I was your age, I was ashamed of the color of my hair and usually kept it covered. I couldn't imagine wearing such a ribbon in my hair."

"But why didn't you tell me your hair was once red like mine?" Priscilla's words sounded more peevish than she intended. Having such an unusual hair color made her feel so different from everyone else.

Granny had obviously anticipated this question. "I waited to tell you about my hair until it was time to give you the ribbon and to share with you the special secret it holds, my dear. The Secret of the Rainbow Ribbon will mean more to you since you have learned from your own experience what it feels like to be different from others and how some people treat you because you are."

Before Priscilla could ask any more questions, Granny lifted the ribbon from the box and handed it to her. "I want you to have this ribbon now, Priscilla, for I believe you are ready to hear its secret."

With a mysterious smile, she revealed the Secret of the Rainbow Ribbon:

**If you learn to love and accept who you are,
one day you will discover that
Your Uniqueness is your most powerful Gift.**

Granny paused in thought for a moment. When she spoke again, her tone sounded grave. "Some people in the world will try to make you less of who you are, Priscilla. They are terrified of their own weaknesses, so they attack those who are different in order to make themselves feel more powerful."

Her round and usually jovial face had grown sad. "If you are unable to stop them, they will take away parts of your spirit until you have only a shadow of yourself left. Much of your life will be spent searching for those lost parts."

Then, as if a dark cloud had passed by, she smiled again. "But today is not the day to think about such things, my dear. Let me see how the rainbow ribbon looks in your hair."

With great ceremony, she leaned over and tied the ribbon into Priscilla's hair. Sitting back, she eyed her granddaughter for a moment. Smiling with satisfaction, she declared, "When you wear the rainbow ribbon, Priscilla, you will remember how beautiful and unique you truly are. By accepting and celebrating your differences, you will become more of yourself, not less. You won't allow anyone to take away parts of your spirit no matter how hard they try."

Granny brought the hand mirror from the dresser and held it so Priscilla could look at herself. The image in the mirror astounded her. The luminous colors of the ribbon emphasized the brilliance of her hair, creating a dazzling sight. Her king-sized freckles beamed with pleasure on her fair skin. For the first time in her life, she really did feel beautiful.

"Priscilla, there is one more thing." Granny's voice sounded so solemn and mysterious that Priscilla wrenched her eyes away from the mirror to look at her. "I have only told you the first half of the Secret of the Rainbow Ribbon. A second and even more important half exists. However, the second half you must discover for yourself. If you wear the ribbon and live out the first half of the secret with honesty and courage, one day you will realize that you have lived into the full Secret of the Rainbow Ribbon."

Leaning over, she gave Priscilla a big hug and whispered in her ear, "Happy Birthday, my little granddaughter!" Then she left the room, leaving Priscilla to puzzle for a long time over what she had just heard.

As the memory receded, Priscilla looked over at the bedroom door, half-expecting to hear a knock and to see Granny coming into the room once more. However, this was impossible. A few months ago, Granny had been in a horrendous car accident. She had died in the hospital without ever regaining consciousness.

Priscilla had been heart-broken. Losing the person she loved most in the world, someone to whom she was "my little granddaughter", words dear to her, seemed almost more than she could bear. It bothered her that she never had a chance to say goodbye to her grandmother.

For as long as she could remember, Granny had lived with them. Priscilla felt closer to her than to anyone else in her family; it never occurred to her to ask why. They shared the same quirky sense of humor. Whatever they did together... cooking and baking, dancing and kicking up their heels, or shopping and going places... it always included plenty of laughter. Granny made the world a better place.

Talking with her grandmother was something she really missed. With endless patience, Granny answered Priscilla's many questions, listened to her troubles, and offered wisdom and support. Even though Priscilla could be stubborn and quick-tempered, and often whined about her brother and sisters, Granny never criticized her. However, she knew when to be firm; then Priscilla was unable to budge her no matter how hard she tried, and she definitely had given it her best shot.

Granny's storytelling was something Priscilla missed most of all. Early every Sunday morning, she would crawl into Granny's bed and snuggle down beside her. There, safe and warm under Granny's comfy homemade quilt, she would listen, spellbound, to the thrilling stories her grandmother had to tell.

The hero of Granny's tales was golden-haired Samuel, a twelve-year-old boy who lived by the seashore in a far-away magical kingdom. His bravery, strength, and fearlessness had made him Priscilla's hero as well.

While Granny recounted what she called *Samuel's Grand Adventures,* Priscilla, in her vivid imagination, stayed glued to Samuel's side as he fought fire-breathing dragons, languished in dark, dank dungeons, scaled towering castle walls, rescued fair princesses, and searched for gold and other fabulous treasures.

When the stories were finished, they would talk and laugh together. Granny would tell her, "One day my ship will come in." Priscilla knew this meant Granny would someday find her own treasure, whatever it might be. It saddened her that Granny had died before this could happen.

For the first few weeks after Granny's death, Priscilla carried her rainbow ribbon with her everywhere, though it hurt too much to look at it. After some time, she took the ribbon out of her pocket to remind herself of Granny's words so she would never forget them. Much to her surprise, this made her feel better.

Recently, she had begun to tie the ribbon into her hair when she was in her favorite place of all, down at the beach. There she felt safe in the privacy of her own little seashore kingdom. But wearing her ribbon around her family or at school was impossible to imagine. The second half of the *Secret of the Rainbow Ribbon* was just going to have to wait.

With a sigh of resignation, she folded the ribbon and put it back in her pocket. Whispering, "Bye Mathilda!" she planted a quick kiss on her cat's furry head. After glancing around her room to make sure all was in perfect order, she smiled and waved farewell to her much-loved stuffed animals and headed off to get ready for school.

While she was in the bathroom combing her hair, Joshua banged on the door. Though there were three other bathrooms in their big house, he wanted this one… probably because she was in it.

"Hurry up, Freckle Face!" he called to her through the door. "Quit trying to scrub off all your ugly spots."

Since he was fourteen, she figured by now he ought to know better, but he continued to tease her and call her names as he always had. Pulling her long wavy hair back from her face, she repeated the

Secret of the Rainbow Ribbon to help drown out his mean words. She tightened the straps of her overalls, took a deep breath, opened the bathroom door, and squeezed past her smirking brother, who was already pushing his way in.

Sneering at her, he said, "It's about time you came out, Missy Prissy. What were you doing in there anyway… playing tic-tac-toe on your freckles?" Pleased with what he considered his little joke, he snickered as he slammed the bathroom door shut.

Not even a "Good Morning" or a "Happy Birthday". That would have been too much to ask. "Boys… yuck!" she exclaimed, as she stomped downstairs. As far as she was concerned, the world could do without them.

Her father had already left for his job in Seattle where he worked with some kind of land development firm. Much of his time, he spent in Washington, DC, meeting with "the bigwigs", Priscilla's name for the important people in government with whom he did business. His company kept a small private jet plane for his use at the local airport, not far from their house.

Though her parents made enough money to afford expensive things, like their big house with all its fancy furnishings, she wished her father worked less than he did. Even when he was at home, he disappeared into his office to work at his computer for hours on end.

Over the years, and particularly since this past summer when they moved to the Pacific Northwest, he spent very little time with his family. In fact, they hardly did anything together anymore. If giving up the house and everything in it meant she could have more time with her father, she would do it in a nanosecond.

Whatever business he was involved in with that nasty Mr. Green kept him busier and more stressed than ever. Mr. Green was the father of Harvey, a boy at her school whom she despised. Horrid Harvey, the name she called him to herself, constantly made fun of her red hair and freckles. From what she could see, the tree was as rotten as the horrid apple hanging from it.

When she reached the bottom of the stairs, her mother rushed over, gave her a quick peck on the cheek, and wished her a cheery "Happy Birthday, Honey!" Calling over her shoulder, "We'll celebrate tonight at dinner, Pris," she grabbed her cell phone and zipped out the door. Her real estate business and shopping for new stuff for the house kept her occupied most of the time.

Though Priscilla tried to feel closer to her mother, it never happened. The two of them had nothing in common. Her mother got along much better with Joshua, Jennifer, and Jessica than with her. At times, Priscilla felt much like Cinderella, though she had never cleaned a fireplace in her life.

Jessica and Jennifer were in the kitchen arguing about who should get the last energy bar and barely acknowledged Priscilla when she walked in. At thirteen, her twin sisters were both as skinny as sticks, and neither of them had red hair or freckles. Priscilla was the only redhead in the family, something she considered extremely unfair.

Adding to the injustice, her sisters had reasonable names, not a quaint name like hers. Granny had once mentioned something about "Priscilla" being the name of her mother's favorite childhood doll. Priscilla figured her mother must have been experiencing an uncharacteristic moment of nostalgia at the time since she was not at all the sentimental type.

Jessica and Jennifer settled their argument by deciding to split the bar between them, "That means fewer calories," they announced with satisfaction to one another as they headed out the door to catch their school bus.

Later, when she was walking down the road to catch her own bus, Priscilla thought about how she and Granny would have giggled over the goofy idea of splitting an energy bar. A familiar feeling of loneliness swept over her. At her new school, she had made few friends and had yet to meet anyone she wanted to know better.

On the way to her classroom, she had to pass Horrid Harvey and some of the other sixth grade boys who loitered in the hallway. When they saw her coming, they hollered, "Here comes Creepy Carrie with her bloody hair! Better stay away from her... she might bring the school crashing down on our heads... hah, hah, hah... Creepy Carrie... Creepy Carrie!"

They were obviously referring to the old horror movie in which some kids dumped a bucket of pig's blood over Carrie's head. As far as Priscilla was concerned, the culprits in the movie got exactly what they deserved. If she could bring the school crashing down on Horrid Harvey and his hateful gang, she certainly would do it. But since she had none of Carrie's secret powers, she just wished with all her might that the horrid boys would vanish into thin air.

Mumbling the *Secret of the Rainbow Ribbon* to herself, she tried to hold her head up high as she walked past them, but when they continued to chant and sneer at her, she lost her nerve. Tucking her head down, she scurried away, the sounds of their laughter echoing in her ears. The *Secret of the Rainbow Ribbon* had been no help at all.

At lunchtime, and at the bus stop after school, Horrid Harvey continued to taunt her without letting up. By the time she got home, she was still feeling upset. Usually she could make herself feel better by going down to the beach. Perhaps it would work its magic on her today. Anyway, it was worth a try.

"At least the beach will help me forget about all the horrid boys in the world!" she muttered out loud, as she made her way across the road and down the steps to the shore. She was heading to the big rock that had become her refuge from the rest of the world.

Chapter Two
The Boy on the Beach

Priscilla did not notice him at first. Her spirits were as gloomy as the fog drifting over the beach. Since gray-and-foggy was her least favorite weather, this only added to her misery. Intent on getting to her rock, she was surprised to find someone, or something, already sitting in her place.

She pulled to a halt and stomped her foot. *Well, that does it!* Her day had been perfectly awful so far. Now someone had invaded her private getaway. A spooky sound came from the rock, and whoever was sitting there appeared as pale and as ghostly as the fog. But no respectable ghost would be caught dead wearing a Harborwood Middle School jacket, and the sound was coming from the guitar he was playing. This was just another stupid boy.

Between Joshua's teasing, and Horrid Harvey and his gang making fun of her, Priscilla was already mad at boys. Now here was another boy thing sitting on Her Rock. This was too much.

Marching up to the rock, she was ready to tell him to get off. When she saw him up close, the words coming out of her mouth were not what she had planned. "Oh my gosh, you are *so* white! No wonder I thought you looked like a ghost. You must be one of those..." She stopped in shame when she realized she had just done to him what she hated others doing to her.

He was an albino. With his wide-brimmed gray hat slung casually over his long silky white hair, he looked magnificent, though she would have died on the spot before letting him know it. Pale blue eyes stared at her over the top of tinted eyeglasses. She might have said he was handsome, except for the nasty scowl spreading across his white face.

"Yeah, and you look like you stuck your head in a bucket of red paint," he sputtered.

Even if she deserved this rude response, his words reminded her of how she felt about boys. Besides, he was sitting on Her Rock. Any thought of his magnificence vanished from her mind. He was sitting where she needed to be.

"You're on my rock, Ghost Boy," she yelled. "Get off. I want to sit there. It's where I always sit. I want my rock back." Even though she sounded childish, she didn't care. After all, it was Her Rock.

He gave her a mean grin. "The beach is public property, Red, not yours. Possession is nine-tenths of the law, or whatever. I was here first, and I'm stayin'. Now get lost."

After trying to stare him down for a moment, she could think of nothing else to say. Walking away in a huff, she plopped down on a nearby smaller rock and glared at him. This other rock was too puny for her to curl her legs under her and pretend to be Queen of the Castle. Besides, today she wanted to be in her own particular place. As far as she was concerned, boys were nothing but jerks.

Since fuming got her nowhere, she decided not to let any more boys, especially this Ghost Boy, whoever he was and whatever he looked like, spoil her birthday or her beach. She took her ribbon from her pocket and tied it in her hair as she thought of Granny's words once more. As usual, this helped her cool down.

"Whatcha doin'?" called out a squeaky voice. A small black and white duck with a huge black head popped up in the water in front of her.

"Well, friend ducky," she answered, as she finished tying her bow, "I was thinking about Granny. Did you know she gave me this ribbon exactly a year ago today, on my tenth birthday?"

"Oh my, my, my. Happy Birthday, Queen Priscilla," the duck quacked. Then all the other birds, even from as far away as the top of the mountain, chimed in with loud singing, cheering, and happy birthday wishes.

"Why thank you all so much. How nice of you to remember," Priscilla giggled. Then nodding regally and imagining she was on her big rock throne, she sat up straighter.

Even though she might want it, she knew that talking for real with birds was impossible. But since she was queen of her seashore kingdom, all the birds and sea creatures were her subjects. In her imagination, she could talk with them whenever she liked, which was often, as she had plenty to say. The best part was pretending that they were talking back to her as well.

The move from California had been easier once she discovered that her new home was across the road from a rocky beach. Granny had given her two special books. One contained pictures of the wildlife of the Pacific Northwest. The other taught her ways in which nature really *did* communicate with people. She had learned to identify birds and sea creatures and discover what messages they brought to her.

Since Granny's death, the beach had become even more significant in her life. Like Samuel, the hero of Granny's stories, Queen Priscilla had her own seashore kingdom. Her lands stretched as far as the snow-covered mountain that she could usually see in the distance, except when it disappeared behind clouds or fog. Her seashore kingdom gave her a safe haven in an ever more frightening world.

"Are you thinking scary thoughts again, Queen Priscilla?" The little duck paddled closer to her. She might have said it was reading her mind except that she knew better.

"Funny you should ask," she answered. "As a matter of fact, I was. There are so many terrible things going on in the world, I hardly know where to begin."

"Well, are you going to tell me about them or not?" demanded the duck.

"My, but you're a pushy duck," she teased. After thinking for a moment, she said, "I could tell you about the wars and all the people who're dying. It all seems so sad. Did you know there are people who kill themselves just so they can kill other people at the same time? Why would anyone want to do that? It doesn't make any sense to me."

"Not to me either, Queen Priscilla," the duck quacked. "If you kill yourself, then you could no longer swim or dive or catch bugs? What would be the fun of that?"

"Other than the part about bugs, it would be no fun at all," chimed in an otter. It had poked its brown nose out of the water to listen for a moment before disappearing into the depths again.

"And that's not all, friend Ducky," Priscilla went on, "what bothers me most is the stuff people do to hurt the earth. The pollution of the oceans harms you and your friends. It's just not right. I wish there was something I could do to help."

No response came from the duck. It had already swum away.

Priscilla sighed. Even though she could imagine her subjects talking with her, she could never count on them to hang around for a whole conversation.

A couple of seals were playing in the water, making loud splashing noises with their flippers. A big old gray whiskery fellow stopped for a moment to look at her. "We heard what you were saying, Queen Priscilla. All of us are worried as well. Things do seem to be getting worse these days. We're glad to know you care about us."

"I wish there was something I could do for you, Mister Seal. No one is interested in what I have to say. Joshua and the twins are always texting their friends or playing video games. My mother is busy at her office or shopping at the mall. Daddy travels all the time. The things that scare me never seem to bother them at all. Since Granny died, I have no one who wants to listen to me or answer any of my questions."

"I'm listening to you, Queen Priscilla," shrilled a big bald eagle flying overhead. "I can look out over your seashore kingdom from up here on high. It helps to see everything from a greater perspective."

"Thanks, Big Eagle," she called after it. "Maybe I would feel better if I could see everything from a different point of view like you do. Besides it sure would be fun to fly." She watched with envy as the eagle soared to the top branch of a tree where it could look down on everything far and wide. Perhaps the world might look a little less daunting from up there.

At least in her seashore kingdom, she felt safe. The beach was real and always there for her. Changes occurred, but this was normal. Nature made more sense to her than the turmoil in the rest of the world. Even the storms, as fierce as they could be, were part of Mother Nature's irrefutable power.

The fog had begun to lift, and she watched the breeze play with the light and currents, creating crisscross patterns on the surface of the water. Sometimes schools of fish transformed the sea into a bubbling witch's cauldron, the tiny dark fish magically turning silver when they leapt out of the water to snatch some bugs or a few rays of sunlight.

On other days, the sea was tranquil, shining with the luster of glass, reflecting clear images of the clouds above and of the trees on Wolf Island, directly across the passage from where she was sitting.

Her curiosity about which of her subjects would show up next kept boredom at bay. As if in response to her thoughts, a massive log transporting a full load of stowaways floated into view.

Five black cormorants, wings extended wide, stood at attention side by side along the log, a row of goofy sentinels in matching regalia. While the log with the wacky squatters sailed slowly past her, Priscilla made up a silly singsong rhyme about them.

Five little cormorants standing on a log,
One disappears in a cloud of fog.
Four little cormorants sailing out to sea,
One flies off since it's time for tea.
Three little cormorants all in a row,
One jumps in 'cause it has to go.
Two little cormorants floating side by side,
One takes off to follow the tide.
One little cormorant left all alone,
Spreads its wings and flies away home.

As if hearing her rhyme, the cormorants flew off the log, one by one, until they had all disappeared. Priscilla clapped her hands and laughed with delight.

Her laughter disturbed a stately blue heron out of its reverie. The skinny long-necked bird had been standing motionless on stick-like legs by the edge of the water not far away. Raucously croaking at her for creating a disturbance, the heron spread its huge blue-tinged wings wide and clumsily flew off to a more private place along the shore.

While checking to see whether her laughter had bothered Ghost Boy, it occurred to her that having pure white hair and skin might be worse than having blood red hair and big brown freckles. The only albinos she had seen before were in movies, and those were all scary characters. Ghost Boy might be a creepy boy, but she would never describe him as scary. People probably teased him as often as they did her. Perhaps he felt lonely too.

After watching him for a moment making his music on top of Her Rock, she no longer cared about *his* loneliness. With all the places available on the beach, why did he have to choose to sit on *her* favorite rock? The world could do without boys, especially this one.

A couple of crows strutted along the beach in front of her, in search of any food the seagulls had left behind. "Hello, Queen Priscilla," they cawed out in their crackly voices.

"Hello to you, too, my black feathered friends. Have you been sharing your magic with anyone today?"

"Always, Your Majesty," the crows cawed in response.

"Keep up the good work," their Queen commanded them.

Until she had read more about them, she thought crows were just stupid noisy birds, and she wished they would go away. Now she knew they were a symbol of magic all around her. As if in homage, they often dropped gifts of crab legs and shells at her feet.

The crows flew away to deliver morsels of food to their families nesting in the trees alongside the road. At the same time, they were keeping an eye out for any birds of prey that might endanger their little ones. Crows took good care of their families.

A kingfisher, patrolling the shore for fish, flew over her with a loud ratchety cry. Her kingdom needed a king, so she was glad to see him. With the speed of a kamikaze pilot, he zoomed down into the water after a fish.

When he rose up into the air again, she called out with respect, "Did you catch anything, Your Highness?"

"Not this time, Your Majesty, but soon," he rattled back at her as he flew farther along the shore. Kingfishers were solitary creatures and did not let humans get too close to them.

Speaking of which, a gray and white seagull had wandered near her on the shore. As a rule, seagulls kept their distance as well, but this big gull showed little unease. She watched with interest as it hopped about on one skinny pink leg.

The one-legged gull differed from all the other gulls that looked so much alike. If she saw it again, she would be able to recognize it, so she named him Pete. She took a cracker from her pocket and tossed it to Pete. He gobbled it up in a hurry.

Most of the time, seagulls were everywhere, in the water, on the shore, and in the air. Often hundreds of gulls squawked at one another as they fought over fish. At other times, only a few gulls were around. All the rest had disappeared.

In her usual way, she asked, "Pete, my seagull friend, where do all the seagulls go when they leave the shore?" He turned his head to look at her as if he had heard her question, which took her aback for a moment.

"That's for me to know and you to wonder," were the cheeky words she finally gave him to say in response. If Pete could have answered for himself, she had an odd feeling he would have said something quite different.

It was time to hunt for rocks and shells to add to her collection, so she got up to walk along the shore. When she said goodbye to Pete, once more he seemed to understand what she was saying, though she knew she was only imagining it.

With glee, she pounced upon a small agate and slipped it into one of her pockets. Having places to put whatever she collected at the beach was one of the reasons she loved wearing her denim overalls. Comfort and practicality came first with her before fashion and fads, another way she differed from the girls at school.

She reserved certain pockets for the special treasures she carried with her everywhere. Whenever she got nervous or upset, she would reach into a pocket to hold one of her treasures. Then she would remind herself of where it came from and what it meant to her. This usually made her feel better.

In addition to her rainbow ribbon, her current treasure trove included a smooth pink quartz heart, numerous tiny pieces of old sea glass, and her favorite shell. The heart stone was a goodbye gift from Rosemary, her best friend at the school she had left behind. She had gathered the multi-colored sea glass during many happy hours spent beachcombing in Victoria, BC where she had gone on a trip with Granny, shortly before her accident. The shell was one Priscilla found on her own beach the same day she arrived in the Pacific Northwest.

This was a unique shell. The outside had the familiar appearance of a clamshell, but the inside was extraordinary. The glossy inner surface pictured a rose-colored bear standing on the shore of a purple sea with waves flowing around its paws. The bear figure held within it the images of a wolf, a seal, an otter, an eagle, an owl, and a raven. If she looked carefully, she could even find a frog and a snake.

The way the shell curved around the bear made her feel as if she were peering into a mysterious cave. There were times when she felt a powerful yearning to shrink down and crawl deep inside her shell cave to discover what secrets lay hidden within it.

As she picked her way over some barnacled rocks, her family came to mind. Soon they would gather for her birthday dinner. Somehow, all of them managed to get together for such special occasions. It was one way they could pretend they were still a big happy family. But this birthday, Granny would not be there, and remembering this made Priscilla feel very sad indeed.

Besides, once she had blown out the candles on the fancy store-bought cake and opened the customary expensive presents, everyone would go about their business. Her father would shut himself in his office; her mother would get on her cell phone; Joshua would play his video games;

and Jennifer and Jessica would hurry off to chat on their computer with their many friends. Priscilla would be on her own as usual.

With a big sigh, she took the ribbon out of her hair, folded it, and put it back in her pocket. Determined to try to enjoy whatever birthday celebration awaited her, she headed for home.

A few days later, when weather and tide permitted, she walked back down to the shore. She was surprised to find Ghost Boy sitting on Her Rock again. This time she ignored him, but she made up her mind to hurry and get there before him on the following day.

Rushing was no help at all. Middle school let out earlier than elementary school, a fact she had overlooked. When she got to the beach, he was already sitting on Her Rock. Even on the weekend, when she figured she would have it to herself, much to her disgust, he was there again.

Pete showed up much of the time as well. Her pleasure at seeing the big one-legged seagull almost helped her forget about Ghost Boy and the loss of Her Rock. She could talk to Pete, and he seemed to like being around her.

One day during the following week, she arrived at the beach at the same time as Ghost Boy. They raced to the rock. When he got there first, she stomped her foot in exasperation and said, "Don't you have anything else to do but come here, Ghost Boy?"

Raising his white eyebrows, he gave her a funny little smirk as he said, "Maybe you oughta ask yourself the same question, Red," which made her feel downright silly.

When she thought about it later, she realized she *had* been going down to the beach a lot more often since she had first seen him. Even though no polite words had passed between them, there was an unexpected sense of comfort in his presence. She felt less alone. Ghost Boy and the sound of his guitar were becoming as familiar to her as the seagulls on the shore.

Then something happened to change both of their lives forever in ways neither of them would fully appreciate for a long time. It was the beginning of what Priscilla would one day fondly recall as the first of her own *"Grand Adventures".*

Chapter Three
The Seagull

It all began on a Friday afternoon. Classes let out early so students and teachers could attend an important school meeting concerning safety during times of war and terrorist threats. Priscilla's mother was required to go with her. Afterwards, she dropped Priscilla off at home and returned to her office.

The afternoon was once again unseasonably warm and sunny. Since Priscilla was home earlier than usual, it was a perfect time to go down to the beach. But after hearing about all the terrible things going on in the world, and what could possibly occur at her school, she was feeling down in the dumps. A cat snuggle might help, so she headed upstairs to find Mathilda.

As she entered her bedroom, she heard an unknown voice inside her head saying to her. "Come on down. Come on down to the sea!" No matter how much she tried to ignore it, the voice kept repeating, "Come on down. Come on down to the sea!" This voice was definitely not one she had created in her imagination.

Once before, an unknown voice had spoken inside her head in this way. It happened when she was walking along the beach one afternoon after a storm. An older female voice asked, "Don't you know how much you are loved, girl?" At the same time, a double rainbow burst through the clouds over Wolf Island, spilling vibrant colors across the sky. She felt as if the rainbow was a precious gift given just to her…

…like Granny's gift of the rainbow ribbon! Never before had she connected these two events. It gave her goose bumps. She decided to listen to the voice and go down to the beach. Anyway, it might help her to feel better.

When she got there, Ghost Boy was already sitting on the big rock, playing his guitar. With an audible sigh, she took her place on what was now her second favorite rock and tied her ribbon in her hair. The school meeting still occupying her mind, she stared absently at the water.

A black mass floating close to shore on the incoming tide grabbed her attention. Forgetting about everything else, she rushed to the edge of the water to see what it was.

A big seagull floated dead in the water. Some sort of gummy tar had blackened its white feathers. All at once, the gull gave a soft mewing sound, and one eye appeared above the water, staring straight at her. The seagull was alive, though just barely. Help was needed right away, but she had no clue what to do.

In desperation, she called over to Ghost Boy, "Could you come here and help me please?"

He ignored her and continued to play his guitar, probably thinking she was trying to trick him into leaving the rock.

This made her angry, so she yelled at him, "Hey, Ghost Boy. This seagull is dying. Can you get over here and help?" Since she really needed his help, she added a beseeching, "*Please!*"

This time the boy looked up. He put down his guitar and hurried over. After studying the gull for a moment, he took off his school jacket and laid it open on the rocks. Gently lifting the gull out of the water, he quickly wrapped it in the jacket. The bird made no move.

"We need to get help right away. I've got a friend who knows what to do. Bring me my guitar and backpack." Ghost Boy called these commanding words to her as he strode off with his bird bundle, heading for the stairs leading up to the road.

For the gull's sake, she obeyed his rude orders and hurried after him, getting to the road just as he was coming out of the bushes pushing an old bicycle; now she knew how he got to the beach so quickly. He had stowed the bird in a wire basket attached to the front of the bike.

Without a word of thanks, he snatched his backpack and guitar out of her hands, slung them over his back, climbed on his bike, and got ready to ride away.

She grabbed hold of the bike, crying out with irritation, "Wait a minute! I want to go with you. I found the seagull first."

"Suit yourself," he snapped, as he rode off.

Grumbling, she followed him. He rode at a reasonable pace, so she was able to keep him in sight, though when he disappeared around the curve of the road, she figured she'd lost him for sure. Even though he was willing to help the gull, her low opinion of boys held firm.

As she rounded the curve, she was relieved to see him still in view, walking his bike up the steep hill. Puffing and panting, she ran to catch up with him. As she drew nearer, she noticed a logo with the letters N.O.A.H. imprinted on the back of his shirt and wondered if this was his name or if the letters stood for something else.

Once she caught up with him, they walked in silence side by side, giving her time to catch her breath and steal a quick peek at him. He was a good head taller than she was, and his thin pale face looked very serious. She guessed he must be around twelve or thirteen. To her surprise, she wanted to know more about him.

He glanced at her and then looked ahead again quickly. Clearing his throat, he asked, without much enthusiasm, "What's your name?"

"Priscilla," she replied, still trying to catch her breath. "Priscilla Anne Wallace. What's yours?"

"Mine's Alasdair McAdams." He mumbled the words, as if he begrudged having to tell her.

After another short silence, she asked, "Where are we going?"

"To my friend's house. She's into birds... used to volunteer at one of those bird rehab centers. You know... the places they help birds caught in oil slicks."

"Do you think the seagull will die?" She wasn't sure if she wanted to hear the answer.

"Don't know." He groused the words at her. "But Mollie will know what to do. She knows lots of stuff about birds."

"Does Mollie live near you?" It sure was hard to keep this sluggish conversation going.

"Yep, Mollie and Jack Gordon... they live next door to me and my mom." As if he was uncomfortable sharing this information, he began to walk faster. The conversation, such as it was, appeared to be over.

At the top of the hill, he turned his bike into a narrow private lane leading to a forest of tall fir trees. Continuing to walk in silence, they passed some large new houses, the kind her mother liked to sell, and entered into the forest. A moment later, they turned down a long curved driveway lined on both sides by huge old rhododendron bushes.

Tucked in the trees at the bottom of the driveway was a charming little cottage that could have come straight out of one of her favorite fairy tale books. It looked so inviting, she felt comforted just by the sight of it.

As they approached the front porch, a riotous barking broke out. An energetic golden retriever bounded out of the house to greet them. After licking Alasdair thoroughly, the dog turned and looked her over with big friendly brown eyes.

"This is Geordie." Alasdair said, giving the dog's head a good rub.

"Hi Geordie!" she whispered, holding herself back. Unfamiliar big dogs scared her. Geordie wagged his tail with exuberance and trotted over to greet her. His joyful welcome soon eased her nervousness.

Alasdair carefully lifted the bird out of the basket. Geordie escorted them into the house and down a long hallway where he presented them to an older woman in a wheelchair waiting to greet them with a welcoming smile. Short silver hair framed the kind worn face gazing at them over a pair of small reading glasses set on the tip of her nose. A cord attached to the glasses hung around the back of her neck.

Priscilla felt drawn to the woman's piercing gray eyes, which seemed to take in Alasdair, his bundle, and her at the same time. When Priscilla felt the intense gaze rest for a moment on her rainbow ribbon, she remembered that it was still in her hair.

"Hi, Alasdair," the woman greeted him in a warm, husky voice. Nodding to Priscilla, she added, "and hello to you too, my dear."

Alasdair, his voice a little rushed, introduced them to each other, "Hi Mollie. This is Priscilla. Priscilla, this is Mollie."

Sensing urgency in Alasdair's behavior and voice, Mollie told him, "Put whatever it is on the dining room table, Alasdair, and let me see what you've brought me." She patted Geordie on the head and sent him to lie down. Then she turned her chair and followed Alasdair as he laid his fragile bundle on a round oak table and opened the jacket.

She rolled her chair closer to the bird. Murmuring, "Oh, you poor little thing," she began examining the gull. Priscilla noticed that Mollie's fingers were badly deformed. Granny's fingers had begun to curve in much the same way from what she said was "her arthritis". Priscilla wondered if Mollie had a similar illness.

While Mollie was busy with the bird, Priscilla glanced around. The dining area was part of a large open space with the living room on one side and the kitchen on the other. Windows and sliding glass doors opened out to a deck where small birds and a brown squirrel nibbled at feeders. The house sat at the top of a steep overgrown hillside with a view of the water and Wolf Island off in the distance.

Gleams of light drew her eyes to a chess set that covered the top of a small table next to the living room window. The intricately carved chess pieces and matching checkerboard were made of black and white marble. Multi-colored jeweled crowns on the heads of the kings and queens sparkled in the afternoon sunlight that streamed in through the glass.

On the far wall, a fire glowed in a stone fireplace. The mantelpiece above it displayed various photographs and a tall ship inside a bottle. Shelves stuffed with books lined both sides of the fireplace.

A telescope, mounted on a wooden tripod, took up the corner nearest the window, while a grandfather clock chimed in the other corner. A well-used upright piano stood against the wall with stacks of sheet music piled on top of it and a couple of guitars and a small electronic keyboard leaning against it.

Geordie had curled up on a braided rug in front of the fireplace. Two large cats, an orange longhair and a calico, snoozed on blankets at opposite ends of a couch. The furnishings, though old and worn, looked cheerful and comfortable. Priscilla felt at home in this cozy room, more pleasing to her than her fancy living room at home with all its brand new furnishings and expensive artwork.

After Mollie finished checking the seagull, she turned to Priscilla and Alasdair. "This gull is badly injured." Though her words were quiet, the fierceness in her tone startled Priscilla. "He's dehydrated and has hypothermia. This doesn't usually happen to birds in this area. Things must be getting much worse. Damn those stupid oil tankers anyway!"

"What can we do to help?" Alasdair asked in a hurry, as if anxious to keep Mollie from getting any more upset.

Mollie took a deep breath. "Right now, nothing except pray. I need to get him into a warm, dark place and give him some charcoal to soak up any oil he has swallowed. After I get him stabilized, we can see if he is strong enough to survive the cleansing of his feathers. Jack will be back from town shortly and can help."

"Shouldn't we get him to a veterinarian?" Priscilla wanted to be helpful.

"I've worked with birds like this before, Priscilla. I have all the equipment I need right here," Mollie said. "I probably know as much as any vet about dealing with this type of problem. Besides, I don't think he should be moved. He's on his last legs… or I guess I should say 'leg', as he has only one leg, poor thing."

Priscilla's heart skipped a beat. It had never occurred to her that the gull could be her friend Pete, and he might be dying. All at once, she felt as angry as Mollie.

As Priscilla tried to calm down and listen, Mollie went on, "However I'll alert the necessary authorities about the gull and the oil to make sure I'm doing whatever is needed."

After gazing in silence at Priscilla and Alasdair for a moment, Mollie added, "If the gull lives, I could use some help from both of you. My hands are not the best, as you can see. The two of you working together could wash the oil off his feathers. I can teach you how to do it."

"His name is Pete," Priscilla said in quiet voice. "He's been hanging around the beach this past week. I think he knows me. It must be the same seagull I call Pete," she insisted, with more stubbornness than usual, as she was uncomfortable with what she was revealing about herself.

"Pete," Mollie repeated, looking at Priscilla with her penetrating gaze. "Thanks for letting me know, Priscilla. Pete it is. I'll do the best I can for him. If I have anything to say about it, we'll soon have Pete well and back where he belongs." Mollie wrapped the gull once more and lifted him into her lap. Rolling her chair through the kitchen, she disappeared through a doorway on the far side.

Left by themselves in the dining room, Priscilla and Alasdair stood in silence, neither knowing quite what to do. Then Alasdair said, in a gruff voice, "She means it, you know. When Mollie sets her mind to something, nothing gets in her way. If anyone can save the gull... er, Pete... she'll do it."

Tears welled up in Priscilla's eyes. Despite his gruffness, she heard kindness in his words. Since she knew his name was Alasdair, she no longer had to call him Ghost Boy. Maybe he was not as horrible as he seemed... just maybe. "Thanks... Alasdair," she whispered, turning away. It would not do to cry in front of a boy.

After agreeing to return the following morning to see how Pete was doing, they left together to go home. At the top of the driveway, Alasdair rode on down the lane to his house, which he told her was just around the bend.

Priscilla walked slowly back to her own house, lost in thought most of the way. By the time she got home, the sun was beginning to set. She went inside and stood by the big picture window in the living room to watch the sunset. As the colors brushed across the sky, they changed from light pink and purple, to rosy peach and orange.

In the background, she could hear the murmur of the television in the family room, so her mother must be home. Joshua and the twins would still be out with their friends. Her father was in Washington, DC at an important conference and was not due back until the following day.

While she took in the sunset, her mind returned to Pete, Alasdair, and Mollie. Pete was an innocent creature, injured by people with no concern for the damage they did to the environment. She felt angry and sad and wished she could find a way to help. The least she could do was to say a prayer for Pete as Mollie had suggested, and so she did.

It had been a peculiar sort of day. Yet, she had a sense it was a meaningful day in her life, even though she had no idea why she should feel this way.

Then, for the first time since she heard it earlier in the afternoon, she remembered the voice inside her head insisting, "Come on down. Come on down to the sea!" With all the excitement, she had completely forgotten about the voice. Whose voice was it, and where on earth had it come from?

Chapter Four
New Friends

"It's really quite lovely, isn't it?" commented another voice. This familiar voice was not in Priscilla's head but came from her father. Much to her surprise, he had come up beside her and stood looking out the window at the sunset as well.

"Daddy, I didn't know you were home yet! I thought you weren't coming back til tomorrow."

"I had some thinking to do, Priscilla, so I decided to leave the conference a day early." His voice was quiet as usual, but he sounded odd. She took a closer look at him. His shoulders slumped forward, and he seemed older and quite worn out. There was a strained expression in his eyes, and his skin had a gray sheen to it. Though she knew he had seemed tense for some time, she had never seen him looking like this.

"You really like this place, don't you, Priscilla." It was more of a statement than a question. "I know how much you love the beach. I hear you're down there almost every day now."

"How do you know that?" She looked at him in astonishment. It had never occurred to her that her father, or anyone else in the family, noticed much of anything she did.

"Oh, I hear rumors once in a while." He smiled at her with great tenderness. "I'm not as unaware of my children's activities as you might think."

"I guess not." This was not how her father had been behaving lately. She wanted to hold on to this moment with him, a reminder of happier times they had spent together before he started working so much.

All at once, a memory of being with her father when she was very young began to push its way into her mind. Before the memory could make itself known, the painful feelings it always brought with it wrapped around her like a heavy cloak. These feelings weighed her down and dragged her places she had no desire to go.

Though these awful feelings were familiar, she did not understand them, nor did she like them. Right away, she did what she had long ago taught herself to do. By concentrating hard on the sunset, she allowed herself to think only of it and of nothing else. Before long, much to her great relief, the heavy feelings faded away, carrying any traces of the memory with them.

As she watched the sky begin to darken, she recalled the bleak expression on her father's face. Turning to look up at him again, she asked, "Daddy is there something wrong? Is there anything I can do to help?"

Her father was quiet for a long time. Just as she decided he wasn't going to answer, he sighed deeply and began to talk. "No, my dear, there is nothing you can do, but thank you for asking. I have a lot on my mind. I must make a difficult decision in the next few weeks. What I decide will have a tremendous effect on our environment and on many people's lives. I need to think carefully before I make my decision."

She stood for a moment, pondering his words and his appearance. Then she reached into her pocket and touched her shell. Her fingers rubbed the well-known curves on the outside and slipped over the sleek inner lining with the bear image. Making up her mind in a hurry, she took it out of her pocket.

Grasping her father's hand, she pressed her shell into it. "Here, Daddy. I want you to have my favorite shell. I found it on the beach when we first moved here. I've been carrying it with me ever since. When I feel nervous or upset, I reach into my pocket and hold it. I remind myself of where it came from and what's important to me. It always makes me feel better. Maybe it will help you to make the right decision."

For a moment, her father gazed down at the shell. When he lifted his head to smile his thanks at her, his eyes glistened. Since she had no recollection of ever seeing her father with tears in his eyes, she stood frozen, not knowing what to say. When he turned away again, she decided what she had seen was just a trick of the light.

He put the shell deep into the pocket of his pants. After patting her gently on the shoulder, he turned and left the room as silently as he had come in.

The following morning she awakened to the sound of rain splattering against the windowpanes. She snuggled down under her quilt to listen to countless tiny raindrop feet scampering across the rooftop. Mathilda, sensing she was awake, crept up from the foot of the bed and curled up next to her. Priscilla stroked her fur, and soon the rumbling sound of blissful contentment welled up from deep within the big cat.

The image of her father's worried face came back to her. What could be causing him so much distress? What was the difficult decision he had to make and how would it affect the environment?

He was an important man; she knew many people in the government depended on him. Other than that, she had no idea exactly what he did.

Speaking of work, even though it was Saturday, both her parents would be working, so no rides were available. But she needed to check on Pete. He was her friend, and she wanted to help if she could. She supposed she would just have to get drenched in the dreary downpour. Anyway, this would give her a chance to try out the expensive rainsuit and matching umbrella her father had given her for her birthday.

Later in the morning, decked out in her new rain gear, she set off along the beach road. Grasping her umbrella, she held it against the wind and rain to keep it from blowing inside out.

The storm clouds hid her mountain making it hard to believe it was still there. Across the passage, Wolf Island floated in and out of the mist, transformed into the legendary Isle of Avalon.

The tide was in, covering the shore with greenish gray water. The wind blew frothy waves over the seawall, sending some light spray in her direction. One other stormy day, when the sea surged up like this, she had been thrilled to discover hundreds of big spidery crabs clinging to the beach side of the seawall. Though she had only seen the crabs once, she continued to look in hopes she might see them again. She leaned over, but the wall was bare.

Granny said some things in nature happened so rarely you could consider yourself lucky to see them once in a lifetime, like the time they visited the Oregon Coast and found the sand sprinkled with so many tiny purple jellyfish that the beach looked like a meadow full of wildflowers.

"It's a good idea to keep your eyes wide open, Priscilla, or you could miss some truly amazing sights," Granny told her.

Priscilla liked this idea a lot. She tried to keep her eyes open most of the time… except when she was asleep, though even then, her dream eyes continued to see some unusual sights as well.

She gazed down at the rocks and shells far beneath the wavering water. It fascinated her how in one moment, she could be walking along the shore exploring its treasures and, in another moment, the sea covered everything, creating a mysterious new underwater world. Her favorite brother in the old story of the five Chinese quintuplets and their unique gifts was the one who could swallow the sea, exposing all the wonders of the deep. If she ever had a chance to explore the bottom of the sea, like the little boy in the story, she too might forget to come back.

There were no other walkers or cars out along the wet road. Only one or two lonely-looking seagulls sat on telephone poles. Wrapped in her protective gear, with the wind and rain buffeting her, she felt as if she were in a still, silent world of her own, a mysterious time and space where nothing was quite the same as before.

Fighting her way through the storm to get to Mollie's house took a while. When she finally walked down the long curved driveway, she wondered if Pete would still be alive. She was a little afraid to find out.

Alasdair and Geordie answered her nervous knock. After a thorough licking by the friendly dog, Priscilla left her wet coverings and umbrella on the hall tree and walked into the dining area. The house smelled of wood smoke, freshly baked bread, and something deliciously spicy that made her mouth water.

Mollie was nowhere in view. An older man stood chatting with Alasdair in the living room. When he saw Priscilla, he strode over to greet her, warmth radiating from his dark eyes and wide smile. He was a large man, tall and sturdy, and she felt tiny when she looked up at him. His curly hair, moustache, and beard were the same gingery gray color as the fur on one of her favorite teddy bears.

"You must be Priscilla," he said in a deep full voice, taking her small hand in his huge paw. "I'm Jack, Mollie's husband. Come and get warm by the fire." He led her into the living room. "Imagine you coming out in this storm. Mollie is with Pete and should be back in a few minutes. Your bird is still alive, you'll be happy to know." And indeed, Priscilla was much relieved to get this good news.

"I know you've already met Geordie as he is our family greeter," Jack laughed. "Now you must meet the rest of the family." He went over to the two cats she had seen curled up on the couch the day before. "This is Copycat," he said, picking up the orange cat and gently stroking it. "And that little girl is Freckles." He smiled and nodded at the calico cat.

Hearing her name, Freckles lifted her spotted face, cocked her whiskers with disdain at Priscilla, and put her head down once more.

Jack went on, "She was Mollie's cat before we got married, and Copycat was mine. Freckles takes a little while to get used to new people, but if you ignore her, she'll get curious about you and come around."

Priscilla giggled. "My cat's the same way. Mathilda won't do anything unless it's her idea." Wanting to include Alasdair in the conversation, she asked him, "Do you have any pets?"

"No, but I'm here so much, Jack and Mollie's pets are like mine." Alasdair bent over and scratched Freckle's head, and she lifted her head for more.

"That's right!" Jack laughed again. He was such a good-natured man; Priscilla couldn't help liking him.

Mollie rolled her chair into the dining area, greeted Priscilla, and echoed Jack's concern about her being out in the storm. Mollie looked even more tired than she had the day before. With whatever was wrong with her, Priscilla guessed it had been difficult for her to take care of Pete.

Mollie's words confirmed these suspicions. "We had a rough night, Priscilla, but Pete made it through. I think he's going to live. He's improving much faster than I would have thought possible. As crazy as it sounds, he seems determined to get well. I think he might even be ready to be washed down tomorrow."

"Could I see him, please?" Priscilla asked, wondering if the older woman might think it was foolish.

"Of course you can, my dear. Come with me." Turning her chair around, she headed off through the kitchen. As Priscilla followed along, she glimpsed some loaves of freshly baked bread on the kitchen counter and a large pot of soup simmering on the stove... the source of the delicious smells.

Mollie led her into a small room at the far side of the kitchen. On a long table, at one end of the room, Pete lay motionless on a pile of soft rags inside a big cage. An electric heater was keeping him warm.

He looked up at Priscilla as soon as she came in and kept his eyes on hers as she spoke to him. Once again, she was sure he understood everything she said. She could even have sworn he was happy to see her.

Mollie said, "Pete does seem to recognize you, Priscilla. That's interesting. I've never seen a gull behave like this one before. Actually," she continued, sounding puzzled, "Pete is not like any other bird I've worked with. There is something different about him, though I can't quite put my finger on what the difference is."

By the time they returned to the main living area, Alasdair and Jack were in the midst of a game of chess. Mollie said, "Alasdair is having lunch with us, Priscilla. Would you like to join us?"

"Oh yes, I'd love to!" Priscilla was delighted, as she liked being in this comfortable home. Besides, she had nowhere else to go. With both her parents working and her siblings busy with their friends, she was on her own as usual.

She set the table and helped Mollie put out the lunch. When it was time to eat, they all sat down to steaming bowls of chunky vegetable soup and thick slices of warm buttered bread.

"We have Jack to thank for baking the bread," Mollie told them. "Let's join hands and give a word of thanks for the meal."

As Mollie said grace, which included a prayer for Pete's recovery, Priscilla was thinking how glad she was to be sitting across the table from Alasdair so she did not have to hold *his* hand. That would have been *too weird*.

Once they began eating, Jack asked, "Why don't you tell us a little about yourself, Priscilla, and about your family. How long have you lived around here?"

Between mouthfuls of tasty soup and bread, she answered Jack's questions. It felt so good to have someone once again interested in what she had to say. After a while, she remembered Granny telling her to be sure not to *mono*... something... the conversation... well, not to talk about herself for too long, so she asked them, "What about you guys?"

Mollie answered. "Jack and I are both retired school teachers, Priscilla. We met about ten years ago on a bird-watching trip. I was living on the Oregon coast at the time, which is where I learned about helping birds caught in oil slicks. I used to do a lot more to help birds before my rheumatoid arthritis got worse, making it necessary for me to use this chair to get around." Mollie did not sound sorry for herself.

She went on, "Jack and I met Alasdair nine years ago when we bought this house. He lives with his mother just down the road. While she was at work, we were lucky to be able to take care of him, until he was old enough to take care of himself, of course. We've been best of friends ever since." Mollie smiled at Alasdair as she said this, and from the glances they exchanged, Priscilla could tell how fond they were of one another.

"My mother's a nurse and has to work long hours," Alasdair added. "I'm really glad Mollie and Jack moved in next door. This is my second home."

"That's right!" Jack agreed. "Alasdair and I spend a lot of time together. We play chess, go boating and fishing… when the weather is not like this, of course…" he gestured toward the window, "and all three of us love music, so we do lots of jamming. Alasdair is a master on the guitar; I can get a bit ridiculous at the piano; and if Mollie feels up to it, she sings and plays the keyboard with us."

"I used to sing with a band, a long time ago," Mollie told Priscilla with a wry smile.

"Of course Alasdair is the real musician around here," Jack announced with great enthusiasm. "In addition to playing the guitar, he writes his own music. Even though he won't tell you himself, Priscilla, he's extremely talented."

Alasdair blushed, his white skin turning almost as red as her hair. "I'm not that good. You're just being nice."

Not about to let Alasdair off the hook, Jack added, "As far as I'm concerned, Alasdair, you're another Johnny Winter."

"Who's Johnny Winter?" Priscilla asked. Though she loved music and knew the names of many musicians, this one was unfamiliar.

Alasdair answered her question. "Johnny, and his brother, Edgar, are long time successful R and B musicians. They started playing when they were kids." Then he looked down as he mumbled, "Both of them are albinos, but they never let that stop them."

He looked so uncomfortable Priscilla thought it might be a good idea to change the subject. Turning to Mollie, she asked, "Do you know how Pete got so much oil on him?"

Before she answered, Mollie took a deep breath, and her expression grew somber. "It probably came from a tanker or freighter carrying oil around Puget Sound somewhere, Priscilla. The owners allow the oil to leak out and contaminate the water.

The waves carry the oil slick to shore, endangering birds and sea creatures in the process.

Such thoughtless leakage of oil and other toxic substances is far too common an occurrence these days," Mollie went on. "It seems to be getting worse all the time and does great damage to our oceans and our environment. We should be protecting our earth, not destroying it."

Mollie took another big breath. Then, to Priscilla's surprise, she smiled. "But you don't want to get me started on all that, Priscilla, as I can become quite heated about it. Jack and Alasdair can attest to that." She smiled at both of them, and they nodded and grinned back at her in agreement. "It is far better to find something to laugh about instead. Laughing doesn't change the world, but it does remind us that a sense of humor makes it easier to tolerate things we don't like."

Priscilla was surprised to see Mollie smile even though she was upset about something so important to her. She was a lot like Granny. It made Priscilla feel better to know that someone as wise as Mollie was as concerned about the environment as she was. Alasdair was lucky to live right next door to the Gordons.

After lunch, Jack said, "Hey, how about a little music? Do you feel up to it today, Mollie?"

She nodded and looked over at Priscilla, "Perhaps for a little while, if Priscilla will help me?" Priscilla readily agreed.

Jack placed the keyboard on Mollie's lap, and Priscilla drew a chair up close beside her. Together they created a spirited accompaniment for Jack at the piano and Alasdair on the guitar. From time to time, Mollie sang along while Priscilla hummed and clapped her hands.

Priscilla loved every minute of it and could have kept going, but Mollie soon grew tired and needed to rest. Priscilla and Alasdair left to go home, promising to return mid-morning of the following day to do the bird washing, if Pete was up for it.

That evening, Priscilla's whole family happened to be at the dinner table at the same time, a rare occurrence these days. While everyone was eating, her parents made an occasional comment about work needed around the house or in the yard, but other than that, no one said much.

Priscilla thought about the lively lunch at the Gordons' house and wished her own family could talk with one another in the same way. Maybe if she told them about Pete it might help. She began to share her story.

Before long, Joshua interrupted her with snorting and laughter. "Why are you worried about one stupid seagull, Missy Prissy? There's a million of 'em out there. If one dies, there's plenty more. I don't see why you want to have anything to do with 'em anyway. Stupid messy birds!"

Jennifer wrinkled her nose in disgust. "Why would you want to wash oil off a bird? It sounds gross!"

In a voice quivering with concern, Jessica whispered, "If you touch a wild bird you could get the bird flu. Be sure you wash your hands, and don't you dare touch me or anything of mine."

"Oil is important in the world, Priscilla," her mother said sharply. "A little spilled oil is just one of the consequences people have to deal with in order to have the things they want, especially cars. I need a big luxurious car to transport my wealthy clients. And cars need oil."

Her father said nothing at all. When her mother started to talk, he seemed to withdraw into himself even more.

Priscilla gave up. After dinner, she went upstairs to her bedroom and threw herself across her bed. Burying her nose in Mathilda's fur, she tried to soothe the ache in her heart. What made her feel better was remembering that she would be going back to Mollie and Jack's house the following morning.

Chapter Five
Lending a Hand

The next day, Priscilla headed out early on her long walk. The storm had passed, and it was another clear winter day. The water shimmered in the sunlight. A brisk breeze lightly kissed her cheeks, bringing with it the pleasant aroma of wood smoke and a powerful whiff of seaweed exposed on the shore by the receding tide.

She had tied her ribbon in her hair. This was the day she was ready to risk wearing it around the few people she was beginning to trust. Knowing that Alasdair and Mollie had already seen it made it easier.

When she came to a narrow strip of fruit trees sandwiched between the road and the shore, she looked over at her favorite pear tree. Since the summer, every pear but one had fallen from the tree. For some reason, this little pear still hung by the thinnest of threads from a bare branch. Even after going through some wild and wicked windstorms, it had not let go. She had watched it shrivel down to a wrinkled brown memory of the juicy pear it had once been.

This stubborn little pear had become her friend, so she was pleased to see that, after yesterday's storm, it still clung to the tree. Holding on to what was familiar was so much easier than letting go and falling into the unknown. Anyway, she knew this was how she would feel if she were the pear. If she let go, she would have no idea where she would land or what would happen to her.

When she arrived at the Gordons' house, Jack met her at the door. "Good morning, Priscilla. Come on in." As she followed him down the hall, he told her, "Pete's ready for the next step. Mollie's in the back room preparing for the washing. You're just in time to join Alasdair for a glass of orange juice and a cinnamon roll if you'd like."

She sat down at the table across from Alasdair. They greeted one another uneasily while Jack set the food in front of them. The gooey cinnamon rolls were right out of the oven, and the orange juice, freshly squeezed. Since Granny's death, Priscilla had not tasted anything so delicious.

After Jack left to help Mollie, Alasdair and Priscilla sat in awkward silence. He was wearing his N.O.A.H. shirt again, and she was just about to ask him what the initials meant when Jack came back to say, "Mollie's ready for you now."

With great relief, Priscilla and Alasdair jumped up and headed for the back room.

Mollie greeted them with a cheerful smile. "Good morning, you two. I'm so glad you're here to help. Come and sit at the table, please. Pete is all ready for you." Pete was inside his cage, which had been set to one side of the table. Two large tubs of warm water... one clear and one soapy... sat on either side of a pile of clean rags.

Mollie directed them to sit on two tall stools in front of the table. She tied long plastic aprons around each of them and gave them rubber gloves to protect their hands. Gently lifting Pete out of the cage, she set him down on the rags in front of Priscilla.

After instructing her how to lift and hold the gull, Mollie had her immerse him in the tub of warm soapy water. While Priscilla lifted Pete's feathers, Mollie showed Alasdair how to agitate the water into the feathers to wash off the oil.

When Mollie had finished teaching them this procedure, she added, "When the water fills with oil, put Pete into the tub of clear water and ring the bell. Jack will bring in fresh water. The water will need to be changed many times before you're done. Just go slowly and follow these steps until all the oil is gone from Pete's feathers. It should take you about an hour or so." After watching them work for a few minutes, and gently tweaking some of their hesitant movements to give them more confidence, Mollie left them to work on their own.

Pete was cooperative. It was almost as if he knew they were trying to help him. Before long, they had all settled into a rhythmic routine.

Spending time alone with Alasdair, yet knowing so little about him, felt awkward to Priscilla. Perhaps it was time to change this. Not sure where to begin, she decided an apology might help. "I'm really sorry about what I said to you when I first saw you at the beach," she began. "I've never seen anyone who looks like you before except in the movies. It was rude. I didn't mean to hurt your feelings."

"Forget it," he said.

Trying another approach, she asked, "What do the letters N.O.A.H. on your shirt mean?"

"It stands for the National Organization of Albinism and Hypopigmentation. It's a group for people like me." He was not helping her out much at all.

"What do you mean by people like you?" She hoped his answer might help her understand what it was like to be an albino.

He turned to look at her as he said in his gruff voice, "Do you really wanna know, or are you just being nosy like everyone else?"

Swallowing her initial angry response to his rudeness, she made every effort to be friendly. "I really *do* want to know. I have no idea what it means to be an albino or how it affects people. I get teased a lot about my red hair and freckles. I don't like it. I guess you get teased a lot, too."

"Yeah, you could say that." The bitterness in his voice felt like a blast of cold wind pushing her away from him.

Pete watched them as if he understood every word they were saying.

Once more, she made an effort at conversation. "I really like Mollie and Jack. You're lucky to live next door to them."

He perked up at the mention of his friends. "Yeah, they're cool. They're like grandparents to me. I don't have any other relatives besides my mom."

Without stopping to think, she asked, "Where's your father?" When there was no answer, she turned to look at him. From the desolate expression on his face, she knew she had asked the wrong question. His mind had gone somewhere else.

"Well, this is not going well," she whispered to Pete. They continued to work in an uneasy silence, taking time out to ring the bell whenever the water got oily. Jack came in each time with a fresh tub of water.

Priscilla decided to give it one last try. "I'm sorry, Alasdair. I keep saying the wrong things. I'm just trying to get to know you better. I didn't mean to hurt you again."

He was quiet for a few moments before he said, "Most kids I run into don't wanna know me better. They just stare at me as if I'm some kind of freak."

While she was trying to decide what to say in response, he sighed and began speaking again, this time in a slightly more friendly voice. "I was born without the gene to make the pigment for color. I have what is called *albinism*. It's an inherited condition I have to live with since I can't do anything to change it." He stopped to take a breath.

Much to her relief, he continued. "Besides feeling like a freak, my biggest problems are my eyes and my skin. I have to wear these tinted glasses and special goggles in the sunlight. If I don't keep my skin protected from the sun, I burn easily, and that can lead to other problems. I always have to wear a hat and skin protection and clothes made from special fabric, like this shirt."

"You don't sound much different from me," Priscilla offered, genuine compassion in her voice. "Maybe the part about the eyes is not the same, but my skin is really fair, so I have to be careful in the sun as well. And my brother and some of the boys at school think I'm a freak because of my red hair and freckles."

As he took in what she said, he looked puzzled. Perhaps he was uncomfortable with such eager acceptance from someone so close to his own age, for he suddenly blurted out, "Why do you always wear that silly rainbow ribbon in your hair?"

This was too much. Any hope of continued friendly conversation went out the window with his thoughtless question. Her quick temper flared up and she snapped at him, "It was a gift from my grandmother who is now dead. It means a lot to me! I'm not going to talk about it anymore with you... you..." She was about to say, "You stupid Ghost Boy," but she stopped herself just in time. The words seemed to hang in the air, as if already said.

In stony silence, they went back to washing the gull. Jack came in and changed the water every time they rang the bell. Pete soon began to look like his old self again which cheered Priscilla a little. When they had checked Pete's feathers thoroughly and felt they had done as much as they could, they rang the bell several times.

Mollie and Jack both came in. Mollie took Pete in her lap and rubbed him with a clean rag, checking to make sure all the oil was gone from his feathers. She looked up at Priscilla and Alasdair and smiled. "He looks really clean. You two did a great job. Thank you both for your hard work."

While Priscilla and Alasdair shed their aprons and gloves, Jack cleared off the table and set up the cage and heater. Mollie put Pete back in the cage as she said, "If Pete continues to do well I think we may be able to release him soon." Priscilla was glad to hear this, and she guessed Pete would be happy as well.

Later when she was walking home, Priscilla felt sad. It had been fun working with Alasdair and getting to know him until he said what he did and she let her temper get the best of her. Trying to become friends with him was *so* hard. All at once, she realized this was what she wanted… to have Alasdair as her friend.

When Priscilla arrived home, she found Mr. Green's humungous black truck parked in their driveway. Knowing that dreadful man was in her house gave her the creepy crawlies. She was heading upstairs to her room when she heard loud voices coming from her father's office. Stopping on the stairs for a moment, she listened.

Mr. Green was shouting, "You must decide now, Wallace. We can't delay much longer." Whatever her father said in reply was not loud enough for her to hear, but then Mr. Green yelled, "That's ridiculous! You know what you have to do. You won't like the consequences if you don't make the right decision. You need to get over this stupid morality stuff. It's just holding us all back."

Someone pulled open the office door so hard it crashed against the wall. Two heavyset men she had never seen before marched out, followed by horrid Mr. Green. He turned around in the doorway and yelled back into the room, "We're giving you one more week to decide, and that's it! If you don't make the right decision, I won't be responsible for what happens. I don't think you or your family will like it very much!"

Her father answered in his quiet voice, "Are you threatening me, Harold?"

Mr. Green growled, "Take it any way you like, Wallace, but hurry up and make the decision. And it better be the right one!" Then he stomped off, following the other men outside and slamming the front door behind him.

Priscilla started to go back downstairs to her father when the door to his office closed, and all became quiet. She considered knocking on the door but decided he probably would not want to be disturbed. Besides, she had absolutely no idea what to say, so she continued up the stairs to her bedroom.

Once she was in bed that night, she lay awake for a long time wondering about what she had seen and heard. What had made Mr. Green so angry, and what were the consequences he had mentioned? Was all this connected to the decision about the environment her father said he needed to make? No answers came to mind. Eventually she grew tired of thinking and drifted off into an uneasy sleep.

After school the next day, she called Mollie to ask how Pete was doing.

Mollie said, "Pete has made an unbelievable recovery, Priscilla. He's healing faster than any other bird I've taken through this cleansing procedure. I think we may be able to release him in a couple of days. Why don't we all meet after school on Wednesday at Sea Wolf dock down at the beach? We can let Pete go from there."

When Wednesday finally arrived, Priscilla could hardly contain her excitement. After school, she hurried down to the beach. Alasdair, Jack, and Mollie were already on the dock. Mollie held a pet-carrying case in her lap, and Jack had Geordie on a leash.

"This is the big day," Jack announced with his friendly smile. "Now we can see if Pete is ready to go. I can't believe what a quick recovery he has made."

Mollie handed the case to Alasdair. "You and Priscilla take Pete down to the shore and release him while we watch from the dock."

There was no way Mollie could maneuver her wheelchair down to the beach, though Priscilla suspected she would have liked to go.

Priscilla followed Alasdair down the steps. He set the case on the rocks near the water and lifted the top. As she was saying goodbye to Pete, Priscilla realized how fond she had become of the one-legged bird. She felt sad to think he would fly off to wherever he came from, and she would never see him again.

At first, Pete remained still, looking about. The way he stared up at her, she imagined he was thanking them and saying goodbye, so she whispered, "You're welcome, and goodbye, Pete."

He stood on his one leg, taking time to find his balance. After another long look at her, and a brief look at Alasdair, he flew up into the sky, circling above them for a moment and then over Mollie and Jack. With a loud squawk, he flew out over the water toward Wolf Island and soon disappeared from sight.

They all cheered for his successful release. Geordie joined in, barking with so much enthusiasm, it made them all laugh. When Priscilla and Alasdair returned to the dock, Jack had mugs of hot chocolate and marshmallows waiting, along with chocolate chip cookies he said Mollie had baked to celebrate the occasion. Geordie was munching on a dog biscuit.

While Priscilla drank her hot chocolate and ate one of the delicious cookies, she stood at the deck railing watching to see if Pete might return.

Mollie rolled her chair up beside her. "I don't think Pete will come back, Priscilla, not after all he has been through. He'll need to finish his healing somewhere else, no doubt."

Then Mollie reached out and touched her arm. "Priscilla, Jack and I hope you will come by and visit us often. We've really enjoyed getting to know you." Jack grinned and nodded in agreement, his mouth full of chocolate chip cookie.

Priscilla leaned down and gave Mollie a big hug. It felt so good to get this invitation. Some of her sadness was because, with Pete gone, she was afraid she would have no reason to see Mollie and Jack again.

"I'll stop by whenever I can," she promised.

After a while, it looked like Pete had gone for good, and the air was starting to get quite chilly. They said goodbye to one another and headed off to their respective homes.

Priscilla walked up her driveway with a heavy heart. It had all been so exciting, but now it was over. Although she could visit Mollie and Jack, and she would probably see Alasdair on the beach, she supposed everything else would just go back to the same way it had always been.

She could not have been more wrong. Nothing would ever be the same again.

Chapter Six
A Return Visit

After school the next day, Priscilla rushed down to the beach to see if, by any chance, Pete had come back, and, though it was hard for her to admit, she wanted to see if Alasdair was there. Pete was nowhere around, but Alasdair was sitting on Her Rock.

Almost as if she had been holding her breath all day, she let out a sigh of relief. Though she was unsure about how to treat him, she did not want things to go back to the way they had been before Pete came into their lives. The least she could do was say something, so she called out, "Hi Alasdair!" as she made her way to the smaller rock.

His quick response of "Hi Priscilla!" made her wonder if he might be a little pleased to see her as well.

A few minutes later, after she'd tied her ribbon in her hair, he walked over and stood beside her. Shifting from one foot to the other, he appeared to be struggling with what he wanted to say. Finally he blurted out, "I guess it's my turn to apologize. I didn't mean to make you angry about your ribbon. It was a stupid thing to say."

She mumbled, "That's okay. We've both said things we shouldn't have."

Then to her disbelief, he added, "If you want to sit on the big rock today, you can. I'll sit where you are."

Surprised by his suggestion, she had no response. Before she could come up with something, he went on, "We can take turns. You can sit there today, and I'll sit there tomorrow."

All she could think of to say was, "Okay, thanks."

So they traded places. Once again, she was able to sit on Her Rock. It felt so good to be back in familiar territory. Curling her legs under her, she smiled with delight. Something had changed between them, not a lot, but something. It felt like a beginning, and she was satisfied.

The following Saturday was another warm sunny day. Priscilla and Alasdair arrived at the beach around the same time in the early afternoon. It was her turn to sit on Her Rock. While marveling again at his suggestion to trade places, she watched a flock of seagulls flying across the water from Wolf Island.

One of the gulls suddenly veered away from the others and headed for the shore. The gull landed beside Priscilla... on one foot.

Pete had come back after all. In great excitement, she called over to Alasdair, "Look Alasdair, it's Pete. He came back."

Alasdair hurried over and stood next to her looking down at the big seagull. "Mollie thought we'd never see him again," he said.

To her amazement, Priscilla heard the same voice that had told her to "Come down to the sea." Now the voice said, "I came back to thank you both for saving my life and to inform you that your help has been requested."

Priscilla knew she had not created this voice, so she looked at Alasdair to see if he had spoken and found him looking at her in a puzzled way.

"Did you hear that strange voice?" he asked.

"Yeah, I sure did," she answered. They looked around to see if anyone else was on the beach, but there was no one in sight.

"I am the one speaking to you both," continued the voice, obviously aware of their confusion. "I am the seagull whom you call Pete. You are both hearing my voice in your heads."

Priscilla and Alasdair turned at the same time to stare at Pete in astonishment. "Are you really talking to us, Pete, or is this some kind of joke?" Priscilla asked aloud. Talking to birds inside her head was one thing. Talking to them and having them answer back for real was quite another.

"It is no joke, Priscilla and Alasdair," said Pete. "You both saved my life. By so doing, you proved you are worthy of the task we have ahead for you."

"But birds can't speak," cried Alasdair. "It's impossible!"

"Well, normally we do not communicate with humans this way," Pete commented, like it was no big deal. "Usually we communicate with your world through the language of symbols, but we thought it was important for me to speak to you in your own language."

"What do you want of us?" Priscilla asked. It was hard to believe she was actually talking to a bird as she did so often in her imagination. Perhaps she was making it up somehow, but she asked the seagull anyway, "You said you needed our help?"

"Yes," Pete said. "Our kingdom is in trouble. We had chosen you to assist us, Priscilla, if you passed our test. When you invited Alasdair to help you, and after he did so with such caring and common sense, we decided to have a look at him as well. We learned he is one of the White Ones and is of Light Heart. He too can be of great help to us."

"What *test* are you talking about?" After zeroing in on this hated word, Priscilla had not heard much of anything else. Taking tests was one of her least favorite things to do.

"We wanted to find out if you had the courage and compassion to help an injured creature, Priscilla, and how you would handle such a predicament," Pete answered her in a matter-of-fact way. "You did not hesitate to help me. Together you got me the treatment I needed. We were pleased with how you dealt with the situation."

Alasdair was still looking stunned, as if he could not believe what he was hearing. He had probably never before had a conversation with a bird, even in his imagination. "What do you mean 'we' and 'your kingdom'? Where are you from and who needs our help? I don't understand any of this. This is nuts!"

"One question at a time, please," chuckled Pete.

Since neither Priscilla nor Alasdair had ever heard a seagull chuckle before, this was quite an unnerving experience. They both grew quiet, which inadvertently enabled them to listen more closely to what Pete had to say.

"I come from the Kingdom Beyond the Sunset," he told them. "We want you to travel to our kingdom as soon as possible. There you will learn why we need your help and what you can do. I will send our transporters to pick you up here on the seashore this afternoon just as the sun begins to set. They will bring you to our kingdom. You will need to wear eye protection, as you will be traveling through bright light. Bring with you only whatever you might need and can easily carry."

"But we can't just go and leave our families," Priscilla protested. "There's no way my parents will let me go off by myself. Besides how can I tell them a little bird told me to do this? They'd think I was being silly!" Alasdair nodded in agreement.

Undisturbed by their qualms, Pete replied, "Our time is different from your time. We will return you here to the seashore before the sun sets today. No matter how long you are with us, it will be as if you have never left. No one will know you have been gone. You need have no concern about it."

Before Priscilla and Alasdair could ask more of the many questions flooding into their minds, Pete took off. He flew back across the water toward Wolf Island.

"What was that all about?" asked Alasdair, staring after the disappearing seagull. "Do you think we imagined all this?"

"I don't know, but if so, we imagined it at the same time, which would be impossible." Speaking almost to herself, she added, "I've always pretended I could talk with birds and animals, but I never knew it could happen for real."

"What do you think we should do? Should we come back this afternoon? Do we tell anyone about this?"

"Well," she thought for a moment, "if we tell anyone, they'll just think we're making it up. It's even hard for us to believe. Why don't we just come back and see what happens? If nothing does, we'll know we made it up. If something does... well... I guess we have to wait and see."

"I don't have anywhere else to go, so I guess it's okay, but it sure feels weird."

Priscilla began to get practical, which was how she handled matters when she was uncertain. "Pete said we need something to cover our eyes. I wonder what else we need to take."

Alasdair paused, and then he said, "I have a couple of pairs of sun goggles I wear in the summer. You can borrow a pair if you want. I need to go home and think about the rest."

"Yeah, me too. I guess I'll see you here before the sun sets this afternoon."

As Priscilla walked up to her house, her mind was full of questions about what she had heard. Immersed in a mixture of thoughts and feelings, she mulled over what they might be getting themselves into. And what on earth would she need to take with her?

When the sun dropped low in the sky, Priscilla returned to the beach. The day had been clear, and soon there would be another lovely sunset.

Alasdair arrived at almost the same time, and they greeted one another nervously. He had on his N.O.A.H. shirt, jeans, tennis shoes, the same gray felt hat he always wore, and a backpack with his guitar strapped to it. In one hand, he carried two pairs of oversized goggles.

Priscilla wore long, striped socks, high-topped tennis shoes, a long-sleeved T-shirt, and her favorite denim overalls. Her special treasures were in her pockets, except for her rainbow ribbon, which was in her hair. If ever there was a time for her to remember her own power, this was it.

She too had her backpack, into which she had put a fleece sweatshirt, snacks and water, tissues, a floppy sun hat and sunscreen, some Band-Aids and antiseptic, string and a pair of small scissors, notebook and pen, her hairbrush and comb, soap and towel, and her toothbrush and small tube of toothpaste. At the last minute, she had tossed in her rainsuit and a change of underwear, just in case. It was all she could think of. Never having done anything like this before, she had no idea what she might need.

Alasdair shook his head as he said, "You know how crazy this is, don't you? How could we possibly be going anywhere? I feel ridiculous."

"Me too." She grinned at him with a sheepish look, and then she laughed. "Oh well, at least we should get to see a great sunset."

He looked at her in surprise. "You're right," he said, grinning back.

The setting sun cast out its net of sparkling diamond lights to indulge in one last merry dance across the water before calling it a day. The great red globe sank slowly behind Wolf Island, leaving behind a spreading rose blush. The color blended with streaming wisps of bluish white clouds, turning the evening sky rosy pink and turquoise.

Something odd caught Priscilla's eye. Two large dark dots hovering over Wolf Island seemed to be moving toward them. Alasdair took a little longer to see what she pointed out, but soon they both knew what it was. Flying across the water, in much the same way as Pete had done earlier in the day, were two huge bald eagles.

Priscilla's heart leapt in wonder. With no awareness of what she was doing, she grabbed Alasdair's hand. He held on, as unaware of their touch as she was. Holding their breath, they watched as the two majestic birds landed right at their feet.

They were the biggest bald eagles Priscilla had ever seen. It was awesome to see their familiar white heads and tails up close, their wing feathers surprisingly multi-colored instead of the brownish gray they looked from a distance. With their hooked yellow beaks and sharp claws, it was easy to see how these birds were capable of tearing small animals and fish to shreds.

Neither Priscilla nor Alasdair moved an inch, not at all sure what they were supposed to do. Once again, Priscilla heard a voice in her head, this one, deeper and scratchier than Pete's voice.

"Hello, Priscilla and Alasdair. I am Ezara the Eagle. Eminore the Eagle and I have been sent to bring you to the Kingdom Beyond the Sunset. Are you ready to go?"

Priscilla and Alasdair let go of one another as they tried to take this in. Alasdair asked in a trembling voice, "What do you mean by 'go'?"

Ezara answered. "Once you have covered your eyes from the light, you need to climb on our backs, grab hold of our neck feathers, and hang on tight. We will take you to our kingdom."

"But we will be too heavy for you!" Priscilla exclaimed.

"What will keep us from falling off?" Alasdair asked, at almost the same time. "I'm not sure I like this idea."

A softer and more feminine voice, apparently the voice of Eminore, reassured them both. "Do not worry little ones. You will be fine. Just climb on. We will take good care of you."

With shaking hands, Alasdair helped Priscilla put on the goggles he had brought for her and then put on his own. Neither of them said a word. They had absolutely nothing to say. All they could do was follow directions.

Without any more hesitation, they climbed aboard the big eagles. Though Priscilla and Alasdair did not know it yet, they were about to take one of the most extraordinary rides of their lives.

BOOK TWO

A STRANGE NEW LAND

Chapter Seven
Beyond the Sunset

Astride the backs of their unusual transporters, Priscilla and Alasdair were soon on their way to the Kingdom Beyond the Sunset, whatever and wherever this might be. The eagles flew in tandem, low over the water at first, then higher into the sky. Far below, their shadowed reflections glistened in rose-colored water.

Priscilla lay across Ezara, clinging tightly to his neck feathers. Tucked between his wings stretched wide on both sides of her, she felt warmed by her closeness to such a magnificent creature. As his soft feathers tickled her nose, she sniffed mixed odors of sun, fish, and sea. Images of salty spray, sun-drenched shores, and treetops with views beyond compare flashed into her mind.

She glanced over at Alasdair. The expression of dazed disbelief on his face mirrored what she was feeling. Her apprehension had vanished. Instinctively, she knew the birds would never let them fall.

The big eagles flew higher and higher. This was probably as close as she would ever get to flying on her own, something she had always wanted to do. If she had not been afraid of scaring the eagles, she would have yelled down to anyone who might hear, *"Look at me! Here I am! I'm flying! Wheee!"* Instead, she whispered the words to herself.

They flew over the tall fir trees of Wolf Island and headed straight into the setting sun. Soon all she could see around her was pure white light. She was grateful for the protection of Alasdair's goggles.

Without any warning, they were flying through what appeared to be the sunset. Everywhere Priscilla looked, brilliant shades of every imaginable color filled the air. Expanding, dissolving, separating, swirling, the colors formed and shifted into intricate patterns all around her. Her breath caught in her throat as wave after wave of vibrant color washed over her.

Almost before she could catch her breath again, the colors were behind them, and they were flying, as if in slow motion, into complete darkness. Something that resembled a massive blob of paint suspended in space drifted toward them out of the blackness.

When it floated close enough to see, what she had thought was only a blob of paint turned out to be a painting of astonishing beauty splashed across the dark sky. The image of a lush green meadow dotted with wildflowers filled Priscilla with a sense of awe. Above the meadow, a dazzling rainbow curved across a brilliant blue sky, so real, she wanted to reach out and touch it. The painting easily outshone the artwork in any of the galleries and museums she had visited with Granny.

One sky painting after another passed by in quick succession. An orange sun, bursting with fiery flames came next, followed by huge single flowers in every brilliant hue. A silvery ocean, with waves glistening under moonlit skies had her gaping with delight.

She loved the peaceful landscape of a meandering river set against a background of dark green forest, snow-tipped purple mountains, and pink skies. Shapes of all sizes and colors in a multitude of unusual patterns drifted past her, one after the other. The eagles were flying them through a virtual reality art gallery.

When she turned to see where the paintings were going, she watched them simply dissolve, one by one, into the sunset, becoming part of the whole. Even though she had always loved sunsets, it had not occurred to her that such unequaled artistic creations could be part of them. Never again would she look at a sunset without remembering what she had seen in this moment.

All too soon, it was over. They had passed through what had to be the greatest art show in the world and were flying in daylight once again. Her disappointment at such a brief flash of glory evaporated when she spied the meadow they were approaching. It looked just like the one in the painting. Vivid wildflowers of every color of the rainbow grew out of grass so thick and luxurious her toes began to wiggle as she anticipated feeling it under her bare feet.

The eagles landed with careful precision in the thick grass. The weather was sunny, and the air smelled fresh and clean. Wisps of soft white clouds floated above them in a sky of pure blue. Every color seemed to glow as if a light burned deep within it.

Ezara announced, "We are here. Welcome to the Kingdom Beyond the Sunset, Priscilla and Alasdair."

Priscilla slid off the back of her eagle while Alasdair climbed down from Eminore. He looked over at her, a foolish grin on his face, and she smiled back.

"We will return to take you home when it is time for you to go," Ezara told them.

As Priscilla and Alasdair waved their thanks and goodbyes, the huge birds lifted off the grass, soared high up into the sky, and disappeared from view. They were all alone in the meadow… or so they thought.

"Well that was one heck of a ride!" Alasdair said. "What did you think of that fantastic art show? I've never seen anything like it before, not even in videos."

"Awesome!" was all she could think of to say. Then she giggled as she announced, "I feel like Dorothy in a strange new land."

He laughed. "So if you are Dorothy, then who am I... the Scarecrow?" Swinging his arms and legs loosely, he pretended to be made of hay. "Or maybe the Tin Man?" Keeping his joints rigid, he marched around her. "Or perhaps I am the Cowardly Lion?" Growling, he screwed up his face, lifted his hands into the air in front of him, and pranced around, pawing at her and making roaring sounds.

Clapping her hands with glee, she giggled at his antics. He had never acted silly like this before, and she liked it. The warmth she felt was what she guessed Dorothy must have felt for her three friends. Cheeks flushing, she took off her goggles, shoes, and socks, and ran barefoot into the meadow.

The cool soft grass tickled her feet and squished between her toes. Soon she was dancing and spinning around. As she whirled with total abandon, hundreds of eye-catching butterflies and dragonflies flew up from the brilliant wildflowers. Spreading her arms wide like wings, she pretended to soar like one of these graceful creatures.

Hordes of curious little brown bunnies peeked out of the grass, twitching their noses as she danced past. When she got too close, they scampered away, cottontails wiggling on tiny behinds. Giggling, she chased after them.

Alasdair watched her with an amused expression. Just as he was about to take off his socks and shoes to join her, a slimy, wheezy, voice out of nowhere called loudly, "Go home! You are not wanted here!"

At once, Priscilla stopped chasing the bunnies. Looking around in bewilderment, she tried to determine where the words had come from. *This* voice was definitely not in her head.

"I'm telling you to go back where you belong!" insisted this unsettling voice. It seemed to come from somewhere in the grass off to the side, but there was no one around.

"Oh, don't ppp-pay any attention to him." From the opposite direction, a much lighter singsong sort of voice with a bit of a stutter entered the conversation. "He's jjj-just an old snake in the ggg-grass! He's always ccc-cranky especially since he often ggg-gets such bad ppp-press."

While they were trying to figure out where this second voice was coming from, Priscilla hurried to put on her socks and shoes. The mention of snakes made her nervous.

"CCC-Come on over here… I'm in the ppp-pond to your rrr-right," the second voice called out.

Following these instructions, they made their way to a small brown pond, which had earlier escaped their notice. A graceful willow tree stood by the edge of the pond, its wispy fronds hanging down like an awning, offering shade to a sizeable dark green lily pad floating on the murky water.

Smack dab in the middle of the pad, and grinning at them from ear to ear, squatted an extremely large pinkish white frog. It had bulging red eyes and a peculiar rectangular grid of multi-colored squares on its back. The squares flashed one after the other in quick succession, reminding Priscilla of the *Simon* game she used to play. It was the weirdest frog she'd ever seen. The lopsided grin on its face had to be, without a doubt, the silliest.

"Hello ththth-there. Welcome to the KKK-Kingdom BBB-Beyond the Sunset!" the frog announced with the same joyous enthusiasm as Kermit the Frog. Only this frog could not be a Muppet since it was speaking for itself. There was no one else around.

"Whoa… this is getting weird," she whispered to Alasdair.

"You're not kidding." He rolled his eyes.

"The weather today will be ppp-perfectly ppp-pleasant," the frog continued. "There will be no ccc-clouds at all and no rrr-rain expected. Of course, every ddd-day here is ppp-perfectly ppp-pleasant, but no matter. There will be no rrr-rain today. But ddd-don't just stand there. What ddd-do you have to say fff-for yourselves? DDD-do you speak?"

"Of course we do," Alasdair answered, a bit sharply, "but we aren't used to speaking to frogs."

"What a ddd-dreadful shame. Frogs are excellent at ggg-giving weather rrr-reports. If you haven't been speaking to any fff-frogs, then you ccc-can't have been getting any ddd-decent weather rrr-reports. I ddd-don't see how anybody can ddd-do without a ggg-good weather rrr-report. You just ccc-can't get a ggg-good weather rrr-report without speaking to a fff-frog. Did I ttt-tell you the weather today will be ppp-perfectly ppp-pleasant?"

"Yes, you did," Priscilla told the silly frog. Before he could start in again on his weather report, she asked, "Are you the one who will be showing us where to go and what we need to do?"

"Oh ggg-goodness me nnn-no," chuckled the frog, grinning even wider, if that were possible. "I'm only the weather rrr-reporter, not the ttt-tour guide!"

"Well, then, who *is* the… er… tour guide?" Alasdair asked this not-very-helpful frog. He was beginning to sound a little irritated.

"Well nnn-now, how should I nnn-know? I'm only the weather rrr-reporter and nnn-not the…"

"We know… we know… you're not the tour guide!" Priscilla interrupted him. "But can you please at least tell us in which direction we need to go to find someone?"

"I'm sure there must be a ppp-path around the MMM-Merry Meadow somewhere. There is always a ppp-path somewhere. You only have to look fff-for it, and you will fff-find it. That's the bbb-best I can do for you, but if you www-want the weather rrr-report, you just have to ask mmm-me. The weather today…" grinning widely, the frog droned on with his weather report, while the colors on his back continued to flash one after the other.

Since she always tried to be respectful of every creature, no matter how ridiculous it might seem to her, Priscilla thanked the frog. Then she and Alasdair looked around the Merry Meadow, as the frog called it, for some sort of path.

And what do you know, they found one. Though they had not been aware of it before, once they started looking, they could see, over to their left, a long path winding through the grass and curving up over some green hills off in the distance. They started toward the path, picking their way with caution and keeping their eyes open for any snakes in the grass.

Speaking of snakes, while Priscilla and Alasdair were making their way toward the path, a long slippery black snake, with a neon purple belly and horizontal rainbow-colored stripes on its back, slithered stealthily around behind them to the edge of the pond. After curling into a coil, the snake lifted its head up high and pompously addressed the frog with the same wheezy voice which had given due warning to Priscilla and Alasdair.

"You didn't tell them about the weather in the Fairy Foressst and the Mara Mountainsss and the Lava Land, did you, Frog?" the snake hissed. "You didn't tell them about the Dreary Drenching Downpoursss or the Horrendousssly Huge Hailstormsss or the Wild Wicked Windstormsss, did you? And I sssuppossse you didn't even think for one moment to warn them about the Legendary Light-Eatersss of the Land, did you?"

"They ddd-didn't ask," the frog countered, still grinning. "Now if they www-were to ask me about the weather in the FFF-Fairy Forest and the MMM-Mara Mountains and the LLL-Lava Land, I'd be ddd-delighted to tell them, but they nnn-never asked. And I ddd-don't know anything about any LLL-Legendary Light-Eaters of the LLL-Land either… ggg-goodness me, no… I only know about the weather. Speaking of which, the weather ttt-today is going to be ppp-perfectly ppp-pleasant. There will be no ccc-clouds or rrr-rain today."

"Tssssk! Tssssk! Tssssk!" hissed the slippery snake as it sneakily stole a glance in the direction Priscilla and Alasdair had gone. Slowly uncurling itself, it slipped away silently, disappearing into the deliciously decadent belly-rubbing grasses of the Merry Meadow.

Meanwhile, Priscilla and Alasdair made their way to a narrow dirt path in the middle of the meadow. Once they stepped onto the path, they had no idea which direction to take. Behind them, a wall of color shimmered, the sunset through which they had just passed. To the left of the meadow a vast green forest lay at the foot of purple mountains where one snowy white peak towered above the rest. Off to the right, an ocean glistened in the sunlight. Ahead of them were the green hills they had noticed before.

Beyond the hills, jagged towers of pale green and rose pink reached high up into the sky. These cathedral-like spires looked as if they were floating in the air. Priscilla and Alasdair had never seen anything quite like them before.

As they stood peering at these structures, trying to figure out what it was they were seeing, a small whirlwind of dust came rolling like tumbleweed over the hills and down the path toward them.

Since this was the only discernible movement anywhere around, other than the twitching noses of a few inquisitive bunnies, they waited for the dust ball to reach them. At the same time, they were wondering what it could possibly be.

Chapter Eight
The Village of the Rainbow

Out of the dust, a miniature horse pulling an equally tiny cart materialized. When the horse pulled to a stop on the path in front of Priscilla and Alasdair, an old and unkempt Hobbit-sized man climbed down from the cart and slowly walked toward them as if he had all the time in the world.

Everything about him drooped with age. His brown skin had thickened into heavy creases, and his bedraggled white beard hung below his knees. Flabby ears dangled under a wide-brimmed black hat; the once high point of his hat flopped over to one side, as if it were too tired to stand up straight any longer. Tiny eyeglasses, ready to slip off at any moment, clung to the end of his sagging nose. They were attached to a string of similar eyeglasses encircling his neck.

A long-sleeved black shirt, billowing black pants, and a multi-pocketed brown vest amply clothed his small frame. A pointy-toed black shoe with a large silver buckle covered one foot; the other was bare and dusty. As he made his way toward them, he bent down to scratch his bare foot.

In one fell swoop, his eyeglasses popped off his nose and his hat fell to the ground. With his left hand he picked up the hat and shook off the dust, while with his right, he pulled another pair of eyeglasses from the string and placed them on his nose. Before putting on his hat again, he scratched his head. The snow-white hair sticking out in all directions suggested he did this on a regular basis.

The only parts of him not timeworn were his mouth and eyes. His round mouth spoke of youthful innocence and good humor, and his dark brown eyes danced with liveliness. When Priscilla felt his intense gaze rest fully upon her, she suspected he was as wise as Mollie.

"Hello, my dears," he greeted them, in a voice unexpectedly resonant for such a small person. "I am so glad you have come to our kingdom. We have been awaiting your visit with great impatience. Did you enjoy your ride?" His eyes twinkled merrily, and he smiled serenely at them, as if he knew there was no way they could not have enjoyed it.

"Hoot Mon!" twittered a high screechy voice.

Priscilla sought the source of this new voice and was astonished to discover a tiny and quite real owl sitting on the old man's shoulder. Gray feathers stuck out in similar disarray to its master's hair. Priscilla thought the owl might have winked at her though she wasn't certain.

Alasdair spoke first, a little on the testy side. "Yes, the ride was fantastic, but we don't know why we were brought here or who is to be our tour guide. Someone yelled at us and told us to go home. Then some sort of silly weather reporter gave us no help at all."

"Ah, yes," the old man chuckled merrily. "You have had the distinct pleasure of meeting Snake and Frog while you were waiting.

Well, I am to be your tour guide, as you call it. I am afraid I am a tad late, as I move much slower these days. My age is catching up with me. Alas, I am often tardy. And I always seem to be forgetting things. Sometimes I cannot even remember what it is I have forgotten."

"Ach aye, like yer ither shoe!" the tiny owl commented. "Ye ne'r 'member to put on yer twa shoes. 'Tis why yer fit is always sae itchy, ye daft old coot. Hoot Mon!"

Though she liked the sound of its distinctive accent, Priscilla thought the owl was a bit rude. But its sassy talk did not seem to bother the old man, who just laughed as he looked down at his bare foot and said, "Oh my! I did forget to put on my other shoe again. My stars!"

He looked up with a sheepish smile. "And another thing I forgot to do was to introduce myself. My name is Wanortu the WiseMaster of the Kingdom Beyond the Sunset. This cheeky fellow on my shoulder is my wee Scottish sidekick, Eideard the Owl." He reached up and gently ran his fingers through the little owl's disheveled feathers, messing them up even more.

"We're pleased to meet you," Priscilla said with great politeness. "I'm Priscilla, and this is Alasdair."

"Oh, yes, we already know." Wanortu smiled warmly at them. "Well now, we had best get going right away." He climbed back up into the cart and said, "Hop in and I will take you into the village. Everyone is waiting to meet you."

Alasdair and Priscilla did not move. They stood staring in bewilderment at the tiny horse and cart in front of them.

When Wanortu turned back toward them and realized they were still standing in the same spot, he asked, "What is the matter? Why are you not getting in?"

"But there's no way we can fit," Alasdair protested. "Anyway, the horse is far too small to pull all of us."

Wanortu scratched his head again. Then he climbed back down from the cart. "What in the kingdom was I thinking? Of course, you cannot fit. We need a much bigger horse and cart. My stars!" Reaching his hand deep inside one of his many pockets, he pulled out a carved wooden stick.

Eideard leaned over and tittered loudly in Wanortu's ear. "Best be careful ye old rascal, ye ken wha' happen the last time! Hoot Mon!"

"Oh posh!" said Wanortu. "I have been doing this for hundreds of years now." He pointed the stick at the horse and pronounced a whole lot of peculiar words in a language Priscilla had never heard before. A puff of white smoke surrounded the horse and cart.

When the smoke dissipated, the small horse and cart were gone. Standing in their place was the biggest horse she had ever seen. It would dwarf the huge draft horses at the state fair, but stranger still, this one was as red as her hair.

Priscilla gaped in amazement at the gigantic red horse, not just because of its unusual color and size, but in total wonder as to how it got there in the first place. Alasdair looked equally dumbfounded. This was like something out of *Harry Potter*.

Eideard snorted and hooted as he bounced up and down on Wanortu's shoulder, "Ach aye, noo there's a horsie of a different color tae be sure! Hoot Mon!"

"Oh dear," lamented Wanortu. "I think he might be just a wee bit big and not quite what we need at the moment. Shoo now! Off you go, horsie," As he spoke, he softly patted the horse's hairy leg, the highest part of the animal he could reach.

The horse immediately thundered off down the path and across the meadow toward the forest, leaving a cloud of dust behind. Priscilla sighed with relief when it obeyed Wanortu's gentle command. She couldn't imagine how they would have been able to get such a giant horse to move if it had decided to be stubborn.

"Hmm, now let me think." Wanortu stood scratching his head for a moment. Muttering more of his peculiar words, he pointed what was obviously some kind of magic wand toward the space recently vacated by the big horse.

This time, when the smoke had come and gone, a pony and cart stood in front of them, facing the direction they needed to go. Though still small, they were at least a reasonable compromise. Everyone got in. By squeezing tightly together, they just managed to fit. Soon they were heading along the path toward the hills.

As they drew closer to the foot of the hills, the pony slowed down. They were approaching a river with a narrow wooden bridge crossing over it. The pony started across the bridge, its shoes making a loud clip-clopping sound on the wide slats.

On the other side of the bridge, three goats of differing sizes grazed on the green grass of the hillside. Giggling nervously, Priscilla peeked over the side of the bridge to see if anything might be lurking underneath. A narrow river flowed gently by with, thankfully, not a single troll in sight.

Wanortu noticed her looking down at the river and said, "We are crossing over the River of Return. It begins up in the Mara Mountains and flows through the Fairy Forest and the Merry Meadow on the way out to join the Ocean of Opportunity. Most of the time, the water is as peaceful as you see it today, but during one of our big rainstorms, it becomes a powerful and fast-flowing river."

The little pony, like *the little engine that could,* did a brave job of pulling the cart with its four passengers up and over the summit of the hills. When they slowly began the descent on the other side, Priscilla stared in awestruck silence.

Below them, a picturesque village lay in the midst of a peaceful valley. A collection of small cottages, each brightly painted in one of the colors of the rainbow, stood on the crest of the hill on one side. From the front door of each cottage, a path curved down the hill and across paint-spattered stone bridges built over a narrow road. On the other side, the paths ended in pools the same color as the cottages. Set side by side along the rocky shores of the ocean, the collection of colored pools resembled a gigantic paint palette.

In his best tour guide voice, Wanortu told them, "Below us is the Village of the Rainbow, the heart of the Kingdom Beyond the Sunset. It is the home of the People of the Rainbow. They live in the cottages on the left. To the right is Paint Pond Park where the colors of the rainbow are turned into paint."

Recalling the paintings in the sunset, Priscilla turned to listen with interest as Wanortu continued. "The People of the Rainbow are responsible for the Paint Pond matching the color of their skin and for adding their particular colors into the sunsets. It is a matter of pride for them to see their artwork in the skies. Everyone works together to create the designs your world enjoys."

When Priscilla turned back to look at Paint Pond Park, a geyser of color had surged up from each pond and merged above into a striking rainbow. The rainbow arched over the village and touched down into the center of the rooftop of a magnificent palace at the far end of the valley.

The palace was all black and white. Most of it was in a checkerboard pattern, except for the tiered roof, which was half-black and half-white. The rainbow disappeared into a round black dome in the center of the roof. Rainbow flags flying from turrets at the corners of the high walls added the only other color. A foundation of huge square tiers of decreasing sizes formed steps all around the palace, creating the impression of a fancy wedding cake.

Wanortu informed them, "The Palace of the Aureole is where the royal family resides. We keep our Sacred Light in the center of the palace. The Royal Rainbow carries the colors from the Sacred Light to the Paint Ponds."

Aha, so the rainbow was actually coming *out* of the palace, not going *into* it as Priscilla had been thinking. She had to revise her idea.

Surrounding the village were pale green and rose pink cathedral-like buildings with long jagged spires reaching high up into the sky. The tops of these spires were what she and Alasdair had puzzled over from the other side of the hills. The blending of green and pink colors wrapped everything in a soft warm glow. The buildings shimmered, as if the walls were moving. She decided this had to be a trick of the light.

"The rose and green structures are our Muses," Wanortu told them. "They are our meeting places where we gather with one another to create Light energy to send into the world. I will tell you more about them later. Right now, we are heading down through the village to the palace. There you will be welcomed by the king and queen and the rest of the royal family."

"Ach aye," put in Eideard, "an' we'd best git movin' as we're late, ye daft old coot, tae be sure. Hoot Mon!" Priscilla now knew that the little owl's tart way of speaking was not rude at all, but only affectionate banter with his master.

The little pony pulled the cart full of passengers down the hill and onto a narrow cobblestone road, which led under the bridges. Priscilla watched in fascination as the little villagers hurried along the paths and across the bridges. The buckets and dripping paintbrushes that each carried explained the paint spatters everywhere.

Except for the younger children, all of them were about Wanortu's size. Priscilla had never before seen people of such colors. Each of them had skin and hair matching one of the colors of the rainbow. She could not see any black, white, or brown people amongst them.

As the little pony and cart journeyed nearer, the villagers gathered by the edge of the road and along the bridges to cheer and wave their paintbrushes. Flecks of paint flew up into the air and sprinkled slowly back down around them like confetti.

"They look happy to see us!" Alasdair cried in mystification. He took off his hat to get a better view of the little folk on the bridges above him.

"Indeed they are," stated Wanortu with great satisfaction. "They know you have come here to help us."

In the next moment, something peculiar began to happen. The rainbow people, who had been smiling and cheering loudly, stopped cheering and gaped at Alasdair, their faces frozen in astonishment.

He had been enjoying the welcoming crowd. At first, he did not seem to notice anything unusual. But before long, he too saw what was happening. Quick as a flash, he put his hat back on and pulled the brim down over his face.

As he hunched down into the cart, Priscilla guessed he was once more feeling like a freak. With his white hair and white face, he stood out in this colorful crowd, where, for the first time in her life, her red hair was not in the least conspicuous.

They continued past a number of quaint little shops in the village and headed toward a small plaza at the foot of the wide steps leading up to the palace. A number of excited children of various ages, all dressed in rainbow colored clothing, had gathered on both sides of a long strip of rainbow carpet laid out in honor of the visitors. As the pony and cart approached the edge of the carpet, the children quieted down and bowed low.

The pony pulled to a stop, and Priscilla and Alasdair jumped down from the cart. After Wanortu joined them, he led the way along the carpet between the two rows of bowing children. Curiosity getting the better of them, the children lifted their heads to sneak a peek at the visitors as they passed by.

It was now Priscilla and Alasdair's turn to be astonished. These children were none of the colors of the rainbow. Instead, they were either black or white, though not all one color or the other. Big freckles of the opposite color dotted their cheeks, black on white and white on black. The girls had rainbow ribbons in their hair, and the boys wore rainbow circlets on their heads. Priscilla smiled with secret pleasure.

On one of the lower steps leading up to the palace, a regal figure stood waiting to welcome them. From what Wanortu had said, this would be the king.

When they got close enough to see him clearly, Priscilla's mouth dropped open in surprise. Now she knew why the People of the Rainbow had been so astonished to see Alasdair.

Chapter Nine
A Royal Welcoming

The king was completely white like Alasdair. His intricately woven robe matched his skin. The only colors were in rainbow threads in his robe, his blue eyes, and the sparkling jewels of every color in the large crown on his head.

The reaction of the crowd now made sense to Priscilla. The People of the Rainbow must have been surprised when they realized Alasdair was white like their king. He was not a freak to them at all. When she turned to say this to Alasdair, she found him staring with admiration as the king regally made his way down the steps toward them. There was no need to say anything.

"Your Royal Highness," Wanortu spoke with great respect. "May I present to you, Priscilla and Alasdair." Then he turned and said, "Priscilla and Alasdair, may I introduce His Royal Highness, King Sol of the Kingdom Beyond the Sunset."

Priscilla had no idea what was an appropriate greeting for a king, so she made a slight curtsey, as she had seen done in movies, and said, "How do you do, Your Majesty."

Alasdair took off his hat, bowed his head, and mumbled, "Your Highness."

King Sol gave a slight nod of his head to each of them. Then he proclaimed in a formal tone, "Welcome to the Kingdom Beyond the Sunset, Priscilla and Alasdair. We are pleased you have come here to assist us." He spoke in the same fussy way as King Friday of "Mr. Roger's Neighborhood".

He led them up a couple of steps to where an elegant woman with skin as dark as the night stood quietly waiting. She was dressed in a magnificent black robe. Her crown matched the king's and gleamed in splendor against her jet-black hair. King Sol took the woman's hand and presented her to Priscilla and Alasdair with a slight bow of his head, "May I introduce my wife, Queen Luminata."

When Priscilla and Alasdair repeated their words and gestures of greeting to the queen, she gave them a shy gracious smile as she bid them, "Welcome, children."

Nodding up the steps to two others, whom Priscilla had not been aware of until now, the king announced with pride, "This is our son, Prince Incandescence, the crown prince of our kingdom, and his betrothed, our future daughter-in-law, Princess Archelita of the Kingdom of the Sunrise."

The prince, a tall teen-aged boy of about sixteen years of age, came down the steps to stand next to the king and queen. His skin was a shiny blue-black color, and he had large black eyes and shoulder-length thick glossy black hair, parted in the middle. When he smiled at them, his white teeth flashed in the sunlight. Priscilla thought he was, beyond doubt, the handsomest boy she had ever seen.

Holding his hand was a lovely teen-aged girl. She was younger and shorter than the prince, and completely white like the king and Alasdair. Soft curls framed her delicate face. The rest of her pure white hair hung down her back in a long thick braid. Alasdair was gazing at the princess like a thirsty person who has just found water.

The prince and princess were more casually dressed. He wore a black open-necked shirt and matching slacks, and she had on a simple short white dress, fit snugly to her slender form. A wide rainbow belt cinched her tiny waist. The princess wore a circlet of diamonds that shone with brilliance on her white hair. The prince wore a circlet of multi-colored jewels, similar to those in the crowns of the king and queen.

King Sol smiled and, with great affection, waved his hand toward the numerous children who had greeted Priscilla and Alasdair in the plaza. "Those who welcomed you are the rest of the royal children."

Turning back to Priscilla and Alasdair, he gave what sounded like a royal command. "Now you must come inside the Palace of the Aureole. You will need to rest and have some refreshment. You must be tired and hungry after your journey." He took Queen Luminata by the hand and led the way up the stairs, with Prince Incandescence and Princess Archelita following right behind them.

Eideard gave a quick "Hoot Mon!" and flew off Wanortu's shoulder, heading in a different direction, probably to find whatever refreshment might be good for an owl.

Wanortu, Priscilla, and Alasdair had just reached the top of the stairs and were moving toward the huge ornate palace doors, when the rest of the royal children, buzzing with excitement and curiosity, came clambering up the stairs. It was apparent they did not want to miss any of the fun.

The inside of the palace turned out to be another surprise for Priscilla. She had expected it to be all black and white like the outside. Instead, it was brilliantly lit and full of color. In the grand entryway, rich multi-colored tapestries hung on light green walls over a floor of pale rose-pink marble. A dazzling crystal chandelier dangled overhead, the many crystals acting as prisms, creating tiny rainbows flitting all around them.

The light came from a sunken circular rotunda in the center of the palace. In the middle of the circle, a brilliant rainbow disappeared like magic into a shiny golden pot. Giggling, Priscilla whispered, "Look, Alasdair, there really *is* a pot of gold at the end of the rainbow!" But he was too busy looking around to pay any attention to her.

The golden pot rested on a glossy black pedestal. Inside the pot, folds of soft black velvet held a small round globe. It glistened with pure white light, so intense it was almost impossible to look at for any length of time. This was the source of the brilliance in the rotunda, and it was into this globe the rainbow vanished.

This had to be the Sacred Light, so from what Wanortu had said, the Royal Rainbow had to be arising out of the Light to carry the colors to the Paint Ponds. The rainbow ascended to the top of the palace and exited through the center of an exquisitely carved ornamental ceiling.

The pedestal holding the precious orb stood on a circular marble floor, divided into seven pie-shaped sections, each a different color of the rainbow. At the outer edge of each section, a single pale green marble pillar extended from floor to ceiling. Carved golden railings connected the pillars, creating a circle of gold around the Light.

In front of each pillar, a small rainbow guard, with skin matching the color of that section of the floor, stood proudly at attention. All seven guards were dressed in formal rainbow-striped uniforms. Seven golden buttons, polished to the finest luster, embellished the front of each of their jackets.

The king led his party along a passageway between this central rotunda and the palace rooms on the other side. At the rear of the palace, the passageways on both sides ended in wide marble staircases curving up and around to higher floors. Priscilla and

Alasdair followed the king and his entourage underneath these massive staircases and through a wide-arched double doorway into a large banquet hall at the back of the palace.

Facing them, a wall of windows overlooked vast orchards and bountiful gardens where many little People of the Rainbow could be seen busily working. The Muses glittered in the background.

In front of the windows, a long narrow banquet table, surrounded by carved wooden high-backed chairs, held a vast assortment of delicacies. Multicolored food, along with vibrant wildflower centerpieces, created a cornucopia of color against the black and white checkered tablecloth covering the table.

Priscilla's mouth watered as she savored the goodies. She spied bowls of fruit of every variety, baskets of eggs of many colors, vegetable salads galore, and open-faced sandwiches on pink and brown bread. Dishes of olives, raisins, nuts, and an assortment of cheeses, as well as crystal jugs filled with milk, juice, or water had been set within easy reach all along the table. An abundance of scrumptious-looking pastries, frosted in rainbow colors, rounded out the feast.

Everyone gathered around the table with King Sol and Queen Luminata at opposite ends and their children in between. King Sol invited Priscilla and Alasdair to sit at his right, providing them with a view out the window. Prince Incandescence and Wanortu sat across from them. Princess Archelita sat to the right of the queen at the other end of the table.

The king stood up and called for quiet. Clearing his throat, he waited while everyone quickly settled down before he spoke. In his dignified voice, he declared, "Priscilla and Alasdair, we are glad to welcome you here to the Kingdom Beyond the Sunset. First of all, we want to thank you for saving the life of our friend whom you call Pete. In our kingdom, we call him Garone the Gull. We are pleased with how you cared for him. Garone will extend his gratitude to you at a later time."

At the mention of Pete, Priscilla and Alasdair looked at one another in surprise. In all the excitement, they had completely forgotten their seagull friend who had made it possible for them to be here in the Kingdom Beyond the Sunset in the first place. Priscilla was glad that she would get to see Pete again. But she couldn't call him Pete anymore. She would have to get used to calling him by his true name, Garone the Gull.

Smiling at them, the king cleared his throat once more and continued, "We have much to discuss of great importance, but for now, let us take the time to enjoy this excellent repast." His voice softened and sounded less formal. "We give thanks for the great bounty of Mother Nature's blessed kingdom. We are grateful to those whose hands have grown, picked, and prepared what lies before us. Let us enjoy it with respect and gratitude as we nourish our bodies and create the energy we need for the tasks that lie ahead of us."

With a small bow of his head and a wave of his hand over the food, he sat down. At once, everyone began to talk and pass the food around. The noise at the table rose to a happy hubbub.

Priscilla and Alasdair hungrily partook of the delicious foods passed their way.

While they ate, King Sol informed them, "The food for the palace is grown in the royal gardens and orchards which you see outside the window. We keep many animals and birds at the palace, though only for enjoyment and for their gifts of milk and eggs. In our kingdom, we do not choose to kill or eat any other living creature."

Prince Incandescence asked Priscilla and Alasdair, "How was your flight on the eagles? Aren't they a remarkable pair?" Apparently, he did not expect an answer as he continued. "By the way, please call me Inky. It is neither as formal nor as long as Incandescence."

With a cheery smile and a wave down the table to his fiancée, he finished with, "And Archelita prefers to be called Lita." He was full of good humor and many questions. Before long, they were chatting like old friends.

Alasdair asked Inky the same question Priscilla had been wanting to ask since they had first arrived at the Palace. "Inky, why are all the members of the royal family black and white instead of the colors of the rainbow like the villagers? I hope my question doesn't upset anyone, but I'd really like to know."

Inky laughed. "You ask a natural question, Alasdair. In the Kingdom Beyond the Sunset it has always been this way. The king or queen is either black or white. The future king or queen marries a prince or princess of the opposite color from a neighboring kingdom. All their children will be a mixture of black and white except for their first child who will be all one color or the other. This child is destined to become the next monarch."

Priscilla and Alasdair listened in fascination as Inky went on. "Because I was the first child, and all black, I will be the next king. I have been training to become king since birth. I have chosen Lita of the Kingdom of the Sunrise to be my queen. It is the duty and obligation of the royal family to live in the palace, to care for the Sacred Light, to watch over the People of the Rainbow, and to govern the Kingdom Beyond the Sunset with love, courage, truth, and wisdom."

Listening intently to every word his son said, King Sol beamed widely, as if his son spoke words any royal father would be pleased to hear.

When they had finished their meal, King Sol stood up once more. "The People of the Rainbow would like to do a welcoming presentation for you, Priscilla and Alasdair. Please turn your chairs around to face the doors through which we entered the room."

The presentation would be an unforgettable experience for Priscilla. She would tuck the memory into a pocket of her heart, the same way she kept her treasures in the pockets of her overalls. In the future, whenever she despaired, she would pull out this memory. Recalling every moment never failed to rekindle hope once more.

When everyone was in position and the room had quieted down, the king waved his hand toward the doorway. Immediately the big doors opened, allowing in a gush of giggles and laughter from the throng of gaily dressed People of the Rainbow squeezed together just outside.

A little red man rushed into the room and hurried forward to face the banquet table. He wore a flared shirt, pantaloons, vest, pointy-toed shoes, and carried a large tri-cornered hat, all the same color as his skin. Bowing down near to the ground, he waved his hat across his knees with a great flourish, first to the king, prince, and Wanortu, then to the queen, princess, and the other royal children, and finally to Priscilla and Alasdair.

Priscilla chuckled to herself as she watched him. Even if he did not have red skin, after all the bowing, the little red man would no doubt be red-faced.

In a melodic voice, he announced, "We, the People of the Rainbow, want to welcome you, Priscilla and Alasdair. To extend our thanks to you for coming to help us, we have prepared some special entertainment for your enjoyment." Turning toward the door, he bowed and flourished his hat yet again. Then he stepped off to one side.

At once, a troop of seven more little people, representing each color of the rainbow, glided in. Dressed in long black robes, each carried a different wooden instrument, none at all familiar to Priscilla. The musicians stood in a row near the little red man, and when he waved his hand, they began to play.

The music was unlike anything Priscilla had ever heard before. It was as if the sweet melodic songs of birds, the haunting calls of wild animals, the whisper of wind, the lapping of ocean waves, the sound of rain pitter-pattering through the trees, the soft whirring of butterfly and dragonfly wings, and the bubbling of flowing brooks, had been captured into these unique instruments. Now, in this precise moment, this array of sounds were being set free to join in a glorious serenade to nature.

Priscilla felt carried away outdoors to the places where each sound had originated. When the music began to change tone, she slowly floated back into the room, bringing with her a new sense of peace which had taken root somewhere deep inside her.

The music swelled, and in marched another seven little rainbow people, this time, dressed in white robes. They took their places in front of the musicians, creating the familiar checkerboard pattern.

As the rainbow chorus began to sing, their lovely sweet voices rose in harmony with the instruments. Their words expressed their gratitude for the hope and promise brought to their land and to the world by the Light and by the Rainbow, hope and promise for a place where all living beings could exist together in peace.

Priscilla again felt the sensation of serenity deep inside her. She turned toward Alasdair just as he looked at her, and they smiled shyly at one another. From the expression on his face, she guessed he was feeling something similar.

The chorus sang of the colors of the rainbow and of courage, truth, wisdom, and love for all life. Whenever the singers named a color, like magic, people of that color appeared in the room. Dressed in striking billowing costumes and long flowing scarves matching their skin, they danced with such grace, eve the air seemed to part to honor them with space.

Priscilla watched in amazement as a beating heart, a blazing fire, and a surging yellow fountain appeared before her. Seeds took root in the earth and grew toward the sun. Trees and meadows, plants and flowers, seas and rivers, mountains and skies materialized in front of her with simplicity and astonishing beauty. The dancers fashioned one breathtaking sunset after another, their colors intertwining in a variety of distinctive patterns.

When the music and singing slowed, the dancers eased toward the doors where they skillfully hopped on top of one another's shoulders to create a perfect rainbow arch in front of the doorway. The pace and tone of the music changed again, becoming lively and full of fun.

Through the rainbow arch and into the room, wearing realistic costumes designed to represent the creatures of their kingdom, danced the children of the Village of the Rainbow. A fuzzy bear twirled in circles, while a sleek silver wolf ran swiftly by its side. An eagle, an owl, a seal, an otter, and a raven followed along. Soon there were far too many creatures to name each one. Laughing, singing, dancing, and playing, the children were having the time of their lives.

When a tiny red toddler dressed as a ladybug, trotted merrily into the room, everyone, especially Priscilla and Alasdair, laughed and clapped their hands with pure delight. After the ladybug, came two small fuzzy yellow-and-black-striped bumblebees with long pointed stingers attached to their rear ends. Flapping gossamer wings, they swung their stingers with pretended menace while buzzing and bumping into one another.

Flowers of all shapes and colors, their petals surrounding the sweetest little faces, sashayed through the arch. Hovering about them were butterflies and dragonflies with gaudily patterned wings. Tiny roly-poly fruits and chunky vegetables bounced in next, looking as proud as any apple, pea, or blackberry could possibly be.

At the tail end of the performance, a magical silky-white unicorn, one long rainbow-striped horn sprouting from its forehead, pranced majestically into the room. Priscilla thought this was the best costume of them all. The performers gathered, arm in arm, around the unicorn, swaying and singing.

When they ended their songs, everyone began to clap and cheer, especially the tiniest of the performers. The little ones laughed and hugged one another as they bowed repeatedly to everyone at the table. Then they all rushed out of the room, bumping into each other along the way, laughing and yelling in their exuberance. It was indeed a merry crowd.

All the younger royal children at the banquet table immediately jumped up and bowed to the king. He smiled and waved his permission for them to leave. With great excitement, they ran out the door after the entertainers. Lita and Queen Luminata, both grinning widely, also bowed to the king and followed along behind the children at a more leisurely pace.

When the room had quieted down once more, only the king, Priscilla, Alasdair, Wanortu, and Inky remained at the table. King Sol stood and spoke to them, "I hope you enjoyed the meal and the performance, Priscilla and Alasdair. Now I would like you to follow me to the conservatory where we can talk. We have important matters to which we must attend."

Chapter Ten
A Shadow on the Horizon

Priscilla and Alasdair followed King Sol, Inky, and Wanortu through a door at the far corner of the banquet hall into a sunny octagonal glass-paned room. Rock gardens filled the many corners, nurturing leafy green plants growing almost as high as the vaulted glass ceiling. Their oversized flat leaves stretched out over the room, offering shade from the sunlight while creating the earthy atmosphere of a greenhouse.

The conservatory extended out on the side of the palace overlooking the ocean; glass doors opened to steps leading down to the seashore. Window seats, thickly cushioned with rainbow-striped fabric, and piled high with soft fluffy pillows, had Priscilla longing for time to curl up with a good book or to just sit and look out at the water.

The same fabric upholstered a tall elegant chair on a raised dais in front of the windows closest to the ocean as well as the bench seats set in rows in a semi-circle in front of it. When King Sol regally took a seat upon the big chair, Priscilla realized it was his throne.

The king waved his hand toward the benches as he royally commanded, "Prince Inky, Alasdair, and Priscilla, please come and sit here in front of me. And Wanortu," he gestured to a tall stool set to the right of the throne, "you will sit beside me in your usual place."

Wanortu had just climbed up and taken his seat when Eideard flew down to his shoulder. After a lopsided landing, the tiny owl wobbled about trying to get a grasp. Without saying a word, Wanortu reached up and steadied his much-loved little pal, gently ruffling his rumpled feathers.

While everyone was settling down, Priscilla thought about what she and Alasdair had been through since they left home. It all seemed far away from this incredible Palace of the Aureole. She had no idea why they were in this strange land or what the king would have to say. So many unexpected things had happened to them, she had not had time to think about it until now.

As if he were reading her mind, King Sol began to speak. "Priscilla and Alasdair, I'm sure you are wondering why we have brought you here." Since he looked directly at them when he said this, they both nodded their heads in agreement.

The King went on. "We have noticed something peculiar happening on the Ocean of Opportunity. The birds and sea creatures have reported activities of great concern to us. If you look across the ocean behind me on my left, you will discern a dark shadow on the horizon." He pointed toward a place far out on the ocean behind him.

When Priscilla looked to where the king pointed, she saw a massive dark shadow ship. Whatever this was, it appeared to be growing even larger while she watched it. Even though she had no idea where or when, she knew she had seen this shadow ship before, and it sent shivers up and down her spine.

Quickly averting her eyes, she reached into her pocket for her favorite shell to help ease her sense of dread. The shell was not in its usual place, and then she remembered she had given it to her father. Taking hold of some of the pieces of sea glass instead, she allowed images of Granny and their visit to the beach in Victoria to come to mind. This helped her regain her composure.

Unaware of her distress, Alasdair asked the King, "What is that strange ship, Your Highness, and why is it there?"

King Sol cleared his throat and began to explain. "Recently, we noticed the arrival of this Dark Ship, which, as you can see, is continuously expanding. It is carrying huge amounts of oil, some of which is leaking into the ocean, causing great damage. The Dark Ship is reaching out toward a marine and wildlife sanctuary in your world. We believe this special place may be in grave danger. However, it is the growing presence of the shadow on the horizon which concerns us most of all."

"But what does it all mean?" Alasdair blurted out, his impatience to know making him forget for a moment to whom he was addressing his question.

King Sol went on, unperturbed by Alasdair's oversight. "The Ocean of Opportunity is the link between our kingdom and your world. When any harm comes to the ocean or to any of her creatures, it is a sign of trouble. The growing shadow on the horizon tells us that there is a dangerous imbalance between the Light and the Dark. This must be remedied as soon as possible."

Priscilla was completely mystified. "I don't understand what you mean by an imbalance between the Light and the Dark… Your Highness." One always needed to be respectful of a king.

King Sol thought for a moment, as if deciding how best to explain. "Let me begin by saying it is the way of life to always have opposites. Think of up and down, in and out, front and back, near and far, give and take." He paused to take a breath and to give them time to get the idea.

Inky chimed in with, "Young and old, life and death, black and white, noise and silence, sunset and sunrise," then looked at Alasdair and smiled.

Getting into the game, Alasdair added, "Fat and thin, tall and short, day and night, add and subtract, this and that"... and looked to Priscilla to continue.

Grinning, she joined in with, "Big and little, hot and cold, sad and happy, kind and cruel, soft and hard, over and under..." She was on a roll...

Before she could continue, King Sol gently interrupted her. "That's right, Priscilla. You could easily keep on going. In the structure of life, something needs an opposite to exist. For instance, how would you know what is up without down, or day without night, or hot without cold?"

This had never occurred to her before. It was such an intriguing idea that she considered it for a moment. The room quieted down. The king was apparently waiting for a reply from one of them, so she said, "You wouldn't know what one was without the other, would you, Your Highness?"

"No, Priscilla, you would not. One is needed to define the other," King Sol agreed. "So it is with the Light and the Dark. When you have one, you must also have the other. The Dark helps to define the values of the Light... love, truth, courage, and wisdom. Living out these values makes the world a better place. The Light defines the values of the Dark... ignorance, hatred, violence, cruelty, and greed. Those who follow these values bring destruction and chaos to the world."

By now, Priscilla and Alasdair were listening intently to everything the king had to say, so he continued. "The struggle between the values of the Light and the values of the Dark is a challenge everyone must face. It allows us the freedom of choice, our most important freedom. As strange as it may sound, our struggles with the Dark help us to develop and strengthen the values of the Light."

Alasdair asked, "So are you saying, Your Highness, that without the Dark and all the bad things that happen, we wouldn't know what is right and good?" Priscilla was glad he had remembered his manners.

King Sol smiled at him. "Yes, Alasdair, that is correct. However, those who choose to live by what is right and good, as you say, must always make sure the Dark stays in balance. If the Dark becomes too powerful, it diminishes the power of the Light. Should this continue for too long, a Dreadful Darkness would descend upon your world. This is a time of great sorrow and devastation for the world and for all humankind. It takes a long time and much hard work to restore balance after a Dreadful Darkness has taken place."

Priscilla thought she understood what the king was saying. She asked, "Is that what happened in World War II?" *The Diary of Anne Frank* was one of her favorite books.

"Exactly!" exclaimed the king, beaming at her, as if she were a smart pupil who had pleased him with her question. "The Dark was allowed to get completely out of balance, and thus it brought a Dreadful Darkness upon the whole world. It was a time of great suffering. Millions of good people died, and there was tremendous destruction while balance was sought again."

Inky eagerly spoke up at this point. "But Father, those who live in such Darkness must only be ignorant of the joys of living in the Light. We just need to make an effort to show them the Light. When they see its power, they cannot help but choose the values of the Light instead of the values of the Dark."

This idea made sense to Priscilla. It was fascinating to hear the prince talk like this to his father, so she listened with great interest to see how the king would respond. At the same time, she was wondering what any of this had to do with her and with Alasdair.

"We have had this conversation before, Prince Incandescence," King Sol answered, with a sigh. "As I have told you many times, my son, there are those who have moved so far into Darkness, the values of the Light no longer exist for them." The king spoke with the familiar toned-down exasperation of a parent. "They have lost all connection to the Light. Showing them the Light will not change them no matter how much you may hope or wish it to be so. As you grow in age and wisdom, Prince Incandescence, you will come to know that this is the way it is."

From the familiar stubborn look on Inky's face, Priscilla knew he remained unconvinced. Her face had looked the same way often enough. She figured Inky probably disliked this royal version of the famous parental statement, "You'll understand when you are older," as much as she did.

Inky tried once more to convince his father. "I believe there is always some Light, even just a little spark, in everyone. Look at what happened to Garone the Gull. The Darkness was overshadowing him, but when we spoke to him and told him what he was doing, he chose to return to the Light. He exhibited great courage by helping us."

Priscilla and Alasdair exchanged perplexed looks. What was this about Pete... Garone the Gull? All this talk of the Light and the Dark was certainly new and mysterious to them.

The king saw the questions on their faces and explained. "Garone the Gull was pulled from the Light into the Dark by poor choices he made. In wanting something belonging to another gull, he allowed his jealousy to consume him. He decided to take what he wanted by attacking and killing the other gull. His leg was lost during the fight.

As a consequence of his act of taking another's life in such a way," the king continued, "Garone the Gull was given the choice of banishment from our kingdom or the opportunity to redeem himself by risking his life to help others. He chose redemption, so we used him to put you through your test. Through his courage and brave actions, he reconnected with his inner Light. He has been rewarded for his effort with the gift of a new leg."

As Priscilla and Alasdair were digesting this, King Sol turned back to Prince Inky and said, "Garone the Gull held enough Light within him to enable him to see the error of his ways and return to the Light. However, this does not mean that all are the same. You are too much of an idealist, my son. There are many who have chosen to let go of the Light inside them. They will never see the Light again. It is essential for the king to know and understand this in his heart as well as his head. If you do not learn this before you become king, you will underestimate the power of the Darkness when it begins to get out of balance."

Inky just sighed and grinned mischievously at Priscilla and Alasdair. He whispered to them in an aside, "Parents, they think they know everything!"

Priscilla looked at him in surprise. She had often had such thoughts about her own parents. Apparently, royal parents also wanted their kids to believe they knew what was best for them. And just like other kids, princes and princesses had the same trouble accepting what their parents had to say, especially if it didn't make any sense to them at the time. They thought they knew more than their parents did. Whether they did or not was always a subject for much argument and testing.

Perhaps because Inky had been brave enough to challenge his father, Alasdair felt free to ask the king, "Why have you brought us here, Your Highness, and what do you think Priscilla and I can do about all this?"

The king turned and nodded to Wanortu, who up until now had been quietly sitting and listening.

"It has come to our attention, Priscilla," Wanortu directed his words to her, "that your father is being pressured to make a decision which would result in the destruction of the marine and wildlife sanctuary King Sol mentioned earlier. The damage this would do to the ocean, the land, and all life forms involved is bad enough. However, unbeknownst to your father, the outcome of this decision is set to increase the power of the Dark in your world in such an exponential way that balance will be difficult to attain again."

Stunned by what she heard, Priscilla recalled the strained look on her father's face when he told her, *"What I decide will have a tremendous effect on our environment and on many people. I need to think carefully before I make my decision."* Was this what Wanortu was talking about? How could these people in the Kingdom Beyond the Sunset know about her father and his decision? It was all too confusing.

Wanortu shifted his glance to include Alasdair as he continued. "We thought if we taught both of you about the Light and the Dark and what can happen if such a decision is made, you could return home and share this knowledge with Priscilla's father. Then you will be able to convince him to make a decision other than the one he is being pressured to make."

"But what will happen if they *cannot* convince him?" Inky cried. "What if he does not *want* to be convinced? If they cannot do it, we *must* have an alternative plan. It is too risky to put all our trust in one plan. I still think we need to do something to show those who have chosen the Dark the error of their ways. We must try to bring them back to the Light!"

"We believe once Priscilla and Alasdair understand what is at stake, they will be able to talk to her father and get him to listen to reason," the king said.

"But I cannot even get *you* to listen to *me!*" Inky shouted, jumping off the bench. "What makes you think *he* will listen to *them?*"

"That is enough, Prince Incandescence!" the king pronounced with finality. Getting up from his throne, he gestured to his son. "Now please take our guests down to the seashore where they will have a chance to visit with Garone the Gull. Wanortu will send for them when he is ready to instruct them further in the ways of our kingdom and in the knowledge of the Light and the Dark."

Inky opened his mouth to speak again, but the king had already turned away, indicating there was nothing more to be said.

Though it was obvious he was still angry, Inky obeyed his father. Priscilla and Alasdair followed him as he stormed out through the glass doors and down the steps to the seashore.

Lita and several of the other royal children were on the rocky shore tossing a small ball back and forth to one another. When she saw Inky, she broke away from the group and ran over to greet them, giving Inky a big hug and welcoming Priscilla and Alasdair with her warm smile.

Laughing at Inky's glowering face, Lita said, "I see you and your father have been arguing again. Come and join us in a game of Bounderball. It will help you work off some steam. We can teach Priscilla and Alasdair how to play." Grabbing Inky's hand, she pulled him along behind her. Her warmth soon dissolved his anger.

They followed Lita to a cleared flat area on the shore where the children were playing. Before long, they were all involved in the game, laughing and yelling at one another as they tossed a soft rainbow-colored rubber ball back and forth. The Light and the Dark no longer existed for them.

Bounderball was a combination of Keep Away and Dodgeball, sometimes trying to get the ball and, at other times, keeping away from it. With beginner's luck, Priscilla won the game, and

Lita presented her with the bounderball as a prize. Blushing with pleasure, Priscilla tucked the ball into her backpack.

Afterwards, they rested on the shore and talked with one another about their lives. Inky and Lita told them they were going to be married in just a few days. They shared some of their plans for what sounded like a fabulous seashore wedding.

The entire time they were sitting together, Alasdair could not take his eyes off Lita. Priscilla guessed it must be unusual for him to see a girl who was as white as he was. Perhaps it was because Lita was so pretty. A twinge of jealousy seized her though she had no idea why.

At that moment, Garone the Gull flew in from the ocean and landed gracefully on the rocks beside them… on two legs. Garone's new leg was a vivid red, quite different from his pale pink one. Priscilla and Alasdair welcomed him with joy.

Alasdair asked in his usual blunt way, "Garone, why is your new leg a different color?"

The gull answered, "It is to remind me of what I have learned." This time he spoke directly to them and not in their heads. "I want to thank you both for saving my life. I'm afraid I did not deserve to be treated so well after what I had done. I had to learn how it feels to be vulnerable and helpless, to know that my fate lay in hands other than my own. I was most grateful when you both cared for me with so much kindness. And I am happy to have two legs again, even if they are different colors."

Alasdair told him, "We just did what anyone would have done. Luckily Mollie was close by."

"Yes," said Garone, with much warmth. "I developed quite a liking for her. She is a wise woman. I liked the big man, Jack, as well. He was always gentle with me."

They chatted a little while longer. Before he flew off again, Garone told them, "If ever there is anything I can do for the two of you, just let me know. I'll be around."

While he was soaring off toward the ocean, a much smaller bird flew in from the opposite direction, though this bird was not quite as graceful. When he landed in front of them, he turned topsy-turvy onto his tufted head. Eideard the Owl had arrived.

The little bird stood up and shook himself off saying, "Ach dear, Hoot Mon!" Gathering his dignity as best as he could, he announced to Priscilla and Alasdair, "I'm here tae tell ye Wanortu the WiseMaster is ready tae see ye noo. If ye follow me, I'll tak ye tae his room. Hoot Mon!"

After saying goodbye to Inky, Lita, and the other royal children, Priscilla and Alasdair followed Eideard up to the palace. He flew ahead of them, leading them in through a different door and up the marble staircase to a room on the highest floor at the back of the palace.

The little owl zoomed toward a tiny flapped opening near the top of the door. At the last moment, he spun his head around to tell them to follow him into the room. This move caused him to miss the flap by inches, and he flew smack into the door.

As he bounced back, he twisted around, saying shakily, "Ach, Hoot Mon!" Priscilla and Alasdair worked hard to stifle giggles.

After telling them, in advance this time, to open the door and follow him inside, Eideard headed for the flap once again, though with a bit more caution. This time he made it through without any trouble and disappeared into the room.

Priscilla and Alasdair opened the door to follow Eideard. After they stepped into the room, they stopped in amazement at what they saw in front of them.

Chapter Eleven
The Light and the Dark

For a moment, Priscilla thought they must be outdoors again. They had entered a forest wonderland. All around the edges of the room, leafy green trees grew toward a ceiling open to the sky. Bird songs rang out from high amongst the branches. Chipmunks and squirrels scurried across the floor. Brilliant butterflies hovered about dark green plants dotted with red, orchid-like flowers; the powerful sweet fragrance of the blossoms mingled with scents of vegetation and moisture in the air.

A miniature waterfall in one corner of the room splashed down over a garden of rocks and plants, spilling into a tiny brook and feeding into a round stone pool sunk into the floor in the middle of the room. A low stone wall surrounded the pool, and a short red wooden bridge provided access to a flat black rock protruding from the center of the pool. Fish of all colors swam in the clear water. Priscilla felt a familiar longing to sit on the rock and watch the fish.

On one side of the room, a hammock hung between two trees. Above the hammock, over a small hole in one of the trees, similar to Owl's house in *Winnie the Pooh*, a painted wooden sign read "Eideard the Owl".

Wanortu called down to them from somewhere in the tree branches above. "Please come up here and join us. The stairway is at the back of the room. You may leave your things by my Pondering Pool."

Priscilla and Alasdair carefully made their way through the room, not wanting to step on any of the little creatures underfoot. After dropping their packs by the pool, they found their way to a spiral staircase, and climbed round and round until they reached the top. They stepped out into a tree house built high in the branches. Everything in it had been sized to fit Wanortu's tiny frame.

"Sweet!" exclaimed Alasdair, looking around with delight.

"Welcome to my workspace," Wanortu greeted them with a warm smile. He was sitting on a low stool next to a short table. Eideard was back in his favorite place on Wanortu's shoulder, looking none the worse for wear after his bump on the head.

An old book with handwriting in a peculiar script lay open on the table in front of Wanortu. Spread out next to the book was a crinkled parchment map. Several measuring instruments and a paperweight shaped like a miniature black cat with one white paw, held the map flat. When the tiny cat raised a quizzical eyebrow at their approach, Priscilla laughed. It was not a paperweight at all but a real cat.

Wanortu saw her eyeing the cat. "This little girl here is PuzzlePuss." He reached out and stroked the cat's sleek fur while Eideard screwed up his face in disgust.

PuzzlePuss, true to her name, continued to scrutinize Priscilla and Alasdair with her perplexed look. Apparently, they passed her thorough inspection, for she lifted her tiny head to allow Priscilla to scratch behind her ears. Mathilda came to mind, and a sudden wave of homesickness washed over her, but she quickly pushed the feeling away. Going home was not an option.

The tree house was a magical museum of curiosities. More ancient books and parchment scrolls were crammed into bookshelves on the wall, exuding the same musty odor as Priscilla's favorite old fairy tale books. Several ornate glass cabinets stood next to the bookshelves. One held a collection of crystal globes and pieces of crystal in a variety of colors. Another was full of assorted sizes of ancient intricately carved wooden sticks, which Priscilla figured had to be magic wands. A collection of rocks and gems of unusual shapes and colors, and a cabinet full of uncommon seashells definitely required a closer look.

Wanortu told them with great satisfaction, "Those are special books and treasures I have collected over the years. Feel free to look around, and you may touch anything you like except, of course, the magic wands. They are always a bit tricky." He smiled with amusement.

Eideard hooted loudly, "Aye, that ye know from yer own experience tae be sure, ye daft old fool. Hoot Mon!"

Priscilla headed for the seashell collection. None of the shells looked familiar, and she studied them in fascination. Alasdair had gone straight to the magic wands, obviously dying to try out a few of them. Wanortu had been wise to issue his warning.

Tiny ribbons of light dancing about Priscilla drew her attention away from the shells and back to the room. Light from the Royal Rainbow that shone above them reflected off numerous pieces of pale lavender crystal scattered on a small round table top, creating miniature rainbows.

Light also came in through windows on the back wall. In front of the windows, a small brass telescope on a wooden stand pointed up to the Royal Rainbow. Next to it, an antique globe displayed the Kingdom Beyond the Sunset and the Kingdom of the Sunrise amongst other places Priscilla did not recognize.

The view from the windows was the same as from the banquet hall, although from this higher perspective, the Muses were more clearly visible. The structures glimmered in the sunlight, looking like multi-colored cathedrals with spires reaching as high as heaven itself.

Wanortu interrupted their explorations. "I wish I could allow you more time, but we have much to do. I want to show you the Muses. Then we can talk further about why we have brought you here. Please follow me." He walked over to the wall and pressed a button beside a low oval window. After the glass slid to one side, he stepped through the opening, and he and Eideard simply disappeared.

Priscilla rushed over, leaned out to look, and immediately squealed with pleasure. Wanortu was walking on a bridge of light leading from his room, over the gardens and orchards, and down to the front of the Muses.

Without any hesitation, she stepped across the threshold to follow Wanortu, with Alasdair right behind her. Both of them were speechless with wonder. The strands of light felt soft and buoyant under her feet. It was like walking on air.

Where the bridge gently curved downwards, Wanortu sat down and slid the rest of the way on his rump.

Priscilla did likewise, hitting the ground with a slight bump. Breathless with excitement, she exclaimed, "I feel like I just slid down a rainbow!"

Alasdair landed almost on top of her, exclaiming, "That was fantastic! I wish we could do it again."

They had arrived in front of the Muses. Much to Priscilla's surprise, these were not real buildings at all. The walls were made of moving strands of rose pink and green light, so close together, they created the illusion of walls. "No wonder the Muses always seemed to be moving," she murmured, as much to herself as to anyone else. "I thought it was just a trick of the light." Well, in a way, this was exactly what it was.

Wanortu led them through the light strands into the space within. Pointing to one of many long wooden benches, he said, "Please take a seat over there."

After she sat down, Priscilla looked about her in awe. The Muses were open to the sky with the spires gleaming up above. The space was full of such quiet holiness it actually felt like a cathedral. Little brown men and women all about the enclosure added to this impression. Some were sitting in pairs or groups and whispering quietly to one another. Others sat alone, writing, praying, or meditating. All of them were about the same size and color as Wanortu and wore similar black and brown clothing.

Wanortu informed them in a hushed voice, "Those of us who are brown-skinned are the WiseElders of the village. It is our job to care for the Muses and the Sacred Light, to provide help and wisdom for the villagers, and to educate the children."

"What is the difference between a WiseElder and a WiseMaster?" Alasdair asked.

"The WiseMaster is the oldest and, one hopes, the wisest of the WiseElders, Alasdair, the one to whom the WiseElders go for consultation," Wanortu answered in a matter-of-fact way, with the usual merry little twinkle in his eye. "The WiseMaster is also the advisor to the royal family and is allowed the privilege of living in the palace."

"Ach aye," snickered Eideard. "Sometimes ye mak me wunder aboot the wisest part, ye old fool! Hoot Mon!" Wanortu tousled the little bird's feathers with great affection.

The Muses continuously brightened and dimmed. A huge circle of light suspended in air in the middle of the space altered in unison with the Muses. Inside the circle, a globe turned slowly, spilling out streams of light and dark colors.

The sense of palpitating power inside the Muses made Priscilla feel all tingly throughout her body. She turned to Wanortu and said, "I have this weird tingly feeling in my body… like electricity running through me. What's going on?" Alasdair must have noticed the same thing for he turned to listen with interest to Wanortu's answer.

Wanortu told them, "We are in an energy field. What you are feeling in your bodies is an increase in Light energy. The people of our kingdom gather here to send Light energy into the Muses and out into your world. The Light Bridge carries Light energy to the Sacred Light."

"What's this Light energy?" Alasdair asked.

"Everything in the universe is made up of energy, Alasdair. All we do or say creates energy of one kind or another," Wanortu said. "When we live our lives with love, courage, truth, and wisdom, even in difficult times, hold positive thoughts, and do loving and kind things for ourselves, for one another, and for nature, we create Light energy. This helps bring about positive changes and healing in the world."

He went on, "When we cause harm to ourselves, to one another or to nature, or think negative and hateful thoughts, we create Dark energy. Dark energy brings pain and chaos into the world. When we deliberately choose to cause harm to others or to the environment, we release even more Dark energy."

As she was listening to Wanortu, Priscilla continued to watch the revolving globe. It looked a lot like planet earth. "Wanortu, is that our earth up there within the circle of light?" she asked.

"Yes, it is, Priscilla." he answered.

She continued with her thought, "Then what are those light and dark colors coming out of it?"

"Your world is constantly sending forth Light and Dark energies, Priscilla. The streams of Light and Dark are those energies," Wanortu told her. "How much of one or the other depends on what is going on at any given moment in all the countries in your world."

The amount of Light and Dark energies seemed to differ in every country on the globe, though none sent out all one or the other. When the Light energy increased, the circle of light shone brighter; when the Dark energy increased, the light dimmed.

Alasdair had been closely watching some areas where masses of Dark energy arose, interspersed with only occasional flashes of Light energy. He asked, "Why is there so much Dark energy coming from some countries?"

"Those are countries where there is tremendous violence," Wanortu told him. "Wars and violence of any kind create excessive quantities of Dark energy. Yet even in the midst of so much Darkness, many act with love, courage, wisdom, and truth, sending out Light energy. It is rare to find a place where only Dark energy exists. If that were to happen, there would be real trouble afoot."

"Aye, an ye wouldna want tae be there! Hoot Mon!" Eideard gave a shudder of his feathers.

"To help you understand how each of you individually sends energy out into the world, let us try an experiment," Wanortu suggested. "First, please close your eyes." He paused for a moment, giving them time to shut their eyes. "Now imagine someone you love, and hold that feeling of love tightly in your heart." He was silent as they did as he suggested.

Right away, Priscilla thought of Granny and all the love she felt for her. She concentrated hard. It was easy to hold tight to these feelings; the hard part was letting go.

Wanortu was speaking again. "Now, please open your eyes and look at the Muses."

With great reluctance, Priscilla opened her eyes. Much to her surprise, the colors of the Muses had grown brighter.

"Now," said Wanortu, "Please close your eyes again and think angry thoughts. Think of someone you don't like who has upset you."

This was easy for Priscilla as well, though in an entirely different way. Images of Mr. Green and his son, Harvey, immediately arose in front of her, and she felt her anger toward them. It was no trouble at all.

"Please open your eyes again and look once more at the colors of the Muses," suggested Wanortu.

This time she opened her eyes in a hurry. The colors of the Muses had dimmed. It was hard to believe that she and Alasdair could have caused such a change.

"Whew! That was intense!" Alasdair exclaimed. Apparently he had no trouble coming up with his images either.

"Hoot Mon!" put in Eideard who had been watching and listening to every word as usual.

Wanortu commented. "Now, if our thoughts and feelings have such an influence, you can see why it is so important to pay attention to what we think and say and how we behave. The choices we make determine the kind of energy we send out into the world around us. We have more power than we realize. When we all work together to send out Light energy, we can accomplish great things."

Alasdair was looking thoughtful. "King Sol said when the Darkness gets out of balance it means something dangerous is happening in the world. Does this have something to do with Light and Dark energies?"

"A good question, Alasdair," Wanortu observed, "and the answer is, yes, it does. If the Darkness is out of balance, it means the Dark energy in the world has increased and the Light energy has diminished. It also means the People of the Dark are succeeding at increasing their power."

Spooked by this unusual name, Priscilla shivered as she asked, "Who are these People of the Dark?"

Wanortu looked uncharacteristically grave as he explained. "The People of the Dark are those who hold only Dark energy within them, Priscilla. Their intent is to increase the Dark energy in the world and destroy the Light energy. They seek out those who have not yet fully chosen the values of the Light to try to pull them into the Dark."

"How do they do that?" Alasdair asked.

"They try to make you give up your own Light and choose the Dark like them, Alasdair. The People of the Dark discourage individual thinking and tolerance of differences amongst people as these weaken their power. By persuading others to believe what they say instead of making their own decisions, the People of the Dark can increase their power which is exactly what they want."

Wanortu's eyes lost their usual twinkle as he went on, "They want you to believe that the acquisition of great wealth, power, and physical perfection are the keys to happiness. How these goals are achieved does not matter to the People of the Dark, even if other people, the earth, and many life forms are destroyed as a result."

Thinking about what Inky had said to his father, Priscilla asked, "But, Wanortu, why would so many choose the values of the Dark instead of the Light?" She could not imagine ever choosing the values of the Dark.

Wanortu said, "Children are not always taught to listen to their own hearts, Priscilla. When they grow older, they can get too busy or too distracted to bother to learn how to do this. It becomes easier to let someone else tell them what to do. Others are afraid to believe in themselves and in their own power. It takes time and a lot of hard work to learn to think for yourself and to have faith in your own beliefs."

As Priscilla and Alasdair listened quietly, Wanortu took a breath. "When people look to others to make their decisions for them, it is easy for the People of the Dark to promote their values. Fear and ignorance are their greatest weapons. Many people choose the values of the Dark without realizing they may never be able to return to the Light. This increases the Dark energy as well as the power of the People of the Dark and can lead to a dangerous imbalance in power."

"But what can be done about these People of the Dark?" Alasdair demanded. He sounded ready to do battle with them, whoever they were.

Wanortu smiled gently at Alasdair. "All of us must work hard to increase the Light energy in the world, Alasdair. We send out as much Light energy as we can from the Kingdom Beyond the Sunset. However, we are not able to send enough Light energy to balance the Dark energy without help from your world. And right now we need all the help your world can manage."

"What does all this have to do with Priscilla's father?" Alasdair was like a dog with a bone, trying to understand what this had to do with him and what he could do about it.

Wanortu said, "Priscilla's father does not know it is the People of the Dark who are pressuring him to make his decision. Nor does he know the decision they want him to make could increase the Darkness in the world in a significant way. This is why it is of great importance for both of you to talk to him and help him to understand the situation."

"But what exactly do we need to tell him?" Priscilla asked. She was trying hard to take in and understand all she was hearing.

"Let us go back up to my room where we can talk more about what your father needs to hear. Then I can answer all of your questions." Wanortu led them outside the Muses once again.

Once they were outside, he took out his magic wand and pointed it at the bridge. Immediately, the light strands transformed from a slide into a set of stairs. In single file, with Wanortu in the lead, and Priscilla and Alasdair following, they climbed up the stairs of light. Soon the stairs began to move like an escalator. In no time at all, they were gliding back to the entry to Wanortu's room,

Priscilla had just stepped through the opening when Alasdair, who was right behind her, yelled, "Help!" Turning around in a hurry, she saw that he had dropped down below the opening.

Alasdair reached up and grabbed hold of the threshold, as Priscilla and Wanortu rushed back to help him.

"Hang on Alasdair! We've got you!" Priscilla cried. She gripped one of his arms while Wanortu took hold of the other.

With Eideard fluttering about in the air above them, cheering them on, they pulled Alasdair up through the opening and into the room. Trembling, he fell to the floor where he lay for a moment, pulling himself together.

Wanortu and Priscilla leaned out the window to see what had made Alasdair start to fall. The Light Bridge was slowly growing dimmer.

"Now that is not a good sign!" Wanortu exclaimed, scratching his head as he looked with concern at the disappearing bridge. "This has never happened before."

"Ach aye, that was tae close fer comfort! Hoot Mon!" burst out Eideard, as he peeked out from on top of Wanortu's hat brim to which he clung.

Priscilla noticed a sudden change in the light in the tree house. Something was different. When she looked up, the Royal Rainbow was no longer shining above them. Just as she was about to mention this to Wanortu, sounds of running footsteps and shouting came from the corridor down below them.

Someone banged on the door and called out loudly, "WiseMaster, WiseMaster! Come quickly!"

Wanortu spoke with composure to Priscilla and Alasdair, "Please wait for me downstairs by the pool while I see what has happened." With Eideard fluttering along behind him, Wanortu climbed down the stairway and left the room.

Priscilla and Alasdair followed him downstairs and sat on the wall by the pool to await his return. At precisely the same moment, each of them jumped up and headed for the little bridge. When they realized what they were doing, they broke into a fit of giggles. Before they had time to decide who should sit on the rock first, voices sounded in the corridor again.

Soon Wanortu came back into the room. The expression on his face was worried as he looked down with puzzlement at the piece of paper in his hand. Scratching his head, he walked slowly toward them.

Eideard was bouncing up and down on Wanortu's shoulder. "Ach, this is nae a gud thing. What's tae be done? Ach, dear, dear!" he muttered. "Hoot Mon!"

"What's going on, Wanortu?" Alasdair and Priscilla asked in unison.

Chapter Twelve
The Disappearance

Wanortu lifted his eyes from the paper in his hand and shifted his focus to Priscilla and Alasdair. His haggard expression emphasized the deep leathery creases on his face, and his eyes had lost their usual twinkle. "I'm afraid I have some disturbing news. It appears Prince Inky has decided to take matters into his own hands. He has borrowed the Sacred Light and disappeared with it!"

"What do you mean, Wanortu?" asked Alasdair in bewilderment. "We were just with Inky. He didn't say anything about going anywhere."

Wanortu showed them the sheet of paper. "According to this letter Inky left behind, he has been secretly planning this for some time. The argument he had with his father today only made him more certain about what he wants to do. He plans to take the Sacred Light to the People of the Dark. He wants to show them the Light and convince them they are choosing the wrong path."

Wanortu went on, his voice heavy with concern. "He has no idea of the danger he will be facing. Someone needs to find Inky and the Light and bring them back before it is too late. Please come with me now. We must go and speak with King Sol."

When they got downstairs, they found a stunned king and other members of the royal family milling about in the rotunda. Where the Light had recently been shining so intensely, it was now dark and gloomy, matching the spirits of those who were present. The Rainbow Guards, protectors of the Sacred Light, were huddled by themselves, looking ashamed.

Only Queen Luminata was not there. King Sol said, "The queen was so upset by the news she has retired to her bed chamber."

"Does anyone have any idea where Prince Inky might have gone?" asked Priscilla, getting practical as she usually did when there was a problem to face.

King Sol shook his head and sighed. "We know he took his horse and headed over the hills toward the Merry Meadow. Why he went that way and what exactly was on his mind, we do not know." He was silent for a moment or two. Then he lifted his head as if he had just had an idea. "There *is* someone who might be able to find out where he has gone."

"Who is that?" asked Alasdair with great excitement.

"Mother Nature," answered the King. "Her kingdom is up on White Mountain in the Mara Mountains. From there, she watches over all the creatures of her kingdom. We must send someone to ask her if she can tell us where Prince Incandescence has gone."

Alasdair and Priscilla looked at each other in surprise. Mother Nature was a popular term used by many people to describe nature. It had never occurred to either of them that Mother Nature might actually be a real person.

"We must be careful whom we send," Wanortu said, continuing with the king's suggestion. "With the Sacred Light beyond the security of the palace, every Light-Eater in the land will be gathering to follow its trail. It will be dangerous for anyone who goes out there now."

"What's a Light-Eater?" asked Alasdair, now thoroughly intrigued.

Wanortu answered, "The Legendary Light-Eaters of the Land are the shadow servants of the People of the Dark. They seek out Light energy wherever they can find it. If you are not prepared and don't know how to recognize them, Light-Eaters will steal your Light energy, leaving you weak and vulnerable, a shadow of your former self."

"We need to send someone with plenty of courage who holds much Light energy inside," stated the king. As he spoke, his eyes rested thoughtfully on Priscilla and Alasdair.

Without stopping to think about it, Priscilla asked, "Is it something Alasdair and I could do?"

The king exchanged a glance with Wanortu. Wanortu answered. "It is too much to ask of you both. The journey would be dangerous as you would have to travel through the Fairy Forest and up into the Mara Mountains to get to White Mountain. It is not an easy trip, and you do not know the territory or the dangers."

"You could give us a map and tell us what to watch out for," Alasdair cried, warming up to the idea of what sounded to him like a glorious adventure. For a boy who had grown up around video games, the idea of these Legendary Light-Eaters seemed like an enticing challenge, not at all something to dread.

King Sol addressed Wanortu, "I do think it might be best to send Priscilla and Alasdair if they are willing to go. Their Light energy will distract some of the Light-Eaters from following Inky's trail. They have the necessary physical stamina for such a journey. Once they find out from Mother Nature where he has gone, they will be better able to find Prince Incandescence and convince him to return home. He may be more willing to listen to them."

Scratching his head, Wanortu settled his eyes on Priscilla and Alasdair for a long moment. Sensing their eagerness, he concurred. "All right, Your Highness, as long as Priscilla and Alasdair are willing to undertake this task, it does indeed make more sense to send them than anyone else. We must go up to my room right away. I need to prepare them for their journey. It will be best for them to leave early in the morning. They will need to get some rest before they undertake such a long trek."

As Wanortu turned to leave, he said, "Come with me, please, Priscilla and Alasdair. I will get you ready to go. Afterwards, I will show you where you can sleep."

Once they were back in Wanortu's room, Eideard flew up to his hole and disappeared inside, probably for a nap. Apparently, he was not used to so much commotion. Perhaps Wanortu was not the only one who felt old.

At Wanortu's suggestion, Priscilla and Alasdair followed him back up the staircase to the tree house where he quickly began clearing off the square table. PuzzlePuss was nowhere in sight. After closing the old book and putting it back on the shelf, Wanortu rolled up the parchment map and placed it with the other scrolls.

He lifted down a different scroll, blew off some dust, unrolled it, and laid it on the table in front of them. PuzzlePuss immediately appeared out of nowhere, jumping up on the table to curl up in her paperweight position on the corner of the scroll.

As Wanortu bent over the scroll, his eyeglasses fell off his nose. While he put on another pair, he told them. "This is a map of the Kingdom Beyond the Sunset." He poked his finger at various places. "Here is where we are now in the Village of the Rainbow. There is where we first met in the Merry Meadow. I will take you back to the same spot. Then you will cross the Merry Meadow to this path into the Fairy Forest. It will lead you through the Fairy Forest and up here into the Mara Mountains."

"Why is it called the Fairy Forest?" Priscilla asked. Fairy tales had always thrilled her, but even though she liked to imagine what a fairy might look like, she had never believed they could be real.

"It is in the Fairy Forest where the little Fairy Folk live," answered Wanortu. "Their homes are in amongst the roots of the trees where they live in safety. Most of the time, the forest is a light and peaceful place, but nasty storms do occur, mostly at this time of year. You may or may not see the Fairy Folk, as they are shy and do not often show themselves to strangers, especially not when the Legendary Light-Eaters of the Land are about. The Fairy Folk are full of Light energy, so they do not care to draw the Light-Eaters to themselves."

"Tell us more about these Light-Eater things," demanded Alasdair bravely. If he were the brash lion he had been imitating earlier, his paws would be up in the air, and he would be roaring, "Let me at 'em! Let me at 'em!"

"They can be quite a challenge," Wanortu began. "You won't be able to recognize them by sight because they will look much like your fellow travelers. They will try to get you to trust them. But once your guard is down, they will begin to ask you specific questions intended to steal your Light energy."

As Priscilla and Alasdair listened entranced, he went on, "Underneath their disguises, they are actually shadow figures and servants of the People of the Dark. You will not know how to discern what they are until they begin to ask you a series of questions. That is when you will know they are after your Light energy."

"What kinds of questions?" Alasdair asked. Priscilla could tell he was getting really excited.

Wanortu smiled patiently at Alasdair as he answered. "They will know your sensitivities, fears, and doubts. Their questions will weaken and confuse you, fill you with uncertainty, and distract you from your journey. In this way, they steal your Light energy. You must…"

"So what do we do about them?" Alasdair cut in.

"You must only answer their questions with questions of your own,' Wanortu continued, as if he had not been interrupted. "If you listen to them, believe what they are saying to you, and try to answer their questions, you will feel your Light energy begin to drain from you. Every time you try to answer any of their questions, you will lose more of your power. Confusion, doubt, and fear will overcome you. Then you will know you are facing a Light-Eater."

Before Alasdair could ask the next question already on his lips, Wanortu went on, "However, if you answer three of their questions with questions of your own, they will lose their power and disappear back to where they came from. Light-Eaters are sneaky and persistent, so you must be careful not to become overconfident, even if you manage to outwit one or two."

Priscilla knew Alasdair had stopped listening and was gearing up to do battle with the Light-Eaters. Touching the rainbow ribbon in her hair, she recalled Granny's words: *"If you are unable to stop them, they will take away parts of your spirit until you have only a shadow of yourself left."* Granny could have been talking about these Light-Eaters.

Wanortu drew their attention back to the map once more. "When you reach the Mara Mountains you will need to make your way here to the Valley of the Moon at the foot of White Mountain. It is not hard to find. All you have to do is follow the well-trodden trail created by the creatures of Mother Nature's kingdom. They all go to drink the healing waters of the Pool of Reflection which lies in the Valley of the Moon."

After he showed them the Valley of the Moon on the map, he pointed at White Mountain. "It is at the top of White Mountain where Mother Nature resides. When you arrive in the valley, you must rest by the pool and wait until she sends you an invitation.

She will know right away when you have arrived and will let you know when she is ready to receive you."

For a moment, Priscilla wondered how they were going to get to the top of such a high mountain, but she decided it would be best to wait until they got there to find out. There were too many other things to think about now. Wanortu obviously had more to tell them.

He pointed to a dark spot on the map between the mountains and the forest as he cautioned them, "This is the Lava Land. It is a dangerous place. You need to avoid it, if possible. The ground is all volcanic rock. Walking on such rock is difficult. The land is flat and barren with no landmarks; it is easy to lose your sense of direction. And it offers no water or protective shade from the sun. If you should happen upon the Lava Land, I recommend you go around it, even if it takes longer to get to where you need to go."

Wanortu scooted PuzzlePuss aside with a gentle nudge as he rolled up the map and handed it to Alasdair. "The storms you must watch out for in the Fairy Forest and the Merry Meadow are Dreary Drenching Downpours and Horrendously Huge Hailstorms. In the Mara Mountains and the Lava Land, the worst storms are the Wild Wicked Windstorms. All these storms strike with little or no warning. None of them is in the least pleasant."

He went on, "You must be especially careful if you run into a Horrendously Huge Hailstorm. The first few hailstones will be small, but others will be as large and as hard as rocks. If you encounter such a storm, seek protection immediately, or the hailstones can do you a lot of harm. In fact, if any of these storms come, it is best to find shelter right away."

"We'll watch out for them," Priscilla said, hoping they would not run into any such awful sounding storms.

Wanortu stood for a moment scratching his head. "I would like to give you some things to help you on your journey. Let me see…"

He walked over to the round table and picked up several pieces of the lavender colored crystal. Without the rainbow shining above, they no longer twinkled.

As he held out his hand to show them the crystals, he told them, "These are called Rainbow-Makers. They will give you Light energy when you need it, especially if you have lost some of your own to Light-Eaters. Just hold the crystals up to catch the Light, and they will create healing rainbows all around you." He handed the crystal pieces to Priscilla, and she put them in one of her pockets.

Then he went to the collection of shells, lifted one from the glass case, and brought it back to show them. The small glossy black shell fit into the palm of his hand. Its papery thin exterior gave it a delicate appearance. When Wanortu opened the shell, an intense ray of piercing white light poured forth from inside, easily lighting up the tree house. So much powerful light coming from such a fragile looking shell took both Priscilla and Alasdair by surprise.

Wanortu closed the shell. "This shell is called a Black Carapas; it is from the deepest part of the ocean. You can use it to find your way through dark places. It shines best underwater, though I doubt you would have such a need. No matter what, you must use the shell sparingly. If it has been open for any length of time, you will need to soak it in water to help it regenerate. The Black Carapas will be of no use to you once it has dried out." He handed the shell to Alasdair.

Alasdair stared at the shell with awe. Opening it gingerly, he tried it out for a moment and then hurriedly closed it. Handling it with great respect, he put it in his pocket.

Wanortu added with a wise smile, "I also want to give you a most important reminder to take with you. Remember that each of you carries within you the best Light Detector in the world… your own heart. If you listen and trust the voice speaking to you through your heart, you will be able to sense when you are in danger. You can determine who has Light energy inside them and who does not. If you listen to your heart as well as your mind, you will be able to make good decisions and find your way through the Darkness."

He started toward the stairway. "Now, please come with me. It is time for you to rest, for you have had a long day and much has happened to you. Tomorrow you will need all your energy for your journey. I will awaken you early in the morning. It will be best if we start out before sunrise."

They went back downstairs. Priscilla and Alasdair picked up their gear and followed Wanortu as he led them to two small rooms next door to his. He showed them where the bathrooms were located and then left them on their own.

Though she was excited and quite sure she would never be able to sleep a wink, Priscilla had no idea how tired she was. She washed and got ready for bed, crawled under the covers, and within moments, fell deeply into slumber with no thought about what tomorrow would bring.

As he said he would, Wanortu awakened them early in the morning. Breakfast was waiting for them in his room when they arrived. Priscilla and Alasdair ate in silence, both far too excited and absorbed in thought to say much or to think about what they were eating.

When they finished, Wanortu instructed them, "Now please gather your things. I will take you back to the Merry Meadow where I will arrange transport to get you to the Fairy Forest."

He called up to Eideard, who awakened with a sleepy "Hoot Mon!" and flew down to sit on his usual place on Wanortu's shoulder.

When they were all set, they made their way downstairs, hurried through the dim passageway and outside to the plaza in front of the palace. The royal children were still asleep, but King Sol, Queen Luminata, and Lita had arisen early to see them off. The queen made sure they both had an ample supply of food and water tucked safely into their backpacks.

Lita, her face grave with concern, told them quietly, "When you find Inky, please tell him I love him very much and want him to come home safely. And remind him that he must not miss our wedding day!" As she said the last words, she gave them a brave smile, but Priscilla could tell how worried she was about her prince.

Alasdair handed Lita his guitar and asked, "Could you please look after my guitar until I return to the palace? I don't know what we're getting into, but I sure don't want it caught in any of those Dreary Drenching Downpours."

"I will take good care of it, Alasdair."

Then Wanortu and Eideard, Priscilla, and Alasdair squeezed into the same little cart they had ridden in before and waved goodbye to everyone.

Within minutes, the pony was pulling them once more along the road through the Village of the Rainbow as they headed toward the hills. The sun was just beginning to rise, along with the villagers who were getting ready to start a new day. It would no doubt be a different sort of day without their Sacred Light.

When the little pony arrived back at the same spot in the Merry Meadow where Wanortu had first met Priscilla and Alasdair, they all got down from the cart. Wanortu put his fingers to his lips and blew out a low piercing whistle.

At once, a huge red cloud rose up far across the meadow and rushed toward them. It was the same big red horse that Wanortu had magically created the day before.

"Oh my gosh," Priscilla gasped, "Surely you don't think we can ride such a huge horse?"

"You will be fine," Wanortu reassured her. "I will add a saddle and a ladder, and I will tell Horse Of Course where to take you. He doesn't need you to lead him, and he travels very fast.

"What's his name?" Priscilla asked.

"It's Horse Of Course," answered Wanortu.

"Yes, I know it's a horse, but what's his name?" she repeated in exasperation, as Eideard hooted loudly.

"Horse Of Course," repeated Wanortu with a gentle smile. "That is his name."

She said "Oh!" sheepishly, as she finally got it. Alasdair grinned at her confusion.

Wanortu took out his magic wand. Speaking more of his peculiar words, he waved his wand at Horse of Course. All at once, a leather saddle appeared across the back of the horse with a long rope ladder attached to one side. Wanortu walked to the front of the horse and, craning his neck, looked up at the big horse and said something. Horse of Course answered with a loud whinny.

As Alasdair started climbing up the ladder with Priscilla right behind him, Wanortu put his hand out and stopped her, saying, "Before you go, there is something more I wish to send with you."

He turned his head and spoke to Eideard, "With your permission, my fine-feathered friend," and then turned back. "Eideard the Owl will go with you. He carries the sun inside him and can help you find your way through the Darkness."

Eideard opened his sleepy eyes wide in surprise and began squirming about on Wanortu's shoulder, sputtering, "Ach w-w-w-wait a bit here. Wha's that ye say? Ach no! I canna go noo. Hoot Mon! I'm tae old fer this game. Besides I canna leave ye, ye daft old coot. Wha' wid ye do wi' oot me? Ach no, I canna go. Who wid look oot fer ye? Hoot Mon!"

Wanortu lifted the tiny bird from his shoulder onto his index finger and looked him squarely in the eye, which can be tricky with an owl. He said with great firmness, "You know I cannot go, Eideard. I am far too old. I need you to go in my place. You will be my eyes and ears and give the gift of your great wisdom to Priscilla and Alasdair."

"Ach aye, if ye sae so, but I dinna know what guid I'll be," muttered Eideard with a sigh, as he continued to fidget. He seemed to know there was no point to arguing. "Ach dear, I wasna expectin' this, tae be sure. Hoot Mon!"

Wanortu gently placed Eideard on Priscilla's shoulder. The tickle of the tiny owl's feathers against her cheek and the sound of his talons scrabbling at the straps of her backpack soon had her chuckling softly.

There did not seem to be anything else to say. So with Eideard sitting on her shoulder, she followed Alasdair up the ladder and swung her leg over the saddle to sit behind him. She pulled up the ladder and folded it across the back of the saddle. Alasdair grabbed hold of the reins and the big saddle horn in front of him, and Priscilla put her arms around his waist.

They called goodbye to Wanortu, who seemed extremely far below them.

He shouted up to them, "Good luck, and have a safe journey!"

Just as they were starting to leave, Wanortu called out to them with an afterthought, "Try not to make Mother Nature laugh."

Priscilla yelled back to him, "Why not?" But there was no time to hear his answer, for Horse of Course had already started to trot and soon broke into a gallop.

She clung tightly to Alasdair as they began their trek across the Merry Meadow, heading toward the forest and the mountains. They were about to discover whatever mysteries lay within them and beyond.

BOOK THREE

SEARCHING
FOR THE LIGHT

Chapter Thirteen
The Fairy Forest

Horse of Course galloped at breakneck speed across the Merry Meadow toward the Fairy Forest. Priscilla clung to Alasdair as they bounced up and down in the saddle. Everything passed by in a blur, giving her no time to admire the wildflowers or watch the quick scattering of butterflies and rabbits as they whizzed past. Wanortu had been right. This was indeed a speedy way to go.

Before long, they arrived at the edge of the forest where they could see the path leading into the trees directly ahead of them. The big red horse pulled to a stop and whinnied at them.

Priscilla took the hint and released the ladder so that she and Alasdair could climb down. After they were on the ground, Horse of Course ambled off into the meadow to munch some grass.

"Well," said Alasdair bravely, as he stood staring at the path leading into the Fairy Forest. "I guess this is it. We're on our own now, and who knows what will happen."

She nodded and gulped, "I just hope we come out of this okay, let alone find Inky and the Light."

"Hoot Mon!" agreed Eideard.

Priscilla jumped in surprise because she had forgotten the little owl was sitting right next to her ear. Knowing he was with them somehow made her feel less afraid.

Alasdair led the way as they started up the path. Before long, they were deep in the forest of tall evergreen trees. The moist air felt heavy and full of the earthy smell of leaves and wood, alive and rotting. The morning sun filtered through the branches, although the farther they walked into the forest, the darker and cooler it became. Wanortu had also been right about the path being easy to follow. It was well traveled and clearly in view.

After they had been hiking for some time, they saw an old man limping down the path toward them. He moved slowly, using a long wooden staff to help him make his way. The weight of the huge pack on his shoulder caused him to stoop over until he bent forward nearly in two.

Stopping to rest, he laid down his pack, lifted his head for a stretch, and seemed only then to notice Priscilla and Alasdair heading toward him.

"Good day to you, children!" he said warmly, in the rasping voice of an old man. "It's a grand day today. No storms at all. And where might you be heading, little ones?" He appeared to be a nice friendly old man.

"We're going to the Mara Mountains to see Mother Nature," answered Alasdair politely.

"Ah," said the old man with a nod. "The Mara Mountains and Mother Nature, you say. Well, 'tis a fine day for a visit. You look like you might be new to the forest. Are you sure you know the right path to the mountains? 'Tis a long way, to be sure."

"I think we do," answered Alasdair, no longer quite as sure as he had been.

"There are many paths in the forest. 'Tis easy to get lost," the old man continued, nodding his head again. "There are wild animals in the forest. You must watch out for them. There are wolves and bears aplenty. Do you know what to do if you happen perchance upon one of these dangerous creatures?" For some strange reason, he no longer seemed quite as old or as bent as when they had first seen him.

Alasdair was about to answer when Eideard began hooting and bouncing up and down on Priscilla's shoulder. He whispered in her ear, "Ken what ye were warned aboot, lassie. Hoot Mon!"

At first, she was doubtful, as this was just an old man. Then she recalled Wanortu saying Light-Eaters looked much like normal people. She looked at Alasdair's confused face and wondered if Eideard could be right.

Before Alasdair could answer, Priscilla asked the old man, "What would *you* do, sir, if you came upon a bear or a wolf?"

The old man seemed upset at her question. In a grouchy voice, he said, "I'm just an old man. I can take care of myself. You are only children and should not be out on your own in the forest."

Turning to Alasdair, he asked, "Do your parents know you are out here by yourself?" Alasdair's face registered shock at this direct question.

"Why do you like frightening little children?" Priscilla asked with defiance. Alasdair looked at her, surprised by her rudeness. Winking at him, she nudged him on the arm and mouthed quietly, "Light-Eater!"

As the old man bent over to pick up his pack, he whined at Alasdair, "What would your father say about you being so rude to a poor old man who is trying to help you?"

Alasdair was ready for him this time. Finally catching on to what was happening, he did not hear this last question directed at him. "Why are you asking us so many questions?" he demanded.

Quick as a wink, the old man faded into a dark shadow figure and vanished amongst the trees.

"Whew, that was weird!" Alasdair gasped in relief. "Thanks for your help, Priscilla. I'd no idea we'd already met one of those Light-Eater things. Come to think of it, I did start to feel weaker the longer he spoke to us."

"It was Eideard who suggested it." Priscilla patted the little owl on the head.

At her touch, Eideard shyly tucked his head down into his neck feathers as he trilled, "Hoot Mon!"

"Did you see what happened to the Light-Eater as soon as you asked the third question?" Priscilla commented to Alasdair. "He turned into a shadow and disappeared." She looked with wonder toward the spot where the old man had simply vanished.

They moved along the path again, though with more caution this time. A few other people of different ages approached them on the path. Priscilla and Alasdair looked with suspicion at each of them. Some nodded, and a few said "hello", but fortunately, all of them passed by without any further comment. Soon Priscilla and Alasdair began to relax again.

The oft-used path enabled them to walk at a fast clip. They were making reasonably good time when they heard a cry in the forest off to one side. Someone was calling for help.

Following the sound of the voice, they ran through the trees until they reached a small clearing. A teen-aged girl stood backed up against a tree, wildly swinging a heavy wooden bucket at a large gray wolf, baring its teeth and snarling as it paced furiously back and forth in front of her.

"Oh no!" cried Priscilla. "The old man wasn't lying. There *are* wolves in the forest!"

Alasdair picked up a branch from the ground. With a loud yell, he threw it at the wolf. It landed in front of the paws of the big creature, causing it to turn and look at Priscilla and Alasdair with huge amber eyes. The movements of its muscles rippled its thick fur like silver ocean waves.

After a moment's hesitation, and much to their great relief, the wolf turned back, growled at the girl once more, and then ran swiftly off into the trees.

Priscilla hurried over to the girl, "Are you all right?" she asked, with her typical concern for someone in trouble.

"I am fine… just a little shaken up," the girl said. "I am *so* glad you came along when you did." As she said these last words, she looked past Priscilla to smile at Alasdair, who had followed along behind Priscilla.

The girl was quite lovely. She was taller than Priscilla, with long golden hair and big blue eyes. "You saved my life," she continued, addressing her words to Alasdair.

"I didn't do much," Alasdair said, bowing his head.

"I was *so* frightened," she told him in a shaky voice. "I knew there were wolves in the forest, but they usually stay with their pack and don't bother anyone. I have *no* idea why this one would want to hurt me. I've never been so scared in my life. *You* were *so* brave." She spoke directly to Alasdair, her big smile lighting up her pretty face and showing off her pearly white teeth.

"Which way are you going?" Priscilla asked abruptly, wanting to be included in the conversation, and at the same time, hoping the girl was not going the same way they were.

"I was heading to the Mara Mountains to pick some huckleberries to bake in a cake for my dear grandmother's birthday," the girl answered, "but I'm a little afraid to go on alone now." She opened her big blue eyes wide and fluttered her long eyelashes at Alasdair.

"You can walk with us," Alasdair said, looking at her with an enraptured expression. "That's where we're going. I'll look after you and make sure the wolf doesn't bother you again."

"Thank you *so* much." She smiled her dazzling smile at him. "I'd like that."

When Priscilla saw Alasdair's awestruck face, she felt even more left out of this exchange. As they headed back toward the path together, Alasdair's attention was focused only on the girl. Priscilla followed along behind them at a slower pace, her head hanging with dejection.

"Ach, I ken a wee green-eyed monster in yer face, lassie," Eideard whispered to Priscilla. "Ye best keep yer wits about ye, lass, for a bonnie face is nae guarantee she's nae up tae nae gud. Hoot Mon!"

She turned toward Eideard in surprise. "You don't mean that she could be a... oh my gosh, it never even occurred to me!" Watching the pair walking together in front of her, their heads almost touching, she added with a scowl, "And I'll just bet it hasn't occurred to Alasdair either!"

She could see how quickly Alasdair had fallen under the girl's spell. Deciding she needed to hear what they were talking about, she hurried along the path to get close to them.

Alasdair was telling the girl about his music and writing his own songs. She was hanging on his every word. "I would *so* love to hear you sing, Alasdair," the girl told him, her words dripping with honey. "You must have a terrific voice." He looked pleased to hear these words.

Her next comment was, "I've never met someone with such pure white skin as yours. Is it difficult to look so different from everyone else?"

Alasdair seemed upset by this question. Priscilla recalled her own insensitivity when she first met him. Shame and embarrassment for her earlier behavior caused her to hesitate for a moment and slow down.

Eideard whispered in her ear, "Hold on, lassie. Stay wi' it. Hoot Mon!" After his gentle reminder, she lifted up her head and moved forward to listen once more.

Alasdair was answering the girl in a sad voice. "Yes, it's difficult because I always feel like such a freak. And I get teased about it all the time."

"I am *so* sorry," the girl said, sounding most sympathetic. "I hope I haven't hurt your feelings. I really like how you look. I'm always attracted to young men who look different. I never like anyone who is just ordinary looking. You have such a nice face and fine-looking blue eyes. Must you wear those thick dark glasses? Your eyes are your best feature. You should never cover them up."

It was clear Alasdair was becoming perturbed with this focus on his looks. Priscilla had a strong sense that something was not right. Wanortu would have said her inner Light Detector was working.

Before Alasdair could answer, Priscilla interrupted, saying the first thing that came into her mind. "What do you like about the way *you* look?"

The girl turned around and smirked at Priscilla as she hissed between her teeth, "The color of my hair!" which stopped Priscilla cold, as she gazed with envy at the girl's perfect blonde hair.

It took some effort and more of Eideard's gentle prompting to get Priscilla to pull herself together again. By the time she did, the girl had turned back to Alasdair and was asking him in a much harsher voice, "How did your father feel about you being born all white like you are?"

Priscilla could almost feel Alasdair's Light energy draining from him in response to this question. Quickly she asked the girl, "How can you ask such a question of someone who is not your friend?"

The girl turned toward Priscilla and, in a vicious voice said, "What makes you think he wants to be friends with someone who has hair the color of blood?"

Priscilla felt her anger rise. Eideard whispered in her ear, "Easy noo, lassie. Ken wha' she is."

"Why would he want to be friends with someone cruel like you?" Priscilla asked through gritted teeth.

Immediately, the girl faded to a dark black shadow and, bucket in hand, vanished into the forest.

Alasdair sank down in the middle of the pathway. "I can't believe she wasn't real… she was one of *them*," he said, hanging his head. "I don't believe I fell for it again. I thought she actually liked me." He put his head in his hands and moaned softly.

Eideard hooted, "Ach aye, ye haf tae watch fer these creatures. They're right sneaky. Ye ken wha' Wanortu telt ye… they'll nab ye wher yer mos' weak. Hoot Mon!"

"Well, that's it," Alasdair whispered. "I'm not going to trust anyone else we run into. I don't feel good."

Recalling Wanortu's crystals, Priscilla hurriedly took a couple from her pocket and held them up so they caught some rays of light still shining through the trees. Rainbows began to dance all around them.

Alasdair eyed the rainbows without much interest, but, after a while, he started to look a little better. The Light from the Rainbow-Makers worked on Priscilla as well, lifting her spirits.

After a few more minutes, Alasdair stood up. In his gruff voice, he said, "We'd better get moving. We can't stay here all day."

They set off once more, this time moving more slowly, with Priscilla and Eideard leading the way. Alasdair dragged along behind, still weakened by his encounter with the Light-Eater, but perhaps even more so by his great disappointment.

As they walked along the path, Priscilla wondered what had happened to Alasdair's father. It was certainly an uncomfortable subject for him, as these Light-Eaters seemed to know. The Light-Eaters knew an awful lot about both of them, like her touchiness about her hair color, and her desire to have friends, as well as Alasdair's sensitivity to his looks. What else did they know? It really bothered her to think that these shadow creatures were aware of her deepest secrets.

They walked on for quite a while with no more travelers passing by, for which Priscilla was grateful. She preferred not to run into any more Light-Eaters. Even Alasdair, who had been so ready to do battle with them, appeared to have had his fill for the moment.

The sun was barely coming through the trees. In fact, it was growing much darker. All at once, a huge thunderclap boomed above them.

"Ach dear, 'tis a sign that a Drrreary Drrrenching Downpourrr is aboot tae start," Eideard told them. "Ye need tae fin' sum shelter, or ye'll be soaked tae the skin."

Up ahead, a narrow path led off into the thick of the forest. Thinking it might lead to some shelter, Priscilla took the path and hurried along, with Alasdair following right behind her.

The rain began to fall, causing them to quicken their pace. Gentle at first, the shower steadily increased in intensity. Priscilla thought with longing of her raingear tucked inside her backpack, but there was no time to stop to put it on.

The path led to a small cottage hidden amongst the trees. The front door was wide open. Sodden leaves all over the porch and steps gave the place a neglected look, but it offered some shelter, so they dashed down the path toward it.

Just as they made it up the steps and onto the covered porch, the clouds opened up. Rain came bucketing down in torrents. It poured and poured, until a river streamed along the path on which they had just been running.

Something hissed. Watching them from a corner of the porch was a golden thick-furred cat with one of the ugliest faces Priscilla had ever seen. As if it somehow knew she was contemplating approaching it, a low growl sprang from its throat. Priscilla stepped back in a hurry. They went inside the cottage and closed the door behind them, shutting the cat outside.

Though she had expected to find the place abandoned, it was obvious someone lived there. They had entered a room furnished with several hand-hewn log chairs set on a homemade braided rug. Faded afghans and needlepoint cushions decorated the chairs. Artistic creations made from rocks, wood, and shells added to the rustic natural feel of the room. The air smelled like Wanortu's room, of wet earth, moist wood, and a sense of being close to nature.

A warm and cozy glow radiated from the fire burning in the fireplace. In front of it, a small wooden table covered with a brightly flowered tablecloth held a teapot, three teacups with saucers and plates to match, and a fancy tin. A gently steaming teakettle hung on a bracket over the fire.

No one seemed to be at home. If there had been three bowls of porridge cooling on the table, Priscilla would have been concerned. The old man had been right about wolves. Maybe he was right about bears.

After shaking off some of the water from her clothes and hair, she sank onto the soft cushion on a rocking chair and sighed with relief.

Eideard flew up above to a rafter near the warmth of the fire where he shook out his sodden feathers and ruffled them back into their usual disarray.

Alasdair plopped down on one of the other chairs, and he too let out a big sigh.

While they sat drying by the fire, they listened to the Dreary Drenching Downpour vigorously rat-a-tat-tatting on the roof. From time to time, they could hear the scrabbling of small animals in the corners of the room. In this tiny cottage, deep in the forest, such sounds seemed quite appropriate.

The cottage was made of wood, not gingerbread, but even so, Priscilla hoped the owner would not be a wicked old witch with a big appetite. Unless they went back out into the downpour, they had no choice but to wait and see if anyone showed up.

It was apparent their journey was not going to be an easy one. They were still in the Fairy Forest, and they had a long way to go before they reached the Mara Mountains and Mother Nature.

Where was Inky? And would they be able to find him before anything bad happened to him or, for that matter, to them?

Chapter Fourteen
Unexpected Help

The front door of the cottage banged open with a resounding crash, startling Priscilla and Alasdair. The warmth of the fire had lulled them into a stupor. A tiny wet mass of clothing piled on top of a pair of big black rubber boots rushed into the room, followed by the golden cat from the porch. Whoever this was closed the door in a hurry, stripped off a dripping wet raincoat, and pulled off the boots, before turning around to see what visitors might have closed the door, known to have been left open on purpose.

A little old woman, brown and wrinkled like Wanortu, stood staring at them with a look of mild surprise on her face. "Well, well!" she exclaimed in a high-pitched throaty voice.

She did not look at all like a wicked old witch. In fact, she looked very much like a shriveled apple doll Priscilla had once made with Granny's help. Her snow-white hair was pulled back into a tight bun, a couple of twigs holding it in place. A crisp white apron covered her faded flowered dress. The wicker basket she held in her hands was filled to the brim with dirty wet mushrooms, offering a clue as to what she had been doing.

"Just who are you, and why are you in my house?" she asked them in a brusque tone.

"We're so sorry." Priscilla said with dismay. "The door was wide open. We didn't think anyone lived here, so we came in to get shelter from the rain. Do you want us to leave?" Though she asked out of politeness, she hoped the woman would not send them outside into the awful downpour.

The old woman looked at her uninvited guests, summing them up. Then she shrugged and made her way over to the fireplace. "No, you may stay until it stops raining. I will make us a spot of tea."

After setting her basket on the hearth, she picked up a potholder, lifted the teakettle, and filled the teapot with hot water. She hung the teakettle back over the fire, pulled a stool from under the table, and sat on it. The golden cat lay at her feet, cautiously watching Priscilla and Alasdair through half-closed eyes.

While the tea steeped, the old woman took chocolate biscuits, cheese, and fruit from the tin, filled two plates, and passed one each to Alasdair and Priscilla. It almost seemed as if she had been expecting company.

When the tea was ready, she gave them each a cup of tea and poured a cup for herself. She took a few long slow sips, giving Priscilla and Alasdair time to eat and to enjoy the savoring warmth of the hot beverage. Priscilla had not realized how hungry she was until she started eating.

After a little while, the old woman leaned forward and asked them, "Now, who are you two and just what are you doing here?"

At this direct question, Alasdair, who had just taken a bite of a biscuit, gave Priscilla a meaningful look, which she immediately understood. Neither of them wanted to answer, as this old woman could be another Light-Eater.

Up above on the rafter, Eideard grew still. Concerned for them, he leaned over to listen more closely.

Instead of answering, Priscilla asked, "What's your cat's name?"

The old woman reached over and scratched the cat's thick fur. The animal scrunched up its ugly face. "This is Purrtyface. Now what are your names, and where are you heading?"

Alasdair had swallowed his bite, so he asked in his most polite voice, "May I please have another cup of tea?"

After she poured him more tea and filled Priscilla's cup as well as her own, the old woman looked carefully at them both, her keen eyes sharp with interest. Setting the teapot on the table, she took off the lid and got up to get more hot water.

"I'm beginning to get the impression you do not want to answer my questions," she said, with what sounded like amusement. While she carried the teakettle to the table, she asked again, "Now who are you and what are you doing here?"

"What's your name?" Priscilla asked her quickly.

The old woman started to tell them, "My name is Baba…"

A screech interrupted her as Eideard, who had leaned over too far, lost his balance and toppled over from the rafter. He landed head first in the teapot with his talons sticking out the top. Fortunately Baba had not yet filled the teapot with more hot water.

Priscilla and Alasdair giggled at the sight, though Priscilla felt anxious, hoping Eideard had not hurt himself.

Baba hung the teakettle back over the fire. With great care, she lifted Eideard out of the teapot and shook him off. When she looked at the little owl, her body quivered, as if she was suppressing laughter, though, when she turned to look at Priscilla and Alasdair, her face showed no hint of mirth.

"Okay," she said with firm resolve. "That is enough. I have answered your three questions in response to mine. Now you know I am not a Light-Eater. Perhaps you are ready to tell me who you are, what you are up to, and why you have Wanortu's little owl with you."

"Oh my gosh, you know Wanortu?" gasped Priscilla.

"Of course I do, and if this little owl had not been so busy protecting you, he would have remembered who I am. Is that not right my little feathered friend?" Lifting Eideard up, she looked him squarely in his tiny yellow eyes just as Wanortu had done earlier.

Eideard was still trying to recover from his embarrassing tumble into the teapot. "Hoot Mon! Ach, I'm that sorry, Baba Yaba. I didna ken it was ye an' that 'tis yer wee hoose we're in. If I'd a ken, I would ha' telt the wee ones. Hoot Mon!" He tucked his head into his neck feathers in shame.

Alasdair, feeling sorry for the little owl, hurried to tell Baba, "My name is Alasdair, and this is Priscilla. We're on our way to the Mara Mountains to ask Mother Nature for help. We need to find Prince Inky. He took the Sacred Light and disappeared from the palace. The letter he left behind says he plans to take it to the People of the Dark to get them to see the Light." After this long-winded speech, he stopped to catch his breath.

But he had given Eideard time to regain his composure. The little owl flew over and settled onto Priscilla's shoulder. She reached up and gently patted him on the head.

"Oh dear," muttered Baba to herself, as she thought about the significance of what Alasdair had shared. She spoke intently to them. "This is not a good thing. You need to find Prince Inky and the Light as soon as possible or they could be lost forever. The Dreary Drenching Downpour will be over shortly. Then you must continue on your journey."

"Will we run into any more wolves along the way?" Priscilla asked Baba, her voice quivering at the thought. "We ran into one on the way here. It didn't look any too friendly."

"You ran into a wolf near here?" Baba looked at her in surprise.

Alasdair told her briefly about their experience with the wolf and the young girl who had turned out to be a Light-Eater, glossing over the more embarrassing parts.

"That is highly unusual," Baba commented. "The wolves do not live in this part of the forest and usually only travel with their tribe. And they do not attack people. Perhaps this wolf had cornered the girl because it somehow sensed she was dangerous, but why it was traveling alone around here, I simply have no idea."

"What shall I do if we run across this wolf again or any other wolves or bears?" Alasdair was preparing to be brave again. He would do whatever it took, or at least give such an impression. Perhaps he felt the need to make up for his pathetic performance with the Light-Eaters.

"You must respect all creatures you come across. Remember you are in their territory only with their permission," Baba told them. "Acknowledge their power, but, at the same time, do not give in to your alarm. When you first look at them, focus on their noses, not their eyes, and send them thoughts of greeting and respect. If they know you are not afraid of them and that you mean them no harm, they will respect you and let you be. We do not harm the creatures in our land, and they do not harm us. We have learned how to live in peace with one another."

The room had become quiet as Baba was speaking. The rain had stopped. It was time to be on their way.

Priscilla and Alasdair thanked Baba for the shelter and food and for her help. With some reluctance at having to leave her wise and safe presence, the cozy room, and the warm fire, they left the cottage.

Outside, everything was dripping wet. The pathway, though no longer a river, was soft and spongy. Their shoes made squishing sounds as they walked along. Moving slowly and carefully to avoid slipping, they returned as fast as they could to the main forest path.

Fortunately, this was not quite as wet, and before long, they were making good progress again.

Without warning, Priscilla felt the hairs on the back of her neck stand straight up. Someone or something was watching them. Looking all around her, she saw nothing except perhaps what might have been a quick movement behind a tree.

"Did you see anyone behind us?" she asked Eideard.

"Nae, lassie. I didna see a thing. Hoot Mon!" Eideard responded.

When she continued to feel the same weird sensation, she called to Alasdair who was up ahead. "Alasdair, I think someone is watching us. Have you noticed anything?"

"Nope, it must be your imagination." He was much too busy staring at the pathway ahead, probably keeping his eyes open for more Light-Eaters.

She could not shake the feeling that someone or something was following them, though when she looked about her, she never saw anyone. Finally, she decided it had to be the shy little Fairy Folk, so she decided to stop worrying.

After walking for some time, they came to a place where the path took them through a wide clearing in the trees. They had gone about halfway across when Alasdair suddenly cried out, "Ouch! Something just hit me on the head."

Priscilla felt something hit her nose, and she too yelped in pain. Little chunks of ice had started to fall all about them. She remembered what Wanortu had told them about the Horrendously Huge Hailstorms. If this was such a storm, they needed to get under cover fast.

Eideard confirmed this when he announced, "Ach, 'tis anither storm aboot tae hit… ye must run tae the trees quickly, lassie. Hoot Mon!"

Alasdair yelled, "Protect your head with your backpack, Priscilla. Follow me to the trees for cover. Hurry!" He took off across the clearing at a fast clip, holding his backpack over him.

Eideard flew off after him, zigzagging between larger hailstones that were dropping in greater numbers.

Holding her backpack over her head, Priscilla ran. The trees were a short distance ahead when her feet slid on the icy hailstones accumulating on the ground. With a crash, she fell down on her stomach. Her backpack dropped over to one side leaving her exposed to an onslaught of hailstones. A large one struck her on the side of the head, and everything went dark.

When she came to, a few moments later, someone or something was pulling her across the ground by her overall strap. Lifting her head a little, she saw gray furry legs in front of her. Some kind of animal was dragging her. Screaming, she tried to wrench herself away.

A gentle feminine voice spoke to her inside her head, "Be still, little granddaughter. I am only trying to help you so you will not be hurt more. Let me get you to the safety of the trees."

The voice was kind. Though the words did not quite penetrate, something in their tone caused Priscilla to relax and trust whatever this was. Soon she was underneath the trees and away from the battering of the hard hailstones. Her head ached with the pounding it had taken.

Rubbing her sore head, she sat up and looked to see what kind of animal had dragged her into the forest. It was the same silver gray wolf they had seen confronting the Light-Eater girl. This time it did not look nearly as frightening. The big creature was sitting back on her haunches watching Priscilla, her huge amber eyes full of tenderness.

"Are you okay, little granddaughter?" the wolf asked. This time she spoke the words aloud.

"Y-y-yes, I think I am f-fine," answered Priscilla, shakily. Recalling what Baba had said, she tried to look at the wolf's nose and not in her eyes. Still trembling from her ordeal, everything else Baba had told them had gone completely out of her head.

All of a sudden, she realized the big wolf had called her "little granddaughter". Her heart constricted in pain at the loving words she had never expected to hear again. She looked up, meeting the kind amber eyes with her own, as she told the wolf, "Thank you for saving me."

The hailstorm must have stopped, for Priscilla could no longer hear chunks of ice hitting the ground. What she heard instead was the sound of someone crashing through the underbrush.

Alasdair charged out of the trees with big stick in his hand. Yelling, he lunged toward the wolf. He too had apparently forgotten everything Baba had said.

"*No, No*, Alasdair, *stop!*" cried Priscilla, jumping in front of him, causing him to slam to a stop. "The wolf saved my life. She didn't hurt me."

The wolf returned Alasdair's intense gaze without moving a muscle. He looked over at Priscilla and then back at the wolf in confusion. After a moment, he dropped his stick on the ground and sat down beside it, trembling with relief. He did not want to take on a wolf, but he wanted to show Priscilla he was capable of protecting her. All he could say was "Oh."

Giving him time to settle down, Priscilla turned and asked the wolf, "Why did you come here so far from your home? We were told wolves don't usually come to this part of the forest."

"I was searching for my lost granddaughter," the wolf answered, her voice heavy with sadness. "She wandered away from our family a few days ago. When you first saw me, I had just come upon her, only to find her dying."

"Oh, I am so sorry," Priscilla whispered, her heart breaking for the big wolf. She knew how awful it felt to lose someone you loved.

"What happened to her?" Alasdair asked with his typical bluntness. He was obviously back to his normal self.

"The Light-Eater girl hit my granddaughter on the head with her heavy bucket. I arrived just as it happened. I was too late to stop it. If only I had arrived a moment sooner, I could have protected her." The wolf spoke with immense sadness. "It was in my sorrow and rage I chased the Light-Eater. The Darkness I saw in her matched the Darkness I felt in my spirit. I wanted to destroy her. I'm glad you came when you did, as it would not have been the right thing to do."

Alasdair looked unhappy. Priscilla suspected he was thinking of his own experience with the shadow girl, someone he liked and thought liked him back.

"Why are you still here, and where are you going?" Priscilla asked the wolf.

"I stayed beside my granddaughter until her spirit passed on to the next world," the wolf answered sorrowfully. "The rainstorm washed away her blood; I dearly wish it could have washed away my pain as well. It filled the stream with enough water to carry her body to the River of Return and out to Grandmother Ocean where she will rest. I was on my way back home when I heard you on the path. I followed along behind you to make sure you were safe."

"So it was you I could feel watching us!" exclaimed Priscilla. "I thought it was the Fairy Folk. Well, I'm sure glad you were around; I might have been killed by those awful hailstones."

"I did not want any more young ones to die," the wolf said softly. "Where are you heading, my dears, and what are your names? My name is Wilinpara the Wolf, but you may call me Grandmother Wolf, if you like, for it is who and what I am."

Priscilla and Alasdair introduced themselves and told Grandmother Wolf about their journey to see Mother Nature. Just as they finished their story, Eideard flew out of the trees and settled with a bump on Priscilla's shoulder. He cast a wary eye at the wolf, but made no comment, so he must have overheard their conversation.

Priscilla reached over and gently stroked his feathers as she said, "I'm glad you are safe little bird."

Eideard the Owl shifted from foot to foot and hooted, "Ach, away wi' ye. Hoot Mon!"

Grandmother Wolf asked them, "Would it be all right if I accompany you on part of your journey? I would like to go to the Valley of the Moon to drink at the Pool of Reflection. The healing waters will help to ease my sorrow. The Light-Eaters will not bother you while I am with you."

Alasdair and Priscilla were more than happy to accept Grandmother Wolf's kind offer. It made them feel a lot safer, especially as it was beginning to get late in the day.

They set off once more along the path, more comfortable now with such a strong companion to protect them. After another couple of hours, and with no further incidents, they finally reached the edge of the forest. Above them lay a large expanse of craggy rock and alpine meadows sprinkled with snow, and beyond that, stood gray boulders underneath a tall white mountain.

They had reached the Mara Mountains. If all went well, soon they would be able to find their way to Mother Nature's kingdom.

Chapter Fifteen
An Awakening

With Grandmother Wolf leading the way, Priscilla and Alasdair followed the pathway up and over the rocky surface. It was not too difficult a climb as the path led across the rocks. Where the path became steeper, there were cracks and crevices for toeholds as well as some hardy bushes to grab hold of as needed.

Grandmother Wolf moved sure-footedly up the path. She kept stopping to wait for Priscilla and Alasdair to catch up to her before moving on again. Priscilla was amazed at how quickly she had developed an attachment to such a patient creature, as protective of her as her own grandmother had been.

The afternoon wore on. They traveled up the path, stopping only to rest and to eat and drink what Queen Luminata had sent with them. While she rested on a rock, Priscilla looked out over the darkening forest below her and beyond the meadow to the silver sliver of ocean off in the distance. She was amazed to see how far they had come. The sun was beginning to set, and a pale moon was rising.

When they came to some larger boulders, they worked their way slowly over and around them; it seemed to take forever. Each time Priscilla thought they had reached the top, there was yet another path ahead and more rocks to climb. All the while, White Mountain loomed up ahead of them, beckoning them to keep going.

It was hard work, and the night air had turned chilly. Priscilla was growing tired. Somewhere she had heard that when things got rough, you should just concentrate on putting one foot in front of the other, so that's what she did. She focused on each step and nothing else. It helped her to keep moving.

By the time they finally reached the top, darkness was upon them, and they were traveling by the light of the moon. Up ahead, Grandmother Wolf stopped moving and stood quite still, looking over the edge of a cliff. Once they joined her and followed her gaze, they too grew quiet.

Eideard gave a soft "Hoot Mon!" which summed up precisely what they all felt.

There, below them, beneath the crags and cliffs of the gleaming White Mountain, lay a lovely little enclosure. Large flat gray and white rocks, haphazardly piled one upon another like stepping-stones, surrounded a dark blue-black pool of water. A glistening thin lace curtain of white mist hung low over the water.

The surface of the pool reflected the brilliance of the risen moon. It was as if the moon had fallen from the sky into the water. At one end of the pool, water tumbled over a pile of flat rocks in a gentle waterfall. At the other end, the water overflowing from the pool meandered around the rocks before flowing in a stream on down the mountainside. Priscilla knew they were looking at the Valley of the Moon and the Pool of Reflection.

Grandmother Wolf started along a path leading downhill into the valley. Priscilla and Alasdair followed, taking care not to slip on pieces of shale strewn along the way. As the pool came more clearly into view, Priscilla could see, all along the edge, various animals standing side by side, drinking the water.

A deer, a fox, a bobcat, a rabbit, and a cougar stood next to one another. Next to them, a family of raccoons sat all in a row from the largest to the smallest. Imagining the raccoons as Russian nesting dolls, with each tucked inside a bigger one until the largest was the only one left, got Priscilla giggling to herself.

When they reached the bottom of the cliff, Grandmother Wolf led them along the edge of the pool to a spot where several flat stones stuck out above the water, forming stepping-stones across the stream. Soon they were all safely on the other side. They had arrived in the Valley of the Moon at last.

The animals sensed their approach, and though they followed the new visitors with their eyes, they showed no obvious concern. Every creature seemed welcome in this place.

Grandmother Wolf validated this when she told them, "In the Valley of the Moon, all creatures may come to drink the healing waters of the Pool of Reflection. No creature will harm any other creature here, even if elsewhere, one may be predator, and the other prey. All come in peace and leave in peace."

Priscilla looked up at the white cliffs soaring above the valley. Mother Nature lived at the top of this White Mountain. While she was wondering how on earth she and Alasdair would be able to get up there, something she glimpsed on a protruding rocky crag caught her attention.

Standing there, as still as the night, loomed a huge white bison. It shone in majestic splendor against the darkening blue of the sky. Grabbing Alasdair's arm, Priscilla pointed up at the animal. "Look at that, Alasdair!" They both gazed in awe.

Grandmother Wolf saw where they were looking and told them, "That is Amara, the Great White Bison, the Guardian of Mother

Nature's Kingdom. No one enters her realm without his awareness. He already knows you are here."

"I wonder what we're supposed to do now," Alasdair spoke his thought aloud.

"You must wait here by the pool until you are invited to see Mother Nature," Grandmother Wolf told them gently. "She usually sends for her visitors before first light in the morning. That way you can get some rest after your long journey. I am going to drink at the pool."

The big wolf left them to take her place at the edge of the pool next to a small mountain goat that had just joined the other animals. All the animals stood together in the silvery moonlight.

As Priscilla and Alasdair watched in awestruck silence, Eideard announced, "Ach, I'm awa tae have a wee drinky too! Hoot Mon!" He flew to the water and took a place close to Grandmother Wolf.

A noisy splash coming from the pool broke the silence. A sleek, whiskered creature poked a pointed nose out of the water and looked at them for a moment with big shining eyes. Then, with what might have been a playful grin, it dove into the pool again and popped up in a different spot. It was an otter. Slithering out of the pool by the waterfall, the otter crawled speedily up the rocks and slid over the falls on its belly into the pool, landing with a big splash.

Priscilla exclaimed with envy, "Oh that looks like so much fun. I wish we could join him!"

"Let's check and see how cold it is," Alasdair suggested with growing excitement. "We could go in if it's warm enough."

"But we didn't bring our bathing suits," Priscilla argued, albeit half-heartedly. She was feeling grubby after their long journey. Rinsing off some of the dust and grime sounded inviting.

"That doesn't matter," Alasdair said matter-of-factly. "We can go in our underwear. There's no one around to say we can't. The animals don't care." He hurried over to the pool and stuck his hand in the water.

"Hey!" he called back to Priscilla, his voice filled with surprise. "It's really warm… smells sulfuric. There must be a hot spring feeding into it. Maybe that's why it's called a healing pool."

He started to strip as he said, "Come on. The water's perfect for swimming, and for once, I can swim outdoors without worrying about my skin. Sweet!"

Within moments, he had taken off his glasses and all his clothes, except for his jockey shorts, and was jumping into the water with great delight. A little embarrassed, Priscilla watched him swim over to the otter. The two of them were soon diving underwater together.

Alasdair popped his head up out of the water and called to her. "Come on down, Priscilla. It feels great! Come down and meet Ogusto the Otter."

It did not take her long to put aside her few reservations. She took off everything except her underwear, folded her clothes neatly, and put them into her backpack. As she did, her fingers brushed against the bounderball, giving her an idea.

She carried the ball to the pool and tossed it to Alasdair. Then she jumped in, and with a blissful sigh, sank under the refreshing water, allowing it to wash away the dirt and stress of the long journey.

When she came up for a breath, Alasdair tossed the ball to her, and she threw it back to him. The otter watched them, with surprise at first, and then with increasing enthusiasm, as he saw possibilities for more fun.

When Alasdair threw the ball to him, Ogusto batted it with his long nose. Soon they were playing a boisterous game of Keep Away.

When they stopped for a breather, Ogusto gestured with his forepaw for them to follow him to his water slide. They eagerly went along. One after the other, they slid over the falls on their bellies.

The animals drinking along the edge of the pool watched them with an interest that soon waned, as one by one they left the edge of the pool to lie down on the rocks to rest.

The moon continued to give everything a silvery otherworldly glow. The water was warm and comfortable. After a while, Priscilla stopped playing and floated on her back, looking up at the moon and stars. It felt good to be in the Valley of the Moon. She could understand why the Pool of Reflection was a healing pool. It would be nice to stay there for a long time.

Alasdair got out of the water and climbed up on a rock to dive in. For a moment, he stood as still as a statue in the moonlight, the water dripping in shiny droplets from his sleek white skin. His wet hair clung in tight curls around his handsome face, which was indeed easier to see without his glasses. The Light-Eater girl had been right about that. He truly looked magnificent to Priscilla now, much more so than when she had first seen him. In fact, he looked like a mythical sea god arisen from the depths.

In that moment, her heart did a weird flip-flop. Perplexing achy feelings she had never felt before, and did not recognize, awakened inside her. As she watched him do a perfect swan dive into the pool, her breath caught in her throat. The new feelings confused her, as did the intensity of the deep longing they brought with them.

Embarrassed, she climbed out of the pool and dried herself as best as she could with her small towel. She pulled on her sweatshirt, plopped onto one of the large flat rocks, and hid her face between her knees. She was afraid what she was feeling was written there for all to see.

When she looked up again, it was just in time to watch Alasdair and Ogusto take a last slide before calling it a night. Eideard and Grandmother Wolf were beside her, though she had no memory of when they had joined her.

Alasdair got out of the water and sat on a rock by the edge of the pool. He was quiet for a little while. Then he began to hum and to sing, his voice reverberating across the valley. All the animals lifted their heads to listen. Ogusto floated on his back in the pool near Alasdair, attentively listening to the song.

The melody seemed vaguely familiar to Priscilla. Then she remembered hearing him strumming the same tune on his guitar on the beach back home, but she had never heard the words until now.

Come on Down

When you're feeling lost and lonely
And you need someone to care
Listen for the one who calls you
Hear her whisper in the air

Come on down my child
Come on down to the sea
Lay your head upon my shore
Lay your body next to me
Feel my breeze in your hair
Feel my sun upon your face
I will always hold you
In the warmth of my embrace

When the world is cruel and scary
And you need somebody near
Listen for the one who tells you
"Little one, I'm always here."

Come on down my child
Come on down to the sea

Lay your head upon my shore
Lay your body next to me
Feel my breeze in your hair
Feel my sun upon your face
I will always hold you
In the warmth of my embrace

When you come down to the shore
You'll feel her magic everywhere
Your troubles will seem far away
For she is waiting there

Come on down my child
Come on down to the sea
Lay your head upon my shore
Lay your body next to me
Feel my breeze in your hair
Feel my sun upon your face
I will always hold you
In the warmth of my embrace

Come on down my child
Come on down to the sea
Come on down my child
Come on down here to me

Come on down
Come on down
Come on down to the sea
Come on down
Come on down
Come on down here to me

As Alasdair sang, Priscilla felt the same bewildering ache in her heart once again. The loneliness of which he sang, she knew as well. Nature seemed to bring him comfort just as it did for her. There was something reassuring in knowing someone she liked so much had feelings similar to her own. It made her feel less lonely inside.

Even though she was terribly tired, she felt mystified by the new feelings tugging at her heartstrings. Wrapping her arms around her chest, she lay on the rock, using her backpack as a pillow. She wanted to examine these feelings and decide what they meant. But exhaustion overcame her; in only a minute she fell fast asleep.

She did not hear Alasdair finish his song, nor did she see him lie down on a rock nearby. He too quickly fell into a deep and worn-out sleep.

Neither of them saw Grandmother Wolf climb up to the highest rocks. So they did not hear her howl her anguish to the moon as she sang out the story of her lost and murdered granddaughter.

Nor did they hear all the other creatures add their own voices of support for Grandmother Wolf after they heard her story. In recognition of her pain, a pain with which they were all well acquainted, they sang out their own stories in comforting solace to one another.

Priscilla was not aware of Eideard taking a guard perch to watch over her. Nor was she conscious of the moment when a depleted Grandmother Wolf padded over and quietly lay alongside her on the rock to keep her warm from the chilly night air.

During the night, she did have a soothing sense of laying her head upon something soft and of feeling a yielding body next to hers. In her sleep, without knowing it, she curled up into the warmth of Grandmother Wolf's embrace and slept deeply and peacefully.

Chapter Sixteen
Mother Nature

"Wake up, Priscilla. Wake up!" a gentle voice was calling her back from her dream world. "Priscilla, it is time to wake up," the voice continued with persistence.

As she slowly became aware of where she was, Priscilla felt the hard rock beneath her pressing into her side. She looked up into the loving eyes of Grandmother Wolf who was leaning over her. "What is it Grandmother Wolf?" she asked sleepily, wanting nothing more than to go back to sleep, especially as she could see it was not yet morning.

"Mother Nature has sent for you, little granddaughter," Grandmother Wolf told her. "It is time for you to go. Alasdair is already up and dressed."

At the word 'dressed', Priscilla became aware of what she was and was not wearing. With great embarrassment, she jumped up and pulled on the rest of her clothes in a hurry.

As she gathered her stuff together and got ready to go, she looked around. The moon was low on the horizon. The white misty curtain had thickened over the still pool water. All the animals from the previous evening had disappeared like smoke, back to their own world, where they would become hunter and prey once again.

Two figures she could not make out stood in the shadows beneath the crag where Amara, the Great White Bison, still kept his faithful watch. Alasdair was walking over toward them.

Eideard flew over to Priscilla's shoulder, and with Grandmother Wolf, they followed along.

"Come on, Priscilla," Alasdair called over to her. "The eagles have come to take us up to Mother Nature. We don't have to climb White Mountain."

"Oh thank goodness!" exclaimed Priscilla, as she happily greeted Ezara and Eminore.

Recalling what she had felt the night before, she stole a quick glance at Alasdair. She had expected to find him different in some way, but he was as he had always been and oblivious to her new feelings. Maybe it had all been a dream, not that it mattered anyway. She needed to tuck her feelings away inside her until she had more time to think about them.

Turning to Grandmother Wolf, she asked what she had been afraid to ask until the last minute. "W...Will you still be here when we come back, Grandmother Wolf?"

Grandmother Wolf's answer was different from what Priscilla was expecting to hear. "Yes, little granddaughter. I will stay here until you return. I need to rest a little longer by the pool. I want to find out where you will be going next."

Priscilla was overjoyed to hear this. Flinging her arms around Grandmother Wolf's neck, she hugged her tightly. The idea of the big wolf leaving them was something she could not bear to think of.

Priscilla and Alasdair climbed on the backs of the big eagles once more. Priscilla lay flat and spread her arms wide in order to pretend she was flying.

Eideard fastened his talons tightly to her backpack as he tittered an excited "Hoot Mon!" He was hitching a ride for the long journey up the mountain.

Priscilla waved goodbye to Grandmother Wolf as Ezara and Eminore whisked them high into the air and soared out around the valley. Then they slowly began making a circular rise up the mountainside. Priscilla watched Grandmother Wolf grow smaller and smaller, soon becoming only a small dot in the distance far below.

On eagles' wings, they flew past the great white bison, close enough to see his massive head and huge hump, his thick shaggy white fur, and his sharp pointed horns. He paid absolutely no heed to them, but, from what Grandmother Wolf had said, there was no doubt he was aware of them.

An old gray big-horned sheep with gnarled, multi-ringed, curled horns followed their progress with sharp eyes as they passed the ridge on which it rested.

On a shelf of rock above, stood an elegant horse with long silky-white hair, its head raised proudly into the air. Projecting out of its forehead was a rainbow-colored spiraled horn. It was not a horse at all; it was a unicorn.

Priscilla called out, "Look Alasdair, it's a unicorn like the one the People of the Rainbow created." Then she whispered in great disbelief, "Except this one is real." Neither of them could take their eyes off the beautiful mythical creature.

She remembered reading in one of her fairy tale books that if you ever saw a real unicorn you should make a wish. Closing her eyes tightly, she wished as hard as she could for Mother Nature to be able to tell them where to find Inky and the Light and for all of them to stay safe. Well, maybe those were two wishes, but she wanted both of them to come true all the same.

The sun was just beginning to rise as they reached the top of the mountain and circled for a landing. The surface of the mountain was surprisingly flat. Covering the mountaintop was a thick gray and white cloud that emitted a cacophony of noisy baffling sounds.

When the eagles landed, the whole cloud lifted off the mountaintop with an echoing shriek. It was not a cloud at all, but hundreds of seagulls. The birds took a moment to adjust to the new arrivals and judge them to be safe. Then, the bird cloud settled back down over the mountaintop once more.

One big gray and white gull separated from the bird cloud and flew over toward them. Priscilla caught sight of a pink leg and a bright red one and knew it had to be Garone the Gull.

"Welcome to Mother Nature's kingdom!" Garone greeted them joyously. "I am glad you found your way here. I just arrived myself."

Priscilla and Alasdair were delighted to see their seagull friend and returned his greeting with great warmth.

Garone told them, "Wanortu and everyone at the Palace will be happy to know you arrived safely. They have been anxious to hear how you are doing."

"We're fine," Alasdair said, "though it has taken us a long time to get here. We ran into a few problems along the way." Anxious to move on, he asked Garone, "Do you know where we can find Mother Nature?"

"Yes, I do." Garone answered. "But first, please join us in welcoming the sunrise and the new day. Early each morning, we all come here to the top of White Mountain for this special moment." Then he added, "You may want to cover your eyes as it will be bright."

As Priscilla pulled her goggles over her head, it occurred to her that this might be one answer to her question of where the seagulls went when they all disappeared from her seashore kingdom. She turned to face the sun as it slowly crept up over the mountains, spreading red and orange fire across the sky. The whole world was lighting up. She felt her heart soar as if it were one of the many birds surrounding her.

There was a moment of absolute silence when the orange sphere rose into view. Considering how many noisy birds surrounded them, such silence was unexpected. Then, all at once, a resounding chorus of noise and song broke out everywhere. The birds were singing their songs to the sunrise. A bright new day had begun.

With a flurry of flapping wings, the bird cloud flew off to wherever the birds were going to spend the rest of the day. After they were gone, Priscilla watched the sunlight spread across the mountaintop, leaving a wake of sparkling diamonds in the hard-packed snow. Something glittered in the distance, catching her eye.

"Oh my gosh!" she exclaimed, grabbing Alasdair's arm and pointing. "Look at that. It's gorgeous."

Alasdair said, "Sweet!" while Eideard hooted at the same time.

In the middle of the mountain plateau, a group of large crystals of assorted sizes appeared to be growing out of the snow. Beyond the crystals, a spectacular crystal castle glistened in the rays of the recently risen sun. An aureole of rainbow lights twinkled around the castle creating the image of a precious jewel set into the crown of the mountain.

Garone the Gull told them, "That is Mother Nature's Castle and her Crystal Garden. In the middle of the garden, you will find the Golden Circle. Mother Nature will meet you there. I will wait here with Ezaro and Eminore for your return. I want to find out where you will be going next so I can carry the news back to the palace."

Priscilla and Alasdair crunched across the snow, the shimmering crystals beckoning them onward. The mountain air smelled fresh and felt invigorating. Priscilla found herself humming *Good King*

Wenceslas as they made their way across the *deep and crisp and even* snow.

In just a little while, they entered Mother Nature's Crystal Garden. Rainbows of brilliant colors flashed all around them as they walked between the crystals. Every crystal was a different size and shape, and each held within it an image of nature.

In one crystal, a garden with masses of flowers was in full bloom. In another, gray whales swam in a shining blue ocean, spouting plumes of water high into the air.

A particularly vibrant pyramid-shaped crystal displayed an erupting volcano, fiery lava bubbling and steaming down the sides. Priscilla could almost feel the melting heat followed by the searing cold when the hot lava sizzled into the ocean at the foot of the volcano.

A smaller crystal drew her attention. In this one, Grandmother Wolf was resting on a rock beside the Pool of Reflection. Priscilla's heart filled with so much yearning, she reached out to stroke Grandmother Wolf's thick fur.

When her fingertips touched the cool crystal, a powerful wave of sadness passed through her, bringing tears to her eyes. She jerked her hand back quickly, as if she had been burned. The incident was puzzling, but she had no time to think much about it.

They stepped out from amongst the crystals onto a gargantuan round golden disk where they were apparently to meet Mother Nature. Ancient-looking symbols graced the outer edges of the circle. Next to the symbols stood golden sculptures of animals, birds, fish, and reptiles. Shadows falling across the circle gave it the appearance of a huge sundial.

All at once, there was a radical change in energy and light. A rumbling sound like an earthquake and a sucking movement of air caused them to look up quickly. Entering the Golden Circle was an unbelievable sight.

Eideard shook and nuzzled closer to Priscilla's neck, whispering, "Will ye look at that? Hoot Mon!"

Swaying toward them was a woman of incredible size and girth. Hundreds of small animals and birds clung like living appliqués to the voluminous white robe she wore. Snakes curled about her thick neck and hung around her wide waist like belts. Lizards sunned themselves on her hefty brown arms. On one of her broad shoulders rode a large, glossy black raven. A pure white dove sat on her other shoulder. Gathered all around her, flying, walking, and swarming, were so many other creatures, it was as if she were a walking zoo.

With every giant step she took, the ground shook. The light became brighter and vibrated with increasing energy. Each ripple of her massive body spun the air around her into a whirling windstorm. Extending out all around her head in a burning halo, her wild mane of flaming red hair swirled and crackled as if on fire. With every toss of her head, a shower of sparks flew into the air.

Her skin was shiny and as nut brown as the earth. Each of her huge eyes was a different vibrant color, one, as blue and fathomless as the ocean, and the other, as green and lush as the Merry Meadow. When Mother Nature allowed her intense hypnotic gaze to upon them, Priscilla had to look away to avoid being sucked into such depths.

"Welcome to my kingdom!" boomed out a deep-pitched, rumbling voice that surely echoed across the mountaintops. "I am Mother Nature."

Priscilla giggled at what seemed to her to be an unnecessary introduction. This could not possibly be anyone but Mother Nature.

Eideard the Owl must have had the same thought as he whispered in her ear, "Ach aye, I didna ken otherwise! Hoot Mon!"

"Why have you come to see me?" Mother Nature asked in her thunderous voice.

Alasdair, in his usual courageous way, stepped forward to answer, though his voice shook as he addressed this commanding personage. "Mother Nature, thank you for seeing us. We are Priscilla and Alasdair. King Sol sent us to search for his son Prince Incandescence. He has taken the Sacred Light and we've no idea where he has gone. We need your help in finding him so we can bring him and the Sacred Light back to the palace."

Mother Nature turned her head and spoke to the big raven on her shoulder, this time, in a surprisingly gentle voice, making a melodic clicking sound with her tongue. The words and sounds were unlike anything Priscilla had ever heard. Spreading his great black wings, the big raven flew off into the sky.

Addressing Priscilla and Alasdair again, she told them, "I have sent my scout, Raldemar the Raven, to search the land for the prince. If he is anywhere in my kingdom, we will soon know, for we have a great network of helpers. While we await Raldemar's return, you must break your fast with some food. You will find a table off to your right already set for you. Please help yourselves, and whatever is left over, take with you for your journey."

With a wide-ranging flourish that caused a small cyclone to blow all about her, she swung around. There was a flutter of wings and the noise of scurrying feet as the birds and animals hurried to stay beside her. As she clumped back the way she had come, the air sizzled with her dynamic energy. The earth shook with each of her steps. She had brought with her so much life that after she had gone, the place seemed dark, flat, and empty.

Priscilla and Alasdair quickly went in search of their breakfast. When Mother Nature mentioned food, they realized how hungry they were. Behind one of the prisms, they found a low crystal table set with plentiful amounts of fruit, nuts, cheese, hard-boiled eggs, a kind of flat bread, and a pitcher of goat's milk.

Eideard began pecking away at a small bowl full of reddish brown globs set on the ground to one side of the food. Priscilla had no desire to know what was in his bowl.

They ate until they were full. Then, as Mother Nature had suggested, they put the leftovers into their backpacks to take with them. It was always an open question as to when or where they would have their next meal.

A bowl and a jug of fresh water enabled them to clean their teeth and wash themselves. Afterwards, Priscilla felt quite refreshed and ready to face the rest of the day.

When they heard the whirring of wings and saw the big raven return, they hoped he brought news of Inky. They hurried back to the center of the garden, arriving just as Mother Nature swept in with her wildlife entourage.

Priscilla and Alasdair politely thanked her for the delicious food.

"You are welcome, my children," Mother Nature told them. "Raldemar the Raven has brought information for you. The prince cannot be found anywhere in my kingdom. This can only mean one thing. He has gone down to the Land of Shadows. I do not have any vision in that region. You will have to make a trip there yourselves to find out what has happened to him."

"Where on earth is this Land of Shadows?" asked Alasdair, sounding frustrated. Perhaps he was wondering, as Priscilla was, if they were ever going to find Inky.

"That is the problem," answered Mother Nature evenly. "The Land of Shadows is not on the earth at all. That is why I cannot tell you exactly where you will find Prince Inky. The Land of Shadows exists alongside our world but is not of our world. All events throughout history, which result in the creation of Dark energy, remain imprinted in this place. Parts of you go there when they disconnect from you. The People of the Dark use the Land of Shadows to harvest these parts for their own purposes."

Mother Nature added, "The Land of Shadows is also where the souls of those who are beyond redemption are kept for all eternity. It is a dangerous place, so you must be careful when you go there."

"But how do we find this place?" asked Priscilla, even though she was frightened by what Mother Nature said. "We have to find Inky and the Light."

"I will send Raldemar the Raven to guide you to the entrance to the Land of Shadows. You must be careful on this journey. Listen to all instructions given to you by any guides you meet along the way. It could be a matter of life and death," Mother Nature cautioned them. Once again, she spoke to Raldemar with the clicking sound.

The big raven flew over and landed beside them. The raven and the owl eyed one another with caution, being natural prey and predator. However, Raldemar was many times larger than Eideard who posed no threat to him, so they appeared to reach an unspoken truce.

Priscilla and Alasdair said their goodbyes and gave their thanks to Mother Nature before turning to leave.

"Hold tightly to the Light within you," Mother Nature bellowed out after them.

This reminded Priscilla of Wanortu telling them about their Light Detectors. Thinking of him, Priscilla recalled his last warning to them. Turning back to Mother Nature, she called out, "Wanortu told us not to make you laugh, Mother Nature. Why would he say that?"

Eideard started bouncing on her shoulder whispering, "Shhh! Hoot Mon!" But it was too late! Mentioning Wanortu was all it took. The damage was done.

Mother Nature stood still for a moment, and for her this was some accomplishment. Then her mouth opened into a huge wide smile as she said, "Why that little old devil... he ought to be ashamed of himself!" Her teeth were white like her mountain and the gap between her two front teeth was as dark as a canyon.

Then with showers of sparks and a crackling of electricity which sent bolts of lightning across the sky, she threw her head back and began to chuckle. The sound reverberated across the mountain like rolling thunder.

As she chuckled, her great mounds of flesh started to sway. All the creatures attached to her flew off in every direction. Alasdair and Priscilla had to duck to avoid the flying critters.

"Ach, you've gone and done it noo, lassie!" hooted Eideard, "Noo, we're in for it! Hoot Mon!"

Soon Mother Nature was roaring with laughter. The wind began to blow in fierce gusts; sparks flew everywhere, and the earth started shaking and rolling. All the animals and birds scattered in a great hurry.

"Let's get out of here!" yelled Alasdair over the roar of sound that filled the air.

It was all they could do to grab hold of the edges of the crystals and pull their way out of the Crystal Garden. They managed to follow Raldemar back to where Garone and the eagles awaited them. The echoes of Mother Nature's roaring laughter ricocheted across the mountaintop. Even as they hurried across the snow, they could feel rumbles in the ground beneath them.

Priscilla was giggling, although she felt embarrassed at the ruckus she had caused.

Alasdair laughed with her, and said, "Well we definitely found out why Wanortu said we shouldn't make Mother Nature laugh!"

Eideard whispered, "Tsk, tsk, lassie! Hoot Mon!" though Priscilla could tell he was not upset.

After they joined Garone and the eagles at the edge of the mountain, they took a moment to catch their breath.

Raldemar croaked, "The eagles will fly you back to the Pool of Reflection. I will meet you there. Then I will guide you to the Land of Shadows." Without any fuss, he flew away.

Garone had heard Raldemar say where it was they were going. He looked at Priscilla and Alasdair with concern as he bade them farewell. "I will let Wanortu know right away that you are safe and are headed next to the Land of Shadows to find Inky. Good luck, and please take great care of yourselves."

Priscilla suspected his concern had everything to do with their next destination. What was it they were getting themselves into? Even with her vivid imagination, she had no idea at all of what lay ahead for them.

Chapter Seventeen
Following the Leader

Priscilla and Alasdair flew back down the mountain on their trusty eagles. Once again, they passed the unicorn, the ram, and the White Bison, but this time, Priscilla barely noticed them. Her mind churned with thoughts about what kind of place this Land of Shadows might be. Mother Nature said it was not on the earth at all. What did that mean? All the talk of Dark Deeds and harvesting parts sounded terribly frightening. She was beginning to wish they had never started on this journey.

In no time at all, the eagles landed them back at the base of White Mountain where Grandmother Wolf patiently waited to welcome them. From the look in her eyes, Priscilla knew the big wolf was glad to see them and relieved that they were safe.

Priscilla and Alasdair thanked Ezara and Eminore once again before the eagles flew away. A moment later Raldemar flew over to join their little group. The wolf and the raven eyed one another with curiosity.

"Grandmother Wolf, this is Raldemar the Raven." Priscilla said, introducing them. "He's going to be our guide to the entrance to the Land of Shadows which is where we need to go next. Mother Nature says that is where Prince Inky has gone."

"Oh no!" cried Grandmother Wolf. "I have heard of this underworld place. It is not somewhere you should be going, especially not alone."

"We don't have a choice," Alasdair declared bravely. "We've got to find Inky and the Light."

"Then I must go with you!" Grandmother Wolf announced firmly, having instantly made up her mind. "You cannot go there without protection."

"Can you really come with us?" Priscilla asked, her face glowing with happiness at the idea. "I thought you would have to go home to tell your family about your granddaughter." This meant she would not yet have to say goodbye to her loving friend. Besides, with Grandmother Wolf accompanying them into the Land of Shadows, she would not be so afraid to go.

"I have already sent word to my family," Grandmother Wolf answered. "They are not expecting me back right away. At the moment, there is nothing more I can do for my little granddaughter, but I can still do something for the two of you." Her huge amber eyes communicated the warmth of her affection for Priscilla and Alasdair.

Alasdair looked pleased as well. "I'm sure glad you're coming with us, Grandmother Wolf."

Eideard was once more sitting on Priscilla's shoulder. Reaching up, she patted the little owl on the head as she told him, "I'm so glad you are with us too, Eideard." She really was. With both the wise owl and the brave wolf along, how could they possibly get into any trouble?

"Ach awa' wi' ye! Hoot Mon!" Eideard whispered meekly, his face feathers turning a light pink. The little owl was blushing.

With Raldemar the Raven leading the way by air and Grandmother Wolf guiding them on the ground, they set off on their trek to the Land of Shadows. Raldemar flew past the pool, across the stream, and then headed toward the same path up the cliff by which the rest of them had entered the Valley of the Moon the night before.

Alasdair and Priscilla hurried to catch up to Grandmother Wolf and Raldemar. As they reached the Pool of Reflection again, Priscilla looked with yearning at the healing waters. Even though she had tried to tuck it away, the memory of the night before still lingered. Feelings she had never felt before had awakened inside her, feelings that intrigued her, and made her feel a little more grownup. It was a night she would always remember.

"Priscilla! Wake up! Wake up, Priscilla!"

Priscilla looked up when she heard Alasdair's voice and was surprised to see that he was already across the stream. Absorbed in her own thoughts, she had stopped moving. Eideard had not said a word. The wise little owl seemed to know she did not need to be disturbed.

Raldemar and Grandmother Wolf were already heading up the path across the cliff. Priscilla decided it was time for her to pay attention. Putting all thoughts of her memorable night away, she hurried to catch up to Alasdair. She concentrated carefully on where to put her feet, jumping from one stone to another, and crossed the water without incident.

Once she drew up to where Alasdair was waiting, she followed along behind him as they began climbing the cliff together. When he began humming and whispering some words to himself, she guessed he might be working on another song. At first, she was going to ask him what it was about, but then she decided to take a lesson from Eideard and not disturb Alasdair's private thoughts.

Climbing back up the cliff took lot of energy. After some time and exertion, they finally reached the top.

While they rested for a moment, catching their breath, Priscilla took one last glimpse of the Valley of the Moon with the healing pool and the White Mountain, home to the ineffable Mother Nature. Then with a sigh of resolve, she turned away and moved on, feeling a mystifying sense of loss at leaving such a tranquil place behind her.

Raldemar led them around the big rocks, heading over the mountains instead of going back the way they had come from the Fairy Forest. He led them along paths they never would have been able to find had they even known they existed.

From time to time Priscilla had the crazy idea that Raldemar created these paths himself in some tricky way, though she knew this was not possible. Still, wherever he flew, as if by magic, a clear path always seemed to open up in front of them. In no time at all, they had started down the mountains and seemed to be making good headway.

By this time, the sun was high in the sky. It was getting quite warm, so they stopped to take a drink and to rest for a moment. Priscilla looked along the path ahead and saw that it led directly toward a solid rock wall. Since there did not seem to be any way to get around this wall, she wondered if they were going to have to turn back.

When they began moving again, Raldemar flew directly toward the face of the rock. Priscilla held her breath, as she was sure he was going to be smashed against the hard surface. But, to her surprise, he simply vanished into the rock.

He had disappeared into a tunnel. Now, she could have sworn this tunnel was not there a moment before when she had looked at the rock wall. However, she knew a raven could not fly through solid rock, so she figured she must have somehow overlooked it... another one of those many tricks of the light.

One by one, they followed Raldemar into the tunnel. Soon it was too dark to see anything at all. Raldemar, in front of them, and Eideard, on Priscilla's shoulder, guided them with their voices. Grandmother Wolf trotted in front of Priscilla to make sure the rocky pathway was safe for walking. Alasdair brought up the rear.

Even with their support, the absolute darkness frightened Priscilla. Moving slowly and tentatively, she felt her way along. It was cold in the tunnel, and it smelled stale and damp. Feeling claustrophobic, she was desperate to be outside in the light again.

From time to time, she complained aloud. Behind her, she could hear Alasdair grumbling. It was obvious he did not like it either.

Raldemar must have heard their whining, for he called back to them, "Just keep putting one foot in front of the other. You will be fine."

"Easy for you to say," Priscilla muttered to herself, with some irritation. He did not have to walk. Besides, like Eideard, he could see where he was going in the dark. It was hard for her to trust and follow along, knowing at any moment she might twist her ankle or fall into a deep dark hole. Anything could happen when she was unable to see where she was going.

They had been traveling like this for what seemed like an eternity when Alasdair let out a whoop, "Wanortu's shell! We forgot all about the Black Carapas." Alasdair took the shell out of his pocket and opened it. Instantly the tunnel filled with light.

Now they could see where they were going without any trouble. Because they had been concentrating on how difficult it was to walk in the dark, they had completely forgotten that they carried with them the exact tool to make their journey easier.

Eideard flew on ahead to join Raldemar with a grumpy "Hoot Mon!" He did not appreciate the intense light the way they did. But for Priscilla and Alasdair, the light made it possible to move at a much faster pace.

After some time, Priscilla was finally beginning to relax when up ahead, Raldemar, Grandmother Wolf, and Eideard came to a dead stop.

As Priscilla and Alasdair drew up next to them, Alasdair asked, "What's wrong?"

"The tunnel ahead is blocked," answered Raldemar. "We are going to have to take an alternative route."

"Okay," said Alasdair. "Let's do it. Which way do we go?"

"It's not quite as easy as that, Alasdair," Raldemar told him. "Look for yourself." The big raven and Grandmother Wolf moved to one side so Priscilla and Alasdair could see the path ahead of them.

A rockslide completely blocked the path ahead, but what lay just a few feet in front of the rocks had Priscilla gasping with horror. The path on which they were walking led right into a deep gaping hole. If they had not stopped when they did, they would have fallen into utter darkness, exactly what she had feared.

"We will either have to go all the way back the way we came or go down through this hole," Raldemar told them. "I will fly down to see where it leads. Wait here for me, please." Before they could respond, he swooped into the hole and disappeared.

When Priscilla peered gingerly over the edge of the hole, she could see no sign of Raldemar or of the bottom of the hole. Since there was no way to climb down such a hole, they would just have to go back the way they had come. Meanwhile she sat beside the others to rest and wait for Raldemar's return. Everyone was hungry, so it was a good time to eat some of the food from Mother Nature's kingdom. Grandmother Wolf and Eideard ate some as well; they did not want to be away hunting when Raldemar got back.

It seemed a long time before the big raven reappeared. A loud whirring noise disturbed the quiet of the tunnel as Raldemar flew up through the hole and landed beside them.

"Well, the hole is a deep one," he announced. Priscilla and Alasdair giggled at one another at his use of these words. "The good news is that it leads straight down from here into another tunnel which will take us closer to where we need to go and will save us a lot of time. I have stretched and tied strong vines across the bottom of the hole so those of you unfortunate enough not to be able to fly, can jump down and land on the vines."

"What do you mean, Raldemar?" Priscilla asked with sudden apprehension. "Are you telling us you want us to jump down into this black hole? We don't even know where we will land. I can't do that," she declared stubbornly. "We need to go back and find another way."

Leaping to her feet, she made as if to go back along the path, hoping the others would take the hint and follow her. When no one did, she stopped and stood, irresolute and trembling with fear.

"The vines will catch you when you jump," Raldemar told her placidly. "They have enough give. You should bounce up and down until you have landed safely. You will be fine." It sounded as if he was describing a trapeze artist's net, something Priscilla had never found the least bit appealing. Her feet remained frozen in place.

Alasdair stepped forward with his usual bravado. "I'll go first," he said. "It sounds like fun!"

When Priscilla shuddered, he looked at her. "We need to hurry. It's getting late. We've got to find Inky. Going back the way we came would take far too long."

Before Priscilla could argue with him, Alasdair handed her the Black Carapas. He looked at Raldemar who gave a slight nod with his beak. Then with a loud holler, Alasdair jumped down into the hole and disappeared, his shouts soon becoming echoes far below them.

Eideard and Raldemar flew down the hole to make sure that he had landed safely and to help him find his way without the light.

Shaking like a leaf, Priscilla walked back over to the hole and stood looking over the edge. There was nothing to see but darkness, and all she heard were some muted sounds coming from far below. Terror-stricken, she sat down by the hole to wait.

After what seemed like no time at all, Raldemar was back telling her, "Alasdair landed just fine, Priscilla. It is your turn now." He perched patiently next to the hole, waiting for her to jump.

Priscilla thought of the stubborn little pear clinging to the branch of the pear tree back home. Like the pear, she did not want to let go. Staying with what was familiar, even if it was uncomfortable, seemed much safer than jumping into the darkness of the unknown.

Grandmother Wolf padded over and lay down alongside her. Gently rubbing her head against Priscilla's arm, she said quietly, "Sometimes it is necessary to follow a leader, little granddaughter, even though you don't know exactly what will happen. The outcome is not something you have control over. You only have control over your choices. It is up to you as to whether or not to trust Raldemar to lead you. The choice is yours."

It was like hearing Granny's voice again. Priscilla remembered Granny saying that true courage is doing what you know to be right even when you are afraid. Grandmother Wolf's wise words gave her similar comfort. Mother Nature had sent Raldemar to guide them, and he had not led them astray. She supposed she could trust him. It helped her to make up her mind.

When she turned and looked into the wolf's gentle eyes, she knew what she had to do, even though she was scared. Giving Grandmother Wolf a big hug, she clung to her neck for a long time.

Gathering her courage, she stood up at the edge of the hole, closed the Black Carapas, wrapped it carefully in her handkerchief, and put it in her front pocket to keep it safe. Even though it was dark, and she would not be able to see a thing anyway, she shut her eyes. Then she took a huge deep breath. With her body quivering from head to foot, she jumped into the black hole.

As she fell through the air, her breath blew out with a great whoosh. She felt like Alice falling down the rabbit hole. Images of Alice's adventures in Wonderland had just begun spinning through her mind when she felt her bottom hit something with a sudden jolt. Whatever it was gave way to her weight. Down and down she sank and then down some more.

Just when she felt she would never stop going down, she was rising up in the air again, her arms and legs flailing as if she were a Raggedy Ann doll. Down she went and then up again several more times until she finally came to rest on her back, where she lay, quivering and breathless.

The tough ropelike fibers of the vines pressed into her back; their earthy smell filled her nostrils, making her cough. But she was safe. And, though she was not anxious to do it again, it was not nearly as bad as she had thought it would be.

Priscilla took out the Black Carapas and opened it. Using the light to find her way, she climbed out of the vine net and wobbled over to where Alasdair and Eideard anxiously awaited her.

Alasdair patted her on the shoulder as he said, "I knew you could do it." She beamed at him with pride as she gave him back the shell.

Eideard flew over to her shoulder twittering, "Hoot Mon, lassie, Hoot Mon!"

They heard a wild howl and looked up in time to see Grandmother Wolf dropping down through the air. Legs splayed, she bounced down on the vines on her belly. After she went through the up-and-down process several times, she jumped down from the vine net and unsteadily made her way toward them. The brave Grandmother Wolf was not used to such crazy shenanigans either.

When they had all gathered once more, they set off in the new tunnel with Raldemar leading the way. Sure enough, just as he had predicted, in no time at all they could see a light at the end of the tunnel. Alasdair closed the Black Carapas and put it in his pocket. They no longer had need of it.

The old tunnel had come to a dead end. In order to go forward, they had made a choice to trust their leader, Raldemar, and take the risk he recommended. Even though they were afraid and had no idea where they would end up, they had chosen to face their fear and follow him down into the unknown. Knowing he had never led them astray before made it easier.

However, it was only after they had made their choice, taken the risk, and arrived safely, that they knew for sure their trust had been well placed. Raldemar had once more led them to where they needed to go.

Chapter Eighteen
The Tree of Innocence

As they emerged from the tunnel into daylight, Priscilla inhaled deep breaths of clean, fresh air. It felt good to be out in the sunshine again. After her eyes adjusted to the light, she saw that the forest lay below them with the meadow on the far side, and she let out a sigh of relief. Even though nothing bad had happened in the tunnel, she hoped it would be a long time before she had to be in such a dark confined space again.

"We are almost there," Raldemar announced. "You just have to climb down these rocks. Then we will make our way through the forest and out into the meadow." Once more, he flew off and, once again, they followed his lead, heading down the rocks toward the forest.

By the middle of the afternoon, having encountered no further obstacles, they finally stepped out of the trees into the meadow. However, this part of the meadow was not what Priscilla had expected. She felt absolutely no desire to bare her toes and dance in the short prickly grass underfoot. No wildflowers grew here, no butterflies and dragonflies flittered about, and no bunnies scampered anywhere. All of this seemed ominous to her.

Shuddering, she turned to Alasdair who stood behind her. "I'm kinda scared to go to this shadow place. It sounds horrible."

He said in his gruff voice, "There's nothing to be afraid of. If we listen to any guides we meet along the way and do what we're told, we'll be fine."

But Priscilla could not be so easily fooled. She knew in her heart that he was as scared as she was. He just wasn't acknowledging it to her… and probably not to himself either. Once more, he reminded her of Dorothy's lion.

Raldemar announced, "We are heading to the lone tree." He had to be referring to the tree with wide bushy branches directly ahead of them, as it appeared to be the only tree anywhere around them.

As they drew closer, Priscilla saw, much to her delight, that it was a pear tree. Ripe golden pears hung in profusion from the branches. A small rustic hut, hidden by the tree before, came into view on the other side.

Raldemar said, "The door on the right side of the hut is the entrance to the Land of Shadows."

The others, including the ever-curious Eideard, moved on to investigate the hut. Priscilla lagged behind under the tree. She pictured the pear tree back home and the little pear she had just been thinking of in the tunnel. These pears looked ripe and ready to eat, and she felt tempted to pick one or two.

A sly, slippery voice hissed, causing her to jump in surprise. "Go ahead, my sssweet, and pluck a pear. And pick one for your sssweetie as well. If you plan to go down to the Land of SSShadowsss, you will need sssome sssustenance." The words had an enticing ring to them, and though the voice sounded familiar, Priscilla could not place it. Looking all around, she saw no one.

"I'm sssitting above you, my sssweet." The way the slimy voice hissed at her made her skin crawl.

Looking up, she saw a long black snake with horizontal stripes of bright colors along its back, curled around one of the branches. As she quickly took a couple of steps backwards, she remembered where she'd heard the voice before. This had to be the same awful snake in the grass that had told them to go away when they first arrived in the Kingdom Beyond the Sunset. Wanortu had called him Snake.

"Don't be ssscared, my sssweetnesss!" Snake continued in his seductive voice. "I want to help you find what you are ssseeking. Now pluck a pear for yourssself and one for your sssweetie. Make sssure that you each take a bite of your pearsss before you go down to the Land of Shadowsss. You will need to partake of the Tree of Innocencesss to help you sssee what you must sssee."

"Why should I trust you?" snapped Priscilla. "After all, you were the one who told us to go home... that we didn't belong here!"

Snake hissed, chortled, and sprayed, "Oh yesss, I ssseee what you mean! Well I warned you away, but you didn't lisssten. Now you will learn why I sssuggesssted you leave our land. You are about to sssee things you will wish you had never ssseen."

Alasdair called out to her, "Priscilla, what's keeping you? Come on!"

Snake hissed once more at her, "Don't forget to pluck and eat your pearsss, my sssweetnesss. Eating the pearsss will make what you sssee more palatable." With these puzzling words, he uncurled, displaying his bright purple belly, slithered up the branch, and disappeared into the tree.

Mother Nature had told them to listen to any guides they met along the way. Even though Priscilla wasn't sure if this sneaky snake was a real guide, or if she should trust him, she picked two large juicy pears and put them in her pockets, just in case. Besides, she was hungry, and they did look mighty tasty. Then she hurried over to the others who were waiting for her.

The hut was a tiny ramshackle structure with two doors in the middle. A chimney stuck out above the roof on the left side, and she wondered who might use such an out-of-the way place.

Everyone was waiting for her just inside the open door on the right. They stood at the top of an old stone stairway leading down into the ground.

"Oh no," Priscilla grumbled unhappily, "We're going to have to go back down into the dark again, aren't we?"

"I'm afraid so," Alasdair answered with a grimace. "This is the entrance to the Land of Shadows." Turning to Raldemar, he asked, "Will we be coming back here again?"

Raldemar croaked, "No. You will be traveling down a river and will end up wherever the current takes you. There will be an exit there. I must leave you now. I need to return to Mother Nature. She will want to know that you have arrived here safely."

With a quick farewell, he flew out the door, which Priscilla still held open, letting in the daylight for as long as possible.

Alasdair watched him go with a wistful look. "I wish Raldemar didn't have to leave us. I felt a lot better having him around." He turned to Priscilla and gave her a shrug and a brave smile, "Well, I guess it's now or never. Let's get down."

Priscilla slowly closed the door behind her and moved further inside the hut. As the darkness enveloped them, her heart began to beat faster, and she could feel Alasdair stiffen beside her.

Grandmother Wolf, sensing their fear, told them gently, "You will be fine, my dears. Though I don't think it will be an easy journey for you, this must be where you need to go to discover what you need to learn. Sometimes you must go into the Darkness in order to find the Light. It is often in the deepest Darkness where the greatest Light is found."

Grandmother Wolf's words sounded profound and gave Priscilla some comfort even if she wasn't sure she understood exactly what they meant.

"Ach aye! Hoot Mon!" hooted Eideard in agreement, as he settled once more on Priscilla's shoulder.

"That's just fine for you," Priscilla whispered snippily to her little owl friend. "Wanortu says you carry your own Light inside you."

"Aye, an' so do ye," Eideard retorted. "Ye jus' don know it yet! Hoot Mon!"

Some sort of slimy mold grew on the hard earthen walls, reflecting a greenish light, and giving a ghostly luminosity to the stairwell. As their eyes adjusted to the dark, this eerie light enabled them to see where they were going. The Black Carapas would not be necessary, which was just as well. They had used it in the tunnel and had no idea how long its light would last.

Alasdair took a deep breath, braced himself, and started slowly down the steps. Priscilla cautiously followed along behind him with Grandmother Wolf at her back.

The deeper they went, the damper the air became. The walls changed from earth to stone. Moisture dripping down the rocky surfaces made the steps slippery, so they had to tread with caution. Priscilla caught a whiff of something nasty that smelled like damp moldy rags and rotten eggs. She could hear the sound of rushing water, so she knew they must be getting close to the river Raldemar had said they would find.

After stepping off the last stair, they entered a short tunnel. It led them out into a dimly lit rock cavern. Illumination came from torches set high on the walls. The flickering flames sent menacing dark shadows leaping across the cavern. Trembling, Priscilla reached down and grabbed hold of Grandmother Wolf's furry neck for comfort.

A narrow river flowed down the middle of the cavern, darker than any river Priscilla had ever seen before. From the horrible smell, she guessed it contained of all sorts of unmentionable things. Shivering, she hoped they would not have to go into this nasty river for any reason.

A shallow, flat-bottomed boat, squared at the front and back, bobbed up and down at the edge of the river, pulling hard on a rope attached to a tall tapered stone on the shore. Next to the stone stood a plump little man wearing a belted brown robe reaching to his ankles. A golden circular medallion hung from a thick gold chain around his neck. He held a long wooden staff in his hand. Except for his brown skin and the wiry gray hair curling all over his head, he might have been a miniature version of Friar Tuck in *Robin Hood*.

"I am Barthos the BoatMaster, and this is the River of Shadows," he greeted them. His angelic voice matched his cherubic appearance but did not fit with this dank, cavernous place.

It sounded even more at odds with what he said next. "Those who undertake this perilous journey down the River of Shadows do so at their own risk and are responsible for anything they see or do. Once we begin, there is no turning back. No one can leave the boat until the journey ends. Do you understand what I have said?"

Priscilla and Alasdair looked nervously at one another. Alasdair answered, his voice barely a whisper, "Yes, we understand."

"What you will see in the Land of Shadows will be shadow images of past events. You will discover what you have come to learn. You will see more than you are expecting to see, though it will belong to you," the odd little personage continued mysteriously. Priscilla had no idea what he meant by this.

He told them with great emphasis, "*Under no conditions must you go into the river!* If you do, I cannot be responsible for what will happen to you. The River of Shadows is *cursed*. Entering it for any reason will have the direst of consequences for you and for your loved ones. Is that understood?"

This time, Priscilla answered. Her voice quavered as she whispered, "Yes, we understand." She knew, beyond a shadow of a doubt, that she had no intentions of going into the dreadful smelly river.

"Now," he smiled at them, and his round, red-cheeked face did indeed light up like a cherub's. As if he had said his worst, he was moving on to better things. "Since you are children, in order for you to undertake this journey, your hearts must be protected by the Veil of Innocence. Have you eaten of the pears from the Tree of Innocence?" he asked.

Priscilla looked at Barthos in astonishment.

Alasdair said, "What pears?" but he stopped when Priscilla drew the pears out of her pocket and held them out for him to see.

She told Alasdair about finding Snake in the pear tree. "I picked the pears, just in case, though I wasn't sure if I should believe what he said. I guess Snake knew what he was talking about and wasn't just being sneaky." She handed Alasdair a pear.

Then a troubling thought hit her. "But it also means he knew what he was talking about when he said we would see things we wouldn't want to see!"

Barthos told them, "Eating the pears will draw the Veil of Innocence around your hearts. It will shield you from the harshness of what you are about to see. Young and innocent hearts still holding so much Light should never be exposed too intensely to the Land of Shadows. You have not had enough experience to teach you how to use your understanding to protect your hearts."

He continued, "Take a couple of bites of your pears before you get into the boat, and then keep your pears close by. If what you hear or see becomes more than you can endure, take another bite. The Veil of Innocence will draw closer around your heart to help shield you."

Barthos waited until Priscilla and Alasdair had each taken bites of their pears. Then he helped them into the boat. They tossed their backpacks under the seat in the middle of the boat and sat down next to one another. Grandmother Wolf jumped in and lay down behind them.

Eideard, as usual, had been taking in everything. Now he whispered to them, "I'd tak anither bite or twa of those pears, if I was ye. I've a wee notion yer goin' tae need all the help ye can git! Hoot Mon!"

Priscilla and Alasdair did as the little owl suggested. Though she could have eaten all the sweet tasty pear at once, Priscilla decided it would be better to wait and see what happened. Her curiosity mingled with her apprehension about what lay ahead of them.

Once they had settled in the boat, Barthos the BoatMaster untied the rope and grasped it in the hand in which he carried his staff. With his other hand, he took hold of his long robe, pulled it up around his knees, and hopped neatly into the bow of the boat. Using his staff, he maneuvered them out to the middle of the river.

The boat immediately caught hold of the current for which it had been hankering. Soon they were heading down the River of Shadows on their way to wherever this next part of their journey would take them.

BOOK FOUR

FACING THE DARKNESS

Chapter Nineteen
The Land of Shadows

With Barthos the BoatMaster at the helm, the little boat carrying its odd assortment of passengers floated along with the flow of the river. Working in silence, his back toward Priscilla and Alasdair, Barthos never once turned his head to check on them. It was almost as if he had forgotten their existence.

Priscilla whispered to Alasdair, "I guess we're on our own now."

At that moment, they entered a narrow dark channel. Moist cavern walls pressed in upon them, nearly scraping both sides of the boat. The rocky ceiling hung so low it missed the little BoatMaster's head by mere inches.

Muffled sounds surged over them in waves, becoming louder as the boat floated down the channel. Before long, they heard terrified cries of pain mingled with torturous moaning and wailing.

Priscilla and Alasdair moved closer together and hunched down inside the boat. Alasdair gloomily commented, "This reminds me of the Pirates of the Caribbean ride at Disneyland, but I don't think it's going to be as much fun."

The anguish in the cries wrenched Priscilla's heartstrings. With shaking fingers, she took several more bites of her pear and heard Alasdair do the same. At once, she felt a sort of protective shawl wrapping around her, making her feel safer. It diminished the effect the sounds had on her.

But when the boat floated out of the channel into a vast cavern, a cacophony of sound crashed over them like a tsunami. Even with the protection of the Veil of Innocence, they could not ignore it. They looked around to see what was causing such an agonizing din.

The landscape on both sides of the river extended off into the distance. All over the land, shadow figures were fighting, wounding, and killing one another in every possible way. From the clothing and armor these figures wore, the weapons used, and the banners and flags flying, these appeared to be images of wars between people of all nationalities, races, and religions.

No noise at all arose from the countless weapons. All those in the boat could hear were howling laments of fear, rage, and anguish. This magnified the depth of the suffering. Dark energy, similar to what they had seen in the Muses, hung in huge black clouds above the mayhem.

As the boat drifted down the river, they saw one horrifying image after another of people acting out their fear, anger, and greed with incredible violence. There were scenes of robberies, murders, rapes, torture, the destruction of magnificent buildings and exquisite artifacts. Dark energy caused these behaviors while creating more at the same time.

When they passed scene after scene of the devastation of the earth, Priscilla felt her heart breaking. She watched, with great sadness, the pollution of the air, the decimation of forests, the massacre of animals, and the contamination of the oceans and subsequent loss of wildlife caused by toxic dumps and oil spills. Those who instigated these acts created massive amounts of Dark energy, yet to them, the consequences of their actions appeared to mean nothing at all.

The boat drifted past shadowy figures committing unimaginable horrors upon innocent children of all ages; some of the perpetrators were parents, whose job it was to love and care for their children. Priscilla and Alasdair quickly finished their pears.

Instantly, Priscilla felt the protective shawl thicken around her, keeping her heart more distant from what was in view. Taking a deep breath, she reached for her treasures in her pockets. Alasdair was humming to himself, and she wondered if his music brought him similar comfort. Without stopping to think about it, she grabbed his hand, and he held hers tightly in response.

She could feel Grandmother Wolf pressing up against her back. Eideard's feathers rubbed against her neck as he whispered, "Hoot Mon!" in her ear. The closeness of her three friends helped soothe her a little.

The Veil of Innocence shielded Priscilla and Alasdair from the total impact of the world of Darkness all around them. Yet Priscilla knew she would never be able to forget the Land of Shadows. The images and sounds seeped through the protection to penetrate into her mind and heart.

Her childhood innocence would never again be the same. She would tuck the memory of the terrifying Land of Shadows away in her heart pocket, though this memory would not bring her hope. Instead, it would remain as a permanent reminder of the destructive power of Dark energy.

Priscilla and Alasdair needed every bit of their concentration to get them through their terrifying ordeal. Consequently, neither of them noticed the boat drifting out of the big noisy cavern into a much smaller chamber. The agonizing wails faded to a low rumbling in the background.

Their state of shock had long overshadowed the purpose for their journey. Eideard the Owl brought them back to the reason they had come to the Land of Shadows in the first place as he whispered to them, "Look yonder o'er to yer left. Hoot Mon!"

Mechanically following his suggestion, they glanced over, not caring what they might see. A familiar figure on the shore soon pulled them out of their dispirited daze.

It was Prince Inky. Priscilla had almost given up hope of ever finding him. Her excitement at seeing him helped her recall why they were here in this awful place. The devastation of the previous images quickly receded into the background along with the noise.

"Oh, look, Alasdair. It's Prince Inky!" she cried. "But what's he doing?" He wore clothing meant for outdoors and had a cap on his head instead of his circlet of jewels.

"I think we are about to see him steal the Light from the Palace, Priscilla," Grandmother Wolf said quietly.

"Then maybe we'll see where he went afterwards." Alasdair too had remembered why they were there and was eager to find out what happened next.

Grandmother Wolf was right. As they watched, Prince Inky strode into the palace rotunda, gathered the Rainbow Guards together and said something to them. The guards immediately left their posts and hurried to the back of the palace.

As soon as the guards were gone, Inky, with gloved hands, grabbed the Light and slipped it under his vest into a thick pouch attached to his belt. The Royal Rainbow immediately vanished. Taking a folded piece of paper from his pocket, he set it in the pot where the Light had been. He hurriedly left the palace by a side door. Mounting a waiting horse, he swiftly galloped down the steps and away from the palace, without stopping to talk to those who called out to him.

Down the road, through the village, and over the hills toward the meadow he raced. Behind him, masses of dark shadows flew after him, like moths attracted to a flame. The shadows stayed with him as he galloped across the bridge, left the path, and rode at a reckless pace across the meadow. Not once did he look behind him, nor did he glance to the right or left along the way, so he never noticed his relentless pursuers.

Inky's destination became obvious when he pulled to a stop at the hut near the pear tree. Jumping off his horse, he gave it a quick thump on the rear to send it away. Then he dashed through the door on the right side of the hut. He was heading down to the Land of Shadows.

"He didn't even stop to pick a pear," muttered Priscilla, with some concern.

Inky leapt into the little boat on the River of Shadows, with a startled Barthos the BoatMaster following right behind him. Alasdair whispered, "Inky seemed to know exactly where he was going. He must have been to the Land of Shadows before."

"At least we know he came this way," Priscilla whispered in return.

Their boat floated out of this chamber and into another about the same size. Priscilla and Alasdair frantically searched the shores for signs of Inky, but he was nowhere in sight. Instead, they saw two even more familiar figures on the shore.

"Look Priscilla, that's you!" Alasdair exclaimed in surprise. "And over there," he added, pointing to the land closest to him, "That's me!" They were looking at shadow figures of themselves. Inky disappeared from their minds for the moment.

At first, Priscilla could not figure out what her shadow self was doing. Then all at once, she got it. "Oh no!" she cried. These were images of her previous bad behavior, much of which she had not remembered, or at least, had tried hard to forget.

Her shadow self behaved in ways of which she was deeply ashamed. In different scenes, she saw moments in her life when she had yelled dreadful names at her brother and sisters, cheated on a test at school, and stolen candy from a store. To her dismay, each of her actions produced masses of Dark energy.

In one image, she threw a temper tantrum, accidentally hitting Mathilda. The guilt she had felt when she hurt her poor innocent cat came back to her in a rush.

She watched a scene of her shadow self with Horrid Harvey and his friends, staring in disbelief. By mocking her, the hateful boys created a lot of Dark energy. However, she was making plenty of her own with her anger and hatred toward them. This did not seem at all fair to her since they had started it.

Alasdair's shadow self misbehaved as well. He screamed at his mother for not buying him an expensive guitar he coveted. When some little kids pointed at him, he swore at them and chased them away. Just to prove he could do it, he stole several items from a grocery store and then teased an elderly, homeless man sitting on the step outside. Repeatedly, he spoke rudely to people who had only been kind to him. Like Priscilla, he had produced loads of Dark energy through his actions.

Both children were stunned to learn that, without knowing it, they had established a history of Dark energy that lived on in the Land of Shadows. Each of them had been inducted into this infamous place not once but many times over. This was quite a revelation and not easy for them to accept.

"I can't believe I made so much Dark energy all by myself," Priscilla groaned, her face flushed with shame.

"Neither can I," mumbled Alasdair, hiding his face behind his hands.

Absorbed in their shame, they did not notice the boat leave the chamber and enter another similar one. When the boat stopped moving, they looked up to see what was happening. Barthos the BoatMaster had pressed his staff firmly down into the river to hold the boat in place.

Grandmother Wolf quietly told them, "There must be something here you are supposed to see."

On the shore, a bunch of boys savagely attacked a boy whose face was a lighter color. The bullies knocked the boy to the ground and continued their beating. Dark energy swirled threateningly above them.

Alasdair leaned forward, and Priscilla turned to look at him. He was staring hard at the scene, oblivious to anything else.

When she turned back to the shore again, an agitated younger boy was pushing and pulling at the bullies, trying with all his might to get them to stop what they were doing. He was much too small to have any effect, and Priscilla sensed his helplessness.

In his agony, he screamed, "Stop hurting my brother! Leave him alone! He didn't do anything to you." The bullies ignored him.

Finally, the group dispersed, laughing and jostling one another while looking smug at what they had done. They left behind a crumpled heap on the ground.

Calling out, "Adam, I'm here," the little boy rushed over to his older brother, knelt down, and took him in his arms. Hugging Adam close to his chest, he began to rock back and forth on his heels. Those on the boat could clearly see the little boy's face as he looked down through his tears at his brother. His face radiated an unforgettable expression of profound love.

With those on the boat watching in sorrow, Adam's light and life slowly seeped out of him. The little boy wailed his anguish. He lifted his head, raised his small clenched fist high in the air, and cursed those who had done this to his brother. A cloud of Dark energy rose out of him and floated up above his head.

Barthos lifted his staff, allowing the boat to move forward, but only for a short distance before he stopped it once again.

Now they were looking at a man, probably in his early twenties. He was standing next to a crib in which a small child lay fast asleep. Like Adam, the child had a light-colored face.

Alasdair stiffened and moved forward, so close to the edge, he was almost falling off his seat.

The man bent over the crib railing and lifted the child into his arms. As he gently rocked the sleeping child, the man's face held an identical expression to the one they had just seen on the face of the boy holding Adam. It was clear that this was the boy now grown into a man.

His face turned angry. Whatever he was thinking caused a familiar dark cloud to rise up and hover above him.

Jerking back, as if something had hit him, Alasdair gasped, "No!"

Priscilla knew the scene meant something to him, though she had no idea what it was. She watched the shore to see what would happen.

With great care, the man laid the child back down in the crib and covered him with a blanket. Those on the boat could clearly hear him whisper, "My precious little son, I won't let anyone do to you what they did to Adam. I will never again be so helpless."

As if he had made a decision, the man turned and walked into a nearby room, pulled a box from the top shelf of a closet, and placed it on a table. Slowly he lifted an old gun out of the box. He sat and stared at the gun for a moment. Whatever he was thinking caused the black cloud above him to darken.

Priscilla glanced over at Alasdair. He sat as rigid as a rock, his eyes glued to the scene in front of him.

The man checked the gun for bullets. It appeared to be empty, for he took a rag and some oil from the box and began to clean the gun. But something went terribly wrong. The gun was not empty after all. It accidentally fired, a bullet striking him in the chest. He fell to the floor.

A young woman rushed into the room. When she saw what had happened, she screamed and ran to the man. Taking him in her arms, she rocked him in much the same way he had once rocked

Adam. He whispered something to her, his words too faint for Priscilla to hear. Then the woman leaned down and kissed him. His head fell back, and he lay still.

Barthos lifted his staff, and the boat began to drift on again.

Alasdair was sobbing. Grandmother Wolf pushed her furry snout under his arm. He buried his face in her thick fur, letting it absorb his tears and the sound of his weeping.

Priscilla heard him whisper, "Daddy, I didn't believe her. Daddy, I didn't believe her. Forgive me, Daddy, I didn't know. I'm so sorry!"

In a flash, it became clear to Priscilla. The children with lighter faces were albinos. The boy in the crib was Alasdair, so the man who died was his father. This explained why Alasdair did not like to talk about him. She hurt for Alasdair, and, for some reason she did not understand, for herself as well.

Just as she was about to reach out to Alasdair, another familiar figure on shore caught her attention. Scooting forward on the seat, she took a closer look. Could it possibly be who she thought it was?

It was. This time she was looking at *her* father on the shore, though he looked very young. He held a beautiful young woman in his arms. She seemed vaguely familiar, but Priscilla could not place her. The couple played with a little curly-haired girl about three years old. The three of them looked very happy together.

The boat moved on to show the same woman lying in bed, obviously very ill. The little girl sat cross-legged on the end of the bed, playing with an old doll. Priscilla's father paced restlessly back and forth by the side of the bed.

In the next scene, the woman had died. Priscilla's father was kneeling by the bed, weeping and raging. A cloud of Dark energy hung over him. The little girl huddled at the foot of the bed, hugging her doll, looking frightened, lost, and alone.

Deep inside her, Priscilla's persistent memory began to stir. The heavy feelings which always accompanied this memory, wrapped around her. She tried to distract herself, just as she had always done before, but, this time, nothing worked. No matter how hard she tried, the uncomfortable feelings would not go away. Instead, they became stronger.

Almost with a vengeance, the uninvited feelings flooded up from within her, spilling over into tears of grief. Her memory surfaced into her heart and mind, bringing with it an understanding of the scene in front of her. Everything began to make sense.

She was the little girl, and the woman in the bed, her real mother. When her mother died, an overpowering sense of loss consumed three-year-old Priscilla, making her unaware of anything else.

No one in the family ever talked to her about her real mother or about her death, so Priscilla had buried the memory and the feelings of loss deep inside her. In this way, she could pretend it never happened and protect herself from pain at the same time.

But whenever something prompted memories of this time, the overwhelming feelings would start to come back. These were the feelings she had taught herself to push away.

It was when her mother died that Granny, her real mother's mother, moved in with them. This explained why Priscilla always felt closer to her than to the woman, who, she now realized was not her real mother, but her stepmother. Joshua and the twins were her stepmother's children from a previous marriage. None of them was related to Priscilla at all. No wonder she had always felt so different from them.

Understanding did not make the hurt go away. Tears streamed down her cheeks. It was her turn to throw her arms around Grandmother Wolf's neck and bury her sobs in the thick fur, already moistened by Alasdair's tears.

In spite of the protection of the Veil of Innocence, what Priscilla and Alasdair had seen and learned in the Land of Shadows pierced their hearts. They wanted nothing more than to get out of this heartbreaking place.

However, their journey through the Land of Shadows was not yet finished. Though they did not know it, what lay ahead of them would be more difficult than they could ever imagine.

Chapter Twenty
The Valley of the Lost Souls

Priscilla instantly became aware of her surroundings. In her grief, she hadn't noticed that they had left the other chamber and entered a new place. This huge dark cavern was cold and menacing; it chilled Priscilla right down to her heart and bones. Intense fear displaced her sorrow. Terror as thick as dust filled the air, and she breathed it in with every shaky breath. Goose bumps raced up and down her spine as she trembled from head to foot.

For the first time since they had stepped into the boat, Barthos the BoatMaster spoke to them. "We have entered the Valley of the Lost Souls," he announced, in a hollow-sounding voice, without looking back at them. "You must remember everything I told you when we started our journey. I warn you once more, under *no* conditions must you leave the boat."

What Priscilla saw on the shore horrified her. Thousands of gruesome figures dressed in long dark robes and hoods shuffled about like zombies. Desolation, as bleak as the barren landscape in which they existed, oozed out of them, leaving behind them an almost tangible toxic trail of slime wherever they went. No life existed in this dreadful valley and definitely not in the loathsome sluggish creatures dragging themselves around.

Priscilla felt sickened by the sight. In a trembling voice, she whispered to Alasdair, "This must be the place Mother Nature told us about, where the souls of those beyond redemption come to spend eternity."

Alasdair replied with a shiver, "They must be the ones who chose the Dark, like King Sol said. None of them have any Light left in them at all."

Priscilla shuddered. "I think you're right. I don't like this place one bit!" She recalled Mother Nature saying the People of the Dark came to the Land of Shadows to harvest lost parts for their own needs. Harvesting parts sounded much like harvesting turnips or potatoes, but even turnips and potatoes had life in them and gave sustenance to others. This horrible place had nothing to give. With no light left in any of these souls, they would bring only destruction to whatever they touched. Perhaps this was exactly what the People of the Dark wanted.

While she was wondering how much more of this she could stand, she spied Inky. He was in a boat, floating down the river in the Valley of Lost Souls just as they were doing. It was confusing to see the boat and Barthos in two places at the same time, until she reminded herself that she was looking at a scene from the past.

Grabbing Alasdair's arm, she pointed, "Look, there's Inky again! He's in the Valley of the Lost Souls just like we are!"

While they watched, Inky reached into the pouch at his waist and lifted out the Sacred Light. Standing upright in the little boat, he proudly raised the brilliant little globe high above his head, illuminating the whole cavern with a sudden blinding light.

Alasdair stared in admiration. "Inky must have come to the Valley of the Lost Souls to show the Light to the People of the

Dark just like he said he wanted to do. He thought they would be drawn to the Light." Indeed, many *were* drawn to the Light, though perhaps not in the way Inky had intended.

Moments after he raised the Light above his head, a piercing shriek echoed through the whole cavern. A harsh blast of violent wind filled with a terrifying mass of dark shadows swooped down like a howling banshee to surround him in a whirlwind of darkness. With a surprised cry, Inky disappeared from view.

Priscilla and Alasdair both screamed, "Inky!" as they ducked down. But of course it wasn't happening to them, nor could he hear them call out. They could do nothing to help him. What they were viewing were images from the past.

Barthos once more held the boat still.

Helpless, Priscilla and Alasdair watched two big ugly black shadows drag Inky out of the boat and onto the shore. Roughly shoving aside anyone in their way, his captors pushed him into the midst of some sort of gathering taking place in the far corner of the Valley of the Lost Souls.

Even though those present at this meeting had no light in them, they did not seem to be the same robed zombie-like creatures as the dead souls all over the rest of the valley. In real life, these men would look horribly evil; as dark shadows, their appearance became even more hideous. All of them carried weapons of one sort or another. Several of the biggest and nastiest of the bunch sat behind a table, the apparent leaders of this dark shadow assembly. Priscilla knew at once that these were the People of the Dark.

Gloating, the two captors thrust Inky toward those at the table, perhaps hoping for some reward.

Inky made another brave attempt to present the Light to the leaders. The way they immediately shielded their eyes and pulled back in anger gave Priscilla the impression that the Light threatened them in some way.

The most frightful of the leaders nodded to one of the captors, who immediately grabbed Inky and silenced him by clasping a huge hand over his mouth. Grimacing in disgust, the other captor snatched the Light and tossed it back into Inky's pouch.

No reward was forthcoming from these dreadful leaders. Instead, they gave their orders to the captors who threw Inky to the ground, rolled him up in a thick blanket, and secured him with a rope. A burly man stepped forward, picked up Inky, flung him over his shoulder as if he were a sack of potatoes, and left the group.

Eideard called their attention to the other side of the river saying, "Look o'er to yer right. Hoot Mon!"

They turned to watch the same man toss Inky into a small speedboat afloat on an expanse of water. The boat was already full of lighter shadowed figures. The man jumped on board, started the engine, and within seconds, he was steering the boat across the water toward a huge dark vessel.

Priscilla shivered in recognition at the same time as Alasdair cried out, "Look, Priscilla… it's the Dark Ship, the one King Sol pointed out on the Ocean of Opportunity. Inky and the Light are being taken out to the Dark Ship!"

The speedboat docked next to the huge shadow ship. The pilot yelled something. One after another, the lighter shadow figures stepped off the boat and climbed up a long metal ladder attached to the side of the ship. The pilot picked Inky up from the floor, slung him over his shoulder again, and clambered up the ladder after them. When he reached the top, he tossed his bundle over the ship's railing, jumped over, and vanished from view.

Alasdair turned to look at Priscilla with excitement. "It looks like we'll have to find a way to get out to the Dark Ship. That must be where they are holding Inky."

Before Priscilla could say anything, more shouting drew their attention back to the other shore where something else was occurring. A light shadow figure was being ushered through the same gathering of the People of the Dark. Unlike Inky, he did not appear to be a captive. Priscilla could only see his back, but she thought there might be something familiar about him.

The man presented himself to the leaders around the table. A conversation ensued, which Priscilla and Alasdair were unable to hear. The man did not appear to be making the leaders happy. The discussion grew heated. One of the leaders placed a lot of money on the table and, as they debated, he kept adding to the pile. Whatever this man had to sell, it was something the People of the Dark badly wanted.

While the man was considering the money on the table, his shadow grew darker. Then he shook his head, and his shadow lightened up again.

Tremendous Dark Energy rose up over the leaders as they argued with him, but the man continued to refuse their offer. His shadow shifted from light to dark to light again, as if the payment they offered tempted him. For whatever reason, he remained undecided.

One of the nastiest of the leaders stood up and spoke emphatically. Then he placed some official looking documents on the table. These documents must have been quite significant, for the light shadowed figure stood motionless for a long time with his fingers tenderly stroking the papers.

As he mulled things over, he drew his hand back, reached into his pants pocket and pulled out a handkerchief to mop his sweating brow. When he was placing his handkerchief back in his pocket, he stopped, startled, as if he had found something unexpected inside. Taking a curved white object out of his pocket, he stood staring at it for some time.

Priscilla gasped. She knew exactly what this object was. He was holding her favorite shell, the one she had given him to help him make his decision. The man was her father. No wonder the shadow figure seemed familiar.

"Daddy!" she called out as she started to get up.

Alasdair pulled her back down whispering, "No Priscilla, these are only shadows of what has happened. He's not really there."

Though she did not try to get up again, she remained focused on the scene. She was terrified for her father. As he gazed down at the shell, he grew a great deal lighter than he had been before, and this time he remained that way. Putting the shell back in his pocket, he straightened his shoulders, said something to the leaders, which caused them to scowl with fury. Then he turned to go, apparently having made his decision.

He did not get far. After a curt nod from one of the leaders, a figure pulled a gun from his belt and hit Priscilla's father on the head. As the injured man started to fall to the ground, the shadow crowd parted to make room for him. Priscilla could clearly see the shock and pain on her father's face.

She screamed, "Daddy!"

Without a single thought or a moment's hesitation, she jumped up from her seat and dove into the dark river. She had forgotten everything Barthos the BoatMaster had warned them about, as well as her feelings about the horrible river. All she knew was that her father was in trouble, and she needed to help him.

Grandmother Wolf and Alasdair yelled in unison, "*No, Priscilla!*" and Barthos called out, "*Come back, girl!*" but she never heard them. Nothing mattered except her father. He needed her, and she had to go to his aid.

A surprised Eideard the Owl sat on the seat where he had landed after Priscilla's sudden movement bounced him off her shoulder. He repeatedly cried, "Hoot Mon!" as he gaped in astonishment at the hole in the river into which Priscilla had suddenly disappeared.

The dense black water closed over Priscilla's head and body, the cold stunning her. Gasping, she bobbed to the surface again. Her sodden clothes acted like heavy weights, pulling her down under the water. Though she kept trying, she could not seem to move through the thick dark water. Her arms and legs felt like rubber. The more she struggled, the more difficult it became. Something was terribly wrong.

As she started to go back under again, she gulped some of the putrid water, which she vomited up straight away. Petrified by her own powerlessness, she tried to scream, resulting in swallowing and coughing up more of the vile water.

She wanted… no… she desperately needed to get to her father, but she could not seem to go anywhere but down… down… down…

Deeper and deeper she sank, even as she tried to fight her way upwards. All at once, a sort of lethargy overcame her, making her want to stop fighting and let go. Her muscles slowly began to relax.

A light sliced through the water toward her. She turned her face into the light. This would be the tunnel of light people talked of seeing when they were dying. As if in a dream, she drifted toward the light. It would be nice to go through the tunnel into oblivion. Then she would not have to struggle anymore.

Before she knew what was happening, something heavy smashed against her chest. Whatever this was pushed her up toward the surface of the water. A blast of cold air hit her face and rushed into her waterlogged lungs. Coughing and retching, she gasped for air like a fish out of water.

In her head, she heard the words, "Hold on, little granddaughter. Hold on. You'll be safe in a moment." Her beloved Grandmother Wolf was there beside her in the river. The big wolf grabbed hold of Priscilla's shirt with her teeth and dragged her toward the boat. Barthos and Alasdair pulled Priscilla into the boat while an exhausted Grandmother Wolf heaved herself over the side to collapse in a puddle on the floor.

Eideard hopped about on the bench crying, "Ach aye, what hae ye done, wee one. Ach, dear, dear! What hae ye done, lassie? Hoot Mon!"

Priscilla lay on her side gasping and gagging. When she started to remember where she was and what had happened, she struggled to get up, sobbing, "I have to go to Daddy. I have to help him."

"No Priscilla, take it easy," Alasdair said holding her down firmly. "He's not really there. You can't do anything for him now."

Barthos muttered with consternation, as much to himself as to anyone else, "This is not a good thing. No one is supposed to go into the cursed river. We must get out of here right away. Perhaps no one will have noticed what happened. Maybe nothing will come of this. That is my hope."

He hurried to the bow of the boat. Leaning his staff down hard into the water on one side of the boat and then on the other, he continued to repeat this practice until, slowly but surely, the little boat began to pick up speed as they headed toward the cavern exit.

All of them were anxious to leave this horrifying place. They were so busy dealing with their own feelings, not one of them thought to look behind them.

So no one, not even Barthos the BoatMaster, noticed one of the nastiest of the black shadow figures leave the group on the shore and slip silently into the river. At a discreet distance, the sinister shadow swam silently along behind the boat.

Chapter Twenty-One
In The Hut

At last, the dreadful Valley of the Lost Souls was behind them. The boat entered a short tunnel that led out into a small, narrow chamber. With deft movements, Barthos the BoatMaster maneuvered them toward the shore. As soon as they reached land, he jumped out of the boat and quickly wrapped the rope around a short stone post.

With Alasdair holding her up and pushing from behind, Barthos tugged a shivering Priscilla out of the boat. Alasdair grabbed their backpacks and scrambled out. Grandmother Wolf leapt onto the shore and shook out her thick wet fur, the whirling cascade of river drops spinning like a wet pinwheel all around her. Eideard fluttered about nearby, muttering "Hoot Mon! Hoot Mon!"

Priscilla managed to walk a few steps on her own, her tennis shoes squishing with water. All at once, her legs simply folded under her, and she sank down to the ground, landing in a soggy heap at Barthos' feet.

He stood rubbing his chin, looking down at her for a moment. Appearing to make a decision, he turned and spoke to Alasdair.

"We need to get this girl out of her wet clothes and warmed up right away or she will catch a chill. My hut is above us. You can stay there tonight. I must go back up the river to make sure no damage has been done."

Alasdair and Barthos, with Priscilla between them, half-carried and half-dragged her to some stairs near the landing. Grandmother Wolf, with Eideard riding on her back, followed along behind.

Priscilla barely knew where she was or where they were going. All she was aware of was how tired and weak she felt. Her body felt numb with cold, and her heavy wet clothes chafed uncomfortably against her skin. Images of light and dark shadows, the Dark Ship and her father, and Inky and the Light flashed one after the other through her mind. Underneath it all, she felt miserably guilty about the trouble she was causing everyone.

Barthos and Alasdair somehow managed to haul her up to the top of a long stairwell. They went out a doorway into a darkened world, too dark to be able to see anything around them.

Barthos led them through another door into what appeared to be a duplicate of the hut by the pear tree, the place where they had begun their perilous journey. It now felt like eons ago to Priscilla.

Grandmother Wolf and Eideard opted to stay outside, possibly to see about getting some supper, though more probably to check and make sure they were safe. They disappeared into the darkness.

Inside the hut, Barthos lit a candle and set it down. With Alasdair's help, he quickly stripped Priscilla of her outer clothing, wrapped her in a heavy blanket, and laid her on a bed. They moved with such haste, she barely had time to feel any embarrassment.

She lay on her side warming up, and dozing off and on for a while. After some time, she could feel the blood starting to flow through her limbs again, and she was able to look around the inside of the hut.

They had put her on the lower of two small bunk beds set against one wall. The candle flickered on a small wooden table in the center of the room. A lost-looking Alasdair sat on one of two short wooden benches drawn up next to the table. A third bench on the far side of the room held a little brown jug, a large pitcher, a basin, and some towels. On the wall above it were shelves stacked with an assortment of tools, dishes, and food.

Barthos had started a fire in an old wood stove set against the back wall. A cooking pot and a large bucket of water were heating on top of the stove. After filling a nearby box with firewood, he unrolled a piece of thick rug and laid it on the floor in front of the fire.

Shadows from the candle flame and the fire danced around the room, though these dark shadows were not at all scary to Priscilla. They made her feel warm, safe, and drowsy. She heard Barthos lift the lid on the pot on the stove to stir whatever was inside. Within short order, the aroma of something tasty blended with the smell of the fire, and her hunger pangs began to revive her.

Watching him through half-closed eyes, she saw Barthos take the bucket of water from the stove and use it to rinse her clothes and shoes. After thoroughly washing and wringing out everything, he hung her clothes on a rope above the wood stove and set her tennis shoes next to it to dry. Then he carried the bucket outside to dump the water.

Once he returned, he set the bucket of fresh water on the stove and said to Alasdair, "The stew will be ready soon. Bread and cheese are on the shelf. Water in the brown jug is for drinking, and the pitcher and basin are for washing."

At the mention of food, Priscilla felt even hungrier. More alert now, she wrapped the blanket tight around herself and sat up on the bed.

Barthos noticed that she was feeling better and told her, "As soon as you feel ready, young lady, I suggest you use the water in the bucket on the stove to rinse the river off you. There are towels by the basin. It will help you feel better."

After a last look around, to make sure he had done all he could, Barthos headed toward the door. Seeming to have an afterthought, he turned and said, "I would recommend you stay inside until morning and keep the door locked. If you have to go outside, it would be best to remain close by the hut. Then nothing should bother you."

"Aren't you going to eat with us?" asked Priscilla. She was trying hard not to think of what might be lurking outside that might want to bother them. "You must be hungry as well." More to the point, she really did not want Barthos to leave them alone.

"I must hurry back to the Valley of the Lost Souls and make sure all is secure," Barthos answered. "I will have supper in my other hut." Already he had gone far beyond his normal duties. It would not be good for him to become any more involved with them.

"Before you leave, Barthos," Alasdair asked, "could you please show us where we are?" He took the map Wanortu had given him from his backpack and spread it on the table.

"You are here at the edge of the Lava Land," Barthos told him, pointing to the same dark spot on the map about which Wanortu had warned them. "Where is it you wish to go?"

"We need to get back to the palace as quickly as possible." Alasdair replied, while Priscilla silently agreed with him. It was time to head back and report to Wanortu. They needed to find out how to get to the Dark Ship to rescue Inky.

Barthos pointed out their route on the map, "You can go across the Lava Land, which, as you can see, will take you directly to the Fairy Forest and then to the Merry Meadow. It is the fastest way, but it is also dangerous, so I do not recommend it. A longer, but much safer way is to by-pass the Lava Land. You will have to go here along the edge of the Lava Land and up into the Mara Mountains to this point here, where you will see the River of Return just below you. If you follow the path along the cliff's edge, it will lead you down to the Fairy Forest."

After Priscilla and Alasdair thanked him and said their goodbyes, Barthos the BoatMaster left them on their own once more. Priscilla was feeling stronger now. Once Alasdair had put away the map, she told him, "I need to wash off the river water. Could you please go outside for a little while? I'll be as quick as I can."

Alasdair did as she asked. After he closed the door, she jumped up and hurriedly washed herself off as best as she could. Then she rinsed out her old underwear, and hung it up on the rope to dry, thankful she had brought a clean set with her.

After washing her hair, she rinsed off her rainbow ribbon. While she was hanging it up, she thought briefly about the second half of the *Secret of the Rainbow Ribbon.* She still had no clue what it could be. With all that was going on, there was no time to think about it.

Once she had wrapped the blanket around her again, she called Alasdair back inside. She sat on the rug Barthos had so thoughtfully provided and dried her hair with the heat of the fire.

Alasdair took the basin of water outside to dump it. He had not been gone for long when Priscilla heard him call out, "Who's there? Is someone there? Is that you, Grandmother Wolf?"

Nothing but silence answered his questions. After another moment, he hurried back inside and quickly closed and locked the door.

Priscilla's voice shook as she asked, "What's wrong?"

"I don't know, but I thought I heard footsteps." Breathing hard, he set the empty bucket down by the fire. "I had the weirdest feeling that someone or something was out there watching me. I thought it might be Grandmother Wolf, but she didn't answer when I called."

All at once, there was a scratching at the door. Priscilla and Alasdair cringed in fear.

The scratching came again, followed by a voice calling gently, "It is I, Grandmother Wolf. Please let me in."

Priscilla and Alasdair looked at one another in relief as each of them whispered at the same time, "Not by the hair of my chinny-chin-chin!" This got them to giggling, which melted away their fear. Grandmother Wolf was definitely not a big bad wolf.

Alasdair opened the door and let Grandmother Wolf into the hut, with Eideard zipping in right behind her. Then he closed and locked the door for the night, shutting out the darkness and anything else lingering outside.

"I thought I heard you call me as I was on my way back, Alasdair," Grandmother Wolf said. "Did you need something?"

"While I was outside I heard footsteps. I thought someone or something was watching me, so I called out to see if it was you. It must have been my imagination, or maybe I heard you in the distance."

"Yes, I'm sure that must have been it," Grandmother Wolf said, though she did not sound convinced. When she lay down on the rug in front of the fire next to Priscilla, she remained alert, keeping her eyes fixed on the door.

Eideard watched her for a moment before perching on the clothesline next to Priscilla's familiar overalls. He, too, kept his hooded eyes on the door.

Priscilla and Alasdair found a couple of empty bowls and some chunks of cheese and bread on the shelf and carried them to the table. They filled their bowls with the hot vegetable stew from the pot and ate a hearty meal. After they finished, they put their dishes into the empty bucket and joined Grandmother Wolf on the rug.

Alasdair added more wood to the fire, and for a time they sat in silence watching the flickering flames. What had happened to them in the Land of Shadows remained present in their minds and in their hearts.

Priscilla was the first to speak. "I'm sorry I jumped into the river and caused everyone so much trouble. I wanted to help my father. I didn't think about anything else. I know he wasn't really there, but he *is* in some kind of trouble. I wish I knew what to do. I hope I didn't cause any harm by what I did."

Reaching over, she flung her arms around Grandmother Wolf and laid her head against the wolf's furry neck. "Thanks for risking your life for me again, Grandmother Wolf. That's the second time you've saved me. You were just in time. I was heading into the tunnel of light like people do when they're dying."

"Actually the light was Alasdair's idea, Priscilla," Grandmother Wolf told her. "He held his shell underwater so the beam of light could find you. That way I could see where you were."

"So that was it!" exclaimed Priscilla. "It wasn't the tunnel of light at all, it was the Black Carapas. Thank you, Alasdair."

He continued to stare into the fire as if he had not heard her.

"Are you okay?" Priscilla asked, reaching out and touching his shoulder.

"Yeah, I'm okay," he muttered, his attention still somewhere else.

"Alasdair." Grandmother Wolf waited until he gave her his full attention. Gently, but firmly, she told him, "I don't think you are okay at all. It will help you to talk about what is on your mind and in your heart. You will feel better. Please talk to us."

After a few moments, Alasdair took her wise advice and began to speak, his voice just above a whisper. "All my life I've believed my father committed suicide. My mother told me his death was an accident, but I never believed her. I thought she made up a story to protect me. Now I know she told me the truth. My father didn't kill himself. It really *was* an accident."

"He just wanted to protect you so that what happened to his brother did not happen to you," Grandmother Wolf told him. "You could see how much he loved both of you."

"Yeah, I guess he did," Alasdair went on in a more normal voice. "I owe my mother a huge apology. I've been rough on her. We've never been able to talk about my father, even though she always wanted to."

"Why didn't you believe your mother?" Priscilla asked.

"It was something my grandfather said to me a long time ago. He was upset and angry with me; I don't even remember why. Anyway, he called me a freak and told me no one could possibly love such a freak. He said it was no wonder my father had killed himself rather than raise such a freak. I never forgot it."

Grandmother Wolf said with great sadness in her voice, "Thoughtless words such as those, when spoken to vulnerable children, become curses. They wound deeply and are difficult to forget. It is one of the reasons we should always be careful what we say to children and to one another, especially when we speak in the midst of hurt and anger. I am glad you learned the truth about your father today, Alasdair."

Priscilla looked pensive. "Granny told me that there are people who try to take away parts of us and make us less of who we are so that they can make themselves feel better. Maybe your grandfather was trying to make himself feel better, Alasdair."

"I guess so," he responded. Then his face changed as if he had just realized something. "But you know what? I don't have to believe his words any more. I can believe my mother. She's the one who told me the truth."

"That's right, Alasdair," Grandmother Wolf told him. "You are old enough now to choose whom and what you want to believe. That way you can break the hold the curse has had on you."

Alasdair sat up, looking much better. In a little while, he turned and said to Priscilla, "What about you? You had a hard time as well."

Priscilla told them about her mother's death and all that she had remembered.

After Priscilla finished talking, Grandmother Wolf said in her soft voice, "It seems each of you lost one of your parents when you were very young. Such enormous losses are difficult for young children to handle."

Priscilla thought about her mother. She knew so little about her. It felt confusing to open this door in her memory again. She was not quite sure what to do with it. Granny and Grandmother Wolf were more real to her than a mother she could barely remember.

They talked on for a little while about what they had seen in the Land of Shadows and how frightening it had been. Before long, Priscilla started to lose track of the conversation. When she nodded off for the third time, she announced, "I need to go to bed. I can't keep my eyes open any longer."

Alasdair agreed. "Good idea. I've had it." He stuffed enough logs into the wood stove to fill it and keep it burning, and then they all said goodnight to one another.

Alasdair climbed into the upper bunk, and Priscilla crawled into the lower one. It had been an exciting, scary, and utterly exhausting day. Before long, they were both sound asleep.

Priscilla dreamed that a fierce wind kept slamming against the hut. Some frightful creature was snarling and growling just outside the door. She was inside with the three little pigs, and the big bad wolf was trying to blow their hut down.

Since neither Grandmother Wolf nor Eideard said anything in the morning about what had happened during the night, Priscilla never knew that much of what she heard did not come from her dreams.

Chapter Twenty-Two
The Reckoning

They arose at daybreak. Grandmother Wolf and Eideard headed out to find something to eat and to scout around to see if it was safe to leave the hut. Priscilla and Alasdair ate some hard-boiled eggs and fruit left over from Mother Nature's breakfast. Figuring Barthos would approve, they packed some of his supply of bread and cheese for their lunch. Since it was going be a long day out in the sun, they slathered on plenty of sunscreen.

After Grandmother Wolf and Eideard returned with the all clear signal, the four of them set out on their journey once again. Heeding advice to avoid the Lava Land, they took the path leading up into the Mara Mountains.

In the gray light of the early morning, the Lava Land looked dry and desolate, much like the Valley of the Lost Souls. Priscilla shuddered at the memory of that horrible place. Just as Wanortu had described it, lumpy gray volcanic rocks covered the ground with no green or shade anywhere in sight. It was easy to see how anyone could get lost in such a place. Thank goodness they had chosen to go a different way.

Once more, they followed Grandmother Wolf's swift pace over the lower rocky formations leading up into the mountains. Priscilla was happy to leave the barren land behind them. They climbed until they got beyond the first set of rocks and sat down to rest. Frog would have said the day was going to be ppp-perfectly ppp-pleasant.

Grandmother Wolf went scouting once more. It was clear she was uneasy. Feeling nervous, Priscilla asked Alasdair, "Do you think we're still in some kind of danger?"

He answered, "I don't know, but Grandmother Wolf and Eideard must think so. They've both been really jumpy since we left." Eideard had been flying in circles above them and had not spent much time on Priscilla's shoulder since they had begun their trek.

When Grandmother Wolf came back, they all set off again. After several hours and a long hard climb, they finally arrived at a path leading along the edge of a cliff. A river gleamed in the sunshine far below them.

"That has to be the River of Return," Priscilla cried. "Barthos said if we stay on the path by the river, we should be able to find our way back down to the forest. It should be easy from here. Let's stop and eat something. I'm starving!" Since they had come this far and not been bothered, she figured they must have left anything sinister behind them.

Priscilla and Alasdair sat down on some rocks near the path to have a snack. Grandmother Wolf and Eideard left to scout around. Alasdair ate quickly and then leaned back against a rock for a short nap while he waited for Grandmother Wolf and Eideard to return.

Feeling restless after her snack, Priscilla walked over to the edge of the cliff to look down once more at the river. The sight of the flowing water sparkling in the sun reenergized her. Anxious to get back to the palace to make plans to rescue Inky, she was ready to be on the move again. Assuming the others would soon follow, she set off along the path. It was such a lovely day that soon she began to run and skip in pure delight.

The path took her along the river to a point where it led up and over a large rock formation. She climbed carefully up the gentle slope and made her way across the top of the rock. From there, the view of the mountains was impressive, so she stopped for a moment to admire it before continuing.

A wide cleft in the rock made it necessary for her to climb down and go through a small enclosure before rejoining the path where it continued up and over the rock on the far side. In great spirits, she decided this would be a fun place to hide and surprise the others when they came along. With great energy, she jumped down into the gap.

After she landed, she looked around. In an instant, her happy smile vanished. Someone, or something, had already used her idea of hiding in this spot. A few feet in front of her, a monstrous black shadow figure loomed up, a nasty smirk on its face. It was one of the evil-looking shadows from the Valley of the Lost Souls.

Her heart leapt into her throat as she let out a piercing shriek. Stepping back as far as she could, she stopped only when her backpack pressed painfully into her back. Rock walls surrounded her, and beyond the figure, the enclosure opened up to the edge of the cliff. She was trapped. As she stood frozen with fright, the terrifying figure gave her a malevolent sneer and began moving toward her.

A silver streak shot like a bullet in front of Priscilla, pouncing on the dark shadow, knocking him away from her. Grandmother Wolf had arrived. Fierce snarls filled the air as the big wolf and the black shadow rolled across the ground, tearing and clawing at one another. They looked evenly matched in size and strength.

Priscilla gasped in horror as they rolled toward the edge of the cliff. She held her breath until they rolled back toward her. Her relief did not last long. The shadow broke free of the wolf and moved once more toward Priscilla. He came within inches of her. The feel and smell of his hot foul breath repulsed her, making her nauseous.

All at once, something dragged him away from her. Bared fangs had chomped into his leg. With a loud grunt, he kicked Grandmother Wolf hard with his other leg, knocking her off. Then he turned and lunged at the big wolf, grabbing her by the throat, and holding her down so she could barely move.

A tiny gray bird flew at the shadow's forehead and pecked him with ferocity. Eideard the Owl's sneak attack surprised the shadow into easing his tight grip on Grandmother Wolf's neck, enabling her to pull out of his grasp. She lay on her side, panting, obviously beginning to tire.

Priscilla stood paralyzed as the creature once again started toward her.

Alasdair hung out over the edge of the enclosure, yelling loudly and waving his hands to cause a distraction. There was no room for him to climb down into the small space without endangering them all.

The monster was oblivious to Alasdair's yelling or to Eideard flying again and again at his head. This time, he simply brushed the tiny owl away as if he were an annoying insect.

Priscilla glanced about for something to throw, but nothing was available. Shrinking back into the rock as far as she could, she wondered if anything could stop him.

Grandmother Wolf must have had a similar thought because she lifted her head and looked fully into Priscilla's eyes for a long moment. Turning away at last, she made a powerful flying leap at the shadow figure, knocking him off balance. Grabbing hold of his upper arm with her teeth, she clamped down and held on tight. The dark figure roared in pain as he struggled to shake the big wolf off his arm, but she would not let go.

As Priscilla watched in horror, Grandmother Wolf dragged him away, toward the edge of the cliff. He pulled back, and they rolled over and over again. This time, when they rolled toward the edge of the cliff, they did not stop. Rolling right over the edge, they both disappeared from view.

Priscilla screamed, "Noooooooooo!" and burst into tears as she ran toward the cliff. "Noooooooooo!" she kept on screaming and crying.

"Priscilla!" Alasdair yelled at her. He jumped down into the enclosure, rushed up behind her, and pulled her back from the edge. They looked over the cliff in time to see the shadow figure plummet like a stone into the river below. But where was Grandmother Wolf? She had not fallen into the river at the same time.

When they leaned out a little farther, they saw why. The big wolf was just beneath them, her claws clinging to a ledge of rock jutting out of the cliff. Priscilla threw herself down on her belly. With Alasdair holding on to her ankles, she stretched down as far as she could, but Grandmother Wolf was just beyond her reach.

"Hold on, Grandmother Wolf! We'll find a way to get to you." Priscilla's words sounded as frantic as she felt.

"No, little granddaughter, it is too dangerous," Grandmother Wolf told her in her gentle but firm voice. "The shadow and the curse will only be satisfied if I go with him. It is the way it must be. Take care of each other, my dears. Remember all you have learned and will continue to learn on your journey. Try not to mourn too much for me. It is my choice to give my life for yours. Goodbye, my dear little ones."

With these loving words, and a last look at both of them, her love for them shining in her soft amber eyes, Grandmother Wolf let her claws scrape slowly off the ledge. Then, like the shadow figure before her, she tumbled down into the river. Grandmother Wolf had saved Priscilla's life for the third and last time.

As the courageous and loving wolf fell to her death, an unearthly soulful howl surged up from deep within Priscilla and echoed across the mountains in a haunting wail. Alasdair wept and Eideard hooted in a sorrowful background chorus.

Slowly, and then with an increasing intensity, resounding off every rock and cliff, plaintive cries and howls arose in waves from every corner of the kingdom, wrapping the sad little trio in a heavy blanket of sound. All Mother Nature's creatures were mourning the loss of one of their Very Own Precious Ones.

For what seemed like an eternity, Priscilla lay sobbing at the edge of the cliff. After a time, numbness replaced her tears. Her weeping stopped. She did not want to feel any more. It was all over. Her life had ended. There was no point in going on.

As she lay there, the same thoughts kept repeating in her mind, *"It's my fault Grandmother Wolf is dead. If I hadn't jumped into the River of Shadows, the monster wouldn't have come after us. Grandmother Wolf wouldn't have died saving me. Everyone I love seems to die... my mother, Granny, Grandmother Wolf. Maybe even Inky and Daddy as well. I can't do anything to stop it. All the people I love die. It's all my fault. I don't want to love anyone any more. I won't love anyone any more. It hurts too much..."*

Alasdair tried to pull her away from the edge of the cliff, as he had done several times before. This time she did not fight him. What did it matter anyway? One thing for sure, she was not going to let herself love him. That would seal his fate for sure.

Eideard flew down to land on her shoulder. He whispered softly in her ear, "Easy noo, ma wee lassie. It hurts ye noo, but the ache, 'twill lessen. 'Twill git better in time. Hoot Mon!"

"It *won't* get better!" Priscilla snapped at the little owl, pushing him off her shoulder onto the ground. Eideard was another one she was not going to love any more. "How could it possibly ever be better again?" she cried, her voice filled with bitterness.

Eideard picked himself up and flew over to a nearby rock. He was wise enough to understand that her anger came from her pain. "Ach aye, lassie, I ken 'tis hard to imagine it noo, but in time 'twill grow easier. And speaking of time, we must move on, lassie. The day is passin', an' we've a lang way tae gae. Hoot Mon!" The wise little owl knew she needed to get up and get moving. It was not good for her to stay in this place any longer.

Alasdair took the hint and helped Priscilla get to her feet. She allowed him to tug her toward the path leading up over the rock and out of the enclosure.

"Wait!" she cried, pulling all her last reserves of energy together. "There is something I have to do." Before Alasdair could grab her, she rushed back to the edge of the cliff.

"No, Priscilla!" Alasdair started to go after her for fear of what she was planning.

Eideard called out to him, "Let 'er go, laddie. She'll be a'right. Hoot Mon!"

Priscilla stood for a moment with tears in her eyes looking down at the river far below. This was the final resting place for her beloved Grandmother Wolf. Reaching into one of her pockets, she took out her favorite heart-shaped stone and held it in the palm of hand.

Lifting it up to her lips, she kissed it as she whispered, "Thank you, dear Grandmother Wolf, for being in my life. I will never forget you. Go now and join your granddaughter in the ocean. May you both rest in peace." With these last words, she tossed her favorite stone down into the River of Return to be with Grandmother Wolf. It was all she could think of to do to honor her beloved friend.

Slowly, she turned and walked back toward Alasdair and Eideard, saying, "I'm finished now." And finished is what she felt, in every possible way. It had taken all the strength she had left to do what she knew to be right for Grandmother Wolf. She had nothing more to give.

They climbed out of the enclosure, crossed over the rock, and found their way down to where the path continued along the river. Priscilla dragged along behind Alasdair and Eideard. She had to focus to lift up one heavy foot after the other.

Somewhere along the way, she sensed Eideard on her shoulder, though she had no idea when he got there. Vaguely aware that Alasdair had taken hold of her arm and was pulling her along, she could not stir up enough interest to care much at all.

A whistling sound began to ring in her ears and kept growing louder. Without much curiosity, she wondered what could be happening. It didn't really seem to matter. Through the thick fog in her head, she heard Alasdair shouting at her, "Priscilla, we've got to find some shelter quickly."

She had no idea why he was saying this or what he meant. Her arm was jerked hard, and at the same time, something pushed against her. It felt as if she were being pulled in one direction and pushed in the opposite direction at the same time. Some force kept slamming against her body, pressing her off the path toward the edge of the cliff. The ringing in her ears had become so loud she could no longer think, even if she had wanted to bother.

Alasdair yelled in her ear. "Up there in the rocks… there's some kind of ledge. It could be shelter. Let's head for it." Grabbing her hand, he pulled her away from the path and up over the rocks.

Somehow, with Alasdair pulling her and Eideard shouting encouraging words in her ear, they slowly made their way. When they got to the ledge, they climbed down behind it into a more sheltered area.

Almost immediately, the ringing in Priscilla's ears stopped, and she could no longer feel the weight pressing against her body. Without the sound and the pressure, she felt bereft. In some peculiar way, they had mirrored the chaos inside her head, giving her a sense of comfort.

Alasdair announced, "At least we have some shelter. This must be one of those Wild Wicked Windstorms Wanortu warned us about. We could've been blown over the edge of the cliff!"

He looked all around him, and then he cried out with great excitement, "Hey, there's an opening in the rock. It looks like an entrance to some kind of cave. Let's see where it goes. Come on!" He grabbed Priscilla's hand again and pulled her into the hole with him. She followed along behind him like a little lost lamb.

Eideard called ahead to Alasdair, "Laddie, ye need tae gae slow as ye've nae idea what lies ahead of ye. Hoot Mon!"

If Alasdair heard Eideard's cautious warning, he gave no indication of it. He continued to go deeper into the hole, pulling Priscilla along behind him. When it became too dark to see, he used the Black Carapas to light the way ahead.

As they made their way along what turned out to be another tunnel, they came to a spot where they had to bend their heads down low and crawl on all fours, like animals. The tunnel curved around a number of times, and then, unexpectedly, it ended.

Pulling themselves forward out of the tunnel, they stood up and looked all around them. Alasdair was right. They had entered a huge cave. Light came from a hole in the roof far above them. A pool of water lay over to one side, and they started to move toward it.

A fierce, growling sound came out of nowhere as something huge and black loomed up in front of them, blocking their path and the light from above.

Priscilla stopped dead in her tracks. It was happening all over again. Here was another horrible dark shadow figure she had to face. She had no strength left with which to fight. And her dear Grandmother Wolf was no longer alive to save her. It was all over. She could hold on no longer.

A thick gooey darkness, as black as the figure in front of her, spread over her mind and her body, like oil spreading across the ocean. She slumped, unconscious, to the floor of the cave.

Chapter Twenty-Three
The Bear Cave

It would be some time before Priscilla would learn that the dark figure in front of her was not another evil shadow. Priscilla and Alasdair had stumbled into the lair of a mother bear and her cubs in the midst of hibernation. The dark figure turned out to be a big black mother bear.

The unfamiliar sound of the Wild Wicked Wind echoing through the cave had wakened the three tiny cubs. Mother Bear was trying to settle them when she heard intruders entering her den. She went to investigate, with the cubs, now thoroughly awake, tagging along behind her.

Mother Bear scooped up the unconscious Priscilla and laid her down on the soft warm bed of dried grass and moss where she and her cubs had been sleeping. The three little bears sniffled and snuffled at Priscilla, curious about this unknown creature lying in their bed.

Their mother gently shooed them away. She turned to a stunned Alasdair and spoke in a deep powerful voice that made him quiver right down to his toenails. "This little one is in shock. Something has depleted her Life Spirit. I will lie with her to keep her warm and safe while she is on her journey to find her Spirit. She must rest until her Spirit returns to her body. Please take care of my cubs while I attend to her."

The huge black bear lay down next to Priscilla. With her paws, she tenderly pulled the lifeless girl close to her warm furry chest and held her in a great big bear hug.

Alasdair stood still, utterly dumbfounded.

Eideard had flown onto Alasdair's shoulder when Priscilla collapsed. He stayed quiet, watching and listening to Mother Bear, trying to determine if Priscilla was safe. Now he whispered to Alasdair, "Trust this Mither Bear, laddie. She has a healin' spirit. The wee lassie is in gud hands. Hoot Mon!"

The three little bear cubs turned their curiosity to Alasdair and Eideard. Sniffing playfully at Alasdair's heels and nipping at his pants, they demanded he pay attention to them. From time to time, they darted quizzical glances at the funny little talking bird.

Alasdair took one last look at Priscilla and agreed with Eideard. She seemed to be in safe hands... well... paws. Anyway, he could think of nothing he could do for her, especially as he had no idea what was wrong. He looked down at the inquisitive little cubs gnawing on his shoelaces and laughed in delight. Priscilla was lost to mind for the moment.

Alasdair and Eideard went off to explore the cave with their fuzzy wuzzy little charges in tow. The excited cubs tumbled and wrestled with one another as they tagged along after Alasdair. Their funny antics made it easy for him to give them names. He called the three little bear stooges, Moe, Larry, and Curly.

Priscilla had disappeared into a dark tunnel inside her mind. The comfortable blackness enveloped her in its invisible grasp. If only she could remain immersed in the dark forever, she would be content. Here there were no black shadows to fear. No longer did she have to fight anyone or worry about anything. She did not have to feel the pain of losing someone she loved. In fact, she felt nothing at all. This was what she wanted… to feel absolutely nothing at all.

Tendrils of a haunting melody wafted out of the darkness to curl their soft sweet sounds gently into her ears. Priscilla tried to ignore the beguiling music but, like one of the Pied Piper's children, she felt drawn toward it and strained to hear more. Amongst the melodious sounds, she thought she could pick out her name being whispered over and over again, "Priscilla, Priscilla, Priscilla…"

Without noticing she had made any decision to do so, she began floating through the darkness toward the music. Though she tried to turn back, she did not seem to have the power to do anything but continue in the one direction. The darkness felt comfortable as she drifted along.

To her dismay, a brilliant white light shone out in front of her, whisking away the comforting darkness, causing her to squint in the sudden glare. The music seemed to be coming from deep within the light.

As she moved helplessly forward, she entered into a light tunnel similar to the one she had seen in the River of Shadows. If this was Alasdair holding the Black Carapas open again, she did not want to go back to him and to all the pain in the world. Yet she seemed incapable of turning away.

Dreadfully tired, all she wanted to do was lie down somewhere and sleep forever, but the music continued to whisper her name. Anyway, the bright light made it impossible to sleep in the tunnel, and since she could not seem to do otherwise, she kept moving.

Ahead of her, at the end of the tunnel, loomed a gaping black hole. This hole did not frighten her, as it might have done once, such a long, long time ago. In fact, she wanted it… no… she needed to fall into the dark hole. The oblivion of darkness was exactly what she needed at this moment more than anything else.

With no fear at all, and with immense relief, she allowed herself to be drawn toward the dark hole with nothing but the hopeful anticipation of finding the long rest for which she yearned.

The music grew louder, puzzling her. Maybe she was in the real tunnel of light and what she was hearing were angel harps, though the sounds seemed too energetic for heavenly music. As carefully as she could, given the state she was in, she listened. She thought she could hear the beating of drums, the tinkling of bells, and the high sweet sound of a pipe. Faint whispers of chanting, singing, and even the rippling sounds of laughter, blended in with the sounds of the instruments.

She sighed deeply. Surely, heaven would not be a busy noisy place. It should be quiet so she could sleep. Maybe she was heading to that other hotter place she had heard about. It did not really matter. All she wanted was some stillness, and ultimately, to rest in the darkness.

When the light tunnel ended, she did not fall into the dark void for which she so longed. Instead, she had entered a deep, dark grove of the widest, tallest, and oldest fir trees she had ever seen. The thick gnarled trunks reached up to the sky and extended wider than her arms could reach. The last time she remembered seeing such huge trees was in an old growth redwood forest in California.

The music and singing appeared to be coming from deeper within the forest. A faint glow radiated out through the trees from the same spot. Again, without her choosing it, she began floating forward toward whatever waited there for her.

Moving swiftly around the trees and through the forest, she lost all sense of time. Before she knew it, she had left the trees and entered an open space. Only then, did she stop moving and feel her feet once more touch solid ground. Openmouthed, she stood motionless, staring at what she saw in front of her.

A fire burned in a round pit in the middle of a clearing. Giant fir trees surrounded the clearing, growing so close together, they seemed to be offering their strength and protection to the blazing circle within, much like the little guards surrounded the Sacred Light in the Palace of the Aureole. Somewhere, deep in that special place inside her, she knew she was about to enter an ancient and holy sanctuary, a cathedral in the forest.

Gathered all around the fire, dancing, chanting, singing, and playing the instruments she had been hearing, were a number of women, most of them about the same age or older than Granny. They were clothed in long richly colored gowns and flowered headdresses. The aura of light surrounding each woman made all of them glow in the dark like fireflies. If it were even remotely possible, their auras shone more vividly than the brilliant flames of the fire.

One glimmering figure left the others, appearing almost to glide across the clearing toward Priscilla. She was dressed in a deep purple gown with matching purple flowers in her headdress.

As she came closer, Priscilla saw her thick chestnut-colored hair and her round jolly face.

With a great shriek of surprise and happiness, she ran toward the woman with more enthusiasm and energy than she had felt in a long time.

"Granny! Granny!" she cried, throwing her arms around her beloved grandmother. "I never thought I'd see you again. I can't believe it! I've missed you so! How could you have left me without even letting me say goodbye?" she laughed and cried and chastised her grandmother all at once.

"Hello, Priscilla, my dear child." Granny smiled at her as she hugged her back. "I am so glad you are here."

"But where am I?" demanded Priscilla, "Am I dead? Am I in heaven? Who are all these people? How did I get here?"

Granny laughed merrily. "I can see you are as full of questions as ever, my little granddaughter, but one thing at a time. First, there is someone who wants to see you and who you will want to see." Taking Priscilla by the hand, she led her toward the group around the fire.

A figure Priscilla had not noticed before stepped out of the shadows and moved slowly toward her. She was much younger than the other women and wore a ruby red gown with red roses entwined in her auburn hair. Priscilla thought she was the most beautiful woman she had ever seen.

Her mind flashed back to the Land of Shadows. All at once, she knew who this woman was… her mother. Tears ran down Priscilla's cheeks as she shyly approached the woman who had given birth to her and yet about whom she knew so little. Her mother reached out, took Priscilla in her arms, and hugged her close to her chest.

The sweet scent of roses and the warmth of her mother's yielding body soon had Priscilla relaxing completely into her mother's embrace. She felt as if she had come home at last. She belonged here.

After a few moments, much too short a time for Priscilla, her mother put her hands on Priscilla's shoulders and gently pulled back from her. Continuing to hold her, she took a long loving look at her daughter. "You are so lovely, my little daughter. Even though you are going through a difficult ordeal, I can see how strong you are. You are everything a mother would want her daughter to be. I am so proud of you." She pulled Priscilla close and hugged her once again.

Taking a still-stunned Priscilla by the hand, her mother led her toward the fire, as she said, "Come, there is someone else here you will wish to see."

A large shimmering four-footed creature arose from the other side of the fire pit and padded around toward Priscilla.

"Hello, little granddaughter," the silver creature greeted Priscilla, love shining in her amber eyes. Grandmother Wolf stood in front of Priscilla once again.

Priscilla could not believe what she was seeing. Shouting with joy, she ran to her dear wolf and flung her arms around her neck. Hugging her tightly, she once again moistened the big wolf's fur with her tears. "Oh, Grandmother Wolf, you don't know how I've missed you and longed to see you. I'm so sorry I caused your death."

Grandmother Wolf lifted her head and looked at Priscilla with great gentleness. "I am glad to see you too little granddaughter. You must not blame yourself. I made a choice to give my life for yours. It is what I wanted to do. I was not able to save my own granddaughter, so I was grateful to be able to save you."

Priscilla did not believe this, but at the moment, nothing else mattered. Grandmother Wolf was here with her again, and Granny and her mother as well. Never before had she felt so happy.

All the other women moved to surround Priscilla and her loved ones. Looking at each of them, she saw only love and acceptance shining in their eyes. She felt as if she were inside a circle of light and love.

She knew instinctively this was where she belonged. Her tired feeling had disappeared. The burden of sadness and loss she had been carrying had been lifted from her, and she felt as light as a feather. This was where she wanted to be and where she planned to stay.

Granny took Priscilla by the hand and led her toward an old hollowed out stump near the fire pit. The shape of the stump reminded her of King Sol's throne. Granny gently set her on the moss and grass cushion that softened the hard wood of the stump seat. Then she knelt on the ground in front of Priscilla. Her mother, the other women, and Grandmother Wolf circled close to kneel or stand next to Granny.

Though she had no idea of what might be about to happen to her, Priscilla's Light Detector told her it was going to be something quite remarkable.

Chapter Twenty-Four
The Reclaiming

"My dear little granddaughter," Granny told Priscilla, "It is time for you to begin to learn who you are and where you come from. It is important for you to know this so that you can go on with your journey."

"Oh, but I don't need to go anywhere else. I am exactly where I want to be right now. I want to stay here. This is where I belong." Priscilla sat up primly and folded her arms in front of her, a look of defiance on her face.

To Priscilla's dismay, Granny said, "This is not your place yet, my dear. You still have much living to do. It is your sacred duty to grow up and become the woman you are meant to be."

"But I don't want to grow up in a scary world where people hurt each other all the time and where people I love keep dying. I don't want to live there," Priscilla cried insistently. "Why can't I stay here with all of you?"

In response, Granny only gave her a patient smile. Priscilla knew from experience with this familiar look that she was not going to get her way. Giving a sulky sigh, she sank back into the mossy cushion. However, she still allowed herself to feel curious about what was going to happen.

Her mother stepped forward and knelt on the grass in front of her next to Granny. She held an old earthenware pitcher cupped in her hands.

Granny took hold of the side handles of the pitcher as she spoke with great solemnity to Priscilla. "This ancient vessel contains Holy Water from our Sacred Spring, Priscilla. With this Holy Water we will now anoint you and bless you, my child."

Dipping one hand into the pitcher, Granny reached out and sprinkled a few drops of Holy Water on the crown of Priscilla's head and then on her forehead, nose, and cheeks. The drops felt cool and fresh as they dripped down her hair and face.

Granny said, "I bless you, my dearest granddaughter, with the wisdom to discern and value your own truth and with the courage to speak out and act upon your truth no matter how hard it might be. May you come to know and trust the voice deep within your heart, allowing it to lead you to the unveiling of your soul. May you learn to trust your inner guidance and your intuitive ability to always find the Light in the Darkness." Granny then held the pitcher while Priscilla's mother followed the same anointing procedure.

As her mother sprinkled Holy Water on Priscilla, she said, "My darling daughter, I bless you with the courage to be able to give and receive love. May you have the strength to keep your heart open, even though it will be broken time and again. May you learn to love others with everything you are and all you will become. May you remember how profoundly loved you are and come to know the full richness of love given and love received."

As her mother stepped back, Granny held the pitcher down low and tipped it to one side. Grandmother Wolf came forward and dipped her snout into the pitcher. With a dripping wet nose, she put her paws on Priscilla's knees. Priscilla bent her head forward, and the big wolf touched her cold wet nose to Priscilla's head, then to her forehead, and moved down to her cheeks and nose.

When she felt the wolf's cold nose touch hers, it tickled. Priscilla started to giggle. Grandmother Wolf sat back on her haunches and looked at her with love, as always, shining in her amber eyes. Priscilla quickly pulled herself together.

The big wolf spoke, "Little granddaughter, I bless you with the wisdom to respect and care for all living things, to know and love Nature as part of you, and to have compassion for all the creatures of the earth. May you remember the world of Nature was created to give you, and all the beings on the earth, sustenance, knowledge, and pleasure. May you continue to care for the earth and all her creatures and work to preserve her gifts so that other generations may in turn enjoy them."

One by one, the other women in the circle followed Grandmother Wolf, anointing and blessing Priscilla. From one woman, she received the blessing of patience and acceptance, some of which she began to use right away, especially since she was not going to get to stay in this place forever as she wished she could.

Another woman blessed her with goodness of heart and loyalty to those with whom her heart connected. Priscilla instantly felt her love for all those who were in her life. After she received the gift of humor and the ability to see the absurd, she laughed with delight. When she was blessed with the gift of caring for those less fortunate, a sense of compassion for others flooded through her body.

The blessing of courage to face whatever was hers in life to face came next. After receiving this blessing, she felt sure she could manage anything that came her way.

Feeling deeply honored by the anointing and touched by the blessings and the love surrounding her, Priscilla took it all in as best as her mind and heart could do at this moment in time. Even though she did not fully understand everything, she tucked each blessing away in the special place inside her.

Granny and Priscilla's mother came forward again and knelt before Priscilla, each holding one of the handles of the vessel of Holy Water. When Priscilla looked into their loving eyes, she sensed that something momentous was about to happen. She began to tremble all over. Even so, she could still feel her heart open up to whatever was coming.

Granny said, "Priscilla now is the time for you to reclaim your true name, the name with which you were born. This name is a secret for you to keep deep within your heart and soul. It will help you to remember who you are and what you are meant to do."

Priscilla sat up straight as she tried to quell the trembling. Her mother and her grandmother gently sprinkled Holy Water on her head and face as they had done earlier.

Granny said, "Priscilla, your mother and I anoint you and bless you with the gift of your true name. You are called *She Who Brightens the World.*"

As Priscilla breathed in her name, her shaking abruptly stopped. Something shifted deep inside the special place in her heart. Her true name slipped in to fill the void she did not even know had existed until this moment. She felt complete. The name *She Who Brightens the World* truly belonged to her. This was who she was and always would be.

Priscilla's mother took the pitcher and carried it away. Then Granny stood up and turned toward another woman who had come up behind her, carrying something large and bulky. When Granny turned back to Priscilla, she held a headdress made from the head of a deer, with the antlers still intact.

"Priscilla, my dear," she began. "You are on the cusp of your journey into womanhood. It is your destiny to grow up to become a woman of great wisdom. You will be a guide and a role model for other women to help them find their way home to their own innate wisdom."

She paused to let her words sink in, and then she continued, "You may not understand all that is said to you in this moment, Priscilla. There will even come a time when your mind will forget everything you hear and experience today, though your heart will hold it all for you. One day in the future, when the timing is right, and when you are ready, all you have learned will come back to you. You will remember who you are and what you are meant to do."

With great ceremony, Granny placed the deer headdress on Priscilla's head. Though it felt big and heavy, Priscilla sat up straight, feeling just like a queen at her coronation. In this moment, she truly became the Queen of the Castle.

Stepping back to look at Priscilla, Granny pronounced, "This deer gave his life so that it could serve us in this way, and we give our thanks to him. The deer reminds you of your innate bond with the wild, Priscilla. This wildness is deep within you and is never meant to be tamed. It is the source of the river of life flowing through you.

The deer is a reminder of the purity of your innocence. Your innocence will remain with you throughout your life, even though you may think you have lost it. There will be dark times ahead for you, Priscilla, as you already know. Your life journey will teach you to face and to hold the Darkness in the world along with the Light. You will have to choose to live knowing full well the kind of world it is in which you live.

From your ever-deepening knowledge of the Dark and the Light, your wisdom will grow. When you are of a greater age, and when it is meant to be, you will unite your wisdom with your innocence, thus creating the powerful wise woman you will become." Granny finished with a smile as she moved to one side.

Priscilla's mother glided forward. She carried a thick, glossy, brown fur cloak in her hands, and she gently wrapped it around

Priscilla's shoulders. Even though Priscilla could feel the weight of the cloak, it did not feel at all uncomfortable. Instead, it helped her to feel safe and solidly anchored in place.

This anchoring had become important because something puzzling was happening to her. She had never experienced anything like it before and had no words to describe it. Part of her body appeared to be rising off the throne while the rest of her remained sitting. She had no idea how this could be happening.

Her mother proclaimed, "This fur cloak is a gift from the muskrats, Priscilla. We extend our utmost gratitude to them. It is a reminder, my daughter, that as a woman you are wrapped in beauty and mystery. You have a timeless connection to the depth and breadth of all of creation. As your Spirit journeys through the challenges it must meet on earth, you will always have within you the ability to find your way home to your true self, a place which is anchored deep within you and yet knows no bounds." Her mother finished speaking and stepped back.

Priscilla felt the wisdom of these words touch the special place deep inside her, a place her mother and Granny appeared to know about as well. However, she had no time to think about what it meant as she was focusing more on what was going on in her body.

Light-headed and free, she felt as if she were floating up into the air, except that she knew her body was still sitting on the stump, solidly held in place with the heavy headdress and thick fur cloak. It seemed as if she were in two places at once, which, of course, was impossible.

In her confusion, she giggled and began singing to herself as she rose higher up into the air, *"Here I am… I am me… I am free… I can be anything I want to be… here I am in this moment… I am me…"* Realizing what was happening to her, she exclaimed, *"I'm flying! Wheeee!"*

Some part of her had left her body to fly through the air. She looked down and giggled with glee at how she could be above everyone, and yet at the same time, see herself sitting on the stump by the fire. Somehow, she really *was* in two places at once.

Even though she did not know exactly where she existed in space and time, it felt as if she had been there forever. Nothing and no one seemed separate from her. In the oddest way, she felt herself becoming part of everything and everyone around her, of all that had been, and all that was ever going to be.

Without noticing how it happened, she was running soft-footed through the forest, in sync with her lithe and muscled deer body, feeling the moist earth beneath her hooves, and smelling the sweet fresh air rushing past her broad black nose.

In the next moment, she paddled her webbed feet and swished her long tail in the cool stream, glorying in the surge of water pouring over her thick luxuriant muskrat fur, as she swam home to her watery cave.

In an instant, she whooshed through the trees, a gusty wind blowing through the forest. Then she reached toward the sky, her ancient fir branches swaying and dancing with the wind, her towering, erect trunk firmly rooted deep in the earth.

All at once she was perching, with her talons wrapped around the tippy top branch of the fir tree, overlooking the forest. Spreading her majestic wings wide, she soared with joy into the open sky above the trees, while through her eagle eyes she looked down on everything far and wide.

For just a moment, she poured out her light as the glorious moon reflecting the sun for the earth, and then as a dazzling hot star, she twinkled across the heavens, viewing the whole world as a small round globe in space beneath her.

Becoming a wispy white cloud, she floated gently across the sky, until her quiet spirit darkened and filled with the fury of a fierce storm cloud. As sizzling lightning, she slashed the cloud in two, when suddenly she burst into a thousand raindrops falling into the wild river far below.

She transformed into the mighty river, her rapids swirling and crashing around the rocks as she wended from mountain to ocean.

For a heartrending time, she knew the fierce determination of the brave mother salmon fighting her way up the raging river, an innate desire to spawn the next generation her one driving force.

Spreading her hands wide she expanded into a glorious rainbow after a storm, shining over all the earth, offering the promise of new life to come.

Very slowly, one at a time, she became her mother, Granny, Grandmother Wolf, and each of the women in the circle by the fire. She saw through their eyes, knew the great wisdom of their hearts, and felt the deep love they had for her and for all of creation. In this moment, she experienced what it was like to be part of all nature and of every being and knew how truly connected to everything and everyone she was. She wanted to hold on forever to this feeling and never let go.

However, this was not to be, for even as she thought of holding on, she could sense the beginning of her reconnection to her body. Soon the hardness of the stump was pressing against her, and once again, she could feel her separateness from everyone and everything around her.

Her moment of freedom and union was now only a memory... another one to tuck away in the special place created inside her heart to hold such joyous experiences.

Yet, she felt different. Something had changed within her. Even though she did not quite understand how or why, she felt more at peace than ever before. She knew who she was, and she knew she could go on. She would be okay. Most of all, she knew she could allow herself to love again.

Priscilla looked around at all the faces watching her. From their serene smiles and the knowing look in their eyes, they were well aware of where she had been. Turning to Granny, she asked, "What happened to me?"

Granny smiled gently at her. "Your Spirit has been on a journey, my little granddaughter. Now you know you are, have always been, and always will be part of Nature, part of all Life. You have learned that those you love never really die. We simply transform into another kind of energy."

Granny went on to tell her, "Deep within yourself, you will always be able to find those whom you have loved, Priscilla. You can ask for and receive our guidance to help you on your earthly journey. We are always with you, even in the darkest hours when you feel most alone."

As she lifted the deer crown from Priscilla's head and handed it to a woman nearby, Granny added, "But for now your Spirit must return to your body so you can continue to do what is needed of you on earth. You have important tasks ahead of you, my little granddaughter."

Priscilla knew her time with her loved ones in this lovely forest cathedral was drawing to a close. Though she felt some sadness, at the same time, she sensed her rising exhilaration mingled with a desire to go back and live the life she had yet to live.

Her mother lifted the muskrat cloak from around her shoulders and gave it to another woman who carried it away with great reverence. Priscilla stood up and hugged her mother in a tight embrace, wishing with all her heart she had time to get to know her better. She knew so little about her mother.

As if discerning Priscilla's thoughts, her mother said, "Priscilla, someday soon you must talk with your father about me. When he is ready, he will tell you all about me. You will be able to learn much of what you want to know through him. He needs you very much."

Priscilla was glad to hear this. She wanted to be able to tell her father what she had learned and how she had been with her mother. She knew it was important to let him know he would be okay.

Next Priscilla turned and hugged Granny with great fierceness. After holding on for as long as she could, with some reluctance, she pulled back. Looking Granny straight in the eye, just like Wanortu and Baba did with Eideard, she said firmly, "Goodbye, Granny." It meant so much to her to have the opportunity to say goodbye to her beloved grandmother.

Granny responded with her jolly smile as she said, "Goodbye, my little granddaughter." Her wise eyes were so full of love and her gaze so serene, that it occurred to Priscilla that Granny's ship had come in. Granny had found her treasure after all.

Priscilla knelt down and put her arms around Grandmother Wolf. Hugging her close, she buried her nose in the wolf's warm sweet-smelling fur for a long time, memorizing her scent and allowing it to sink into her every cell. She never wanted to forget it. "Goodbye, dear Grandmother Wolf," she whispered.

"Goodbye, little granddaughter," Grandmother Wolf answered in response, her love for Priscilla, as always, shining in her amber eyes.

When Priscilla got up again, she knew each of them felt her love for them in the same way she felt their love for her. With new resolve, she stated, "Thank you for being here for me and for teaching me what I need to know. I won't let you down."

Using some of the courage with which they had blessed her, she turned and walked across the clearing. As she drew near the trees, she looked back once more and waved goodbye to the glowing group in the midst of the sacred forest cathedral.

Then she turned and stepped in amongst the big trees, knowing, beyond a shadow of doubt, she could now find her way back where she needed to go… in either direction.

BOOK FIVE

FINDING THE WAY BACK

Chapter Twenty-Five
The Lava Land

Priscilla opened her eyes. The first thing she saw was a pair of big black eyes looking down at her with great tenderness. For a moment, she was puzzled as to where she was until she realized a furry black bear held her in a warm embrace. She did not feel afraid. In fact, she smiled when she remembered how often she had cuddled her stuffed bears in just this same way. It felt wonderful.

"Welcome back, my child. I am Mother Bear, and you are here in my bear cave. You have been on quite a journey." Somehow, she knew where Priscilla had been.

With a grateful smile, Priscilla reached up and gave Mother Bear a great big bear hug. Under the circumstances, it seemed entirely appropriate. "Thank you, Mother Bear," she whispered into a fuzzy ear.

Having heard their mother's voice, Moe, Larry, and Curly scampered back to her. Sniffing at Priscilla, they pushed her aside with their noses so they could take their place by their mother once more. Tired from play, they were ready to nap again.

Priscilla was delighted to see the three tiny cubs. Giggling at their antics, she got up to give them room. Anyway, it was time for her to go.

The little bears nuzzled in close to Mother Bear, and all four of them settled down for a long winter's nap. It was time to catch up on some hibernating.

Alasdair and Eideard had followed behind the triplets, anxious to find out how Priscilla was feeling. When they heard her giggle at the triplets, they knew she was okay. She smiled happily at her waiting friends.

"Hey, Priscilla," Alasdair gave her a warm smile in return. "I'm glad to see you're feeling better."

"Hoot Mon!" Eideard flew over and settled on Priscilla's shoulder. He blew out his breath in what sounded like a tiny sigh of pleasure at being with her again.

"Hello, little owl." Priscilla stroked his feathers. Recalling her past behavior, she felt ashamed of herself. "I'm sorry I got angry with you, Eideard," she whispered. "I was terribly rude. You were only trying to be helpful."

He blushed and tucked his head into his feathers as he said, "Ach, awa' wi' ye! Hoot Mon!"

Not wanting to embarrass him further, Priscilla exclaimed, "I'm starved! I need to eat something." She asked Alasdair, "Have you eaten yet?"

"Yeah, I did. You were out like a light for a long time. It's way past noon." Alasdair showed her to a big rock by the pool as he said, "You can sit there and eat something, and then we've got to get going. We've got a long way to go, and if we don't hurry, we could get caught in the dark."

He went on talking as she ate her lunch. "While you were sleeping, Eideard and I played with the cubs. They liked hearing a song I wrote about Mother Nature. We checked out the cave, and after you finish eating, there's something cool you've gotta see." He seemed to be bursting with excitement.

As quickly as she could, she gobbled up what was left of the food from Barthos' hut. Alasdair told her the water in the pool came from a spring and was safe to drink, so she quenched her thirst and refilled her water bottle with fresh clear water. While he waited, Alasdair kept fidgeting. Whatever he wanted her to see had to be something special.

Once Priscilla was ready to go, she glanced with fondness at the softly snoring bears, and then she followed her impatient guide along the edge of the pool toward the back of the cave. Where the pool ended, he turned and made his way along a narrow path leading to the far side. The spring he had mentioned bubbled up in the middle of the pool, reminding her of the Holy Water from the Sacred Spring with which Granny and the women had anointed her.

They were halfway around the pool when Alasdair drew to a stop and pointed above them on the rock wall and said, "Look up there!"

Some faded paintings covered the face of the wall above them. They were obviously quite old, but she had no idea what they were, how they got there, or why Alasdair was so excited about them.

With great pride, he announced, "Those are ancient pictographs. I heard about them in my history class. Paintings like these are rare. They tell the stories of people who lived here a long time ago."

Priscilla dutifully admired the paintings without paying much attention. There were more pressing thoughts on her mind. Alasdair continued to watch her intently, as if waiting for her to see something in particular.

As she turned around to head back along the path, one of the paintings caught her eye. It portrayed the figure of a small girl with long wavy red hair, much like her own. The girl was looking up at a big black bear. Priscilla examined it more closely, and then she took a step back and quickly scanned the rest of the paintings. In total bewilderment, she stared at the wall.

Pictured there on the wall was the whole story of her inner journey. Everything was there, from her fainting and Mother Bear holding her, to the forest cathedral and the circle of figures around the fire pit, Granny, her mother, Grandmother Wolf and the crowning ceremony. There were even images of her as a deer running through the forest and as a muskrat swimming in the river. Her whole story had been painted on the wall a long time ago.

Alasdair was looking pleased with himself. "Doesn't that look like you in the bear cave with Mother Bear? Isn't that an incredible coincidence? And this painting here," he reached up to tenderly touch the painting of Grandmother Wolf, "sure looks like Grandmother Wolf, though of course it couldn't be," he whispered, his voice filled with sadness.

He has no idea how incredible it really is! There was no way he could know what this meant to Priscilla. She was not yet ready to share her inner journey with him, or with anyone else, for that matter.

The cave paintings were another reminder of how everything was connected. Pete… Garone the Gull… had told them that time was different in the Kingdom Beyond the Sunset. These paintings clearly showed how time was not at all what she had once thought it was. She stood in awestruck silence.

Unable to draw her eyes away from the paintings, she heard Alasdair say something about his discovery of a different way out of the cave. Her mind preoccupied, she paid scant attention to him until he touched her arm and said, "Come on, we've got to get moving."

With great reluctance, she tore her eyes away from the wall. Glancing back at the paintings several times, she followed Alasdair back along the path. Wrapped in a sense of mystified wonder at what she had just seen and what it all meant, she felt again the sense of being in another time and space.

Alasdair led them back along the edge of the pool, but instead of turning toward the way they had come in, he took them in the opposite direction. Priscilla followed along without thinking much about it.

They entered another long tunnel. Alasdair opened up the Black Carapas to light the way ahead saying, "I remembered to rejuvenate it in the pool," Priscilla made no response, her mind still focused elsewhere.

It was some time before they reached the end of the tunnel. Stepping out into the light and feeling fresh air finally got Priscilla's attention. The tunnel in the cave had led them right through the mountain. From where she was standing, the Fairy Forest did not look far away. However, in order to get there, they would have to cross the dreaded Lava Land, which lay right below them. Wanortu and Barthos had both cautioned them against this inhospitable place.

"I know we were told to avoid the Lava Land, if at all possible," Alasdair began, reasoning against any possible objections she might have, "but we don't have much time. If we go back the way we came, it'll be dark before we get down from the mountains, and we could get lost. The Fairy Forest isn't that far from here. If we hurry, maybe we can even make it back to the Merry Meadow before dark. I think we should try it."

Eideard protested, "I've been arguin' wi' the laddie tae nae avail, Lassie. I think ye need tae gae back an' follow the river. Hoot Mon!"

Priscilla was hesitant. Twice, they had been warned against crossing the Lava Land. But it was her fault they were late, and she felt guilty for using so much time for herself. Alasdair thought it was okay to take this shortcut, and she felt as anxious as he did about finding Inky. Besides, her father appeared to be in some kind of danger as well. The more time they took, the worse it might be for him.

"It doesn't look all that far," she wavered, "though I don't much like the idea of being in that awful place." Turning to Eideard and stroking his feathers she said, "Anyway, how can we lose our way if you are with us, little owl!" She did not want him to think she was ignoring his advice.

"Ach aye, if that's the way 'twill be, we best get goin', but I dinna like this vera much. Hoot Mon!" muttered Eideard, knowing he had been overruled.

With Alasdair once again leading the way, they climbed down the rocks. The sun was still high in the sky as they made their way to the barren volcanic land below them.

By the time they had started across the Lava Land, Priscilla had already begun to feel uneasy. Climbing down the rocks had taken longer than they expected. Now that they were actually in this flat, unpleasant place, the Fairy Forest seemed farther away. In fact, the ground had begun to slope down into a sort of valley. Before long, they would be unable to see the trees ahead of them at all.

The Lava Land turned out to be a thoroughly nasty place. No paths were available to follow, and the jagged lava rocks made it hard to walk. It was necessary to watch where they stepped to avoid twisting an ankle. Thinking that snakes, scorpions, and other creepy crawlers would find this type of landscape most appealing, worried Priscilla.

The sun bore down on them with no respite and no shade in sight. She was glad they had put on their goggles and hats and added more sunscreen before leaving the cool darkness of the tunnel.

Alasdair seemed a little less confident now. He stopped for a moment, pulled a pale blue bandana out of his backpack, and used it to wipe the sweat off his brow. Then he drank some water and lathered on more sunscreen. Priscilla did the same.

They kept going in the direction they had begun, or at least they assumed it was the same direction. The trees in front of them and the mountains behind them were no longer in view. It was easy to understand how anyone could get lost in a land that looked the same in all directions.

After they had been walking for some time, Priscilla noticed Eideard had begun shifting from one foot to another on her shoulder whispering, "Hoot Mon!" repeatedly to himself.

Finally, he announced, "I'm awa tae see if we're goin' the right way, wee ones. I'll be bak soon. Cheerio! Hoot Mon!" He flew off in the direction they were heading.

Priscilla watched him fly out of sight with an even greater sense of unease. Her body was beginning to tingle with some sort of anticipation. It was as if she were gearing up for something, though she had no idea what it could possibly be. She supposed some of Eideard's nervousness had rubbed off on her.

With no advance warning whatsoever, a loud sound whistled through the air. Something slammed against her, pushing her so hard she nearly fell over. The deafening noise and the feeling of being shoved back and forth at the whim of something beyond her, was not unfamiliar, but she could not recall where she had encountered it before.

She grabbed onto Alasdair's arm and cried, "What's happening, Alasdair?"

"It's another of those Wild Wicked Windstorms," he yelled, trying to make his voice heard over the noise of the now roaring wind. "We've got to find a place where we can lie down. There won't be any caves to hide in here."

Grabbing her hand, and shielding her with his body, he slowly pushed his way ahead. Suddenly he yelled, "My hat!" as something flew past her, lightly brushing against her cheek. There was no way they could stop to find it. Priscilla snatched off her own hat and her ribbon and stowed them in one of her pockets so that she wouldn't lose them as well.

The wind picked up the volcanic ash from the ground and blasted it at them. Soon the air became so thick with the gray dust, it was impossible to see much around them. The ash stung Priscilla's eyes, nose, and throat causing her to cough and gasp. They struggled to move forward against what was beginning to feel like insurmountable odds.

Priscilla tripped. If Alasdair had not been holding her hand, she would have fallen. What had caused her to stumble was the edge of a shallow crevice. It extended off to one side where it opened wider, possibly offering a little protection from the wind.

She tugged at Alasdair's hand and pointed. He nodded. Slowly maneuvering their way along, they found a place where the crevice widened into a slightly deeper indentation in the ground with barely enough room to accommodate them both. It wouldn't be much protection, but it was better than nothing.

Alasdair gestured for her to lie down on her stomach with her backpack under her head. She did as he said, wondering what other little creatures might already have found their way into this spot. She quickly put the thought aside. They had no other choice.

Alasdair lay down on top of her, again using his body to shield her. He put his head next to hers and pulled his backpack over both of them. Shouting in her ear, he said, "Hold on. It should be over soon." Gratitude filled her for his kind words as well as for his closeness.

For some time, they lay together with wind and ash whirling all around them. Priscilla figured Alasdair had to be taking the brunt of the storm since he was shielding her from the worst of it. Her head hurt where it pressed into her backpack. Parts of her body were sore from pushing against the lava rocks, and with all the ash in the air, she could scarcely breathe. But with the wild whistling of the wind droning above and the warm comfort of Alasdair's body, she soon dozed off to sleep.

Chapter Twenty-Six
Lost and Found

The silence awakened Priscilla. The wind had died down, and the howling and blowing had stopped. Alasdair was above her, attempting to brush ash off his clothes, which soon had him coughing and sneezing. For once, he was not all white. Gray dust covered him from head to foot making him look much like one of the lighter shadow figures.

She giggled. "We must look like a couple of dust bunnies." Brushing the ash off herself, she said, "Thanks for protecting me," before she went into a coughing and sneezing fit of her own.

When she was able to catch her breath again, she realized he had not said anything.

She asked, "Are you okay?"

"I think so," he answered, in his gruff voice. "I've been wondering about Eideard. I just hope he made it to the trees before the storm hit. He's so tiny the wind would toss him about."

Priscilla responded with more certainty than she actually felt, "He's a tough little bird. I'm sure he'll be okay." She hoped this was true.

They cleaned off as much of the ash as they could from their clothes and their backpacks. Since they needed to save water, washing was not an option. When they looked around, they had no idea in which direction to go. The air was still thick with the gray dust, making it impossible to see any distance in front of them.

"I think we're better off moving than staying where we are," Alasdair said. After looking down at the crevice to try to figure out the lay of the land, he pointed, "I think it's this way."

With no better idea to offer, she agreed. "Okay, though one direction looks much like another to me. Anyway, Eideard should be back soon to guide us."

They walked on in their chosen direction for some time. The sun burned through the gray filter. Alasdair seemed to be having a hard time with the heat, especially without the protection of his hat. His fine hair swirled all around his head.

Priscilla offered her hat to him, but he refused to take it, saying, "You need it."

While they rested for a moment, he wrapped his towel around his head like a turban. Neither of them cared how funny they looked.

The ash slowly started to dissipate, and soon the air became clear enough for them to see where they were. Priscilla stopped walking and stood staring in front of her, flabbergasted. She could see nothing but volcanic rock. Not a single tree was in view. Looking around, she saw the mountains off to their right instead of behind them where they should have been. They had been walking deeper into the Lava Land, not across it.

"Oh no!" cried Priscilla. "We've been going in the wrong direction!"

There was no response from Alasdair, so she turned to look at him. Something was wrong. His goggles were off, and he was dabbing his bandana to the back of his neck. The cloth came away red with blood.

"You're bleeding!" she cried. Hurrying over to him, she checked his neck and was shocked to find his skin burned and full of pockmarks where something small and sharp had cut him.

"I'm all right. I just got hit with some flying rocks. I'll be okay." But his expression did not match his words. He seemed weak and disoriented. She touched his forehead, the way Granny used to do to her when checking for a fever. He felt hot.

"Sit down!" she ordered, in her fiercest Granny-like voice.

When he obeyed her, she took his bandana from him and soaked it with some of her precious water. Then she washed his face and neck as best as she could. Once the dust was off, she saw that there were cuts and blisters on his face as well.

After an anxious search through her backpack, she found the Band-Aids and antiseptic cream she knew she had packed. She rubbed some cream into his cuts and put Band-Aids on the worst of them. Wetting the cloth once more, she spread it across the back of his neck, tucked it under his shirt, and tied it in front. Then she wet his towel turban with the rest of her water. Maybe it would help to cool him down. It was all she could think of to do.

The sun was beginning to set, so at least it would cause no more damage to his skin. However, this meant the light would soon be gone. They needed to get moving, or they would still be in the Lava Land in the dark, not a pleasant thought. She got him up, and they began walking, this time in the right direction.

They trudged on for some time, their progress slowing, as he grew weaker. Taking his arm, she placed it around her shoulders, telling him, "Lean on me."

When he did this without any argument, she knew he really had to be feeling ill. He soon began to lean on her more heavily, making it harder for her to walk. They could only travel at a slow pace. Every now and again, she had to stop to catch her breath.

Her fear increased along with her thirst and exhaustion. Her legs hurt, and her back and feet ached. Recalling the many times Alasdair had watched out for her gave her the courage to keep moving. She had managed the long climb in the Mara Mountains by putting one foot in front of the other and focusing on taking one step at a time, so she did the same thing again.

Soon it would be too dark to see anything. She asked Alasdair for the Black Carapas and put it in her pocket, intending to open it only when she had no other choice. Even though he had rejuvenated the shell in the cave, they had used it in the tunnel, and she had no idea how long the light would last.

Eideard was much on her mind. He should have been back by now. It was hard not to imagine the many things that could harm such a tiny bird. She did not share her fears with Alasdair; he had enough to worry about.

Tonight there was no moonlight, and within a short time, full darkness fell upon them. Priscilla had to open the shell. The brilliant light lit the way ahead so they could see where they were stepping. However, it did not project far enough into the distance to be able to determine their direction. One misstep and they would veer away from where they needed to go.

With stubborn determination, relying purely on her inner Light Detector, Priscilla kept them moving forward. Spending the night on the soft moist floor of the forest would not be much fun, but it was infinitely more appealing than sleeping on lumpy lava rocks. Even with this incentive, she did not know how much longer she could hold out.

The night brought a chill to the air, and they stopped to put on their jackets. Alasdair continued to shiver, and she had no idea if it was from cold or fever. She felt even more frightened and alone.

Granny's words to her in the forest cathedral came back. "*We are always with you, even in the darkest hours when you feel most alone.*" Whispering a quiet plea, she asked for help from Granny, her mother, Grandmother Wolf, and all the others in the Sacred Circle.

An answer came right away. She could almost hear their voices on the night air chanting softly, "*You can do it, Priscilla! You can do it!*"

Their words gave her renewed strength. She would keep going as long as it took. It helped her to say the chant over and over with every step she took. "You can do it, Priscilla… you can do it… you can do it, Priscilla…"

A loud sound of flapping wings cut through the deadly quiet, interrupting her words and causing her to pull up short in panic. An enormous black shadow zoomed down into the light as if it was about to dive-bomb them.

Priscilla screamed and closed the shell, engulfing them in complete darkness. Pulling Alasdair with her, she ducked down close to the ground where they stayed, trembling.

A familiar voice called out to them, "Priscilla and Alasdair, have no fear. It is I, Raldemar the Raven. I have come to help you."

Shaking with relief, Priscilla opened the shell again just in time to see the big black raven land in front of them. She got up and helped Alasdair to his feet, exclaiming, "Oh, Raldemar, I am so glad to see you. Alasdair is ill, and we're having a hard time finding our way out of this horrible place."

Then a thought struck her. "How did you know we were here? Did Eideard send you?" she asked with hope in her voice.

"Mother Nature was walking in her garden and saw you in one of her crystals," Raldemar said. "She sent me to help you. I am to stay with you to guide you back to the Village of the Rainbow."

Alasdair grunted. Though he did not have the energy to speak, he was as pleased as she was to have their trusted guide with them again.

"You are headed in the right direction," Raldemar told them. Priscilla was happy to hear that her Light Detector had kept them on course. "You are not far from the Fairy Forest. If you follow me, I will keep you on the right path. Your light will help you see where to walk."

With no more conversation, Priscilla and Alasdair moved on. They needed all their strength to keep going. Raldemar flew in the spotlight of the Black Carapas, making it easy for them to follow him. With his help, Priscilla did not feel so alone. Having a trusted guide made their difficult journey much easier.

After a time, the shell light began to flicker. "Oh no!" Priscilla cried. When the light went out, they were once again in complete darkness. The Black Carapas had dried up.

Raldemar flew down and stayed close in front of them, calling out so they could follow the sound of his crackly voice. Since Priscilla and Alasdair were unable to see where they were putting their feet, the going was much slower. Every step required great caution. Alasdair had little strength left; Priscilla felt as if she were dragging him along.

Even though she had no idea how much farther she could go on like this, she kept moving just the same, losing all sense of time, conscious of nothing but her next step. She focused on listening for Raldemar's voice and feeling her way with her feet, as she continued to whisper to herself, "You can do it, Priscilla! You can do it!"

Raldemar called back to them, "Look out in front of you now, Priscilla and Alasdair. See what lies ahead!" His crackly voice somehow managed to sound pleased.

Priscilla lifted her tired head to look. In front of them, two long rows of lights created a pathway much like an airport runway. This lighted path led all the way into the dark forest, now visible to her in the distance.

"Oh Alasdair, look!" Priscilla cried in her excitement. "You've got to see. We'll be safe now."

Alasdair slowly lifted his head and stared in front of him. His eyes were tired and blurry, but he could just make out the lighted path. Looking down at her, he gave her a lopsided grin, reminding her of Frog. With his strength almost all gone, he was struggling just to hold on.

They made their way toward the lighted path. After what had seemed like an eternity to Priscilla, they finally stepped between two rows of flickering lights. In her exhaustion, she was only vaguely aware of the way the lights danced about like little clusters of fireflies. Though she was grateful for the lights, she had no energy left to wonder where they came from.

As they walked between the shimmering lights, a sense of peace spread over her, making her steps a little lighter. Even Alasdair, as sick and tired as he was, seemed to lean less heavily on her shoulder. Their pace picked up a little.

Before long, the flickering path led them into the forest. The branches of the trees hung down over them in what felt like a welcoming embrace. With great joy, Priscilla stopped to breathe in the moist forest smells. The ground under her feet had changed from the hard prickly lava rock to the soft spongy grasses of the forest. They had made it out of the dreadful Lava Land at last.

The lighted path continued through the trees. Raldemar flew ahead without stopping, so Priscilla and Alasdair, using their rekindled energy, followed along behind him, losing track of time once more. They had no idea where they were going, but they trusted the big black raven.

All at once, Priscilla realized where it was they were heading. She stopped moving as she cried out with gladness, "Look Alasdair! Oh, Alasdair, you must look up now!"

He lifted his tired head to see. The path ahead led up to the back door of a little cottage. Standing there at the bottom of the steps was the owner of the cottage herself. It was Baba.

Priscilla burst into tears.

Chapter Twenty-Seven
Baba's Cottage

The door of the cottage was open. Baba, with Purrtyface at her feet as usual, stood waiting at the bottom of the steps to greet them. Priscilla had never felt so glad to see anyone or to be anywhere in her life. Pulling Alasdair along, she hurried toward the cottage.

After seeing Purrtyface raise her back and hiss at him, Raldemar announced he would remain outside and flew to a nearby tree. Priscilla called a quick thanks to him for leading them to safety.

Baba greeted them without any fuss as she could see Alasdair's condition. Together, they got him up the stairs and into a little bedroom just inside the back door.

After they laid him on the bed, Priscilla told Baba about the Wild Wicked Wind and showed her the wounds on Alasdair's face and neck. Baba removed his towel turban and examined his scalp. Then she checked his arms, legs, and back. Everywhere, she found damage to his skin.

Priscilla was dismayed to see how badly hurt he was. No wonder he was feeling so ill.

After she finished her assessment, Baba turned from her charge to ask, "Are you okay, dear? Did you get hurt?"

"I'm tired and sore and really thirsty, but I think I'm okay."

"I am glad to hear it. I will need to attend to Alasdair for a little while. Why don't you go into the living room and have a cup of tea? I just made a fresh pot. You can rest until I come to you." Before Baba turned back to tend to Alasdair, she added with a little smile, "Someone is waiting there who will be pleased to see you."

Feeling curious, Priscilla walked into the living room. At first glance, she saw no one else in the room. The fire was burning, and the room felt cozy, just like she remembered from her previous visit. As before, the table in front of the fire held a teapot and teacups. Something with a delicious smell bubbled in a big pot hung over the fire.

A quiet little cough interrupted her thoughts. The sound came from the chair behind her, and she turned to see who had coughed. There, on a soft cushion, sat Eideard the Owl, an itsy bitsy tartan ice bag nestled rakishly between the tufts on his head.

"Eideard!" Priscilla screeched his name in delight and rushed over to him. "I was so worried about you. What happened? Are you okay?" Leaning over, she gently stroked his wing feathers, trying not to disturb his tiny ice pack.

He looked up at her with a rueful grin. "Aye, lassie, I'm right guid tho' my head hurts, and I'm still a wee bit peely wally. That blasted wind caught me jist as I was flyin' in tae the forest and blew me headfirst intae a tree, knockin' me oot cold. I woke up here in Baba's wee hoose. Hoot Mon!"

"But how did you get here?" asked Priscilla, as she went over and poured herself a cup of tea. Her throat was dry, and tea sounded good. Cup in hand, she sat down on the rug beside Eideard's chair to drink her tea and hear his story.

"The same wee Fairy Folk who helpt ye and the laddie foun' me and brought me here. Hoot Mon!"

"What do you mean the same Fairy Folk who helped us?" Priscilla looked at the tiny owl in bewilderment as she sipped her refreshing tea. "I've no idea what you're talking about."

"'Twas the wee Fairy Folk who lit yur way to Baba's wee hoose. Did ye no ken that, lassie? Hoot Mon!"

"You mean the lights along the path were Fairies?"

"Aye, lass. When I got ma senses back agin and foun' mysel' here wi' Baba, the wee Fairy Folk were still waitin' aboot tae hear me tell ma tale. When they heard how ye twa were lost in the Lava Land, they poot oot a call tae all the rest of the wee Fairy Folk o' the forest tae make a path tae help ye find yer way here. Hoot Mon!"

"Oh my gosh!" Priscilla was astounded to think she had actually seen Fairies without even knowing it. They were not what she had come to expect from her storybooks, but then she had been too tired to look closely at the twinkling lights.

Recalling how she felt as she walked between the rows of lights, she asked, "Did the Fairies have something to do with the feeling of peace when we walked along between them?"

"Aye, lassie. They're mostly made of Light energy like the Muses. They put oot guid energy where e'r they gae. It made ma head feel better just tae be aroond them. Hoot Mon!"

At that moment, Baba came into the room. She was tying a small woven rainbow-striped bag to the belt of her apron. When she saw Priscilla look at the bag with a questioning look, she smiled. "This is my medicine bag, Priscilla. It holds my healing tools. I put some of my salve on Alasdair's skin and gave him herbs to prevent infection. He is sleeping peacefully and will probably not wake until morning. That is best for him right now. Tomorrow I will bathe his skin properly. Then I should be able to determine when he will be ready to travel."

Baba went to the fireplace, picked up a ladle, and scooped some of whatever was simmering in the pot into a bowl. After setting it on the table, she pulled out a chair, and said to Priscilla, "Come and sit here, my dear, and have some mushroom soup. You must eat and then get some sleep as well."

Priscilla ate the hot tasty soup, along with buttered bread Baba set out for her, her head nodding over the bowl. Before long, her hunger pangs were satisfied enough for fatigue to take over. A watchful Baba took her by the arm and helped her up.

Blowing a sleepy goodnight kiss to Eideard, she allowed Baba to lead her to another tiny bedroom at the back of the cottage. Baba pointed out where to find everything she might need and left her on her own. Before much time had passed, a much cleaner and thoroughly exhausted Priscilla lay fast asleep in bed.

The sound of a door closing awakened Priscilla in the morning. For a few moments, she lay still, wondering where on earth she was. Her sore legs and feet brought everything back to her. It was barely light and she wanted nothing more than to go back to sleep. But she was anxious to know how Alasdair was faring, so she got up, dressed quickly, and went to find Baba.

The old woman was busy cooking breakfast on an ancient wood stove in her homey little kitchen. Scents from bunches of dried herbs and flowers hanging upside down from the rafters, mingled with the delicious smells of cooking.

When she saw Priscilla, Baba smiled and said cheerfully, "Good-morning, dear. Did you sleep well?"

"Yes, thank you, Baba. Good-morning to you too. How is Alasdair doing?"

"He rested well through the night, and his fever is down, but his skin still needs a lot of care. It will take time to heal. I have washed and fed him and put more ointment on his skin. He is asleep once again." Motioning Priscilla to sit down at a small table,

Baba set a plate of cooked eggs, vegetables, toast, and fruit in front of her.

"Now, my dear," Baba said, pulling a stool up to the table to sit beside Priscilla, "while you eat, we must put our heads together and decide what needs to be done. I have been thinking about it since Eideard told me where you have been and what you have learned. It seems you must find your way out to the Dark Ship to rescue Inky and the Light. I cannot see any other solution."

"We've been thinking the same thing." Priscilla chewed a piece of toast. "But we didn't make any plans other than to get back to the palace."

Baba paused in thought, giving Priscilla a chance to eat. "I think a better idea would be to first go and visit my friend, Grandmother Ocean. She will know what the Dark Ship is up to and can show you how to get on board. However, once you are on the ship, you and Alasdair will have to use your own resources to rescue Inky and the Light. None of us will be able to give you much help there." Baba gave Priscilla an apologetic smile.

"Who's this Grandmother Ocean, and where do we find her?" Spearing a forkful of eggs, Priscilla mulled over this peculiar name. Grandmother Wolf had mentioned the name, but Priscilla had just assumed it was a term used for the ocean.

"She lives at the bottom of the ocean and keeps in touch with all that goes on in her domain and with all her creatures."

Priscilla stopped, fork raised in mid-air, her face registering this unusual information. Before she could ask any questions, Baba went on, deep in thought, "You can take my boat down the River of Return to the Ocean of Opportunity. Sami and Sumi will meet you there and guide you to Grandmother Ocean."

"B-B-But how could we do that?" Priscilla stammered, "We can't stay underwater for any length of time, and the ocean would be too cold. Besides, even though Alasdair can swim, I'm not a strong swimmer."

"Oh, you need not worry about that," Baba laughed, "Sami and Sumi will give you all you require to go underwater. Being a strong swimmer is not necessary." Then her voice filled with concern. "But, Priscilla, I am afraid Alasdair will not be able to go with you. With his skin the way it is now, it would not be a good idea for him to go into salt water. You do not have time to wait until he has healed."

Priscilla heard this news with dismay. It meant she would have to take the boat down the river to the ocean all by herself.

Baba gave her an understanding smile and touched her lightly on the shoulder. "I know it must be frightening to imagine doing this on your own, Priscilla, but you must remember you are never really alone. There are other forces at work, looking out for you. You have been to the cave of Mother Bear, so I know you have learned this."

Priscilla's look changed to one of astonishment. So even Baba knew what had happened to her in the cave. Somehow, when it came right down to it, this should not surprise her. Baba was another wise woman, just like Granny and Mollie.

For a few minutes, Priscilla thought about all she had learned in the bear cave. Once more, she heard the loving voices whispering to her, "You can do it, Priscilla! You can do it!"

She took a deep breath and forced herself to say, "Okay, I'll go, but you must tell me what to do." Her voice sounded as shaky as she felt inside.

While Priscilla finished her breakfast, they made plans. Even though most of her appetite had gone, she continued eating because she knew she would need her strength. And who knew when she would be eating again.

All was prepared for her to leave as soon as possible. Once Alasdair awakened, he joined them. He and Eideard, who said he was still feeling "a wee bit peely wally", were to return to the palace as soon as they felt well enough to travel.

"Raldemar left earlier to recover my hat from the Lava Land," Alasdair told her. "After he returns, and once Eideard and I are ready to go, he will fly ahead to ask Wanortu to meet us in the meadow with a *large* cart," he added with a grin.

"Wanortu will know what to do to complete the healing of Alasdair's skin," Baba said.

After her visit with Grandmother Ocean, Priscilla was to return to the palace and reconnect with Alasdair. With the help of Wanortu's wise counsel, they would make plans for rescuing Inky and the Light.

"I'm sorry I can't go with you," Alasdair told Priscilla. "I feel like a jerk letting you go on alone."

"Hoot Mon!" Eideard added, his head tucked down in shame.

"I wish you were going as well, but it's not your fault you can't go." Priscilla tried to sound braver than she felt. "You two just need to hurry and get well. When I get back to the palace, we can decide how to rescue Inky and the Light."

Goodbyes said, Priscilla and Baba left the cottage by the back door and set off on a path through the woods. They made their way to the edge of a narrow stream where a small wooden boat was attached by a rope to a tree on a nearby bank. Baba peeled back the canvas cover on the boat and handed Priscilla a pair of oars from inside the boat.

Without untying the rope, she pushed the little craft down the bank and into the water. While Baba held the boat still, Priscilla tossed in her backpack, climbed in, and put the oars into the oarlocks.

"You will only have to row until the stream meets the River of Return, Priscilla. It is not far from here. Once the boat enters the river, the current will carry you all the way down to the ocean. You will not have to do a thing. The boat will not tip over, so you will be perfectly safe."

Baba added one caution. "The only time you need to be concerned is if there is a Dreary Drenching Downpour. You already know what such a storm is like. The good news is, if it does rain, the river will rise and carry you downstream to the ocean much faster.

However," Baba continued, lifting up the canvas still attached to the back of the boat, "as soon as you feel the first drop of rain, you must pull this cover over you and the boat right away. Hook it all the way around so no water can get in. Then you must stay under it until the rain stops, no matter what." She showed Priscilla how to hook the canvas to the boat and had Priscilla try it a few times.

Fortunately, Priscilla knew how to row a boat. Her father had taught her. Thinking of him gave her a pang of anguish, making her anxious to be on her way.

In her farewell words, Baba said, "Have faith and courage, little one. Remember you are not alone." Before Priscilla could change her mind, Baba untied the boat and tossed her the rope. Giving the boat a gentle shove, she stood back and watched Priscilla row the boat out into the stream.

"Please give my regards to Grandmother Ocean." She waved to Priscilla as the boat started to pull away.

"I will, Baba. Goodbye and thank you!"

Priscilla rowed along, singing a silly little round she remembered from kindergarten: "Row, row, row your boat, gently down the stream. Merrily, merrily, merrily, merrily, life is but a dream." Rowing was fun since she knew it was only for a short time. It felt good to stretch out her arms and legs. The methodical movement of the oars, along with the dreamlike silence of the forest around her, helped to drain away some of her worry.

It was only once Baba was out of sight that Priscilla realized she had forgotten to ask who Sami and Sumi were or what they looked like. Well, it was too late now. Maybe they were whales like Jonah's whale in the Bible, and one of them would swallow her and the boat and carry them down to the bottom of the ocean. She didn't much like that idea at all.

Since she had no idea where she was going, or what was going to happen to her, she would just have to take things as they came, a lesson she seemed to be continuing to learn on this journey. Anyway, she did not appear to have any other choice.

Chapter Twenty-Eight
Into the Depths

Since the sun was out, Priscilla was not at all concerned about a Dreary Drenching Downpour. The boat had been gliding along smoothly when the oars hit choppier water. The stream had widened, and the water was moving much more rapidly. Figuring she must have reached the river, she stopped rowing and pulled the oars inside the boat.

The little craft adjusted to the flow of the river, settling into the faster current. Now she had nothing to do but let the boat drift, so she figured she might as well get comfortable. Sliding down onto the floor behind her, she leaned against her pack and put her feet up on the seat in front of her. She laid her head back and looked up beyond the trees to the clear blue sky.

The white fluffy clouds floating overhead brought back images of what it was like to be such a cloud. She remembered when she was an eagle, soaring high in the sky. Within moments, she was lost in the pleasurable memories of her time in the forest cathedral.

In the midst of recalling what it felt like to be a powerful storm cloud, she realized she was gazing at something real, not just a memory. There actually *was* a storm cloud above her. She sat up in surprise. The fluffy white clouds had disappeared, and the blue sky had turned dark gray. It was hard to believe the weather could have changed so quickly.

A drop of water touched her cheek, so lightly she thought it might have splashed up from the river. When more drops fell on her head and dripped down her face, she could no longer deny what was happening. A Dreary Drenching Downpour had begun. She was going to have to go through yet another storm.

Calling to mind Baba's instructions, she hurried to batten down the hatches. By the time she had hooked the cover all the way around the little boat, the rain was pouring down. The raindrops pounded away at the stretched canvas, creating a tremendous racket. The boat bumped up and down in the rough water and began moving much faster.

Under the canvas, it was dark and confining, and the fact that she had no control over what was happening, terrified her. Completely at the mercy of the river, there was nothing left to do but trust.

Baba's words, so similar to Granny's, came back. *"Have faith and courage, little one. Remember you are not alone."* Once more, she prayed for help from God, Granny, her mother, Grandmother Wolf, Mother Bear, Baba, and anyone else who might hear her. Then she grabbed her backpack and clasped it tightly to her chest.

The rain battered away at the canvas, and the little boat shook, as if it were about to split apart. Using her pack as a pillow, she curled up in a tight little ball on the floor as she had done in the Lava Land. If only she had Mathilda curled up next to her, she might feel less alone and scared.

Thinking of Mathilda made her wish she was at home, safe in her own bed, with her beloved cat beside her. Her pent-up tears burst forth in a torrent and flowed down her cheeks, mimicking the rain pouring over the canvas.

After a long time, her tears spent, she fell into an exhausted sleep.

Priscilla dreamed of dogs. Someone had locked the animals outside her house, and they kept barking and scratching at the door to get somebody to let them in. Nobody seemed to hear them, so they barked louder and louder. The barking awakened her from her dream.

It took her a moment to remember where she was. Her body felt stiff from being in such a cramped position. Uncurling her legs, she listened to see if the rain had stopped. Once again, she heard barking which made no sense. If she was no longer dreaming, why was she hearing the same noise? Dogs did not belong on a river.

Unhooking some of the canvas, she peeled it back and peeked outside. What she saw so astounded her, she quickly unhooked the rest of the canvas, sat up on the seat, and looked around in disbelief. The rain had stopped and the river was gone. She was somewhere far out on the ocean. Water was everywhere around her with not a single tree in sight.

Then she spotted the dreadful Dark Ship on the horizon. It loomed larger than ever. One of its long ugly arms was stretching out toward some land in the distance. A tremor of terror rippled through her.

A scratching sound on the side of the boat made her cry out in fear. She shook for a moment or two before she managed to pull herself together. Gathering her courage, she edged to the side of the boat and leaned cautiously over the rim to see what had caused the noise.

Two little faces with black eyes, blunt snouts, and long whiskers peeked up at her. It was a pair of young seals. The barking had come from seals, not dogs. She burst out laughing, causing her fears to dissipate.

The little seals watched her uncertainly. Then, in sudden delight, they clapped their flippers together and smacked them on the water. The loud resonant sound cut her laughter short, enabling her to recollect her manners.

"Hello," she said politely to the little seals, "My name is Priscilla."

The seals both said "hello" back to her. The larger of the two, a shiny gray seal, spoke to her in the voice of a young boy aware of the importance of his duty. "I am Sami the Seal." Gesturing with his flipper to the slightly smaller seal, who had a sweet, spotted black and white face, he continued, "And this is my sister, Sumi the Seal. We are here to take you to Grandmother Ocean when you are ready to go."

"What do I need to do?" Priscilla asked, her voice quaking, as fear set in again. She did not feel ready to go anywhere at all and only wanted to be safe at home.

"You must put this on," Sami told her, with as much authority as the little fellow could muster. With his nose, he pushed what looked like a bundle of seaweed through the water toward the boat. "Once you put it on, please come and join us in the ocean." He made it sound as if this ought to be the most natural thing in the world for her to do.

Well, for a seal, it might be natural, but it sure did not feel that way to her. Wrinkling her nose in disgust, she reached down, grabbed the slimy stuff and pulled it into the boat. It brought with it the powerful scent of the sea.

Expecting it to be slippery like seaweed, she was surprised to find it felt more like soft furry rubber. When she unrolled the bundle, she discovered it was a sealskin just her size. In the movie, "The Secret of Roan Inish", seals called *selkies* shed their skins and became human. What she was doing seemed to be the opposite, putting on a sealskin to become a seal.

Quickly she stripped off her outer clothing and her rainbow ribbon so they would stay dry and odor free. Then she began the process of climbing into the furry suit. As she pulled the wet slick skin over her feet, she cried out, "Yuck, ish, ish, ish!" and began to hop around. When the boat started to wobble, she had to stop this in a hurry.

The sealskin was cold, and just the idea of putting it on her skin gave her the creeps. Soon she had no more time to fuss about it. The suit took on a life of its own, molding close to her body like a wetsuit. Once she had tucked her hair into the hood, only her eyes, nose, mouth, and palms of her hands remained uncovered. The sealskin felt surprisingly warm and comfortable, even if it did smell fishy. She hoped the smell would go away once she took it off.

She climbed over the edge of the boat and slipped down into the water next to the little seals. For a moment, she panicked, remembering the horrible dark water of the River of Shadows. Then she reminded herself that this was the Ocean of Opportunity, not the Land of Shadows. Baba had said she would be okay. Besides, she had been a muskrat and a salmon, so she knew what it felt like to be at home in the water.

The sealskin was buoyant, enabling her to float on the surface. The furry skin on her feet expanded into flippers, giving her more power in the water. Though the ocean was icy cold, in her sealskin suit, she felt toasty warm.

It eased her fears when Sumi swam up beside her and in a high singsong voice said, "Sami and I will give you the breath you need to go underwater, Priscilla. First you must take three deep breaths of fresh air, breathing in through your nose and out through your mouth. When you breathe out the last time, you must try to let go of all the air inside you."

Priscilla obeyed. Taking in a deep full breath, she filled her lungs, much like she had learned to do at swimming lessons at the Y. Then she blew the air out through her mouth. With each subsequent breath, she became a little more relaxed and not quite so scared. After the third breath, she blew out all the air until she felt as if there was nothing left in her lungs.

Sami and Sumi pressed their noses up against her cheeks. Sumi told her gently, "Now please keep your mouth open, Priscilla, and breathe our breath into your lungs. Do not be afraid. Sami and I will take good care of you."

Feeling much like a little bird in a nest, Priscilla did what they asked of her. As Sami and Sumi blew into her mouth, she swallowed deep gulps of their sweet fishy seal breath. Her lungs filled up to a peculiar fullness, unlike anything she had ever experienced before. They breathed like this for a few moments. Then Sami and Sumi turned away, signaling with their front flippers for her to follow them into the depths.

As soon as Priscilla submerged herself in the water behind the little seals, the peculiar feeling in her lungs disappeared, and she discovered she could breathe comfortably underwater. Her sealskin clung snugly against her. She felt just like one of the sleek shining seals swimming in front of her.

Even though she remained a little shaky, she was thrilled. Baba had been right. It did not matter if she could swim well. Since she could breathe underwater, she could do whatever worked. Stretching and kicking her flipper feet, she slipped through the water as easily as if she had been born into this aquatic home.

The water was murky, so she could only see a short distance around her. At first, she wished she had brought the Black Carapas. Her second thought was that she was better off not seeing what creatures might be lurking around her.

At a slow pace, giving her plenty of time to adjust to her new surroundings, the two little seals led her down toward the ocean floor. Deeper down, the water became clearer. Ahead of them,

Priscilla could see a large mass of jumbled rocks covered with barnacles and sea anemones. Sea creatures teemed all around the rocks.

Clinging to one of the rocks was a large brown octopus. Priscilla looked at it with nervous interest as they swam over it. An ugly eel stuck a huge pouched head out of a hole in one rock and watched her with its protruding eyes as she passed by. It exhilarated and scared her at the same time. Starfish of many different colors had attached themselves to the rocks; some with too many legs to count.

Several large silver salmon swam past. A rusty-colored jellyfish floated above her, and she watched it breathe in and out. Schools of tiny dark fish swam all around her, seeming to accept her as one of their own.

A flat fish disappeared down into the ocean floor below, sending up a storm of particles. When the water cleared, she saw numerous crabs. Some were hermit crabs carrying their shell houses on their backs. Others were much bigger crabs with lumpy dark reddish-brown shells. They looked like the same kind of crabs her parents liked to eat, a thought she quickly stifled out of respect for where she was.

Sami and Sumi swam into a channel between the rocks. Priscilla followed, entering into what appeared to be a deep-sea canyon hidden in the rocks. With a ripple of excitement, she saw where it was the little seals seemed to be heading.

Just in front of them, wedged deep in the canyon, lay the wreck of an old fishing boat. It looked to Priscilla much like one of the many fishing boats in the harbor at home. Underwater, it took on a much more mysterious appearance. It too was covered with barnacles and swarming with all sorts of crawling and swimming creatures.

Sami and Sumi swam past what Priscilla guessed was the pilothouse in the stern of the boat and headed toward the bow.

Priscilla followed slowly, trying to take it all in. Underwater wrecks fascinated her, especially after seeing "Titanic". It was hard to believe she was actually getting a chance to see one for herself.

Sami and Sumi were patiently waiting for her next to a small hole in the side of the wreck; it looked big enough to allow her room to swim through it. When the seals gestured with their flippers that this was where she needed to go, she was ecstatic. She was going to get a chance to see inside a wreck.

Wondering what she was going to find, and feeling giddy with excitement, she waved gaily to the little seals as she swam past them and dove through the hole into the wreck.

Chapter Twenty-Nine
Grandmother Ocean

Once inside the wreck, Priscilla looked around. She appeared to be in some kind of storage tank. Even though the space was large, it certainly was not big enough for Grandmother Ocean to be equal in size to Mother Nature, as she had imagined. There was no one about... just the continual flow of little fishes and other sea creatures to which she had already grown accustomed.

Two large cage-like contraptions sat on the floor in the middle of the tank. More of the same were stacked on every wall around the space. Each cage contained huge books, giving the tank the look of an underwater library. What was most peculiar, lights of many different colors flickered out of each book, indicating some kind of movement was going on within them. These lights lit up the tank with a supernatural glow.

"Hello Priscilla," a squeaky voice spoke inside her head.

Priscilla quickly looked around to see who or what was speaking. All she could see were little fishes swimming to and fro.

"I'm Grandmother Ocean," the high-pitched voice continued.

Puzzled, Priscilla looked around her again. Perhaps Grandmother Ocean was only going to be this funny little voice in her head. If so, she would be terribly disappointed. "I can't see you," she cried in frustration. "Where are you?"

"I am all around you," Grandmother Ocean replied enigmatically, "but I am also right in front of you."

Again, Priscilla peered carefully all around her, especially in front of her. A miniature rainbow-striped seahorse caught her eye. No bigger than her index finger, it was extremely cute. With great delight, she watched the little seahorse flit about, forgetting for a moment to look for Grandmother Ocean. The seahorse display at the aquarium was a particular favorite of hers.

The tiny seahorse darted right up in front of Priscilla's nose as Grandmother Ocean's voice said, "Now you can see me, can't you? I'm right in front of your nose!"

"B-B-But Grandmother Ocean... you can't possibly be just a little seahorse!" Priscilla stammered.

"And why ever not?" The voice warbled with laughter, as the sea horse zipped back and forth. "I can be anything I want to be. Besides, there are great joys in 'just being a seahorse', as you say. You should try it sometime."

"I'd like to!" exclaimed Priscilla, with great enthusiasm, as she thought about what fun it would be. But she had not come here to play.

Addressing the seahorse... well... Grandmother Ocean, she said, "Baba sends you her regards, Grandmother Ocean. She said you could tell me about the Dark Ship and what it has been doing."

Instantly the seahorse disappeared. Priscilla searched everywhere, but the tiny striped creature was nowhere in view. Now she was completely mystified as well as disappointed. Where had Grandmother Ocean gone? "Where *are* you Grandmother Ocean?" she cried.

From nowhere in particular, she heard a gravelly, sour-sounding voice say, "I'm here below you, Priscilla. Talking about that nasty ship makes me feel downright crabby."

Looking at the floor, Priscilla saw a huge reddish brown crab. It was similar to those she had seen earlier, only this one was much bigger. Two large pincers swinging about wildly caused her to move back out of range in a hurry.

Oh my goodness, now Grandmother Ocean was a crab. What was next? Aloud, Priscilla mumbled in confusion, "But, I thought you were a seahorse."

"Sweet little seahorses have nothing to do with that Wicked Ship. It is so much easier to complain when I'm a crab," Grandmother Ocean grumbled. Poking one of her large pincers toward the two cages on the floor, she commanded Priscilla, "Have a seat on one of those nasty old crab traps over there, dearie, while I see what I can do for you."

Obediently, Priscilla climbed onto the top of one of the traps. Her feet dangled over the edge. From the number of similar traps all around, she realized she must be in the wreck of a crab boat. Granny had watched a program on public television about the many crab boats lost at sea in the Pacific Ocean. This might even be one of those boats.

"First, I must tell you about that Evil Ship," crabby Grandmother Ocean said. "It is up to no good as you know. We have been watching it grow larger every day."

As she talked, her voice grew even crabbier. "It has been stealing huge quantities of oil from beneath my ocean floor. Oil and sludge are leaking out, causing damage to my ocean and hurting my friends. Now the Nasty Ship is trying to grab a special place where many of my seabirds and sea creatures make their home. Those on the ship want to destroy this sanctuary so they can reach the rich oil reserves beneath it. This makes me angry!"

At once, a huge gush of inky black liquid squirted into the water. A surprised Priscilla could no longer see anything in the darkness. Since she did not know what else to do, she sat still, nervously waiting to see what might happen next. Grandmother Ocean was as changeable as the Northwest weather.

After a few moments, the cloud of ink dispersed, and there in front of her, a giant red octopus floated in the water. All eight arms hung down from an oversized bulbous head. The bulging eyes were wide-open, staring right at Priscilla. She quickly pulled her legs up under her onto the crab trap. Shrinking back, she asked in a tremulous voice, "I-I hope the octopus is you, G-Grandmother Ocean?"

Changing in color from red to brown to a soft cream, the octopus answered in a loud deep bass voice, quite fitting for its size, this time speaking directly to Priscilla. "Yes, I am here, dearie. You do not need to be afraid. No creature in this ocean will do you harm. We know you are here to help and not to harm us."

The octopus, who was indeed Grandmother Ocean, swished over to the traps along the wall. "It is time for me to show you what I've been talking about. Let me find what I need." Grandmother Ocean began to mumble to herself as she stroked her chin with one of her arms and scratched her big head with another. "Hmmm, where in the ocean did I put it?"

All eight octopus arms began opening different trap doors and flipping through the lighted books within. Each time an arm pulled out a book, there was a loud sucking noise. Whenever she opened a book, more lights flashed from within. "Hmmm, not under *Ark, Bad, Black, Boat, Dark, Environment, Evil, Monster, Nasty, Oil…*"

When Grandmother Ocean decided a particular book was not what she wanted, she discarded it, letting it float away. Soon the tank was full of flickering lights and floating books, fast becoming what Priscilla imagined would be a deep-sea librarian's nightmare.

Grandmother Ocean went on muttering to herself. "Well, let me see if it might be filed under *Priscilla*."

Priscilla looked up in surprise when she heard this. She had no idea why her name would be in one of these books.

"*Patricia, Paul, Persephone, Persimmon, Pointdexter, Precious,* aaah, *Pri*scilla!" the Octopus exclaimed happily. One of her eight arms lifted out the book. Another arm opened it up, and she glanced at what was inside. As a third arm turned pages, the lights flickered and flashed. Then she closed it, saying, "Nope, not there."

Filled with curiosity, Priscilla asked Grandmother Ocean "Is that book about me?"

"Of course, my dear!" Grandmother Ocean answered, letting go of the book. "These are Life Books. They hold the stories of all that has occurred and will occur in everyone's lives."

Priscilla stopped her with an excited, "Wait, wait a second! What does it say about me?"

Grandmother Ocean reached out one of her arms and grabbed the book as it drifted away. Opening it once more, she looked inside, more closely this time. Stroking her chin with one arm, scratching her head with another, rubbing her belly with one more, she turned each page and looked at it, making all sorts of little exclamations at the same time. "Ooh, aah, oh, oh my, uh oh, oh my goodness, oh yes, oh no, good grief, oh dear, aha!" her voice going up and down and her octopus face changing with each expression as if she were smiling, frowning, or puzzling over what she was reading.

Priscilla watched with great concern, wondering what could be in the book and what it was saying about her life. Finally, she could stand it no longer. In a petulant voice, she asked, "So what does it say about me and my life?"

Grandmother Ocean closed the book firmly. This time, she allowed it to float away from her.

Turning, she looked at Priscilla and gave her what might have been a wise smile, though it was hard to tell on an octopus. With some of Granny's firmness, she said, "It says you must live your life and let it unfold the way it is meant to, Priscilla. Life is a mystery that reveals itself in its own time." Then she turned and went back about her business, arms flying right and left, up and down.

Priscilla felt a little sheepish. It was obvious she was not going to find out anything else. Oh well, maybe it was better not to know. If she knew something bad was going to happen, she would be waiting for it to happen, expecting it, and worrying about it all the time. If good things were going to happen, it would be better not to know about them either, as it would spoil the fun of the surprise… or the mystery… as Grandmother Ocean had said. She would prefer something nice to happen without any warning at all.

"Aha, here it is under *Wicked*!" shouted the octopus, in triumph. "Now I can show you what I was talking about." Tucking the large book under one of her arms, she swirled over to Priscilla. With another arm, she set the book on the trap. Using the suckers on a third arm, she began flipping through the pages.

Immediately, lights began to flash. When Priscilla looked down at the book, she saw what caused the lights. There were no words on the pages, only living pictures. Grandmother Ocean found what she was searching for and pointed with one of her arms at the pages she held open, directing Priscilla's attention to what she wanted her to see.

Priscilla gasped with awe. What lay before her was an exquisitely beautiful ocean bay with the sun reflecting off sparking clear blue-green water. High jagged rock cliffs surrounded the bay. Extending out from the tops of the cliffs, long green grass covered an expanse of gentle rolling hills and fields dotted with small shining ponds. Forests of tall evergreen trees extended beyond the fields as far as her eye could see.

Different species of birds could be seen everywhere. Some circled overhead while others floated in the water, sang sweetly in the trees, wandered along the shore, nested on the cliffs, paddled in the ponds, or rustled through the grasses. Seals and otters swam in the sea or basked in the sun on massive rocks protruding from the water. Salmon soared up above the waves, the sun reflecting off their silver scales, the water rippling out in ever-widening circles when they splashed down again.

Priscilla heard every sound and smelled the freshness of the air, the plants, and the water. It was so real, she felt as if she were there inside the book. This place was heaven on earth; it was a peaceful haven, undisturbed by any humans. Such a paradise would bring only contentment to any creature privileged to live there.

Grandmother Ocean told her, "You are looking at a marine wilderness sanctuary on both land and sea, Priscilla. The Wicked Ship wants to use this place for evil purposes. Take your time so you will remember how it looks now."

Priscilla had no problem taking her time; she felt as if she could stay there forever.

Then Grandmother Ocean slowly turned the page and said with great sadness, "And this is how it will look if the Wicked Ship and all those connected with it are allowed to have their way."

When Grandmother Ocean's octopus arm set the new page down, an unbelievably different landscape met Priscilla's eyes. She stared at it in absolute horror. The peaceful paradise had vanished. In fact, it was difficult to believe it had ever existed at all.

A wasteland of oil derricks and sludge had taken its place. Everything, including the water, was filthy dirty. The air was thick with smoke and gave off cloying smells of petroleum and dust. A cacophony of loud mechanical noises quickly overloaded Priscilla's senses. There were no sweet sounds of birds to be heard anywhere, and no sea creatures swam in the blackened water.

The only life left was what little existed in the robotic drivers of many large oil trucks. The long line of grayish vehicles snaked along a dusty gravel road, built over land once green and filled with trees before clear-cutting had laid it bare.

"Oh no!" Priscilla exclaimed with a horrified gasp. "I can't believe anyone would want to do this to such an incredible place."

Grandmother Ocean turned another page.

There, right in front of her, Priscilla saw the Dark Ship. With eight arms stretching out in all directions, it had become a terrifying sea monster attempting to devour the ocean. Oil drilling platforms dotted the water everywhere. Some of these giant ugly contraptions stood in a line leading across the water toward the marine reserve. They looked like the Dark Lord's vicious orcs on the march, destroying anything that lived and breathed in front of them.

Black pools of oily slime and sludge leaked from the ship and the platforms, spreading in increasing quantities over the surface of the ocean. Birds and fish struggled to make their way through the toxic quagmire, already strewn with the bodies of other creatures forced to give up their brave fight.

"It isn't right!" Priscilla cried out. "It just isn't right. We've got to do something to stop this from happening!"

Chapter Thirty
The Black Pearl

"I agree, my dear," sang out a lovely sweet voice. In surprise, Priscilla turned away from the dreadful images in the book to see where this new melodious voice had come from. The octopus was gone. In its place was something so captivating, Priscilla could only stare.

Swimming in front of her was a stunningly gorgeous mermaid. Masses of curly green hair flowed down from her head and clung all around her body like layers of silky sea grass. Her greenish blue eyes were as bottomless as the deepest part of the ocean. Her teeth glistened like strings of fine pearls. Garlands of shells of all sizes and shapes hung around her neck.

The breathtaking creature pushed the book to one side and took a seat on the crab trap next to Priscilla, her long shiny fish tail swirling through the water. A fat catfish with oodles of whiskers swam into her arms. While the mermaid softly stroked its back, the catfish blew out bubbles of contentment. Priscilla continued to stare in disbelief at both of them.

The mermaid spoke again to Priscilla in a voice, so soothing, she might have been singing a lullaby. "I think it will help you to know more about the Wicked Ship, Priscilla. Would you like to see what it looks like on board?"

Priscilla barely nodded assent, as she continued to stare open-mouthed at Grandmother Ocean's most recent transformation into such a fabled figure.

Tucking the catfish under one arm, the mermaid reached out to the book and turned another page. Nodding her head toward the page, she smiled as she gently invited Priscilla's attention toward what lay inside the book.

Dragging her eyes away from the mermaid with some difficulty, Priscilla looked down. The deck of the Dark Ship was there in front of her. Shadow figures, in shades from dark black to light gray, were everywhere on deck. They were a tough looking bunch. Many were arguing and fighting with one another. Others were busy piling thick ropes and dirty metal barrels into the middle of the deck.

Several lighter shadow figures broke away from the others and ran up the stairs to a catwalk that wound around the deck. They jumped over the railing and disappeared down into the ocean without a sound. The ship seemed to shrink in response.

Priscilla looked up at the mermaid to ask, "What just happened, Grandmother Ocean? Why did those shadows jump overboard?"

Grandmother Ocean said, "As you know, Priscilla, this Ship belongs to the People of the Dark. They send emissaries to the Land of Shadows to gather parts of Spirits. Most of these parts still have some Light left in them. If a part gives up the Light and chooses the Darkness, the ship expands. If a part chooses to return to the Light, or if its owner reclaims it, then it jumps ship, so to speak, by diving overboard into the ocean. This causes the power of the Dark to diminish."

"What do you mean by an owner reclaiming a part?" Priscilla asked. This was something new to her.

"You saw on your journey, Priscilla, that shadow parts of your Spirit live on in the Land of Shadows. When you make a choice to live by the Light, you can reclaim those parts of your Spirit. You can turn the Dark energy into Light energy."

Priscilla was relieved to hear this. She did not want parts of her to live on in the Land of Shadows forever. This would take some thinking about, but she had other questions on her mind.

"I don't understand why the Dark Ship is growing so much right now, Grandmother Ocean." Her brow knitted into a puzzled frown as she thought of some of the worrisome things going on in her world. "Why are so many people choosing the values of the Dark?"

"Well, it is difficult to give a simple answer, Priscilla, but it has much to do with the loss of individual power. Too many people want to be like everyone else. Your world is growing more complex all the time. People get overwhelmed. They forget to take the time to listen to their own hearts and end up turning to others for direction. This makes it easy for the People of the Dark to manipulate them. The world needs individual thinkers who are willing to take the time to learn to stand up for what they believe and to do the hard work of bringing their own special gifts into the world."

Priscilla listened to what Grandmother Ocean had to say. She remembered what Wanortu had told them about their inner Light Detectors. Then she thought about Granny, the *Secret of the Rainbow Ribbon*, and her journey in the bear cave. There was so much more going on than she understood. It made her want to know more. But for now, this had to be enough. She needed to concentrate on rescuing Inky and the Light and finding out what had happened to her father.

Grandmother Ocean obviously thought so too. Pointing to a cabin sitting high above the deck in the middle of the ship, she told Priscilla, "That is the bridge from where the captain controls the ship. Underneath the bridge, you will see a large wooden door. We know they took Prince Inky through that door. That is where you must go to find him."

She turned and looked at Priscilla as she said gravely, "I think you know by now, Priscilla, just how important it is to rescue the Prince and restore the Light safely to the palace. If this does not happen, the power of the People of the Dark will continue unchecked and will be difficult to stop."

Priscilla's stomach clenched as she thought about the great responsibility lying ahead of her. When she tried to picture herself and Alasdair on board the Dark Ship, the knots in her gut tightened. How could they possibly avoid being seen? She felt sick with dread.

"But how will we get out to the Dark Ship, and what will keep them from seeing us?" she whispered weakly, trying to dispel her anxiety in her usual practical way.

Grandmother Ocean replied, "You must use Baba's boat and travel out to the ship in the dark." She pointed to a ladder attached to the side of the boat, the same ladder Inky's abductor had used. "You can climb up this ladder and over the railing onto the catwalk. There are stairs down to the deck all the way around."

"But how can we move about on deck without being seen?" Priscilla almost moaned with despair.

"I will give you the sealskin you are wearing now as well as one for Alasdair," Grandmother Ocean told her. "All I ask is for you to return them to my ocean once you are finished with them. The sealskin will make you close to invisible in the dark. You will look like one of the shadows. If anyone comes near you on deck, hide amongst the ropes and barrels and no one will notice you.

How you rescue Inky and the Light will depend on your courage, determination, and inspiration."

The mermaid took hold of a large wrinkled shell on one of her garlands and plucked something from inside it. She opened her hand to show Priscilla what it was. "I want you to have this, Priscilla. It is a gift for your courage and will remind you that you are not alone." These were familiar comforting words to Priscilla.

When she saw what Grandmother Ocean held in her palm, Priscilla blew out bubbles of pleasure just as the catfish had done. It was a large, shiny gray pearl, glistening with iridescent light. Carefully lifting the pearl, Priscilla held it in her hand and stared down at it with awe.

Grandmother Ocean said, "That is a black pearl, Priscilla, one of the rarest of the pearls. As you may know, a pearl grows within an oyster's shell. A small speck of grit or a microscopic creature finds a way inside the oyster, causing irritation. The oyster wraps a film around the irritant to ease the pain. When this does not help, the oyster continues to wrap it. In this slow and meticulous way, a precious pearl forms. The pearl is a symbol of the beauty that results when we give gentle attention to those parts of ourselves which irritate us in some way."

Grandmother Ocean continued, "If a black pearl has a blemish on it, workers known as peelers carefully peel back the layers of the pearl until the blemish is gone. The pearl will be smaller, but it will be perfect, and thus, infinitely more valuable. This is a symbol, Priscilla, of the perfection lying within each of us. By slowly and carefully peeling away our blemishes, we will one day uncover our true perfection and our real value."

Then the mermaid opened a clamshell on a different garland and lifted something from it. Taking Priscilla's other hand, she gently pressed whatever this was into her palm and closed her fingers around it. This was flatter, not round like a pearl, and the shape felt familiar to her.

When Priscilla opened her fingers to look, much to her surprise, she saw her pink heart stone, the one she had tossed into the river to honor Grandmother Wolf. At least, she thought it was the same one. She stared at it in wonder. Could it possibly be?

"This stone belongs to you, I believe." Grandmother Ocean confirmed it did indeed belong to Priscilla. "Grandmother Wolf wanted you to have it back again."

Feeling completely overwhelmed, Priscilla did not know what to say. Her stomach began to unknot, and she felt much better. Grasping her old and new treasures, one in each of her tightly rolled fists, she whispered with gratitude, "Thank you, Grandmother Ocean, for your help and for your gifts."

"It is time for you to return to the palace now, Priscilla," Grandmother Ocean said. "You have much work ahead of you. Sami and Sumi will escort you back to your boat where Waleutius the Whale is waiting for you. He will speed you back to the shore. Good luck, my dear, and remember to have courage and to trust your own resources. You are never alone."

With these last comforting words, the mermaid, who was Grandmother Ocean, simply disappeared. Priscilla, feeling amazed by what she had seen and learned, slowly followed behind the fat catfish as it swam toward the hole. The catfish turned and raised a couple of whiskers at her, as if to say goodbye, before it swam through the hole. Priscilla had a feeling Grandmother Ocean was now a catfish.

Sami and Sumi were waiting for her outside the wreck where she had left them. They nodded their heads shyly at her in greeting and then swam off ahead of her as before. This time they led her directly up to the surface of the water and back to the boat. The scenic route they had taken on the way down must have been for her benefit. Such kindness from the little seals touched Priscilla's heart.

With their snouts, Sami and Sumi pushed her from behind as she pulled herself back into the boat. The sealskin Grandmother Ocean had promised for Alasdair was already there in the boat. She thanked the friendly little seals and waved goodbye to them as they disappeared into the depths once more.

Her ocean visit was over. It was another experience she would never forget and would probably never have again. Feeling a little sad that it was over, she peeled off her smelly sealskin, dried herself off with her towel, and pulled on her clothes.

Once her pink stone was back in the pocket of her overalls where it belonged, she put the precious black pearl into the pocket where her favorite shell had once been. Rolling up her sealskin, she wrapped it and Alasdair's sealskin in a towel and tucked the small bundle into her pack.

While she was tying her rainbow ribbon back in her hair, the boat began to move swiftly across the surface of the ocean. She looked over the side and saw that a small black and white whale was ferrying the boat across the ocean.

The whale called out to her in a young voice, "My name is Waleutius the Whale. Hold on, Priscilla. I'll carry you back to shore."

Laughing in delight, she clung to the sides of the boat as Waleutius whisked it across the water. Before long, the beach and the palace came into view. It was a great relief to see them again.

Soon she would see Alasdair as well. She had been too busy to think much about him, but now she was eager to know how he was doing. The same feelings she had felt in the Valley of the Moon surfaced in her heart once more, and she trembled with anticipation.

When they drew closer to the shore, Waleutius gently let the boat back down in the water. He rose to the surface at the back of the boat and told her, "When you are ready to go out to the Dark Ship, I will be available to take you. Just come down to the sea and call for me."

With his curved black and white snout, he gave the boat a great push just in time for it to catch a ride on a big wave that took it almost all the way in to the shore.

BOOK SIX

FIGHTING FOR THE LIGHT

Chapter Thirty-One
Preparing to Board

Priscilla did not have a chance to thank Waleutius the Whale, nor did she have time to worry about how she would get the boat onto the shore. Several People of the Rainbow rushed into the water to meet her and, quick as a wink, pulled the boat up on the beach. When she stepped out on the rocks, her legs buckled. She had to stop for a moment to get her land legs back.

Wanortu, Eideard, and Raldemar were there to greet her. Smiling at them in delight, she said, "I'm so glad to see you all again!"

Raldemar croaked his greeting while Eideard gave his usual "Hoot Mon!"

Wanortu hugged her and said, "I am happy to see you looking so well, Priscilla. You have been many places and learned much since we were last together, my dear. Come inside the palace and have some food and rest a little. Later we can talk."

The mention of food made her realize she had not eaten a thing since breakfast at Baba's cottage. Alasdair was nowhere around. As they made their way up to the palace, she asked Wanortu, "How's Alasdair? Is he okay?"

"His health is much better," Wanortu told her, his voice sounding uncharacteristically solemn. She wondered if something might be wrong.

Before she could ask why Alasdair had not come to meet her, Wanortu added, "He has been working with Lita and the Royal Children on some special entertainment. If we hurry, we should just be in time to catch their performance. We have already finished our lunch, but we saved some food for you. You can eat while they are performing."

She was relieved to hear that Alasdair was fine. The reason he had not come to greet her must have been because he was busy getting ready for the performance.

Raldemar and Eideard flew off together as Wanortu led Priscilla into the banquet room. King Sol and Queen Luminata greeted Priscilla warmly and invited her to sit beside them while she ate and watched the entertainment.

Priscilla filled her plate with food. She was just about to take a bite of a plump strawberry when the banquet room doors opened with a flourish. Alasdair strode into the room, guitar in hand. He was dressed all in white, except for a small rainbow circlet on his bare head. Bowing low to the King and Queen, he lifted his head and stepped back for a moment.

Seeing him standing so tall and proud, looking so much better than when she had last seen him, Priscilla's heart leapt with joy. Calling out, "Alasdair!" she lifted her arm to wave to him, but he had already turned away. Intent upon what he was doing, he had not even noticed her. Feeling embarrassed, and with a sense of disappointment, she let her hand fall back down. Returning her attention to her food, it was with much less enthusiasm than before.

After seating himself on a tall stool, Alasdair began to play and then to sing. Through the doors sailed a mountainous figure, so much like Mother Nature, Priscilla had to do a double take. A long white gown completely covered a form built on wheels with someone neatly tucked into the top. After a few moments, Priscilla realized it was Princess Lita.

Her white skin had been colored nut brown, and she wore a red wig. When she shook her head, sparkles whirled off the wig in every direction. Lizards, snakes, and all sorts of other small creatures clung to her robe, neck, and arms. To Priscilla's great relief, these were not real but made of cloth. The Royal Children, dressed in animal costumes, danced and frolicked in delight all around the figure of Mother Nature.

As Alasdair sang, Priscilla recalled him mentioning something about singing a song about Mother Nature to the cubs in the bear cave. The performance was full of laughter and fun. Everyone involved was having a great time.

Big Mamma

When the earth starts a shakin'
And your knees start a quakin'
And the lions and tigers start to roar
When the birds fly thither
And the snakes start to slither
Big Mammas comin' through that door

Oh Mamma, Big Mamma
You never wanna make her roar
Oh Mamma, Big Mamma
She's more woman
Than you've ever seen before

When the thunder starts a rumblin'
And the ground starts a tumblin'
And flames go shootin' through the air
When the wind is a whistlin'
And your neck hairs are a bristlin'
Big Mammas gonna be right there

Oh Mamma, Big Mamma
You never wanna make her roar
Oh Mamma, Big Mamma
She's more woman
Than you've ever seen before

When you hear her start a chucklin'
And your knees start a bucklin'
And critters come flyin' cross your path
You'd better skedaddle
As fast as you can paddle
Big Mammas gonna start to laugh

Oh Mamma, Big Mamma
You never wanna make her roar
Oh Mamma, Big Mamma
She's more woman
Than you've ever seen before

Priscilla loved the song and the performance and laughed along with everyone else. Yet watching Alasdair smile and sing to Lita, his unwavering gaze following her every move, she felt alone and left out, much like she had felt with the Light-Eater girl in the forest.

When the performance was finished, the bowing completed, and the performers roundly applauded, Alasdair started to follow Lita and the children out of the room.

Wanortu called out to him. "Alasdair, could you please come here for a moment?"

With obvious reluctance, Alasdair turned and walked over to the table. He looked at Priscilla in surprise. "I didn't think you'd be back so soon," he said, without much enthusiasm. "I'm glad you're okay," he added, almost as an afterthought.

Priscilla wondered what was going on with him. It was as if he had not even noticed how long she had been gone. He did not seem at all pleased to see her and showed no curiosity about where she had been or what she had found out.

"Alasdair," Wanortu told him in a pleasant but firm voice, "that was an enjoyable song and a great performance, but now we must find out what Priscilla has learned from Grandmother Ocean. Then we need to make plans to rescue Inky. Please come and meet with us in the conservatory as soon as you have changed."

Alasdair agreed with a sulky sigh. After a slight bow to the king and queen, he turned quickly and, without another word, walked out of the room. Priscilla looked at Wanortu and saw him watching Alasdair with a look of concern on his face.

Feeling her eyes upon him, Wanortu smiled at her as he said gently, "Come Priscilla, let us go to the conservatory. You can catch me up while we wait for Alasdair to join us."

They took their leave of the king and queen, and together they went into the sunny room and sat side by side on a bench. Priscilla and Alasdair had been so many places and had done so much, it seemed like a long time ago when they had been in this same room listening to King Sol and Inky argue with one another.

She told Wanortu about what had happened once she left Baba's cottage, and then she showed him the black pearl. Wanortu whistled softly through his teeth as he took the pearl and held it for a moment. Handing it back with a big smile, he said, "You must have impressed Grandmother Ocean, Priscilla, for her to honor you with such a rare gift."

Flushing at his words, and wanting to cover her embarrassment, she asked, "Why isn't King Sol meeting with us?"

"The king and queen heard everything Alasdair shared with us about your journey, Priscilla," he answered. "Right now, in the absence of the Light, they are spending as much time as they can in the Muses sending out Light energy. Most of the villagers have been gathering there as well. King Sol entrusted to me the task of helping you and Alasdair figure out how to rescue Prince Inky and the Light."

While they waited for Alasdair, Priscilla decided to ask Wanortu something that had been troubling her since her visit to the Land of Shadows. "Wanortu, I don't quite understand about these shadow parts. Grandmother Ocean explained some of it, but I'm still confused. Was it my father who was hurt?"

"You saw a shadow part of your father, Priscilla. Probably it was the part of his Spirit he lost when your mother died." He went on to explain, "It will be harder for your father to make the right decision while this part is separated from him, especially when he is being pressured by the People of the Dark."

"But how can I help him?"

Wanortu was thoughtful for a moment before he spoke. "From all you have told me, Priscilla, your father's shadow no doubt was taken out to the Dark Ship as well. You may be able to rescue him when you rescue Inky. If this part reconnects with your father, it would be easier for him to make the right decision."

This made some sort of sense to her. Even though she had no idea how to do it, or how long it would take to find Inky and her father's shadow, or for that matter, how to rescue them, she felt an urgency to get started doing something. "But what will happen if we can't find his shadow part or convince him to reconnect?" she asked, thinking of Inky's words. She did not like to think about failing, but she knew it was always a possibility.

"All will not be lost, Priscilla. You can still talk to your father when you get home and convince him to reclaim his shadow part. The loss of this part is probably what made him more vulnerable to the People of the Dark in the first place."

The door suddenly swung open, and Alasdair charged into the room. Though he had changed back into his own clothes, it was obvious he had not changed his attitude. Flopping down on a bench across from them, he announced rudely, "Here I am. Let's get on with this. Everyone's waiting for me. I said I'd be right back."

Holding back her anger, Priscilla briefly told Alasdair what she had learned from Grandmother Ocean. When she finished, she took his sealskin out of her pack and handed it to him. "You'll need to wear this when we go out to the Dark Ship."

Alasdair took the sealskin with a look of disgust and said, "Yuck! I don't want to wear this smelly stuff."

Priscilla remembered feeling the same way when she had first seen her sealskin, but she also knew how much it had helped her. Before she could open her mouth to say anything, Wanortu began speaking.

In a gentle but firm tone, he told Alasdair, "Not only will you have to wear the sealskin, Alasdair, but you will need to darken your skin as well. Otherwise, you will shine out like a beacon on the Dark Ship. Priscilla, you will need to do the same." Reaching into one of his big pockets, he took out a couple of small tins and gave one to each of them, saying. "Here is some blackening to put on your exposed skin."

After some discussion about how to rescue Inky, it became apparent that not much could be determined beforehand other than to take Baba's boat and, with Waleutius the Whale's help, head out to the Dark Ship. Once on deck, they needed to remain invisible and make their way to the door under the bridge as quickly as they could. The rest, as Baba and Grandmother Ocean had both said, would be up to them.

Wanortu reminded them, "Don't forget to use your Light Detectors. They will help you make the right choices, tell you what you need to know, and show you how to find the Light in the Darkness."

The three of them agreed that it would be best to wait until after dark to head out to the ship, though Priscilla and Alasdair disagreed about what time to leave. She wanted to go in the late afternoon as soon as it got dark. He wanted to wait until later in the evening when he thought most of the crew would be asleep.

"But the crew will have different shifts. Guards will be watching all the time," Priscilla insisted. "It won't matter when we go as long as it's dark. We need to go as soon as we can." She was beginning to wonder if Alasdair was stalling because he was afraid to go. Even though she was scared, she knew she could not stop until they had rescued Inky and her father.

"There should be fewer guards later in the evening," Alasdair argued. "Besides, I'm in the middle of working on songs for the wedding. I need to finish them before we go. The performers must have time to practice."

Ah, so that was it. He had other, more important, things on his mind. "But there won't *be* any wedding if we don't rescue Inky!" Priscilla retorted, her anger bursting forth at last.

Once again, Alasdair did not seem to hear her, or perhaps he chose not to. Maybe he was hoping the wedding would not take place so he could have Lita all to himself. A feeling of discouragement overcame Priscilla, causing her to wonder if they could even do this at all.

Wanortu offered a compromise. "Why don't you both take the next few hours until it is dark and do what you need to do. Priscilla, I suggest you get some rest as you have had a busy day, and you still have a long night ahead of you."

He pointed to one of the cushioned window seats that she had longed for the last time she had been in the conservatory. "You can curl up in here on one of the window seats. There are blankets tucked inside the seats."

Then he turned to Alasdair. "Alasdair, perhaps you can hurry and finish your rehearsals so you will be ready to go as soon as possible after dark."

With nothing else to say or do, Priscilla and Alasdair agreed, neither one at all satisfied. Without even saying goodbye, Alasdair hurried out of the room. Priscilla stared after him in distress.

Wanortu started to get up. Then he seemed to think better of it and sat back down beside her. "I know you are troubled by Alasdair's behavior, Priscilla," he told her, taking her hand in his. "I want to tell you something. Perhaps it will help you understand him a little better."

Stroking her hand, as gently as if he were stroking Eideard's feathers, he told her, "Alasdair is getting something here in the palace which he has never had before and has long desired. For the first time in his life, he is receiving admiration from his peers just for being who he is. He is the center of attention, not because he looks unusual, but because he is well liked and willing to share his considerable talents. Here Alasdair feels accepted. Much like a starving lion that has just found food, he wants to keep on eating for fear there will be nothing left for him tomorrow."

Priscilla thought about this for a moment. It made a lot of sense to her, and her spirits began to lift. She asked a question she found difficult to put into words. "Wanortu, this thing... this strong feeling Alasdair seems to have for Lita… is it part of what you're talking about?"

"Yes, my dear, it is." Wanortu spoke with great kindness, somehow understanding the pain she was feeling in asking such a question. "Lita is so like Alasdair physically. He sees in her a reflection of himself… one he is able to love. It is a kind of narcissistic love. This, too, is something new for him. He will no doubt get over it in time, but for now, it helps him begin to love himself."

"Thanks for telling me this, Wanortu," Priscilla said, her eyes filling up with tears of gratitude. "It gives me something to think about even if I don't quite understand it. I feel like he no longer cares about Inky and the Light. And I don't seem important to him at all. It's like he doesn't even see me."

"That is true, Priscilla. Right now, he is in his own world and not aware of what he is doing. I am sure he will see the Light soon. Then he will recognize how his behavior is affecting you. Do not give up hope, little one." He patted her on the shoulder. "Now you must get some rest."

After Wanortu left the room, Priscilla sat for a moment longer thinking about what he had told her. Her mouth slowly opened into a huge yawn, becoming almost as wide as the gap between Mother Nature's front teeth, and the idea of sleep seemed quite appealing.

A multiplicity of thoughts bounced around inside her head as she made her way to one of the window seats, found a blanket, and snuggled down amongst the soft pillows. She lay on her stomach looking out at the ocean as her mind continued to wander. Before long, her head relaxed into the inviting pillows and sleep caught up with her.

Chapter Thirty-Two
Just Plain Ducky

When Priscilla awoke, it was late in the afternoon. The conservatory was beginning to darken. She sat up and stretched her arms and legs. Well rested, she felt ready to meet whatever challenges lay ahead. The first thing she needed to do was to find Alasdair, so she walked out into the corridor to look for him.

The center of the palace looked different from the first time she had seen it. Back then, the Sacred Light had been shining brilliantly with the Royal Rainbow rising out of it. Now everything was dark and felt so bleak, she was reminded of how important it was to get to the Dark Ship as soon as possible.

While she stood wondering which way to go, she heard laughter and singing coming from a room off to one side. Following the cheery sounds, she entered a small room where she found Alasdair, with Lita by his side, sitting in the midst of all the Royal Children. They were talking, laughing, and singing together as Alasdair strummed his guitar. No one noticed Priscilla as she walked in, so she had to speak in order to get his attention.

"Alasdair," Priscilla said quietly, at first, and then louder so that she could make herself heard over their voices, *"Alasdair!"* It came out with such force that everyone turned to look at her. "It's starting to get dark. We need to get ready to go."

"It's not night yet, and we're not done here." Alasdair's impatience with her showed in his gruff voice. "As soon as we've finished our rehearsal and the choirs have a chance to practice, we'll go. There's still plenty of time."

Lita gave her a smile of welcome. "Hello, Priscilla! Why don't you come and join us while you wait?"

Having nothing better to do, Priscilla sat down on the floor behind the children. The song Alasdair was working on was one she had never heard before. Relaxed and confident in himself and in his music, he was obviously enjoying all the attention. If Wanortu was right, this was what he had been craving all his life.

As she watched Alasdair working with everyone, Priscilla felt the same powerful longing rise up in her as it had at the Pool of Reflection, only now it was much stronger. This surprised her because she thought she had tucked the feeling away. Even in its hidden place, the feeling seemed to have developed a life of its own.

After a while, Alasdair, Lita, and the children stood up to begin rehearsing the performance for the wedding. Since they all had a specific part to play and a place to be, Priscilla felt like she was only in the way. Unnoticed, she slipped out the door and walked in misery back to the conservatory. She stood by the glass doors in the conservatory, staring out at the darkening ocean, thinking of home and how the beach always made her feel better. Alasdair could find her there as well as anywhere, so she grabbed her pack and headed out the door and down to the shore.

She sat on the rocks and looked at the water. After a while, she pulled her knees up to her chest, and rested her head on her knees.

Closing her eyes for a moment, she thought about Alasdair and the mixture of feelings she felt for him.

"Whatcha doin', Love?" a peculiar male voice interrupted her thoughts, startling her, and causing her to look up in surprise. These were somewhat familiar words, but she knew she did not speak them to herself. This was not her seashore, and here she was not queen of the kingdom.

Waddling up the beach toward her was the oddest duck she had ever seen. His feathers were a curious combination of colors, and the word *waddling* had to have been created in order to describe just such a creature. For when he moved, his large behind wiggled from side to side, giving him a comical lurching gait.

Pulling to a dramatic stop in front of her, the duck studied her with great intensity, his round dark eyes shining out above his vivid yellow beak. His head was an iridescent green, and around his neck was a wide band, the same glowing color as his beak. There were white feathers on his breast and a mixture of gray, brown, and black feathers on his back and hind end. An array of dark red feathers on the tip of his tail added the final flourish.

"Whatcha doin', Love?" he repeated, plumping his big behind down on the rocks in front of her and looking up at her, his large eyes filled with interest.

Priscilla looked down at this strange duck and did not know quite how to answer, so she said, "Sittin' on the beach, doncha know, doncha know?" wondering why on earth she had answered in such an absurd way. Perhaps it was because she was feeling a little embarrassed about the thoughts he had interrupted.

"Oh my, but aren't you the thathy one!" he said.

It took her a moment to get that 'thathy' meant sassy and that this fat duck apparently had a lisp. He sounded like Daffy Duck.

"I thought maybe you could uthe thome good company, thithter. You look a little down in the mouth," As he made this last comment, he started to quack. When he quacked, his huge downy behind quivered from side to side. "Did you get it, *down* in the mouth?" he quacked and quivered again at his little pun.

"Who are you anyway?" Priscilla cut him off bluntly. She was in no mood for this kind of nonsense. Besides, she had heard this silly joke many times before.

"Jutht plain Ducky," he said, quacking and quivering again.

"I didn't ask *how* you are," Priscilla snapped at him, "I asked *who* you are."

"And I jutht told you, my name ith Ducky".

"Oh!" said Priscilla. To cover her embarrassment, she added grouchily, "Well, I think that's a very silly name and that you're a very silly looking duck." What had gotten into her anyway? Usually she was much more polite.

"Well, I am a thilly duck," he responded affably, with another quack and quiver. "Whatth your name?"

"Priscilla," she practically groused her name at him.

"Prithilla, Prithilla, Prithilla," the duck seemed to be rolling her name around on whatever he rolled it around on; she had no idea if ducks had tongues. "Thatth the thilliest name there ever wath."

"It ith… it is not!" Priscilla exclaimed with unexpected vehemence. "My mother gave me that name. It was the name of one of her favorite dolls."

All at once, a light dawned. It was her *real* mother, not her stepmother, who had given her the name Priscilla. Now it made sense. Suddenly, she knew how happy she was to have her name. She smiled to herself. "I *like* the name Priscilla," she announced with great pride to the duck. "So you'd better not say another bad word against it," she scolded.

"Oh my, but you are quite the little thpitfire!" Ducky said. "Okay, okay, you win. Prithilla ith a beautiful name. Now tell me Prithilla, Love, why are you thitting here alone on the beach looking

tho thad? Anyone with a name ath beautiful ath Prithilla thouldn't
be looking tho thad. Too bad, tho thad."

At this pronouncement by the thilly duck, Priscilla started to
giggle and then to laugh. Ducky began to quack. With each quack,
his behind jiggled and wiggled. This made Priscilla laugh and Ducky
quack and quiver even more. Soon they were both rolling around
on the beach laughing and quacking together until it was apparent
that in short order they had become the best of friends.

"Oh my," gasped Priscilla, as she pulled herself together again.
She sat up and grinned at Ducky. "I haven't laughed like that in a
long time. It felt good."

"Why haven't you laughed like that in a long time?" Ducky
asked her in all seriousness. "Itth a good thing to laugh, Prithilla.
Laughing makth everything eathier and much more fun."

Ducky's words made her think of Mollie. When she looked in
his eyes, she knew he was just as kind and as wise as Mollie. He
really *did* want to know the answer to his question. So they sat and
talked together. They talked on and on as it grew darker and darker.

Priscilla told Ducky about the search for Inky and the Light and
about her feelings for Alasdair. When she expressed her concern for
her father and her fear of the Dark Ship, she shared how scared she
really was, something she had not even acknowledged to herself.

Ducky listened closely. He seemed to understand everything
she told him. What she was thinking and feeling no longer felt
abnormal. This made her feel so much better.

Then Ducky told her that he and his singing group, the Witty
Winkers, were going to be performing at the wedding. He told her
of his secret love for one of the other ducks in the group. "I don't
thay anything becauth I'm afraid no one could love me with my
thilly lookth."

Hearing this, Priscilla felt terribly guilty. "Ducky, I'm so sorry
for calling you a silly looking duck. I just said it because I was

feeling bad. You don't look silly to me at all… you look just right. You're kind, gentle, and understanding, and that's what counts. I'm sure your duck friend knows this as well." Though Ducky had come to shore to attend a rehearsal, when he saw how unhappy she was, he had stopped to see if he could help. This was just the kind of duck he was.

When it came time for her new friend to leave, they said good-bye, and he waddled off to find the rest of the Witty Winkers. As she smiled and waved to him, she thought about how much he had helped her. The silly lovable little duck had made her laugh. She had been able to open up and talk to him. He had listened to her and understood her longings and her fears, some so much like his own. Now she felt much better, and she was not nearly as scared as she had been before.

Out of nowhere, it came to her what she had to do. Wanortu would probably say her Light Detector was working. Alasdair did not have to go with her to the Dark Ship. He could stay in the palace and get the attention he needed. She would go alone to rescue Inky and her father. Anyway, one person might not be seen as easily.

Making a decision felt good. Waiting around had been hard on her. She needed to be doing something useful. Before she could change her mind, she pulled off her rainbow ribbon and her outer clothing. She took the sealskin and the tin of blackening from her backpack and put her carefully folded ribbon and clothes in their place.

Within moments, she was wearing her sealskin once more. After she blackened her face and the palms of her hands, she knew she would be almost as invisible as a shadow figure in the dark, just as Grandmother Ocean had said. It was a good thing her sealskin-covered feet did not turn into flippers as they did in the water, so she could walk on the rocks with ease.

After putting her backpack on the highest step, to keep it safe from the incoming tide, she hurried down to Baba's boat. The People of the Rainbow had wrapped the rope around a rock, so she unwound it and shoved the boat down the shore and into the water.

Without stopping to wonder if she was doing the right thing, she hopped in and began rowing out to sea. When she had rowed out a short distance, she quietly called across the water, "Waleutius".

Almost immediately, the graceful black and white whale rose out of the water and swam toward her. He had been watching for her as promised. In a few moments, he was underneath her boat, and they were zooming out to the Dark Ship.

When they drew nearer the huge shadow ship, her bravado began to falter. Having made her decision in the spur of the moment, she had not stopped to think about what she had to face. The immensity of the dark shape looming up ahead sobered her up in a hurry. Soon she was shaking and quivering all over.

Shaking and quivering made her think of Ducky and Mother Nature when they laughed. Then she thought of Alasdair, Lita, and the children performing his song about Mother Nature. These images made her giggle, helping her to breathe a little easier. Ducky and Mollie were right. Laughing did make things easier. She could do this. Anyway, she no longer had much of a choice.

"I just need to take it one step at a time. The first thing I have to do is climb up that ladder," she said, taking herself firmly in hand. "I'll think of that and of nothing else."

Waleutius slid the boat silently alongside the ladder on the huge ship. When Priscilla looked up at the dark, rusty metal hull above her, she gulped, feeling very small indeed. Well, no matter how ridiculous it seemed, or how small she was, she was going to do this.

The story of David and Goliath came to mind. Just like David, she was small and determined. Even though she did not have his ability with a slingshot… for that matter she did not even *have* a slingshot… she was not going to let her fear of this dark Goliath stop her.

Tying the boat to the bottom rung of the ladder, she whispered her thanks to Waleutius and received his guttural "good luck" in response. Then she bravely grabbed the rough, cold rung of metal above her, swung herself out of the boat and stepped onto the ladder. The sticky sealskin on her fingers and feet helped her cling to the rungs. The ship reeked of oil, rust, mildew, and slime, and she wrinkled her nose in disgust.

As she stood on the ladder for a moment watching Waleutius glide away in the darkness, she realized how alone she was. What on earth did she think she was doing? Then she remembered that she was not alone… not really… not now… not ever…

With a great effort of will, she turned back to the ladder. By taking it one rung at a time, she began slowly and with stubborn determination to climb up the side of the Dark Ship.

Chapter Thirty-Three
The Dark Ship

The rungs of the ladder on the side of the Dark Ship seemed to go up and up forever. Just when Priscilla was sure she could not take one more step, she found herself at the top. By lifting her head up a little way, she could peer through the railing and see the catwalk with the deck below.

Keeping her head low, she stayed still and listened. Trembling, she felt the knots in her gut turn into butterflies doing multiple jumps and cartwheels. A heavy sense of darkness pressed down upon her shoulders, making her shudder. There was no doubt she was about to enter a very evil place.

To distract herself from this uncomfortable feeling, she peeked through the railing again to see what was happening below on the deck. Black shadow figures were hurrying back and forth, shouting and yelling at one another as they tossed ropes and heavy barrels into the middle of the deck. Everything looked much like what she had seen in Grandmother Ocean's big book.

A glow of light from above illuminated the deck. The light came from the windows of the bridge. Beneath it, she saw the wooden door Grandmother Ocean had pointed out… where she needed to go to find Inky. The door looked terribly far from where she was. While she was pondering how she could get to it unseen with so many shadow figures around, a loud whistle blew.

Thinking that the whistle was a warning of an intruder on board, she immediately pulled her head back down in a panic. Clinging to the ladder, she shook from head to foot as she heard the sound of running feet and the babble of voices, expecting at any moment to hear a yell indicating that she had been discovered.

But nothing happened. Before long, everything above her became quiet. Once her heartbeat slowed enough for her to breathe, she raised her head again to peer through the railing. All activity on deck appeared to have ceased. No dark figures were about at all. They had all disappeared.

Acting purely on instinct, she climbed over the railing and jumped onto the metal catwalk. Running swiftly down the nearest steps, she reached the wooden deck. She was just starting toward the door when she heard footsteps coming from both directions and realized too late that not everyone had gone.

Recalling Grandmother Ocean's suggestion, she dove in amongst the ropes and barrels in the middle of the deck and curled up as tight as a ball. Scarcely daring to breathe, she lay without moving an inch.

The footsteps grew louder. They crossed paths right where they passed her hiding place. Whoever these footsteps belonged to stopped to talk to one another. Priscilla took a deep breath and pretended she was invisible, as she tried to quell her quivering body. If she had wanted to, which of course she did not, she could have reached out and touched them.

"Hey, Grungeball, I sees you got stuck with dinner guard duty too. Whad ya do to deserve it this time?" snarled a low surly voice.

"Nuttin' as bad as you, Dogface, I'm sure," a bad-tempered voice responded. "Hey, what's that yucky smell… smells like somethin' bad out of the sea. You been bathin' in the ocean again, ya dirty mutt?"

Priscilla froze as she realized the men behind the voices could smell her sealskin.

A low cursing was the response to this insult. The two men started pushing each other around.

More footsteps sounded close by, and a third voice growled, "You two better stop that fighting or you'll both be smellin' the fishes. Get back to your rounds now."

More cursing and grumbling went on as all the footsteps faded away. Priscilla released her breath as she slowly uncurled. Staying low amongst the barrels and ropes, and at the same time listening for voices or footsteps, she eased her way toward the large door.

Just when she was about to step out into the open, the sound of footsteps came closer once more. Hurriedly, she curled up tightly until the two guards passed in front of her. This time they did not stop, though they continued to snarl and hurl curses at one another.

While waiting to see if the third guard showed up, she glanced up at the windows of the bridge. What she saw there almost made her heart stop beating.

Through the lighted window shades, she saw the silhouette of a monstrous stubby figure. Its huge head bobbled up and down as it paced furiously back and forth. If this was the captain of the Dark Ship, then it had to be the most evil creature of all. With such a bizarre silhouette, Priscilla could only imagine how hideous it would look up close. She hoped she would never have occasion to see it.

Hearing only silence, she tore her gaze away from the frightening figure and slipped swiftly across the deck, the sealskin on her feet serving to cover the noise of her steps. With all her strength, she swung the heavy door open just enough to allow her small frame to squeeze through before closing it quietly behind her.

Breathing a huge sigh of relief, she leaned back against the door, listening. At least she seemed to have accomplished her first step unnoticed. Finding herself in a dark passageway, she let her eyes adjust to the dark and checked to make sure no one was around. Strips of dim lights marked the middle of the floor and the edges of the walls, but they offered little illumination. Having no clue as to where Inky could be, she saw no alternative but to open every door along the passageway to check inside.

At each door, she listened for any movement within. Then she tried the door, thinking if Inky were inside, most likely it would be locked. The first few doors opened into small cell-like rooms with bunk beds. Fortunately, they were unoccupied. All the crew appeared to have gone to dinner.

As she was about to open another door, she heard footsteps ahead of her, around the corner. Flattening herself against the wall, she stood perfectly still, holding her breath, her heart fluttering like a bird.

A door opened, and a loud male voice called out "Chow time!" Priscilla edged down the hall and peeked cautiously around the corner. Midway down the hall, a door on the right was open with light streaming out into the hallway. Priscilla listened intently, but could hear nothing coming from within.

When a dark shadow figure stepped out the door, Priscilla pulled her head back in a hurry. She looked once more when she heard the shadow figure say to whoever was in the room, "I'll be back to get yer tray when I've finished with me own chow."

A second voice spoke. This voice was familiar. Her legs sagged with relief and her heart jumped for joy. It was Inky! She had found him at last. He was pleading with the guard, "Please, you must help me get out of here. My wedding day is tomorrow. I cannot miss my own wedding. You do not need to keep me here. I meant no one any harm. I only wanted to help."

The guard answered rudely, "Too bad, Yer Highness, but the cap'n gives the orders, and we just obeys 'em. Eat yer chow as it's all yer gettin'." With that, he closed the door and locked it. He hung the key up on a hook on the wall to the right of the door.

Priscilla cheered to herself when she saw the guard hang up the key. Apparently, they did not anticipate any uninvited visitors coming aboard. She quickly stepped into a doorway in case the guard came her way and was relieved to hear his footsteps moving off in the opposite direction. Another door opened and closed, followed by silence again.

As swiftly as a deer, she ran around the corner and down the hall. When she reached Inky's door, she jumped up and grabbed the key, unlocked the door and stepped inside, closing the door quietly behind her. She had entered a tiny cell containing only a bed and a small table with two chairs. Inky was sitting at the table eating from a tray of food in front of him.

He looked up in surprise. His look changed from puzzlement to total amazement when he realized who she was. Dropping his fork, he jumped up, crying, "Priscilla, is that you? What are you doing here? Why are you dressed like that? Oh, I am so glad to see you. Are you alone?"

Priscilla laughed at this outpouring of questions, confusion, and gladness. She gave Inky a big smelly, hug. Looking into his eyes, she asked, "Are you okay?" He certainly looked okay. His black clothes were rumpled and dirty, but he was as handsome and regal as ever. However, there was a kind of weariness in his eyes which she had never seen before, making him appear much older than she remembered.

"Yes, I am okay," Inky answered, with a sigh of resignation. "They have not hurt me, Priscilla, but I have been so worried about

Lita and my family and the little People of the Rainbow and how they are all managing without the Light."

Looking even more pained, he touched his hand to his forehead and added with a groan, "I am afraid I have made an awful mistake, Priscilla. And now the Light is gone."

"The Light!" Priscilla cried in response. "Oh my gosh! There's no time to talk now, Inky. We've got to get moving." The Light had to be found and then her father. After that, they needed to get off the ship. Explanations and discussions would have to wait until they safely returned to the palace. "What have they done with the Light?"

"I don't know. They took it from me when they first brought me on the ship. I have not seen it since." His eyes were full of sadness and his shoulders slumped. Pausing in thought for a moment, he added, "But they did seem to be terribly afraid of it, so my guess is they have put it somewhere well out of sight. They must have covered it with something else because they did not take the Light Protector from me." He lifted his vest to show Priscilla the pouch still around his waist.

Wondering what Nancy Drew would do in such a situation, Priscilla gave the matter some thought herself. Then she said, "They wouldn't need a protector if they hid the Light somewhere in the darkest part of the ship. It would have to be in a place where no one would ever be able to see it or know it was there. I wonder where that would be…"

Inky connected with her train of thought as hope began to rise in him again. "Somewhere down below us, I imagine, Priscilla, where few crew members are likely to go… maybe in the cargo hold or the engine room. The cargo hold would have a great many hiding places, but I think there would be far too many people coming and going in there for the Light to stay hidden for long. The engine room is probably our best bet."

"Well, wherever it is, we need to find it as fast as possible and get you back here before the guard comes to pick up your tray. I can lock you in and hide until he's gone. When it's safe, I can let you out again. We don't have much time before he finishes his 'chow'."

She had started toward the door as she was speaking, but she stopped as a thought struck her. "But how on earth do we find the engine room?"

"Actually, I think I might know where it is," Inky said, with excitement. "When I was being escorted to the shower room, a door opened farther along the hallway. I could hear the sound of the ship's engines below. The way down could be through that door. I hope I can remember which one it is."

Inky looked into the hall to make sure no one was coming before stepping out and hurrying along the hall. Priscilla followed, stopping for a moment to close the door and hang the key back on the hook in case someone came by while they were gone.

Turning to go after Inky, she was surprised to see him down the hall, laughing as he looked at a door. Filled with curiosity, she quickly joined him, looking to see what had made him laugh. The door was clearly marked "To Engine Room".

"Well, that helps," she said, giggling. "Let's hope finding the Light is as easy!"

As soon as they opened the door, they were assailed with the rumble of the ship's engines from somewhere far below. They stepped over the high doorsill and entered a short corridor. A second door opened out to the top of a steep metal stairway. The ship's engines were pounding away below, even louder now.

They climbed down the stairs, trying to be as quiet as possible until they realized the noise of the engines made such caution unnecessary. No one could hear them. Keeping an eye out for any shadow figures, they hurried down. Below them several dark figures were busily working with the machinery, but they all seemed involved in what they were doing and oblivious to anything else.

When Priscilla and Inky reached the bottom, they looked around them with absolutely no idea where to go next. In a flash, Wanortu's words came back to Priscilla. She shouted into Inky's ear so he could hear her, "Inky, we must both use our inner Light Detectors. Perhaps they will lead us to the Light. It's all we have right now."

Inky looked at her in surprise, but he smiled as he shouted, "I see you have been learning from Wanortu, Priscilla. Yes, that is a good idea."

They both stood for a moment in silence. She was not exactly sure what she was supposed to do or what would happen. Inky closed his eyes, so she closed her own as well. Picturing the Sacred Light in her mind, she asked inside, "Is it here?" In an instant, she got a strong sense they were in the right place with the Light not far away.

Opening her eyes, she looked doubtfully at Inky. But when he told her, "It is here somewhere. I can feel it," she knew they had both sensed the same thing.

Nodding in agreement, she asked him, "But where? This is a huge place."

"I got an image of a wooden crate filled with rags," Inky said. "I think that is where the Sacred Light is hidden, in a crate under a pile of rags. Let us make our way around and see if we can find such a crate."

They slowly began to move around the edges of the space, the noise of the huge engines in the middle masking any sound they made. Near one of the engines just ahead of them, a wooden crate the size of a large trunk sat in plain sight. Priscilla grabbed Inky's hand and pointed.

As they started toward the crate, a dark shadow figure stepped into view, causing them to hurriedly pull back behind a post and remain perfectly still. Fortunately, he was turned away from them, working on the machinery in front of him. Since he appeared to be fixing something, they would have to wait until he finished.

When the figure reached into the crate and took out a rag to wipe oil off his hands, Priscilla was relieved to know it did indeed contain rags. Then her heart sank. Surely, the Light would not be in such an easily accessible place. There could be many such crates around. Yet, there was little time left to look anywhere else.

As they waited, she was impatiently aware of precious seconds ticking by. Maybe they needed to hit the shadow figure on the head and knock him unconscious. She looked around for a possible weapon.

Inky, deducing her thoughts, put his hand on her shoulder. "We cannot harm him, Priscilla. If we do, we are no different from them. Let us wait just a little longer. I think he is almost done."

So… they waited. Priscilla closed her eyes to determine if they were in the right place. All at once, she saw an image of…

… *a dark shadow figure hurrying down the stairs with the Light under his arm. He had it wrapped in an oily rag. Anxious to get rid of his burden as quickly as possible, he was looking right and left for the first hiding place he could find. When he spied a nearby crate, he headed straight toward it…*

Before she could see what happened next, Priscilla felt a tug on her arm. Inky was pulling her forward as he called to her, "Come on, Priscilla. He has gone. We can get to the crate now." The shadow figure was no longer in sight and the crate was accessible. Quickly they rushed over to it.

Inky carefully felt all around inside the pile of rags, but he could not find anything. "I think we'll have to look in another crate, Priscilla," he groaned in discouragement.

As he slowly lifted his hands out of the rag pile, Priscilla thought she might have glimpsed a tiny ray of light just to one side of where his hands had just been. "Wait a minute... I think I saw something!" she cried with excitement as she reached in and felt around.

Impatiently, she shoved the rags first to one side and then to the other. Just as she had begun to think she had been mistaken, her fingers touched the edge of something round and hard. Moving her hands quickly around it, she grabbed whatever this was, pulled it out, and held it up for them to see. It was the Sacred Light!

They stood in awestruck silence looking at what she held in her hands. Even under an oily film, the Light still glowed from within. With great reverence, Priscilla handed the sacred globe to Inky. He wiped off the oily film with one of the rags. Then he chose a cleaner rag and wrapped it around the Light before slipping both into his pouch. Smiling his gratitude, he nodded at her, and she grinned at him in triumph.

She moved the rags in the crate back in place so they would look undisturbed. Continuing to exercise caution, they hurried back up the stairs. Once they were in the hallway again, they dashed down to Inky's room. Priscilla grabbed the key, unlocked the door, and held it open while Inky slipped inside.

After a whispered, "I'll be back," she closed and locked the door.

Just as she was reaching to hang the key back on the hook, she heard a yell from down the hallway, "Hey youse slimbeball, what do youse think you're doing?"

With a sickening feeling, she turned toward the voice. Inky's guard was coming through the door. Key in hand, she turned and ran down the hall away from him, but he was too fast for her. He grabbed her from behind. Kicking and screaming, she tried to fight him, but he was bigger and stronger than she was. Her sealskin covered feet had no impact on him whatsoever.

"Trying to get in to rescue the prince were you, you smelly little creature," he chided her as he dragged her back down the hall toward Inky's cell. "Well we'll see what the cap'n 'll have to say about this. But it'll have to wait 'til he finishes his dinner and gets his bit of rest. He don't like to be interrupted and can get real nasty, if yer gets my meanin'."

Grabbing the key from her hand, he unlocked the door, and opened it, saying, with a malicious leer, "Here, now you can go on in and visit the prince real nice and cozy like. When he's done with his rest, I'll bet the cap'n 'll be real interested to hear about this." Shoving her inside, he laughed with cruel delight as he banged the door shut and locked it.

Priscilla stood clumsily where she had stumbled into the room. Inky had heard what the guard said. His voice gentle, he told her, "Well at least he thought you were coming in to rescue me. He does not know we have the Light. It is some comfort, I think."

But it was no comfort to her. Now she was just another helpless prisoner on this horrible Dark Ship. How on earth were they going to find her father and get away now?

She sank down to the floor and promptly burst into tears.

Chapter Thirty-Four
Caught in the Dark

Inky knelt in front of Priscilla. He put his arms around her and hugged her tightly. "Dry your eyes, little Priscilla. You have been incredibly brave and have done as much as anyone could do. We must put our heads together once more and see what we can come up with to get ourselves out of this situation."

The calm, regal voice of the Prince quieted her weeping. He was right. Priscilla gave him a weak smile to let him know she would be okay. All was not lost yet. They ought to be able to think of something if they just got practical again.

Inky helped her up, and together they sat at the table. He asked her about his family. Briefly, she told him that everyone at the palace was okay, though concerned about him, especially Lita, whose message she passed on to him. She gave him a quick overview of their journey to find him and told him of her need to rescue her father's shadow as well.

Just as they had begun to talk about what to do to escape, the door banged open, startling them both. The same guard yelled "In youse go, ya dirty mutt!" as he roughly shoved someone else into the room before slamming the door and locking it. Whoever this was wore a sealskin suit just like Priscilla's.

She stared at the dark-faced figure in astonishment before asking in a halting voice, "Alasdair? Is that you?" Without his glasses, and with his black face, it was hard to tell for sure.

Alasdair got up from the floor where he had landed unceremoniously and answered angrily, "Yeah, I'm sorry to say it is. I wanted to help you and Inky escape, and now here I am, captured as well." He was scowling at them in his frustration.

"Oh Alasdair, I'm so glad to see you!" Priscilla cried, restraining her impulse to rush across the room and hug him.

Inky added, "I'm so sorry they caught you, too, Alasdair, but now we have three heads to think of how to get us out of here. That will work even better."

Alasdair sat down on the edge of the bed. "You both okay?" he asked, in his gruff voice, looking straight at Priscilla. "They didn't hurt you, did they?"

"No, we're fine," she told him. His concern pleased her. This was so much better than having him ignore her as he did the last time she had seen him. "What happened to you? How did you get here?"

Alasdair sighed and said, "I'm not sure where to start." He thought for a moment, and then he continued with great reluctance, "I guess I need to begin with when I got back to the palace."

He took a deep breath. "Everyone was glad to see me, and even though we hadn't found Inky, they were pleased that we knew where he was and had plans to rescue him. I told Lita and the kids about our adventures. They were excited to hear my stories and kept begging me to tell them more. Then they wanted me to sing my Mother Nature song…"

He looked up at Priscilla with a remorseful look. "Well… one thing led to another. Soon I was working on songs for the wedding.

I was enjoying myself so much, I barely noticed when you got back. I was really rude to you, Priscilla."

Though she felt sorry for him, Priscilla was glad he had apparently "seen the Light", as Wanortu hoped he would.

"Lita was worried when I didn't rush off to rescue you right away," he continued, looking at Inky with some embarrassment, "but I told her that it was better to wait until the evening. I really did believe it was better to wait. Plus, it gave me time to finish my songs for the wedding so the children and the choirs could practice while I was away."

He stopped for a moment and sighed again. As if gathering the courage to go on, he sat up straight and clasped the side of the bed, "But the truth is, I just didn't want to let go of all the attention I was getting. I'd never had anything like it before. I guess it's what I've wanted all my life. It felt so great, I didn't want it to stop." He looked down at his feet in shame.

Inky's said with great kindness, "You don't have to tell us all this, Alasdair."

"Oh yes I do!" Alasdair spoke with vehemence. "I need to be able to say it." Keeping his eyes on his feet, he went on, "Anyway, I met to rehearse with the duck chorus. Just as we were about to start, one of the ducks waddled up to me and demanded to know what I was doing there and why I wasn't with you, Priscilla."

This time he looked up at her. "He was the funniest looking duck… spoke with a sort of lisp like Daffy Duck. He was so angry, he sputtered and spit at me, and his whole body shook like a bowlful of Jell-O." The memory made him smile as he added, "I had a hard time not laughing at him."

Then his face grew serious once more, "But as funny as he looked, he was speaking the truth. He said I was selfish for leaving you hanging out on your own, Priscilla, and that I had forgotten what was important, which was to rescue Inky and the Light. He told me I ought to be ashamed of myself." Alasdair hung his head once more in his heartfelt shame.

Priscilla smiled to herself as she thought of dear Ducky. He would say he had given Alasdair a good 'drething down'. Then he would quack merrily at his little pun. Even though he thought he looked silly, it would not have stopped him from speaking up. That is what friends did for one another, and she was his friend. It made her feel good to know she had a friend who would stand up for her no matter what.

Aloud, she said, "Yes, I'll bet he gave you a hard time, but he meant well." And she knew he did.

"He was right!" Alasdair cried, lifting his head and looking straight at her. "He told me you were sitting alone on the shore in the dark, bravely waiting for me, while I was selfishly soaking up attention. It made me see what a jerk I'd been. I felt disgusted with myself. I'm really sorry, Priscilla."

"It's okay, Alasdair," she said. It was easy to forgive him since he was here now. Wanting to let him off the hook, she went on in a hurry, "But how did you find out where I'd gone?"

Alasdair continued with his story. "I left the Witty Winkers to practice on their own and went to find you. I was so upset that on my way down to the beach, I tripped over your backpack. Your ribbon and overalls fell out. Seeing them made me remember all we'd been through together and how you helped me when I was hurt." The warm way he looked at her as he said this made her heart skip a beat.

"That's when it hit me!" he exclaimed. "If your clothes were in your pack, you had to be wearing your sealskin. I looked to see if you were waiting for me in the boat, but it was gone. I figured you must have already gone on your own, though I hoped I was wrong."

His energy returning, he sat up to finish his story. "I ran back to the palace to look for you, but, of course you weren't there. Raldemar flew out to the Dark Ship to see if he could find you. While he was gone, I got ready to go. By the time I had my sealskin on, he was back. Waleutius the Whale told him where you were, and Raldemar flew over the ship in time to see you disappear through the door. I knew I needed to hurry to help you and Inky."

He looked at them both, his disappointment with himself showing on his face. "And then I stupidly got myself caught. I thought I was going to make it through the door without anyone seeing me, but I bumped into a guard coming out. So here I am… not much help to you now, I'm afraid." He shook his head in despair. "I'm really sorry."

Priscilla asked, "But how did you get here without the boat?"

He smiled with genuine pleasure this time. "Waleutius the Whale brought me out on his back. It was quite a ride."

Priscilla told him their one piece of good news. "At least Inky and I managed to find the Light before I got captured. Now we just have to figure out how to find my father and get us all out of here, so we can get the Light back to the palace."

Inky had been listening quietly. When he spoke, his voice sounded troubled, "You have both been so brave and have gone to so much effort to help me after I did such a stupid thing. I am sorry you got involved in this. Even though I hate to admit it, my father was right. I am just a foolish idealist. Trying to share the Light and our values with those who have already turned to the Dark seems to be a useless enterprise."

Priscilla did not like hearing the prince speak like this. "You don't know that, Inky," she told him, using some of Granny's firmness. "You only showed the Light to those who don't have any Light left. There are others, like Garone the Gull, who still have some Light left in them. Maybe they can learn before it is too late." Looking into Inky's eyes, she pleaded with him. "Please don't give up on your beliefs!" She hoped with all her heart that she was right about what she was saying to him.

Before they had a chance to talk any more or to think about what to do next, the door opened, and this time, the guard swaggered into the room. Shaking a heavy stick at them, he sneered at them maliciously as he snarled, "Okay youse guys, hurry up and come with me. The cap'n 's ready to see youse now. He'll decide how to dispose of youse, if yer gets my meaning."

Obeying seemed their only choice. Trembling, the three prisoners moved slowly toward the door. Once he got them all out of the room, the vicious guard prodded them along the hall with the stick. Since they outnumbered him, he was taking no chances.

"Git along there now… out on the deck youse go… the cap'n wants to see you… hurry up there, don't want to keep 'im waitin' if yer know what's best for you… not that it matters much now." He let loose a nasty chuckle, reminding Priscilla of Horrid Harvey.

Inky led the way, with Priscilla following. Alasdair brought up the rear, receiving the full brunt of the stick against his back. The constant prodding kept them bumping into one another. They were not a happy threesome.

What came to the forefront of Priscilla's mind was the terrifying silhouette she had seen in the windows of the bridge. Even in her warm sealskin, she began to shiver. Her legs shook so much she could barely walk. Having to face the monster of a captain was something she had hoped she would never have to do.

When they got to the door to the deck, the guard reached around in front of them and banged his stick on it. Immediately, the heavy door swung open. Another dark shadow guard held the door open, leering at them with his nasty face as they passed him by. He too carried a big stick and did not hesitate to use it to push them out onto the deck.

The moon had risen while they had been imprisoned, bathing the deck in silvery light. Under other circumstances, it would have been a beautiful sight. On this particular night, it only enabled them to see all the scary dark shadows milling about. For so many to be out on deck, word must have spread that something unusual was about to happen.

Even in her fear, Priscilla could not help but notice the different shades of the shadow figures. Many were not dark like the guards, but lighter shades of gray, just as her father's shadow had been when she had last seen him. Her heart constricted at the thought of her father, and she wondered if he were here amongst the crowd. It made her sad to think she might die without him knowing she was close by. Trying to hold back tears, she searched for the familiar face of her much-loved father.

A hush swept over the crowd. The shadow figures stood still, looking up at the windows of the bridge. Priscilla looked up as well, dreading what she would see, but drawn to look all the same. In the window was the same hideous silhouette, more terrifying now than when she had first seen it.

The light went out, and the frightening monster disappeared from view. A door opened and banged shut, so loudly that she jumped. Heavy footsteps started down the stairs leading to the deck. Priscilla's heart began to hammer like a woodpecker pecking on a tree trunk. When the creature she was expecting to see finally came around the corner toward them, she stared in disbelief.

Instead of an ugly horrible beast, what she saw was a shrunken man who looked as if every ounce of moisture had been squeezed out of him. A grotesque hump on his back caused him to bend into a permanent forward position. An oversized tri-cornered hat covered a head that seemed far too big and heavy to belong to such a thin body. It was not surprising that his silhouette produced such a beastly form.

With his wire-rimmed spectacles on his shriveled nose, he reminded Priscilla of a miserly accountant who spent every minute of his life pouring over his account books and counting his money.

He matched her image of Uriah Heep, the greedy sniveling clerk she loathed in *David Copperfield*. For some reason, she felt strangely relieved.

However, her relief was only momentary. As the captain drew closer to the three of them, Priscilla experienced a horrible cold chill throughout her whole body, unlike anything she had ever felt before, even in the Valley of the Lost Souls. This captain was no storybook character. He was real. And she had no pear from the Tree of Innocence to protect her heart from the full effect of such a man.

The Darkness in him was so absolute that her Light Detector could not detect one iota of Light left in him. His withered heart had to be as black and as hard as a lump of coal. Though he might be just a thin shrunken man, the captain of the Dark Ship was the epitome of pure evil.. There would be no mercy from him.

Instinctively, Priscilla shrank back and sensed everyone around her doing the same. Reaching out she took hold of Inky's hand on one side and Alasdair's hand on the other and held on tightly to them both.

The captain came to a stop in front of his three prisoners. The expression on his face was one of cold scientific curiosity. "Well, well, well, what have we here?" he asked, in a crushingly powerful voice. Not expecting an answer to his question, he continued with a nasty sneer, "Two little innocents who no doubt came on board to rescue their prince, unsuccessfully of course, as no one ever takes prisoners off my ship. We couldn't let that happen, now could we?" He seemed to enjoy asking questions that no one would dare answer.

Stepping forward, he carefully scrutinized each of them, as if they were squirming laboratory specimens pinned to a board. When he reached Inky, all at once, he recoiled, taking a couple of steps backwards. Recovering himself immediately, he turned away from them as he reached with deliberate casualness into his pocket and took out a pair of dark glasses. These he slowly exchanged for his spectacles.

Watching him, Priscilla instinctively knew what was happening. The captain was trying to hide his discomfort with the Light he sensed inside the three of them. Plus he did not know Inky carried the Sacred Light, so he had not been prepared for the full effect of so much Light. It was obvious he could bear no Light at all. The Sacred Light would do to this evil man what Kryptonite did to Superman.

For Priscilla, there was an odd sort of power in this knowledge about the captain. In that special place deep inside her, she felt a seed of hope sprout and begin to grow.

Inky spoke up bravely. Nodding toward Alasdair and Priscilla, he pleaded, "Please captain, spare these two children. They mean nothing to you. Please let them go. You can do what you want with me, but let them go. They are young and innocent and only tried to help me. You must let them go. Please, I beg of you."

"No, Inky!" cried Alasdair and Priscilla at the same time, knowing they could never leave Inky behind, especially not after all they had gone through to find him.

The captain laughed. It was a brittle, harsh, and humorless laugh. The sound made Priscilla's blood run cold. "You are funny, my little prince. Of course, they mean nothing to me, just as you mean nothing to me. The fact that you are all young and innocent is good reason to get rid of the three of you. You bring far too much Light into this world. What we need is more Darkness, not more Light. No, I think it is time to send the three of you down to the bottom of the ocean. It is dark enough there to douse your Lights once and for all."

Turning to the guards, he ordered them to get three barrels of oil and some rope. "Soon we will have as much oil as we want. The loss of a few barrels to the bottom of the ocean will mean little," he muttered, with malevolent enjoyment.

The guards pushed their way through the crowd, heading to the center of the deck where the barrels of oil and rope were stored. As the crowd parted to let them through, Priscilla finally saw the face she had been hoping and praying to see. It was her father, or at least, his shadow part. She had to stop herself from crying out, "Daddy!"

He was standing in the crowd not far from her, but it was clear that he had no idea who she was. This was no surprise, as with her dark face and her sealskin, she looked very little like the Priscilla he knew. From the look in his eyes, he appeared to be unaware of exactly what was going on anyway.

An idea came to her, and she decided to act on it at once. There was not a moment to lose. She could hear the guards rolling the barrels of oil across the deck behind her.

Trembling, she stepped forward and faced the captain. "Mr. Captain, Sir," she projected her voice as loudly as she could so that it would carry over the crowd, as she had learned to do in her communications class. Once she had his attention, she waited for the crowd to quiet down to listen to what such a little girl would dare say to their terrible captain.

Mustering up every speck of courage she could, Priscilla spoke out again. "It seems, Mr. Captain, Sir," she hoped she was building up his opinion of himself with this respectful address, "you are about to dispose of us. But, before we die, could you please answer one last question?" In movies, prisoners about to be executed usually got a last request. She hoped this evil captain would give her one.

"I would really like to know exactly what you plan to do with the marine and wildlife sanctuary you have gone to so much trouble to acquire. Since you don't intend to keep us around any longer, surely it can do no harm to tell us what you plan to do with it.

What makes this land so important to you?" She really *did* want to know the answer to her question.

The captain glared at her as he deliberated for a moment. If he was surprised at her knowledge of his plans, he did not show it. He seemed to be trying to decide if it was worth his time or trouble to say any more.

Fortunately, his arrogance got the best of him. He appeared to decide it could do no harm to answer her question. "Well, my little innocent, I suppose there is no reason not to tell you. Perhaps it will make it even harder for you to leave this world knowing what kind of place it will become after you are gone." He laughed again, his horrible laugh, causing Priscilla to tremble right down to her sealskin-covered toes.

Warming up to his spiteful task, he went on. "The reason we want this piece of land is because the decision to turn it over to us will make it possible for the People of the Dark to acquire all other such places across the nation and eventually around the world. Everything is primed to go into action as soon as this first decision rules in our favor. There will be a most magnificent domino effect." Leering at her, he rubbed his long bony fingers together, reveling in his lust for power.

His voice rose even louder. "All we need is to get this one place. Then all others like it will be ours. We will be able to drill for oil wherever we want, land and sea. It will give us all the money and power we need. The People of the Dark will rule the earth, and the Light will be lost forever." Once more, he laughed his hideous laugh. "Now let's get on with this." He waved his hand commanding the guards to begin.

At his signal, one of the guards rolled a barrel of oil up alongside Priscilla. He was beginning to unravel a length of rope wrapped around his shoulder, when a lighter shadowed figure moved up behind him and laid a hand on his arm, stopping him.

It was Priscilla's father. This was exactly what she had been hoping for with her question. She knew her father, and she believed in him, so she was positive the People of the Dark had never given him all the details of their plans.

"Wait just a moment," he said in his quiet voice to the captain. "Are you telling me that my decision will start all of this change happening across the country and around the world? Why did you never tell me about this before? I thought my decision only had to do with drilling in this part of the country. And you never mentioned these so-called People of the Dark."

"You fool," the captain dismissed him angrily, "you and your stupid questions about morals and your worries about preserving the land and wildlife. All you have to do is make the right decision, and you will have all the money and power you desire. Believe me, Wallace, you would not be here now if you had not let yourself want it so much. If you make the right choice, you will have a chance to join the People of the Dark in ruling the world."

Priscilla saw her father's shadow waver and then flash darker at the captain's seductive words. Suddenly remembering something, she called out to him in her loudest voice, "Daddy, reach into your right pocket and feel the shell."

Perplexed, her father looked over to where this somewhat familiar voice had come from. He seemed to recall something. As if in a trance, he reached into his pocket and pulled out the shell she had given him and stood looking down at it.

Once again, she watched her father's shadow grow lighter. Without a doubt, he was remembering what was important to him. Then he looked over and finally seemed to see her clearly for the first time. Crying out, "Priscilla?" he started to move toward her.

The captain, seeing the obvious change in him, commanded his guards, "Grab him!" Before her father could move, a huge black figure came from behind, grabbed his arms, and held him. Even though he fought to pull away, it was no use. Her father was as helpless as the rest of them.

"I'm sorry, Priscilla. I didn't know about all this," he told her with a look of great distress.

"I know that, Daddy," Priscilla told him, her love for him shining in her eyes.

The captain looked smug. "This is working out even better than I'd expected. I did not know this little piece of fluff was your daughter, Wallace. How absolutely delicious. Once we get rid of these three, you will know we mean business. You will make your decision the way we want it made." With as much ghoulish glee as such an emotionless man could muster, he rubbed his hands together again, looking every inch the evil greedy accountant.

He nodded to the guard with the rope. The guard grabbed Priscilla by the arm and pulled her forward toward the barrel. Then the captain turned to her father and, in a voice dripping with venom, said, "When you see us destroy your daughter and her friends, Wallace, you will know what will happen to the rest of your family if you choose not to decide our way."

Shaking like a leaf, Priscilla felt the hope that had been steadily growing inside her begin to wither. Out of the corner of her eye, she watched her father struggle helplessly to get free of the guard who had him pinned so tightly.

It looked like it was over for all of them.

Chapter Thirty-Five
The Power of the Light

Out of nowhere, a large black projectile, as dark as the blackest shadow, whirled through the air and crashed into the guard who held Priscilla. With an outraged cry of pain, the guard let go of Priscilla's arms and stepped back.

Almost at the same time, a similar-sized white missile smashed into the guard who was holding Priscilla's father. He too yelped in pain and immediately released his grip.

Something whizzed by them like a gray bullet and hit the captain smack in the head, knocking off his hat and laying bare his ugly wrinkled bald head.

In the confusion that erupted following these attacks, Inky was the first to gather his senses. Grabbing an astonished Priscilla by the hand, he pulled her back to where he was standing as he whispered to both her and to Alasdair, "Hurry, we must make our way toward the ladder and get down to the boat."

She cried, "But what about my father. I need to help him."

Inky's reply was steady and sure, "He will be okay now, Priscilla. He knows what he must do."

They began pushing their way quickly through the agitated crowd when they heard the captain's loud voice cry out, "Stop them! We cannot let them get away."

Once again, the darkest of the shadows standing around them caught and held onto them. The crowd drew back to make room for the captain as he angrily stomped across the deck. Minus the hat on his huge warped head, his face and body brimming with fury, he looked even more terrifying. Everyone backed away to make room for him.

From above them rang out a voice with unquestionable authority, "I think you need to let them go." Priscilla thought there was something familiar about the voice. Along with everyone on deck, she looked up to see where it had come from.

There on a rope high overhead sat Garone the Gull with Raldemar the Raven right next to him. And there beside them, bless his tiny little heart, perched Eideard the Owl. These three birds had bravely propelled themselves into the captain and the guards. Priscilla's heart filled with love for their three friends who had come to rescue them.

However, the captain was not giving up so easily. Immediately taking control of himself and the situation, he sneered at Garone and the other birds. "You may have surprised us once, you twitty little birdbrains, but you will not interfere again." He turned and nodded toward three dark guards who climbed up on the catwalk next to the bridge. Each of them held a gun, and they took careful aim at the birds.

"I do not think your guns will help you much," Garone the Gull said coolly. "Take a look above me."

Everyone, including the captain and the guards with the guns, looked up. What they saw caused them to open their eyes wide.

A thick white and gray cloud was rapidly moving down through the sky and spreading over the ship, bringing with it a tremendous shrieking noise. It was the seagull cloud from the top of White Mountain.

The massive cloud of birds descended until it hung just above them like an immense storm cloud ready to burst over the Dark Ship. Without any hesitation whatsoever, the guards dropped their guns, jumped down from the catwalk, and slunk off into the crowd. Priscilla and Alasdair cheered.

Inky grabbed them both and pulled them away from their guards who were still looking up at the bird cloud. Together they slipped through the shadows, unnoticed, as all other eyes focused on the obvious threat from above.

Quickly they ran up the stairs to the catwalk. Priscilla was already on the railing getting ready to head down to the ladder, when Inky stopped on the catwalk and pulled himself up to his full height. Alasdair tried to pull him toward the railing.

Inky said quietly, "No, Alasdair, there is something I must do. I must try at least once more." When he said these last words, he smiled fondly at Priscilla. Then he turned around and faced the crowd with a regal stance.

Priscilla knew at once what Inky was about to do. Stepping back down from the railing, she walked over and stood beside him. Lifting her head high, she tossed the sealskin hood off her head and shook out her long red hair, letting it fall down around her shoulders.

After she whispered something to him, Inky reached into his pouch and handed her the rag he had wrapped around the Light. Using the cleanest part of the rag, she wiped the blackening from her face until her freckles stood out clearly against her pale skin.

Following her lead, Alasdair took his place on the other side of Inky. He too released his long hair from the sealskin hood. Priscilla passed him the rag, and he wiped the black off his face. With his white hair and white skin, he did indeed shine like a beacon on the Dark Ship, just as Wanortu had said he would.

In a powerful voice, Inky called down to the crowd. The bird cloud became silent for a moment. All faces below turned from the threat of the bird cloud to look up at the prince and then at Priscilla and Alasdair standing on either side of him. What they saw on the catwalk caused all of them to stand as still as they had earlier when they had looked up at the terrifying silhouette of the captain.

For there above them stood a brave and handsome prince whom everyone knew, beyond a shadow of a doubt, would one day become a great and wise king. He was as black as the darkest of them, but there was such deep intense Light shining out from within him, that his skin gleamed as indigo blue as a deep dark pond reflecting the moonlight.

On his right side, stood a small but courageously defiant girl, teetering on the edge of her womanhood. Her wavy, vibrant hair was the color of the blood of life itself. Her large brown freckles stood out on her fair cheeks, an earthy reminder of the purity of her innocence.

To the left of the prince stood a proud silver-white boy, resembling a young Greek god. He was on the verge of becoming a truly loving man. His hair and skin blazed out of the darkness like the sun, his fiery passion radiating heat on his friends beside him and upon those who stood gazing up at him.

The three of them cast so much Light across the Dark Ship that any shadow figures too Dark to bear so much Light, like the captain, quickly averted their eyes. Those who still had Light left inside them stared in fascination. Already stirring deep within them was a yearning to feel more of their own Light once again. They stood with their eyes glued to the trio.

Inky spoke out to them in a majestic voice, the voice of a once and future king. "I call upon those of you who still have Light left inside, those of you who can still feel hope and love, and who have a memory of your own innocence, to leave this Dark Ship now. Go back home where you belong. Let your Light shine out once more. It is not too late. There is always hope, even in the darkest times."

He waved his hand over them as if he was giving them a royal blessing. "You must not let the Darkness overcome you, terrify you, or seduce you into believing it will make you happy. Money, power, and success may draw you toward them, but accompanying them is always the fear of losing them and a desperate need to hold onto them. This only leads to violence and death. The pursuit of such values creates nothing but Darkness inside you and Darkness in the world."

He went on, his voice soaring across the deck yet touching down gently to spark the Light inside those who had a glimmer left. "By bringing your own unique Light into the world, you will learn to love yourself and all life. You will be giving the world a gift it sorely needs. When we each in turn shine our Light, the glow we create together will spread across the world and create a place of love and beauty for all of us, for our children, and for generations to come."

He stopped and looked at them for a moment, his own Light spreading over them like warm sunshine after a long dark winter, softening and melting the Darkness in those who still had the capacity to hear his words. He had said all he needed to say.

There was a sudden flurry of wings. Garone the Gull flew down and settled lightly on Inky's shoulder, followed by Raldemar who landed on Alasdair's shoulder. Eideard took his favorite perch next to Priscilla's ear. Reaching up, she stroked his feathers. He blushed in pure delight as he curled his head down into his neck with a "Hoot Mon!"... music to her ears.

"Thank you all so much," she whispered to the three courageous birds. Inky and Alasdair added their thanks as well.

The little group turned toward the railing to make their way down to the boat. Priscilla had just climbed over the railing when she heard a huge ruckus behind her. A fight had broken out. The lighter shadows were trying to escape while the darker figures fought to hold them back.

She saw her father amongst the melee and yelled to him, "Daddy!"

He looked up at her and called out, "Go on, Priscilla. Save yourselves. I will be okay." Turning around, he was just in time to dodge a blow from a dark figure who was swinging at his head.

As she hesitated, Alasdair whispered in her ear, "Listen to your father, Priscilla,"

Garone told her, "Do as he says, Priscilla. We will watch over your father. Have no fear." The three birds lifted off their shoulders and flew back down to the battle.

Reluctantly, she made her way down the ladder, followed by Inky and Alasdair. She could not help feeling worried about her father. Now she had her three dear bird friends to worry about as well.

She had climbed about halfway down the ladder, when something big and heavy hurtled past, so close by, she could feel the air whistle beside her. Whatever this was barely missed the three of them and landed smack dab in the middle of Baba's boat down below, smashing into it with such force, the little craft split apart like a walnut. Water rushed in through the cracks.

The thrown object was a barrel of oil. When she looked up to see where it had come from, she saw their guards leaning out above them, attempting to stop their escape. Another barrel soon followed, and the three of them had to pull quickly to one side of the ladder to avoid being hit.

This barrel too, made a bull's-eye hit. Baba's sturdy little boat could not hold out against such a bombardment. Chunks of wood sank down into the ocean depths along with the heavy barrel. Shattered pieces of wood slowly floating away were all that was left of Baba's boat.

Priscilla exclaimed, "Wow! And they wanted to tie us to those barrels!" In all the excitement, it never occurred to her that the guards had just destroyed their means of transportation back to land.

Loud squawking sounds mingled with cries from the shadow figures above announced the descent of the huge cloud of seagulls upon the ship. The birds were intervening to protect them from the guards and to help the lighter shadow figures. From the vast number of birds in the cloud, there was no question as to which way the battle would go; the fighting would be over in short order. The lighter figures would be free to go home, if that was what they chose to do.

After the fracas above quieted down, it seemed safe to begin making their way down the ladder again. They had just started to descend when something peculiar began to happen all around them. At first, Priscilla thought it had begun to rain. Groaning, she wondered if this was the start of yet another Dreary Drenching Downpour. However, what was falling all around them did not look anything like ordinary raindrops. These were huge. Something else was going on.

It was raining shadow figures. For a long time, the shadow rain fell in cascade after cascade. Priscilla's image of raindrops was most appropriate, for as soon as the falling shadows hit the water below, they dissolved into the ocean. Many of the lighter shadows had apparently chosen to go home to where they belonged. She hoped her father's shadow was amongst them.

Inky was watching the shadows rain down, an amazed look on his face. When it dawned on him what it meant, he looked down at Priscilla and grinned happily, his white teeth glinting in the moonlight.

At least part of his plan had worked. Trusting his own beliefs, especially when they differed from those of his father, had been a risk, but one he had the courage to take. In standing up for his own ideas, he had discovered that his father was indeed wise and had much to teach him. However, even though the king might be older and wiser, he too had some things to learn. Inky had something to teach his father as well.

As time passed, the number of raining shadows decreased until only an occasional shadow figure fell every few seconds. Finally, the shadows stopped falling altogether. Those who wanted to live by the Light again had gone home. The night became silent. Even the birds were no longer squawking.

Priscilla started to climb down the ladder, thinking about her father, Garone, Raldemar and Eideard, praying that they were all safe.

Without warning, a tremendous shudder rumbled throughout the ship, followed by several smaller shudders. The ladder started to shimmy and shake. They had to hang on for dear life.

Alasdair cried out, "Something weird is happening to the ship. Let's jump off."

"But we don't have a boat!" Priscilla yelled back, the reality of their situation finally hitting her. "How are we going to get back to shore?"

Her question went unanswered. The ship gave a massive violent shudder and started to vibrate intensely without stopping. The bottom of the ladder suddenly snapped free from the ship, springing the ladder up into the air with such great force that it flicked the three of them off the rungs like flies. They flew through the air, away from the ship and far out into the ocean.

One by one, they splashed down into the cold water. Priscilla took a deep breath just before the water closed over her head. As soon as she could slow her downward plunge, she kicked her way back up to the surface. After her visit with Grandmother Ocean, she was much less fearful of being underwater. In her sealskin, she knew she could stay afloat with no trouble at all.

Alasdair would be okay since he also wore a sealskin, but she was worried about Inky who was not dressed for swimming in the ocean. She looked around to find him.

When her gaze fell upon the Dark ship, she stared in amazement. The enormous ship had shrunk and was continuing to shrink at a rapid pace. Now it was closer to the size of the crab boat wreck. The eight appendages sticking out from its sides were shrinking and gnarling at the same time into what looked like giant ugly claws. The bird cloud still hung above it, making the ship even smaller by comparison.

"Priscilla, are you all right?" It was Inky calling to her. Relieved to hear his voice, she turned to see him sitting astride the back of Waleutius the Whale, looking as regal as ever. Worrying about him had been unnecessary.

"Yes, I'm fine," she answered, "But where's Alasdair?"

"Right behind you," called out a cheerful voice. Alasdair was just a few yards away from her, discovering the joys of wearing a sealskin in the ocean.

Inky said, "If both of you climb onto the net behind Waleutius, he will take us all back to shore." Waleutius swam over to show them a crystal net attached to his tail and fanning out over the ocean behind him. It glittered in the moonlight like diamonds sprinkled across the water.

The corners of the net were held firm in the mouths of Sami and Sumi. Priscilla greeted her friends with great delight and introduced the two little seals to Alasdair.

Another creature popped a pointed nose out of the water between the seals, grabbed the net in its teeth, and gazed at Priscilla and Alasdair with playful eyes.

Alasdair exclaimed, "Look, Priscilla, it's Ogusto the Otter! He must've swum all the way down the river." They joyfully welcomed the little otter.

Priscilla and Alasdair pulled themselves onto the sparkling net and lay across it. Waleutius began swimming toward the shore, pulling his passengers along behind him.

With a noisy flurry of wings, the bird cloud left the ship and flew over them, heading toward shore. Priscilla, Alasdair, and Inky looked up and waved. Two birds left the cloud and flew down toward them.

"Inky, Priscilla, Alasdair!" called out a voice that had become dear to Priscilla. Garone the Gull was flying toward them with Raldemar following behind him. But where was the third bird? Priscilla's heart sank as she searched the sky for the little bird that should have been with them.

When Garone and Raldemar landed on the net, Priscilla cried out in panic, "Where 's Eideard?"

Before the birds had time to answer, Raldemar's back feathers parted, and a small gray face, feathers in even more disarray than usual, peered out at them and said, "Hoot Mon!"

Priscilla laughed with relief. All her friends were safe, but most especially the goofy little gray owl of whom she had grown so fond.

Soon the great Orca whale was swimming toward shore with the net skimming across the waves behind him. As light sprays of water gently splashed over them, Priscilla knew they were having yet another once-in-a-lifetime experience, made even better by the presence of their bird friends safely beside them.

When they got closer to shore, they found that the bird cloud had landed in the water just offshore, joining many other birds already gathered there. Waleutius had to make his way through a thick soup of gulls, cormorants, and ducks. Slowing his pace, he gave the birds time to move aside to create a pathway for the whale and his entourage.

"Prithilla, Alathdair!" called out another voice Priscilla was delighted to hear. "We are tho proud of you both!" Paddling his way toward them, the birds immediately giving way to his determined progress, came Ducky. In the water, where he was completely at home, he looked perfectly normal and not at all funny. In fact, he looked as regal as a swan.

Close behind Ducky swam a big black and white duck with a thick fuzzy head. "Prithilla and Alathdair, thith ith Thilly Willy," Ducky told them proudly, giving Priscilla a little wink. She grinned mischievously at Ducky as they greeted Silly Willy.

Lining the edge of the shore were herons, crows, and all sorts of other shore birds. Priscilla thought she heard the familiar ratchety sound of a kingfisher over the din. Then, from high above them, a piercing eagle call rang through the air as Ezara and Eminore flew over them, their air escort arriving to bring them safely in to shore.

Immense cheering arose from the shore. Waiting by the edge of the water were King Sol and Queen Luminata and all the royal children. Wanortu the WiseMaster was there with his WiseElders. Even dear Baba had come from her home in the Fairy Forest. All the People of the Rainbow had gathered with them.

An ecstatic Lita waded out in the water in great excitement, wanting to welcome back her beloved prince who had indeed made it home in time for his wedding day.

Inky stood up to his full height on the back of Waleutius the Whale. Taking the Sacred Light out of his pouch, he lifted it high above his head. The Light gleamed out over the water, the shore, and all who were there. It shone more intensely than ever, having picked up the Light energy released when so many chose the Light and left the Darkness behind.

Such a resounding cheer burst forth in response, Priscilla was sure the whole world could hear it. She felt incredibly proud to know that she and Alasdair, with lots of help of course, had found Inky and the Sacred Light and had brought them both back home where they belonged. Together they had done it.

Once Priscilla stepped onto the shore, everything became a complete blur. Her relief at being safely back on land, coupled with the full realization of all she had been through, swept over her in a wave of exhaustion. All the congratulations, questions, and exclamations blended together in noisy confusion. About all she took in was that the wedding was to take place at sunrise the following day, and, after the wedding feast, she and Alasdair were to leave for home.

With no knowledge of how she got there, she was back in the palace, peeling off her smelly sealskin and getting into a hot bath. Afterwards, while she was eating a little something, her head began to nod over her plate. Someone kind picked her up, carried her to her room, and tucked her into bed. For the next few hours, she was not aware of another thing.

Chapter Thirty-Six
A Royal Wedding

A knock on the door awakened Priscilla. Though she was definitely not through sleeping, she called out, "Come in."

When the door opened, a little blue woman entered and set Priscilla's freshly laundered clothes on the bed as she joyfully announced, "Good morning, Priscilla. It is time to get up and get ready for the wedding." She slipped out of the room, returning in an instant with a cup of hot cocoa and a warm roll and set these on the bedside table next to Priscilla, saying kindly, "This will help tide you over until the breakfast feast after the wedding." Then she left Priscilla alone to get up.

The hot cocoa tasted delicious, and the buttered fresh roll practically melted in her mouth. After her refreshment, Priscilla felt more awake, so she got up and reached for her pile of clothes. Her rainbow ribbon glistened on top of the bundle.

Next to it was a small woven rainbow-striped bag exactly like Baba's medicine bag. Peeking inside, Priscilla found all the treasures from her pockets. There was a note from Baba pinned to the outside. Baba had written, "I thought you might like to have a medicine bag of your own to hold all your healing treasures."

Priscilla stared at the note and then at her treasures. It had never occurred to her to think of them as healing treasures. Yet that was exactly what they were. They belonged together in the richly colored bag. The idea of having her own medicine bag appealed to her. Perhaps, from now on, she would keep her treasures together in the bag instead of in separate pockets.

After she dressed, she tied her rainbow ribbon in her hair and tucked her new medicine bag filled with her healing treasures into one of her pockets. Then she went out into the corridor.

Her room was on the first floor near the Sacred Light. With the Light back in the golden pot where it belonged, the rotunda shone with brilliance once more. An even more dazzling rainbow than usual soared up through the roof.

As she stood admiring the rainbow, Wanortu, with Eideard once more on his shoulder, came to stand beside her. "We would not have our prince and our Light back if it had not been for you and Alasdair, Priscilla," Wanortu told her, giving her a hug. "You have helped bring back the Light, my dear. Now the Darkness has shrunk to a more manageable size. No one could have done more. We chose well when we chose you and Alasdair."

"Hoot Mon!" agreed Eideard.

Priscilla giggled when she saw that he was dressed for the wedding in a tiny tartan vest with a thistle embroidered on it. He looked happy to be back home on Wanortu's shoulder where he belonged. She smiled at both of them.

"Come," said Wanortu, "Let us go down to the seashore. It is getting close to sunrise, which means it is almost time for the wedding." They chatted companionably as they went out through the conservatory doors.

At the top of the stairs, Priscilla stopped. A lot had gone on while she had been sleeping. The night shore shone with breathtaking beauty, lit by the Light from the Royal Rainbow borrowed from the Paint Pots for the wedding. The rainbow curved from the roof of the palace across the shore to the water's edge.

Underneath it curved a smaller rainbow, creating a lovely archway. A pathway strewn with flower petals led up to the arch. All along the edges of the path were painted pots of green plants and colorful flowers. Hordes of birds were still in the water and on the shore, where the busy People of the Rainbow, dressed in their fanciest finery were bustling about. The seashore had become an enchanted sea garden, teeming with color and life.

Wanortu left Eideard with Priscilla while he went off to prepare for the marriage ceremony. Though it was delightful to once again have her little friend on her shoulder, she felt sad knowing it was probably for the last time. She gently stroked the little owl's feathers, leading him to blush and twitter, "Hoot Mon!"

Baba came over and greeted them cheerfully. She took Priscilla's arm and tucked it under her own so that they could walk together.

"Thank you so much for the beautiful medicine bag, Baba," Priscilla told her friend. "I'll treasure it forever."

"I thought you might like it," Baba smiled.

As they walked down to stand near the rainbow arch, Priscilla brought Baba up to date on her adventures. With great regret, she shared what had happened to Baba's little boat.

"It is not a problem, Priscilla," Baba told her amicably. "I will build another one. I'm just glad you all got home safely."

"Me too," said Priscilla, thinking that this place did indeed feel like a second home to her.

After glancing over the people on the shore, she asked Baba, "Is Lita's family coming for the wedding? I don't see any unfamiliar faces around."

"No," Baba told her, "After the wedding and all the festivities here, Inky and Lita will travel to Lita's home where they will have a second wedding with even more festivities. In the Kingdom of the Sunrise, the wedding will be held at sunset in honor of Inky, just as here it is held at sunrise in honor of Lita. This makes it possible for all the villagers in both kingdoms to attend a royal wedding, so everybody is happy."

"I like the idea of having a wedding at sunrise and sunset," Priscilla mused. "I hope I remember that when I grow up. Of course, I don't even know yet if I'll ever get married."

"Oh, I suspect you will," Baba told her with a secret smile. "And by the way, where is Alasdair?"

"He's helping with the music for the wedding, so I guess he must be with the performers." Priscilla looked around to see if she could spot him.

About a dozen or so ducks, each a mixture of different vibrant colors, stood in rows on the steps leading up to the palace. They had to be the Witty Winkers. Priscilla smiled when she spotted Ducky on the top step with Silly Willy right next to him.

Alasdair sat on a tall stool near the duck chorus. Guitar in hand, he was dressed once more in his own clothes, also freshly cleaned and pressed. He was without his familiar hat, and his silky hair stirred gently in the soft breeze. When he saw Priscilla looking at him, Alasdair smiled and waved to her. Pleased to have him notice her, she waved back happily.

Everyone quieted down. The same little black and white robed musicians and singers who had performed at their first banquet silently took their places behind the rainbow arch. Wanortu followed behind and climbed up on a short platform set in front of them. With quiet dignity, he faced the crowd through the arch.

Eideard whispered to Priscilla, "Will ye look at that? He remembered tae poot on his twa shoes fer once. Hoot Mon!"

Wanortu did indeed have on two shoes. In addition, he was not wearing his hat and had obviously tried to tame his wild hair a little in honor of the ceremony. Other than that, he looked like the same old Wanortu Priscilla had come to know and love.

The musicians and singers began to play and sing, and soon their captivating music and singing filled the air with magic. The ceremony had begun.

King Sol and Queen Luminata, wearing exquisite velvet robes, imperially made their way down the petal-strewn pathway toward the arch. Following behind their dignified parents, the royal children walked or skipped down the path, trying to be as serious as they could manage in their great excitement. King Sol took his place to the left of the path in front of the arch. Queen Luminata stood to the right. The royal boys stood near the king and the royal girls stood next to the queen.

From somewhere off in the distance behind her, Priscilla thought she detected the faint sounds of hoof beats. As the sounds became louder, the royal family turned around, and the rest of the crowd followed suit. It was, indeed, hoof beats Priscilla had heard, but what created them had her gasping in awe.

Emerging out of the Darkness and entering into the Light, trotting at a measured pace along the edge of the water, was none other than the unicorn from White Mountain. On the back of the gorgeous silken-haired creature rode Prince Incandescence and Princess Archelita. Inky sat astride the unicorn holding Lita sidesaddle in front of him; his long black cloak, which he had wrapped around both of them, accentuated the brilliant whiteness of the unicorn.

Watching the slow dreamlike movement of the mythical beast carrying its enchanted passengers along the shore, Priscilla felt something again touch the special place deep inside her, and she slowly blew out her breath with approval.

Lifting its legs high, like a proud Lipizzaner stallion, the unicorn pranced majestically up the shore and along the path toward the rainbow arch, placing its hooves with such care the rose petals barely shifted as it stepped amongst them. When the magnificent creature reached the rainbow arch, it bowed its horned head and front legs down to the ground, honoring the king and queen, while at the same time allowing Inky and Lita to slip gracefully off its back. One of the little WiseElders stepped forward, deftly caught the reins and cloak Inky tossed to him and led the unicorn off to one side.

Inky took Lita by the hand as they turned toward the crowd and nodded in greeting. A soft hush swept over everyone, followed by a shared soul-deep sigh of admiration.

Inky had chosen to honor Lita by wearing white, heightening the blue sheen to his dark hair and skin. His trousers were dove white silk. Over a matching frilled shirt with long billowing sleeves, he wore a short waistcoat of exquisite white brocade. The collar peaked around his neck, and the padded shoulders stood out in front and back. Woven into the heavy material, wavy rainbow threads radiated out in circles around seven carved gold buttons. The sparkling jewels on his head added the final regal touch.

Priscilla thought he looked just like one of King Arthur's elegant knights, every inch the handsome prince of all her favorite fairy tales.

Lita returned the honor with her long elegant flowing black gown worn against her pure white skin. Nothing could have shown off her beauty more vividly than the distinct contrast created by the multiple layers of shimmering black fabric. Gathered around her neck, like the petals of a flower, and riddled lengthwise with sparkling rainbow threads, the dark material glistened in the light with her every graceful movement. Her long white hair, released from its tight braid, flowed in soft waves over her shoulders and down her back. Her diamond circlet and a stunning silver sunrise medallion hanging around her neck served as her only royal jewels.

The courtly prince took his lovely princess by the hand. After nodding once more to the crowd, they turned and walked forward to stand between the king and queen under the rainbow arch, facing Wanortu. Inky lifted his circlet of jewels and, with a bow, gave it to his father, while Lita curtsied and handed her circlet of diamonds to the Queen.

The crowd quieted down as Wanortu began to speak. His rich full voice easily reached out to everyone on the shore. "Your Royal Majesties… King Sol and Queen Luminata." He bowed his head to each of them, formally acknowledging the elder royal presences before he commenced.

"Welcome to our beloved royal family and to all our loved ones and dear friends. On this auspicious occasion, we are here to celebrate the union in Love and Light of our beloved Prince Incandescence of the Kingdom Beyond the Sunset and our cherished Princess Archelita of the Kingdom of the Sunrise. At this moment in time, we are honored not only to bring together these two treasured young people, but to create yet another connection between our two blessed kingdoms."

He waved his hand toward the rainbow above. "Prince Inky and Princess Lita exchange their vows at sunrise today beneath our glorious rainbow. Both the sunrise and the rainbow are eternal reminders of the hope and promise of new days to come. Even when our lives fill with Darkness, as they sometimes must, we continue to hold before us our symbols of the promise of another day. Each new day brings with it the possibility of new Light and new life to the world."

Reaching down with a smile, he gently placed his right hand on Inky's head and his left hand on Lita's. "The Light and the Dark joining together teach us about balance. By holding on, never too tightly nor too loosely, through our love and affection for one another, we create new patterns of Light and Dark in our lives. Together in this way, we continue our sacred work of preserving the Light energy in the world. Our greatest desire and chosen duty is to make the world a better place for ourselves, for our children, for all people, and for all life. Together we create new possibilities in each and every moment of our lives." As he finished speaking, he lifted his hands and stood back on the platform.

King Sol and Queen Luminata handed the jeweled circlets back to Inky and Lita and stepped back, leaving the young couple to stand alone under the rainbow arch.

Looking down at Lita with a loving smile, Inky gently placed his circlet of multi-colored jewels on her head, and Lita, on tiptoe and with a slight giggle, reached up and placed her circlet of diamonds on his head. Then, beneath the brilliant rainbow arch, they quietly gave their promises of love to one another. When they had finished, Inky took Lita's hands in his, and they stood smiling at one another with love shining in their eyes.

Wanortu looked over at Alasdair and nodded.

Alasdair began to play his guitar and to sing. The musicians and singers joined in the chorus. Listening to the music echoing across the shore, Priscilla felt her heart fill to overflowing. When Alasdair came to the final chorus, he waved for everyone on the shore to join in the singing, which, of course, they did.

Forevermore

In this moment here we stand
Where the ocean greets the land
And creates this magical shore

In this moment full of love
While the rainbow shines above
Sunrise and Sunset are joined forevermore

Forevermore, forevermore
Our love will last forevermore
Like the mountains and the seas
And the meadows and the trees
Our love will last forevermore
Forevermore

In this moment filled with Light
We cheer the passing of the night
And welcome in a bright new day
In this moment we are near
To all those who we hold dear
And we know our love is here to stay

Forevermore, forevermore
Our love will last forevermore
Like the mountains and the seas
And the meadows and the trees
Our love will last forevermore
Forevermore

In this moment we can see
Just how bright our world can be
When we hold one another's hand
In this moment we all know
We have the power to make it so
To bring peace and love throughout our land

Forevermore, forevermore
Our love will last forevermore
Like the mountains and the seas
And the meadows and the trees
Our love will last forevermore
Forevermore

While the last words of the chorus resounded across the water, with great eloquence Wanortu made his pronouncement. "In the name of the Light, we bless this marriage and pronounce Prince Incandescence and Princess Archelita to be husband and wife, now and forevermore."

Inky took Lita in his arms and tenderly kissed her as the crowd clapped and cheered merrily. The cheering went on and on because, as the newlyweds were kissing, the sun was rising into the sky behind the arch. The birds began to sing out their greeting to the sunrise as they had done on White Mountain. Inky and Lita stopped kissing and joined everyone else in singing to the sunrise. A bright new day had begun.

The newly married couple turned and bowed to the king and queen and the royal children. Then they waved happily to the crowd who cheered even louder.

The royal children took this opportunity to slip away to get ready for their part in the musical performance which was to come next. Everyone turned to face the musicians on the steps. The crowd on the shore quieted down once more.

Alasdair put his hat on at a jaunty angle and, with great confidence, made his way slowly down the stairs. As he reached the shore, he began to strum his guitar and then to sing. Soon he was walking amongst the wedding guests on the beach, a wandering minstrel singing to the crowd.

He sang the first three verses in this medieval style while the Witty Winkers harmonized with him. The incredibly high sweet sounds of some of the ducks, contrasting with some deep voices of others, soon had Priscilla smiling.

Sing Your Song to the Sunrise

There is a land... a most enchanted land... far beyond the deep blue sea
Where people live with Nature in peace and harmony

There is a land... a most enchanted land... where the rainbow shines above
And people of all colors live with wisdom, truth, and love

There is a land... a most enchanted land... where the Light shines all night long
To guide us through the darkness as we learn to sing our song

To her great delight, individual ducks began to sing each of the lines of the next verses. The uniqueness of each duck voice, especially Silly Willy's thunderous bass voice, which came as a complete surprise to Priscilla, had everyone laughing aloud with glee. During the singing, the royal children and the children of the People of the Rainbow danced and mimed the words.

Sing your song to the sunrise
Paint your colors in the sky
Fly on eagles through the sunset
Slide down rainbows from on high

Dance barefoot in the meadow
Wear bright ribbons in your hair
Gallup on a big red horse
Snuggle down with a bear

Make friends with a duck
Hear what a gull can say
Put an owl on your shoulder
Let a raven lead the way

Go swimming in the moonlight
Chase an otter down a slide
Ride a whale across the ocean
Stand by your friends with pride

Confront every shadow
In the darkness shine your Light
Seek a path through the desert
Grab a friend and hold on tight

Learn wisdom from a wolf
Listen to the wisest guide
Go deep into your heart
Find the Light that shines inside

Alasdair continued to stroll as he sang another couple of verses:

There is a land… a most enchanted land… far beyond the deep blue sea
Where people live with Nature in peace and harmony

There is a land… a most enchanted land… and you can go there too
For the land beyond the sunset lives inside of me and you

Everyone sang the final chorus together. Even those who had not been singing could not help but join in the last repeat.

Sing your song to the sunrise
Paint your colors in the sky

Fly on eagles through the sunset
Slide down rainbows from up high

Sing your song to the sunrise
Paint your colors in the sky
Fly on eagles through the sunset
Slide down rainbows from up high

As she sang, Priscilla thought how lucky she was to have come to this place and to have been on such a fantastic journey. There had been some rough times, but they had helped her learn about herself and her own strengths. Along the way, she had met many fascinating characters and made good friends whom she would never ever forget.

After the singing, everyone congratulated the happy couple and the ecstatic performers, and then it was time for feasting. The joyous People of the Rainbow speedily carried tables covered with all sorts of delicious foods and drinks down to the shore. Priscilla and Alasdair, along with everyone else, tucked in and ate until they were fit to burst.

After she finished eating, Priscilla found a few minutes alone with Ducky. They sat on the steps near where they had first met. While they talked and laughed together, Priscilla told Ducky about her capture on the Dark Ship and thanked him for helping to set Alasdair straight.

"Well," Ducky told her conspiratorially, "You wouldn't believe it, Prithilla, but it wath me thetting Alathdair thtraight, ath you thay, that brought Thilly Willy my way. It really impreththed him that I would thtick up for you the way I did. It gave him the courage to tell me tho after Alathdair left. It turnth out he hath liked me all along, but he wath a little thy. That wath the beginning of what I think will be a beautiful friendthip, ath they thay. Thingth do work out, don't they, if we do what we think ith right?"

"Yes, they certainly do," said Priscilla. Leaning down, she gave the little duck a big hug and a kiss on the head. He blushed, just as nicely as Eideard might have done, and said, "Oh, thuckth!" Priscilla had to laugh at how this sounded when it came out.

It was beginning to feel like the right time to head for home. Though it was hard for her to leave all her new friends, she was anxious to find out if her father was safe and to see if he had made the right decision.

This had indeed been an incredibly grand adventure. She knew she would never forget this experience. However, she wanted to be home once again. Home was where she belonged.

Chapter Thirty-Seven
Coming Home

When Priscilla went in search of Alasdair, she found that he had been looking for her. He too had been thinking it was time to go home.

With some embarrassment, he told her, "I've had my fill of all the attention. Now that I know I can make music others like to listen to, I really want to learn to do it at home, especially with everyone at school. And I need to make things right with my mother. I'm definitely ready to go home."

Wanortu, with Eideard once again on his shoulder, approached them just as Alasdair was saying these last words. He said, "I thought you might be ready to go, so I had your packs brought down to the seashore. Ezara and Eminore will fly you back from here. You might like it a little better than going by horse and cart." He grinned at Alasdair. "The eagles are waiting for you down by the water."

It was time for goodbyes, and none of them would be easy. King Sol and Queen Luminata, with their usual royal formality, thanked Priscilla and Alasdair for all they had done. The Royal Children begged them not to go so soon. The little People of the Rainbow thanked them profusely for rescuing their Prince and their Sacred Light, bowing to the over and over again.

Baba advised Priscilla to remember everything she had learned. In passing, she also mentioned that she would be in her cottage if Priscilla ever needed her. What Baba meant by this, Priscilla wasn't sure, though there was something comforting in her words all the same.

Ducky told Priscilla she would always be his friend, and she happily responded with the same. She winked at him and teased, "Have fun with Thilly Willy!" The funny little Ducky winked back at her. He had changed their lives with his courage, and she would never forget his friendship.

They thanked Raldemar for his guidance and asked him to give Mother Nature their greetings. When Garone the Gull thanked them once again for saving his life, they enthusiastically returned the favor. He was a good and courageous friend.

Inky and Lita hugged them and told them how grateful they were, saying they would always be there for Priscilla and Alasdair whenever they wanted to come back to the Kingdom Beyond the Sunset.

"In fact," Inky suggested, "Why don't you come back for my coronation when I become king? We can send Ezara and Eminore to bring you to us again."

Even though Priscilla thought such an event was probably a long way off, and a whole lot could happen before then, she was happy to hear this. Knowing they could return to the Kingdom Beyond the Sunset made it easier to leave.

It was hardest to say goodbye to Wanortu and to Eideard. As she hugged Wanortu, Priscilla could no longer hold back her tears. He was a wonderful, warm, and wise little man, and she had grown to love him very much.

"I want you to keep the Rainbow-Makers as a reminder of the Kingdom Beyond the Sunset, Priscilla," Wanortu told her. "I have given Alasdair the Black Carapas to keep. Remember to trust the Light inside you above everything else." He smiled warmly at her, his eyes twinkling as usual.

When she reached over and kissed the little owl on the head, his typical "Hoot Mon" with a blush was all the response she expected. He did not disappoint her.

But then to her great surprise, he looked up at her and winked. "Niver be ashamed of yer rare red hair and those braw fernitickles on yer cheeks, lassie. They make ye right bonny. Hoot Mon!"

Now it was her turn to blush, making her fernitickles, as he called her freckles, stand out on her pink cheeks.

Turning away in embarrassment, she got her goggles out of her pack and put them on. Alasdair did the same. He climbed on Eminore, his guitar once more tied to his pack. Before she climbed on Ezara, Priscilla bent down and whispered something to the big eagle. After she stood up, she looked at Ezara for a long moment, a perplexed look on her face. She turned back to Wanortu.

"I just thought of a question I want to ask you before we go, Wanortu," she said. "Why on earth did Alasdair and I need to go on our long journey when we could as easily have flown from here to Mother Nature's Kingdom on the eagles? Well, for that matter, why didn't you just send Garone the Gull to ask Mother Nature where to find Inky? Wouldn't it have been much easier?"

Wanortu smiled, his lively eyes twinkling even more than ever. "Yes, Priscilla, we could have done that, but then you and Alasdair would not have had your *Grand Adventure,* would you?"

Priscilla stared at him in astonishment, and then she started to laugh. She was still chuckling as she climbed on Ezara. The time had definitely come to leave. They waved their goodbyes to the crowd on the shore as the eagles flew out over the ocean. Priscilla and Alasdair waved and called down their thanks to the birds and to Waleutius and Ogusto, who looked up at them from the water.

As Priscilla had requested of Ezara, the eagles flew low over the little seals, Sami and Sumi, who were waving their flippers. Priscilla and Alasdair smiled and waved back. Then they leaned over and dropped their sealskin suits into the water next to the seals. As Grandmother Ocean had requested, they were returning the sealskins to the ocean where they belonged.

Farther out on the ocean, they flew over all that was left of the Dark Ship, now only a small shadow on the horizon. Like an obnoxious weed, it would grow again. But with luck, caring, and a lot of hard work, it would be a long time before it grew very much. Perhaps if all those who loved the values of the Light joined together, they could keep it from to growing as large again.

The eagles banked and turned around. They flew high over the shore and over the Village of the Rainbow where the magnificent palace held the Sacred Light that created the Royal Rainbow. The Muses were shimmering even more intensely than usual with the increase of Light energy. Their spires reached high into the sky, and Priscilla felt as if she could almost reach out and touch them. Of course, there was nothing there to touch, but the Muses had incredible power just the same.

Ezara and Eminore flew them over Paint Pond Park, the bridges, and the colorful little cottages, then over the green hills and across the shining River of Return. Once they were above the Merry Meadow, Priscilla looked down and recalled the joy of dancing amongst the many wildflowers with all the wonderful creatures around her.

Something huge and red stood in the middle of the meadow. It was Horse of Course, leisurely chomping the luscious green grasses. As they flew over him, he looked up. Priscilla waved to him, and he responded with a loud whinny before resuming his munching.

She looked beyond the meadow toward the Fairy Forest where Baba and the little Fairy Folk had their homes and where she had met her dear Grandmother Wolf. Knowing her beloved wolf was still alive in the special place inside her made her feel less sad. Any time she wanted to, she could visit Grandmother Wolf, Granny, and her mother as well.

Maybe this was what Baba had meant. Perhaps Priscilla could go deep inside herself and visit Baba in her cottage as well. Sometime, after she got home, she would have to try it and see if it would work.

The Mara Mountains, with the great White Mountain guarded by Amara, the Sacred White Bison, were off in the distance. Priscilla waved just in case Mother Nature was walking in her crystal garden watching them fly past.

And somewhere, deep in those mountains, dear Mother Bear and her three precious little cubs would still be fast asleep in their cave… an incredibly sacred space where the ancient paintings on the wall held the eternal inner journey Priscilla had taken while she was there.

They passed over the little brown pond where the silly grinning Frog would still be giving his ppp-perfectly ppp-pleasant weather report to no one in particular. Priscilla was even quite positive she could see sneaky Snake sticking his head out of the grass nearby to watch them pass overhead. Without a doubt, he never missed a trick.

The pear tree and Barthos' hut, where they had started on their journey to the Land of Shadows and the Lava Land, were somewhere off in the distance out of sight. Even though this was the hardest and darkest period of their journey, it had taught them much of what they had most needed to know. As dear Grandmother Wolf had said with her great wisdom, *"Sometimes you must go into the Darkness in order to find the Light."*

Ahead of them, the colors of the sunset blazed intently. In a moment, they were flying once more through another amazing art show. The People of the Rainbow had clearly outdone themselves with their creations this time. Priscilla thought of how much had happened since they had flown through the sunset in the opposite direction and had seen the Kingdom Beyond the Sunset for the first time.

Before long, they were flying over Wolf Island. It sparkled like a jewel in the evening sun. As they headed toward her beloved beach, Priscilla knew they were coming home at last.

Ezara and Eminore left them on the shore, carrying away with them Priscilla and Alasdair's gratitude and good wishes. The sun was just beginning to set. As Garone the Gull had said, it was as if they had never been away. However, now they both knew that time was not always what it seemed.

Priscilla and Alasdair looked at one another. After going through so much together and so many recent goodbyes, it was difficult to add this one last goodbye to all the rest. They stood unmoving, neither knowing quite what to say or do.

All at once, Alasdair reached out and gave Priscilla a quick awkward hug. As she hugged him back, she felt the special bond between them that could never ever be broken. What they had shared was extraordinary. No one else could possibly understand, let alone believe what had happened to them.

Leaving the shore, each headed in a different direction toward home. As King Sol would have said, they had important matters to which they must attend.

Priscilla was drooping with exhaustion by the time she got to her house. However, she was not too tired to remember to take off her rainbow ribbon and put it in her pocket. Any decision regarding wearing her rainbow ribbon around her family would have to wait until she got some rest and had a chance to think about it.

Several unfamiliar cars were in the driveway. Something unusual was going on. Puzzled, she went into the house. As she was heading toward her father's office, Joshua came down the stairs.

He called to her. "Hey, Ugly! Dad's in his office with some really important people, so don't go in there. He doesn't want to be disturbed." His pompous manner made her think of Snake.

She was relieved to know that her father was safe at home. This was all she needed to hear, as she was too tired for anything else. She told Joshua, "Please tell Mom I don't want any dinner. I'm really tired... not sick... just tired, so I'm going up to bed."

And that is exactly what she did. Half asleep, she dragged herself upstairs where she only took time to give Mathilda a great big hug and a good scratch, say hello to her stuffed animals, pull off her clothes, and put on her pajamas, before crawling into bed. Moments later, she was out like a light.

The sounds of voices yelling, people arguing, and car doors slamming outside in front of the house, awakened her early in the morning. Trying to ignore the noises at first, she pulled her quilt over her head, but the commotion seemed to go on and on.

Finally, her curiosity got the better of her. Climbing out of bed, she slipped over to the window and peered between the curtains to look down at the front of the house. Three vehicles sat in the lighted driveway, including the big truck belonging to Mr. Green. The other two were police cars.

Before she even had time to think about what this could mean, Mr. Green, and the two men she had seen him with before, shuffled out of the house. Each of them had his hands handcuffed behind his back. Police officers followed behind them and pushed them into the back seats of the police cars. One of the officers got into Mr. Green's truck. Then all three cars drove away, and everything became quiet.

Priscilla smiled to herself. Now she knew for sure her father had made the right decision. Daddy had made the world a better place. Still exhausted, she crawled back into bed, cuddled up with Mathilda, and went back to sleep.

The next time she awakened, the house was silent. After she got up and showered, she decided it was time to put on some different clothes for a change. It felt like she had been wearing the same thing for days. Well, theoretically, she guessed she had.

Before tossing her overalls into the laundry hamper, she took her rainbow ribbon and her medicine bag out of her pockets and laid them on the bed. While she was reaching into her closet for fresh overalls, it occurred to her that, with her medicine bag, she would not need so many pockets to carry her treasures. So instead, she took out a brand new pair of blue jeans and a new shirt and put them on.

When she was dressed, she sat on the bed and spread the contents of her medicine bag on the quilt. The lavender Rainbow-Makers from Wanortu, the black pearl from Grandmother Ocean, and the medicine bag from Baba were reminders that her adventure had been real and not just the dream she had thought it might have been.

Her familiar treasures were all there, except of course, her favorite shell, which had helped her father make his decision. Her pink heart stone was more precious than ever after undertaking an unexpected journey in the ocean. As she was slipping her treasures back into the bag, there was a knock on her door.

"Come in," she called out. The door opened, and her father walked in. His appearance was entirely different from when she had last stood beside him watching the sunset. He stood tall and straight before her, with more color in his face than she had seen in a long time. In fact, he looked many years younger, more like the dear father she remembered so well.

"Good morning, sleepyhead," he smiled at her warmly. "You must have been really tired. I didn't think you were ever going to get up."

"I was terribly tired, Daddy, so I just decided to sleep as long as I could. I feel much better now. Did I miss something?" she asked, with a Wanortu-like twinkle in her eyes.

"Not much, my dear, but I wanted to return this to you. Thank you for sharing it with me. It was most helpful." He walked over to where she sat on the bed and handed her the shell.

She rubbed her fingers delightedly across the familiar surfaces once again and asked mischievously, "Did you make your decision, Daddy?" even though she already knew the answer to her question.

"Yes, I did, and I know for sure it was the right one. However, your mother is not at all pleased about it. She has taken Joshua, Jennifer, and Jessica, and they have all gone away for a few days to think things over. You and I are on our own, Priscilla. I thought perhaps we could spend the day together, if you don't have anything else planned. We really haven't had much time together over the past few years. I think we need to talk about why that has been and how things are going to change in the future. What do you think?"

She smiled happily at her father. "I think I'd like that very much, Daddy."

"Well, you finish whatever you're doing. I'll meet you downstairs in a few minutes for some breakfast. Then we can plan our day." He went out and closed the door.

She had a good idea what he wanted to talk about… her mother. It was definitely time. Granny and her mother would be pleased to hear that, at long last, Priscilla and her father were going to talk about what they had needed to talk about for years.

As she started to add her shell to her medicine bag, she took a moment to look at the bear figure and all the other creatures it held within it. When she saw how many of the friends she had met on her journey were there in the shell cave, she smiled. Now that she knew how everything was connected, she guessed this was not too surprising.

Picking up her rainbow ribbon, she wondered if she should begin wearing it with her father. Granny and the *Secret of the Rainbow Ribbon* came to mind. Perhaps now she would have time to think about the second half of the secret, which she had yet to discover.

Then, out of the blue, it came to her. She already *knew* the second half of the secret. Just as Granny had predicted, she had lived into the knowledge of the full *Secret of the Rainbow Ribbon*.

The first half of the secret was to be more of who she was, even though she was different from everyone else, and to learn to see her uniqueness as her most powerful gift. But this was not enough by itself.

She needed to share her unique gifts with others. Giving her shell to her father, rescuing Garone the Gull, making new friends, helping Alasdair, sharing with Ducky, saving Inky and the Light, standing up with him on the Dark Ship… all this had helped others. This was the second half of the secret. Not only did she have to sing her own song, she had to sing it out into the world.

So to the first half of the *Secret of the Rainbow Ribbon*:

> ***If you learn to love and accept who you are,***
> ***one day you will discover that***
> ***Your Uniqueness is your most powerful Gift.***

She could now add the second half:

> ***When you share your gifts with others,***
> ***You make the world a better place.***

From now on, she was going to shine her own light and sing her own song. She would wear her rainbow ribbon, remember who she was, and find ways to share her gifts with others. Living up to her true name, she planned to brighten the world wherever and whenever she could, especially in the darker times. Even if she couldn't change what was happening, she could make the world a better place. She no longer felt helpless.

Perhaps if she and Alasdair gathered with others who believed in the values of the Light, they could send Light energy out into the world at the same time, just like they did in the Muses in the Kingdom Beyond the Sunset. Wanortu had said, *"When we all work together to send out Light energy, we can accomplish great things."* Maybe by working together they could keep the Darkness in balance.

This was something she would have to think about tomorrow, but for now, she had other important matters to which she must attend.

After tying her rainbow ribbon in her hair, she put her medicine bag into the pocket of her jeans. Then she headed downstairs to join her father.

Epilogue
A Bright New Day

On Monday morning, Priscilla walked down the corridor at her school with her rainbow ribbon tied in her hair. She was no longer afraid to wear it at school. In fact, she planned to wear her ribbon wherever and whenever she wanted.

As usual, Horrid Harvey and his friends were loitering in the hallway. As soon as they saw her, they caught sight of the rainbow ribbon. Laughing in anticipation, they looked thrilled to have something new to add to their boring repertoire.

"Hey, Creepy Carrie has a sissy ribbon in her hair," yelled Horrid Harvey. "Maybe she thinks her hair and freckles look better. But her hair still looks like pig's blood and her freckles are as big as raisins. Look at the sissy ribbon on sissy Prissy!" They all began to chant at her, "Sissy Prissy! Sissy Prissy!" while they laughed and sneered.

This time Priscilla did not tuck her head down and scurry on past them. Instead, she marched right over and stood in front of them, glaring, her hands on the hips of her brand new jeans. The boys grew silent, gaping at her in surprise.

Loudly and slowly, she spoke directly to them, as if they were foolish children with no understanding of anything at all. "Don't you think it's time you stupid boys found something more interesting to keep your boring little minds busy? Do you think I'm remotely interested in hearing what you have to say to me? Do you feel so bad about yourselves that you have to make fun of other people to make yourselves feel better?"

Each time Priscilla asked one of her three questions of these Light-Eater boys, her power grew. No matter what they said in response, she knew she would never again let them drain any of her Light energy from her. She had faced much worse and survived. These horrid boys did not scare her any more.

The boys stood with their mouths hanging open without saying another word. After she finished, she simply turned on her heel and walked away, her head held high and her rainbow ribbon dazzling in her blood red hair.

However, this one confrontation was not enough to stop Horrid Harvey. After school, when Priscilla passed him on her way to the bus, he came at her once again. "Hey, Raisin-Head. Do you think that sissy ribbon makes you look better? Missy Sissy Prissy with her raisin-spotted face! Ha, ha, ha!"

Priscilla had simply had enough. Allowing her temper to get the best of her, she turned and looked him straight in the eye with a dark glare. With as much nastiness as she could muster, in her best slimy Snake voice, she hissed at him, "If you and your friends don't stop teasing me, I'll tell everyone in school about your father and what he's been up to. I'll tell them he's in jail and why. I don't think you'd like it!"

Horrid Harvey turned pale and immediately shut his mouth. Turning around, he tucked his head down and vanished into the crowd. This Light-Eater boy would not be bothering her any more, or anyone else if she had anything to say about it.

Priscilla was grinning even wider than Frog when she got on the school bus. Maybe she should not have done that to Horrid Harvey, as it probably was not at all nice. Certainly, she did not add any Light energy to the world. In fact, she guessed she might have increased the Dark energy a little. But it sure felt great.

When she thought about it a little more, she laughed, as she whispered quietly to herself, "Well, I'm still young, and I guess I have a lot to learn."

After she arrived home, she did her chores as quickly as she could, and then hurried down to the beach. All day long, she had been wondering if Alasdair would be there.

And he was. Her heart sang when she saw him sitting on the big rock. When he saw her coming, he jumped down and hurried over to welcome her. "I'm glad you came today, Priscilla. I've been dying to talk to you." He smiled at her happily.

"I'm really glad to see you too," she said, with genuine enthusiasm, "I've so much to tell you."

"Me too," he said. Then he looked at her shyly as he suggested, "Why don't you come and sit beside me on the big rock? There's enough room for both of us. It'll be easier to talk."

So… Priscilla joined Alasdair on what had become Their Rock. They sat together, side by side, and talked and talked.

Priscilla told him all about her day with her father. "Daddy told me about my mother's death. When she died, he was tremendously hurt and angry. He thought if he made himself forget her, it would help stop the pain. So he made a decision to never think about her or talk about her, and he would not allow anyone else to talk about her either, not even Granny. That way he thought he could protect me from hurting as much as he did."

Alasdair, listening intently, asked, "So what changed his mind?"

She answered. "Now he realizes he was mainly protecting himself. Keeping everything all bottled up inside wasn't good for him. He doesn't want me to do the same thing. His way of dealing with the pain was to work hard to become rich and powerful so he could give his family everything he thought they wanted. If we were happy, then he figured he would be happy too, but it didn't work. Instead it caused him to make some major mistakes in his life and to almost make one which would have had everlasting consequences for the world."

Alasdair nodded somberly as he said, "We know about that one, don't we?"

She smiled. "Yes, we do. Anyway, he said that he needed to do some grieving and some thinking about what was right before making some needed changes in his life."

Sometime soon, she knew she would tell her father about her adventures and about meeting her mother. Maybe it would help him decide what to do. She also wanted to ask him to tell her all about her mother, just as her mother had suggested.

"What about you, Alasdair?" she asked. "How did it go with your mother?"

"Mom and I talked about my Dad." Alasdair said. "I told her why I didn't believe her.

Apparently, after my Dad's death, my grandfather turned into a bitter old man, filled with rage at life. He blamed albinism for the death of his two sons. She was surprised and sad to hear what he had said to me. Anyway, I found out that my father was an extraordinary man, and he really loved me. I saw pictures of him, including some of him with Adam. Can you believe everything we saw and learned in the Land of Shadows was for real?"

"I know. It feels like a dream. I have to hold the Rainbow-Makers and my black pearl to convince myself it really happened."

Alasdair went on to tell her with great excitement, "And guess what? My dad was a musician and played the guitar as well. Mom kept his guitar for me so that I could have it when I was ready to receive it. Here it is."

With great pride, he showed her his new guitar. "And I heard they're going to have a huge talent show at my school. I'm going to audition. I've already been working on the song I want to perform." He gave her a bashful look, as he said shyly, "Maybe you'd like to hear it?"

When she gave a huge smile and answered, "I'd *love* to!" he jumped down in front of her, his father's guitar in his hand. Using the shore as his stage, he got ready to perform his song for her, while she watched him with enchantment shining in her eyes.

And then, he blew her away when he broke out into a fast rap song, break dancing across the rocky shore, with his precious new guitar held close to his heart.

Get Down

If the kids are mean at school and no one really cares
And they're always being cruel and everyone just stares
Get down

If your mother makes you cry and your father's never there
And your sister's always high and your brother takes your share
Get down

If no one's ever home and you're always all alone
And every time you call you hear a busy tone
Get down

Get up, get down, get out the door
Get up, get down, get down to the shore
Get down

If you got things you wanna say but no one wants to hear
And you really wanna play and they don't let you near
Get down

If life is rough and tough and you don't like being you
And you think you've had enough and you don't know what to do
Get down

If you can never get it right no matter how you try
And you lie awake at night thinking you should die
Get down

Get up, get down, get out the door
Get up, get down, get down to the shore
Get down

If you can't find a shore… find a river or a pond
There's always something more… you just gotta look beyond
Get down

You can rap with a bird… a crow, a seagull, or a duck
I know it sounds absurd, but birds will bring you luck
Get down

So you're havin' a bad day and life is such a bore
Remember what I say… I'll say it just once more
Get down

Get up, get down, get out the door
Get up, get down, get down to the shore
Get down
Get down
Down
Down
Down
Down to the shore

With these final words, Alasdair landed on his knees on the rocks, looking up at her, his new-found courage shining in his pale blue eyes.

Priscilla laughed and clapped her hands with pure pleasure. All the kids at school were going to love his rap and the way he performed it. Even if he didn't win the contest, he was finally taking his stand and letting them all know, "This is who I am and this is what I can do!" just as she had taken her stand with her rainbow ribbon.

Out of breath, Alasdair got up and joined her on Their Rock. They talked and laughed as the sun dropped lower in the sky. Neither of them noticed the sun beginning to set and the unbelievable colors of a truly spectacular sunset spreading across the sky. An extra special celebration appeared to be underway.

They were so busy talking and laughing that they did not even notice the big gray and white gull circling around above them, looking down on them as they sat together on the rock. If seagulls were capable of smiling, this one was smiling for sure. In fact, it might even have been chuckling.

As the seagull made one last wide circle over the shore, something peculiar happened. From within the gull's white tail feathers, a tiny gray bird poked out a tufted head and peered down at the figures far below.

This funny little creature made an odd noise. It sounded something like "Hoot Mon!"

The seagull gave one last loud squawk. Then, with the little gray hitchhiker once again tucked safely inside its feathers, the seagull turned and flew out across the water toward Wolf Island and beyond the sunset.

The End
of this
Grand Adventure

and also

The Beginning
of a
Bright
New
Day

Acknowledgements

Dear Readers,

I hope you enjoyed reading *"The Kingdom Beyond the Sunset"* as much as I enjoyed writing it. If you did, please give a copy to someone you think will derive pleasure from it as well.

The Kingdom Beyond the Sunset could never have been written without the many gifts I have received from all of you who have touched my life in some way. If you are such a person, please know that your gifts have become part of my story.

I thank my parents (now deceased) for teaching me to love stories, reading, and writing, and for all my family for loving me, even if they didn't always understand me or know what I was up to in my life. The abiding love of my siblings keeps me grounded. I thank my first husband, Roger Adams, for my wonderful children and for sharing part of my spiritual journey with me.

I will be forever grateful to my many mentors who taught me so much of what I needed to know as I developed in my personhood and in my career as a pastoral counselor and psychotherapist, especially Jerry F. Smith, STD, Terrill L. Gibson, PhD, Jim Anderson, M.Div., Donna Smith, PSYD, and Douglas R. McLemore, M.Div. I thank them all for their inspired teaching, spiritual direction, and loving support.

Most specifically, I honor Stephen Gilligan, PhD, for sharing his incredible knowledge and healing skills with those of us who attended his annual supervision retreats in Leavenworth, WA for well over a decade. Stephen asked me the important question "Where do you feel most in touch with yourself?" When I answered, "In my writing", he blessed me with his prophetic words, "Then you must write more."

In addition to the psychological and spiritual growth I experienced at these retreats, I gained treasured friends from around the world and deepened my relationship with my dear friend, Patti Carter, whose nurturing of me and my writing has been a special gift of our friendship.

Bouquets of thanks go to all my clients who have honored me through the years with their presence and their trust. I can never offer enough homage to those of my clients who were forced to grow up facing more Darkness than any human being should ever have to face. Entering into the Darkness with them to help in their healing has increased my awareness of the dark realities of our world. At the same time, these courageous clients continue to teach me that the resilience of the human spirit can overcome unbearable trauma. Love is the one true healing force.

I am so grateful to the many authors whose works have been beacons in my writing process and in my spiritual journey. I especially honor Ted Andrews for *Animal-Speak* and his other fine works on understanding the symbolic gifts that nature and wildlife bring to us.

I am deeply indebted to author and teacher, Val Dumond, my editor, whose patient teaching, delightful sense of humor, and expertise in grammar and publishing helped me to improve my manuscript as she gently guided me toward getting it out into the world. I am so grateful to my good friends, Jeff and Jill Rounce, publishers of the South Sound Business Examiner, for referring me to Val. She is a terrific role model for how doing what we love in our lives makes us seem fully alive and ageless.

I extend immeasurable thanks to the loving women of my Women's Spirit Circle who continually listen to me and sustain me as I share my struggles and joys on becoming a writer.

For those dear friends who read my manuscript and gave me feedback, I am profoundly appreciative. It meant so much to me, and I am grateful for all those who were willing to take on this challenge. A special thanks to Marlaina Mohr of N.O.A.H. for making sure I portrayed Alasdair's albinism with caring and authenticity.

Oceans of kisses and hugs go to my two youngest grandchildren, Sam and Mara, for asking me to tell them my story and then begging me not to stop. It was their love of my book that finally got me to follow up on six-year-old Sam's open-hearted suggestion, "Grandma Di, you should publish your book. I want to take it to school to share with the other kids."

One reader I want to single out for my everlasting gratitude is my dear friend, Sheila Anderson. Sheila was the first friend I trusted to read my manuscript, and I could not have made a better choice. Her heartfelt enthusiasm for the story and characters and her delight in my book, along with her reassuring words, served to keep me going through many of my most discouraging moments. Her vibrant paintings of Priscilla sitting on "her rock" on the shore kept me smiling as I worked. Sheila has been "my rock" throughout this journey.

I am grateful to my dear children and their loved ones and to all my wonderful family and friends for their continual love and support as they listened patiently to me talk about my book and my writing for so many years without ever seeing any tangible results.

My church provides me with a beautiful sacred space to worship and a community of open-hearted people who uplift me, giving me the confidence to share more of myself and my gifts with the world. I especially want to thank Terry Gibson, for his constant generous help with my computer and website needs, and Karla Jo Tupper, for sharing the gifts of her hard work and inspiring musical talents to help bring my song melodies to life. I feel truly blessed to have found such a loving and giving church community.

It is difficult to find the right words to express my gratitude to my beloved husband, Dwight, whose encouragement in the development of my writing career and in my life has been phenomenal. With his willing consent and financial assistance, I was able to cut back my work hours in order to write, and with his ever-present love and belief in me and my capabilities, along with his patient listening, I have always felt fully supported in my choices. His brave and honest critique brought me face to face with some tough truths about my writing skills and, as hard as it was at the time, this was invaluable in my learning process. His expertise in photography and his wonderful sunset photographs inspired the design for the book cover. I feel truly blessed to be sharing my life with this cherished man.

These acknowledgements would be incomplete without offering my thanks to each of the much-loved characters in my book for presenting themselves to me, inviting me to write about them, and believing in me when I had absolutely no idea that I could do this.

I thank God for honoring me with bringing this project to life, even though it has taken ten years of difficult labor to teach myself to write, to learn to believe in myself as a writer, and to birth this book into the world.

I am so grateful for God's gift of this incredibly beautiful world and for the opportunity to share my images of the magnificent Pacific Northwest with others. I hope we will all listen to Grandmother Wolf's wise words, *"I bless you with the wisdom to respect and care for all living things, to know and love Nature as part of you, and to have compassion for all the creatures of the earth. May you remember the world of Nature was created to give you, and all the beings on the earth, sustenance, knowledge, and pleasure. May you continue to care for the earth and all her creatures and work to preserve her gifts so that other generations may in turn enjoy them."*

With Love, Light, and Gratitude for all,
Diane H. Larson

About the Author

Diane H. Larson was born in Glasgow, Scotland. At age six, she immigrated with her family to Victoria, BC, Canada, and at age twelve, to Oakland, CA. She graduated from Oakland Technical High School and received her B. A. in Social Welfare from the University of California, Berkeley, during the wild sixties. While raising her children, she went back to school and earned her M.Ed. in Pastoral Counseling from the University of Puget Sound, Tacoma, WA.

For over twenty-five years, she has worked as a pastoral counselor and psychotherapist, currently maintaining a small private practice from her home office. Through the years, she has done extensive training and work in trauma healing, including Dissociative Identity Disorder (formerly Multiple Personality Disorder). She specializes in trauma recovery, life transitions, older women's issues, and spiritual growth. Her life's purpose is to be a healing presence in the world.

In addition to years of journaling her spiritual journey and writing poetry, she has written newspaper articles, newsletters, community theater promotions, and a weekly newspaper column for women. *The Kingdom Beyond the Sunset* is her first novel.

With her husband, and her beloved wee dog, Archie, she takes daily walks along "Priscilla's Beach" on Puget Sound and watches the sunsets from her living room window. Her two children and four grandchildren live close enough to visit and are her great delight as well as her favorite audience.

14478589R00245

Made in the USA
Charleston, SC
13 September 2012